PENGUIN BOOKS

Richelle Mead, the *New York Times* bestselling author of the Vampire Academy series and the Bloodlines series, lives in Seattle in the USA.

www.richellemead.com

D0683389

Books by Richelle Mead

Bloodlines series
BLOODLINES
THE GOLDEN LILY
THE INDIGO SPELL
THE FIERY HEART
SILVER SHADOWS

Vampire Academy series
VAMPIRE ACADEMY
FROSTBITE
SHADOW KISS
BLOOD PROMISE
SPIRIT BOUND
LAST SACRIFICE

A *Bloodlines* NOVEL

RICHELLE MEAD

PENGUIN BOOKS

PENGUIN BOOKS

Published by the Penguin Group
Penguin Books Ltd, 80 Strand, London WC2R 0RL, England
Penguin Group (USA) Inc., 375 Hudson Street, New York, New York 10014, USA
Penguin Group (Canada), 90 Eglinton Avenue East, Suite 700, Toronto, Ontario, Canada M4P 2Y3
(a division of Pearson Penguin Canada Inc.)
Penguin Ireland, 25 St Stephen's Green, Dublin 2, Ireland (a division of Penguin Books Ltd)
Penguin Group (Australia), 707 Collins Street, Melbourne, Victoria 3008, Australia
(a division of Pearson Australia Group Pty Ltd)
Penguin Books India Pvt Ltd, 11 Community Centre, Panchsheel Park, New Delhi – 110 017, India
Penguin Group (NZ), 67 Apollo Drive, Rosedale, Auckland 0632, New Zealand
(a division of Pearson New Zealand Ltd)
Penguin Books (South Africa) (Pty) Ltd, Block D, Rosebank Office Park,
181 Jan Smuts Avenue, Parktown North, Gauteng 2193, South Africa

Penguin Books Ltd, Registered Offices: 80 Strand, London WC2R 0RL, England

www.penguin.com

First published in the USA in Razorbill, a division of Penguin Group (USA) Inc., 2014
First published in Great Britain by Penguin Books 2014
001

Printed in Great Britain by Clays Ltd, St Ives plc

British Library Cataloguing in Publication Data
A CIP catalogue record for this book is available from the British Library

ISBN: 978–0–141–35018–9

www.greenpenguin.co.uk

MIX
Paper from
responsible sources
FSC® C018179

Penguin Books is committed to a sustainable
future for our business, our readers and our planet.
This book is made from Forest Stewardship
Council™ certified paper.

For the #VAFamily

CHAPTER 1

SYDNEY

I WOKE TO DARKNESS.

This was nothing new, as I'd been waking to darkness for the last . . . well, I didn't know how many days. It could've been weeks or even months. I'd lost track of time in this small, cold cell, with only a rough stone floor for a bed. My captors kept me awake or asleep, at their discretion, with the help of some drug that made it impossible to count the days. For a while, I'd been certain they were slipping it to me in my food or water, so I'd gone on a hunger strike. The only thing that had accomplished was a forced feeding—something I never, ever wanted to experience again—and no escape from the drug. I'd finally realized they were piping it in through the ventilation system, and unlike with food, I couldn't go on an air strike.

For a while, I'd had the fanciful idea that I'd track time with my menstrual cycle, the way that women in primitive societies synced themselves up to the moon. My captors, proponents of cleanliness and efficiency, had even provided feminine hygiene products for when the time came. That plan failed as well, though. Being abruptly cut off from birth control pills at the time of my capture reset all my hormones and spun my body into irregular cycles that made it impossible to measure anything, especially when combined with my wacky sleep schedule. The only thing I could be certain of was that I wasn't pregnant, which was a huge relief. If I'd had Adrian's child to worry about, the Alchemists would've had unlimited power over me. But it was just me in this body, and I could take whatever they threw at me. Hunger, cold. It didn't matter. I refused to let them break me.

"Have you thought about your sins, Sydney?"

The metallic, female voice reverberated around the small cell, seeming to come from every direction at once. I pulled myself up into a sitting position, tugging my rough shift down over my knees. It was more out of habit than anything else. The sleeveless garment was so paper thin that it offered no warmth whatsoever. The only thing it provided was a psychological sense of modesty. They'd given it to me partway through my captivity, claiming it was a token of goodwill. In reality, I think the Alchemists just couldn't handle keeping me there naked, especially when they saw it wasn't getting to me the way they'd hoped.

"I slept," I said, stifling a yawn. "No time to think." The drug in the air seemed to keep me perpetually sleepy, but they were also sending in some stimulant that made sure I stayed awake when they wanted, no matter how exhausted I might be. The result was that I never felt fully rested—as was their intent. Psychological warfare worked best when the mind was weary.

"Did you dream?" the voice asked. "Did you dream of redemption? Did you dream of what it might be like to see the light again?"

"You know I didn't." I was being uncharacteristically talkative today. They asked me these questions all the time, and sometimes I just stayed silent. "But if you want to stop feeding me that sedative for a while, maybe I'll get some real sleep and have some dreams that we can chat about."

More importantly, getting real sleep that was free of these drugs meant that Adrian would be able to locate me in my dreams and help me find a way out of this hellhole.

Adrian.

His name alone had gotten me through many long, dark hours. Thoughts of him, of our past and of our future, were what had helped me survive my present. I often lost myself in daydreams, thinking back to the handful of months we'd had together. Had it really been so short? Nothing else in my nineteen years seemed as vivid or meaningful as the time I'd spent with him. My days were consumed with thoughts of him. I would replay each precious memory, the joyous and the heartbreaking, and when I'd exhausted them, I'd fantasize about the future. I'd live out all the possible scenarios we'd imagined for ourselves, all our silly "escape plans."

Adrian.

He was the reason I was able to survive in this prison.

And he was also the reason I was here in the first place.

"You don't need your subconscious to tell you what your conscious already knows," the voice told me. "You are tainted and impure. Your soul is shrouded in darkness, and you have sinned against your own kind."

I sighed at this old rhetoric and shifted, trying to make myself more comfortable, though it was a losing battle. My muscles had been in a perpetual state of stiffness for ages now. There was no comfort to be found in these conditions.

"It must make you sad," the voice continued, "to know that you've broken your father's heart."

That was a new approach, one that caught me off guard enough that I spoke without thinking: "My father doesn't have a heart."

"He does, Sydney. He does." Unless I was mistaken, the voice sounded a bit pleased at having drawn me out. "He greatly regrets the fall you've taken. Especially when you showed such promise to us and our fight against evil."

I scooted over so that I could lean against the rough-cut wall. "Well, he's got another daughter who's much more promising now, so I'm sure he'll get over it."

"You broke her heart too. Both of them are more grieved than you could ever know. Wouldn't it be nice to reconcile with them?"

"Are you offering me that chance?" I asked cautiously.

"We've been offering you that chance from the beginning, Sydney. Just say the words, and we will gladly begin your path to redemption."

"You're saying this hasn't been part of it?"

"This has been part of the effort to help you cleanse your soul."

"Right," I said. "Helping me through starvation and humiliation."

"Do you want to see your family or not? Wouldn't it be nice to sit down and talk to them?"

I made no answer and instead tried to puzzle out what game was afoot. The voice had offered me many things in captivity, most of them creature comforts—warmth, a soft bed, real clothes. I'd been offered other rewards too, like the cross necklace Adrian had made for me and food far more substantial and appetizing than the gruel they currently kept me alive on. They'd even tried to tempt with that last one by piping in the aroma of coffee. Someone—possibly that family that cared so much about me—had tipped them off to my preferences.

But this . . . the chance to see and talk to people was a whole new thing altogether. Admittedly, Zoe and my dad weren't exactly at the top of the list of whom I'd want to see right now, but it was the larger scope of what the Alchemists were offering that interested me: a life outside of this cell.

"What would I have to do?" I asked.

"What you've always known you had to do," responded the voice. "Admit your guilt. Confess your sins, and say you're ready to redeem yourself."

I nearly said, *I have nothing to confess.* It was what I'd told them a hundred times before this. Maybe even a thousand times. But I was still intrigued. Meeting with other people meant that surely they'd have to turn off that poison in the air . . . right? And if I could escape that, I could dream. . . .

"I just say those words, and I get to see my family?"

The voice was irritatingly condescending. "Not right away, of course. It has to be earned. But you would be able to move on to the next stage of your healing."

"Re-education," I said.

"Your tone makes it sound like a bad thing," said the voice. "We do it to help you."

5

"No thanks," I said. "I'm getting used to this place. Shame to leave it."

That, and I knew re-education was where the real torture would begin. Sure, it might not be as physically challenging as this, but that was where they really honed in on the mind control. These harsh conditions were a setup, to make me feel weak and helpless so that I'd be susceptible to when they tried to alter my mind in re-education. So that I'd be grateful and thank them for it.

And yet, I couldn't shake that thought again, that if I did leave here, I might be in a position to sleep and dream normally again. If I could make that contact with Adrian, everything might change. At the very least, I would know he was okay . . . if I survived re-education itself. I could make guesses at the kind of psychological manipulation they'd try on me but didn't know for sure. Would I endure it? Could I keep my mind intact, or would they turn me against all my principles and loved ones? That was the risk of leaving this cell. I knew also that the Alchemists had drugs and tricks to make their commands "stick," so to speak, and although I was *probably* protected against them, thanks to regular magic use before I'd been imprisoned, the fear that I might still be vulnerable nagged at me. The only certain way I knew to protect against their compulsion was through a potion I'd once made and successfully used on a friend—but not on myself.

Further ruminations were put on hold as I felt fatigue wash over me. Apparently, this conversation was over. I knew enough now not to fight and stretched out on the floor, letting thick, dreamless sleep wash over me, burying thoughts of freedom. But before the drug took me down, I said his name in my mind, using it as a touchstone to keep me strong.

Adrian . . .

I woke at an unspecified time later and found food in my cell. It was the usual gruel, some kind of boxed hot cereal that was probably fortified with vitamins and minerals to keep my health up, such as it was. Calling it "hot cereal" might have been generous, however. "Lukewarm" was more adequate. They had to make it as unappetizing as possible. Tasteless or not, I ate automatically, knowing I needed to keep my strength up for when I got out of here.

If I get out of here.

The traitorous thought reared up before I could stop it. It was a longtime fear that had nagged at my edges, the terrifying possibility that they might keep me here forever, that I would never see any of the people I loved again—not Adrian, not Eddie, not Jill, not any of them. I would never practice magic again. I would never read a book again. That last thought hit me particularly hard today because as much as daydreaming about Adrian carried me through these dark hours, I would've killed to have something as mundane as a trashy novel to read. I would've settled for a magazine or pamphlet. Anything that wasn't darkness and that voice.

Be strong, I told myself. *Be strong for yourself. Be strong for Adrian. Would he do any less for you?*

No, he wouldn't. Wherever he was, whether he was still in Palm Springs or had moved on, I knew Adrian would never give up on me, and I had to match that. I had to be ready for when we were together. I had to be ready for when we were reunited.

Centrum permanebit. The Latin words played through my mind, strengthening me. Translated, they meant "The center will hold" and were a play off a poem Adrian and I had read. *We are the center now*, I thought. *And he and I will hold, no matter what.*

I finished my meager meal and then attempted a cursory washing at the small sink in the cell's corner, feeling my way in the dark to where it sat by a small toilet. A real bath or shower was out of the question (though they'd used that as bait before, too), and I had to clean myself daily (or what I thought was daily) with a rough washcloth and cold water that smelled of rust. It was humiliating, knowing they were watching with their night vision cameras, but it was still more dignified than staying dirty. I wouldn't give them that satisfaction. I would stay human, even if that was the very charge they were questioning me on.

When I was clean enough, I curled back up against the wall, my teeth chattering as my wet skin shivered in the cold air. Would I ever be warm again?

"We spoke to your father and sister, Sydney," said the voice. "They were so sad to hear that you didn't want to see them. Zoe cried."

Internally, I winced, regretting that I played along last time. The voice now thought this family tactic had some leverage over me. How could they think I'd want to bond with the people who'd locked me up here? The only family I might have wanted to see—my mom and my older sister—probably weren't on the visitor list, especially if my dad had gotten his way in their divorce proceedings. *That* outcome actually was something I would've liked to hear about, but no way would I let on to that.

"Don't you regret the pain you've caused them?" asked the voice.

"I think Zoe and Dad should regret the pain they caused *me*," I snapped back.

"They didn't want to cause you pain." The voice was trying to be soothing, but mostly I wanted to punch whoever was behind it—and I wasn't the kind of person usually given to violence. "They did what they did to help you. That's all we're trying to do. They'd love the chance to talk to you and explain themselves."

"I'm sure they would," I muttered. "If you even talked to them." I hated myself for engaging with my captors. This was the most I'd spoken to them in a while. They had to be loving it.

"Zoe asked us if it would be okay if she brought you a skinny vanilla latte when she visits. We told her it would. We're all for a civilized visit, for you to sit down and truly talk, so that your family and especially your soul can heal."

My heart beat rapidly, and it had nothing to do with the lure of coffee. The voice was confirming again what had been suggested before. A real visit, sitting down, drinking coffee . . . that had to take place out of this cell. If any of this fantasy were even true, there was no way they'd bring my dad and Zoe here—not that seeing them was my goal. Getting out of here was. I still maintained that I could stay here forever, that I could take whatever they threw at me. And I could. But what was I accomplishing? All I proved was my own toughness and defiance, and while I was proud of those things, they weren't getting me any closer to Adrian. To get to Adrian, to get the rest of my friends . . . I needed to dream. To dream, I needed to get away from this drugged existence.

And not just that. If I were somewhere that wasn't a small, dark cell, I might be able to work magic again. I might have a clue about where in the world they'd taken me. I might be able to free myself.

But first I had to leave this cell. I'd thought I was brave staying here, but suddenly, I wondered if getting out was what would truly test my courage.

"Would you like that, Sydney?" Unless I was mistaken, there was an edge of excitement in the voice—almost an eagerness—that contrasted with the lofty and imperious tone I'd grown used to. They'd never sparked this much interest from me. "Would you like to begin the first steps toward purging your soul—and seeing your family?"

How long had I languished in this cell, moving in and out of agitated consciousness? When I felt my torso and arms, I could tell I'd lost a considerable amount of weight, the kind of weight loss that took weeks. Weeks, months . . . I had no idea. And while I was here, the world was going on without me—a world full of people who needed me.

"Sydney?"

Not wanting to sound too eager, I tried to stall. "How do I know I can trust you? That you'll let me see my family if I . . . begin this journey?"

"Evil and deception are not our ways," the voice said. "We relish in light and honesty."

Liars, liars, I thought. They'd lied to me for years, telling me good people were monsters and trying to dictate the way I lived my life. But it didn't matter. They could keep their word or not about my family.

"Will I have . . . a real bed?" I managed to make my voice

choke a little. The Alchemists had taught me to be an excellent actress, and now they'd see their training put to work.

"Yes, Sydney. A real bed, real clothes, real food. And people to talk to—people who'll help you if you'll only listen."

That last part sealed the deal. If I were going to be put regularly around others, surely they couldn't keep drugging the air. As it was, I could feel myself being especially alert and agitated now. They were piping in that stimulant, something that would make me anxious and want to act rashly. It was a good trick on a worn and frazzled mind, and it was working—just not how they'd expected.

Out of old habit, I put my hand on my collarbone, touching a cross that was no longer there. *Don't let them change me,* I prayed silently. *Let me keep my mind. Let me endure whatever there is to come.*

"Sydney?"

"What do I have to do?" I asked.

"You know what you have to do," the voice said. "You know what you have to say."

I moved my hands to my heart, and my next internal words weren't a prayer, but a silent message to Adrian: *Wait for me. Be strong, and I'll be strong too. I'll fight my way out of whatever they've got in store. I won't forget you. I won't ever turn my back on you, no matter what lies I have to tell them. Our center will hold.*

"You know what you have to say," the voice repeated. It was practically salivating.

I cleared my throat. "I have sinned against my own kind and let my soul become corrupted. I am ready to have the darkness purged."

"And what are your sins?" the voice demanded. "Confess what you've done."

That was harder, but I still managed the words. If it got me closer to Adrian and freedom, I could say anything.

I took a deep breath and said: "I fell in love with a vampire."

And like that, I was blinded by light.

CHAPTER 2

ADRIAN

"DON'T TAKE THIS THE WRONG WAY, but you look like crap."

I lifted my head from the table and squinted one eye open. Even with sunglasses on—indoors—the light was still almost too much for the pounding in my head. "Really?" I said. "There's a right way to take that?"

Rowena Clark fixed me with an imperious look that was so like something Sydney might have done. It caused a lurch in my chest. "You can take it constructively." Rowena's nose wrinkled. "This *is* a hangover, right? Because, I mean, that implies you were sober at one point. And from the gin factory I can smell, I'm not so sure."

"I'm sober. Mostly." I dared to take off the sunglasses to get a better look at her. "Your hair's blue."

"Teal," she corrected, touching it self-consciously. "And you saw it two days ago."

"Did I?" Two days ago would've been our last mixed media

13

class here at Carlton College. I could barely remember two hours ago. "Well. It's possible I actually wasn't so sober then. But it looks nice," I added, hoping that would spare me some disapproval. It didn't.

In truth, my sober days at school were about fifty-fifty lately. Considering I was making it to class at all, though, I thought I deserved some credit. When Sydney had left—no, been taken—I hadn't wanted to come here. I hadn't wanted to go anywhere or do anything that wasn't finding her. I'd curled up in my bed for days, waiting and reaching out to her through the world of dreams with spirit. Only I hadn't connected. No matter what time of day I tried, I never seemed to find her asleep. It made no sense. No one could stay awake that long. Drunk people were hard to connect to since alcohol dampened spirit's effects and blocked the mind, but somehow I doubted she and her Alchemist captors were having nonstop cocktail parties.

I might have doubted myself and my own abilities, especially after I'd used medication to turn spirit off for a while. But my magic had eventually come back in full force, and I'd had no difficulties reaching out to others in their dreams. Maybe I was inept at a lot of other things in life, but I was still hands down the most skilled dream-walking spirit user I knew. The problem was, I only knew a few other spirit users, period, so there wasn't a lot of advice I could get on why I wasn't reaching Sydney. All Moroi vampires use some sort of elemental magic. Most specialize in one of the four physical elements: earth, air, water, or fire. Only a handful of us use spirit, and there's no well-documented history of it like there is of the other elements. There were a lot of theories, but no one knew for sure why I wasn't reaching Sydney.

My professor's assistant dropped a stack of stapled papers in front of me and an identical one in front of Rowena, jarring me out of my thoughts. "What's this?"

"Um, your final exam," said Rowena, rolling her eyes. "Let me guess. You don't remember this either? Or me offering to study with you?"

"Must have been an off day for me," I muttered, flipping uneasily through the pages.

Rowena's chastising expression turned to one of compassion, but whatever else she might have said was swallowed by our professor's orders to be quiet and get to work. I stared at the exam and wondered if I could fake my way through it. Part of what had dragged me out of bed and back to college was knowing how much education meant to Sydney. She'd always been envious of the opportunity I had, an opportunity her controlling asshole dad had denied her. When I'd realized that I couldn't find her right away—and believe me, I'd tried plenty of mundane ways, along with the magical ones—I'd resolved to myself that I'd carry on and do what she would have wanted: finish this semester at college.

Admittedly, I hadn't been the most dedicated of students. Since most of my classes were introductory art ones, my professors were usually good about giving credit as long as you turned something in. That was lucky for me because "something" was probably the nicest description for some of the crap pieces I'd created recently. I'd maintained a passing grade—barely—but this exam might do me in. These questions were all or nothing, right or wrong. I couldn't just half-ass a drawing or painting and count on points for effort.

As I began making my best attempts at answering questions

on contour drawing and deconstructed landscapes, I felt the dark edges of depression pulling me down. And it wasn't just because I was likely going to fail the class. I was also going to fail Sydney and her high expectations of me. But really, what was one class when I'd already failed her in so many other ways? If our roles had been reversed, she probably would've found me by now. She was smarter and more resourceful. She could've done the extraordinary. I couldn't even handle the ordinary.

I turned in the exam an hour later and hoped I hadn't just wasted an entire semester in the process. Rowena had finished early and was waiting for me outside the classroom. "You want to get something to eat?" she asked. "My treat."

"No thanks. I've got to go meet my cousin."

Rowena regarded me warily. "You aren't driving yourself, are you?"

"I'm sober now, thank you very much," I told her. "But if it makes you feel better, no, I'm taking the bus."

"Then I guess this is it, huh? Last day of class."

I supposed it was, I realized with a start. I had a couple other classes, but this was my only one with her. "I'm sure we'll see each other again," I said valiantly.

"I hope so," she said, eyes filled with concern. "You've got my number. Or at least you used to. I'll be around this summer. Give me and Cassie a call if you want to hang out . . . or if there's anything you want to talk about. . . . I know you've had some rough things to deal with lately. . . ."

"I've dealt with rougher," I lied. She didn't know the half of it, and there was no way she could, not as an ordinary human. I knew she thought Sydney had broken up with me, and it killed me to see Rowena's pity. I could hardly correct her, though. "And I'll definitely get in touch, so you'd better sit by your phone. See you around, Ro."

She gave me a half-hearted wave as I walked off toward the nearest campus bus stop. It wasn't that far away, but I found myself sweating by the time I reached it. It was May in Palm Springs, and our fleeting spring was being trampled into the ground by summer's hot and sweltering approach. I popped the sunglasses back on as I waited and tried to ignore the hipster couple smoking beside me. Cigarettes, at least, were one vice I hadn't returned to since Sydney went away, but it was hard sometimes. Very hard.

To distract myself, I opened up my bag and peered inside at a small statue of a golden dragon. I rested my hand on his back, feeling his tiny scales. No artist could've created such a perfect work of art because he wasn't actually a sculpture. He was a real dragon—well, a callistana, to be precise, which was a type of benign demon—that Sydney had summoned. He'd bonded to her and to me, but only she had the ability to transform him between living and frozen forms. Unfortunately for Hopper here, he'd been trapped in this state when she was abducted, meaning he was stuck in it. According to Sydney's magical mentor, Jackie Terwilliger, Hopper was technically still alive but living a pretty miserable existence without food and activity. I took him everywhere I went and didn't know if contact with me meant anything to him. What he really needed was Sydney, and I couldn't blame him. I needed her too.

I'd been telling Rowena the truth: I was sober now. And that was by design. The long bus ride ahead gave me the perfect opportunity to seek Sydney. Even though I no longer tried to reach out to her in dreams as voraciously as I once had, I still made a point to sober up a few times a day and search. As soon as the bus was moving and I was settled into my seat, I drew upon the spirit magic within me, exalting briefly in the glorious way it made me feel. It was a double-edged joy, though, one that was tempered by the knowledge that spirit was slowly driving me insane.

Insane is such an ugly word, a voice in my head said. *Think of it as obtaining a new look at reality.*

I winced. The voice in my head wasn't my conscience or anything like that. It was my dead Aunt Tatiana, former queen of the Moroi. Or, well, it was spirit making me hallucinate her voice. I used to hear her when my mood dropped to particularly low places. Now, ever since Sydney had left, this phantom Aunt Tatiana had become a recurring companion. The bright side— if you could even look at it that way—was that some of the bipolar side effects of spirit had become less frequent. It was as though spirit's madness had shifted form. Was it better to have mental conversations with an imagined deceased relative than to be subject to wildly dramatic mood swings? I honestly wasn't sure.

Go away, I told her. *You aren't real. Besides, it's time to look for Sydney.*

Once I'd connected with the magic, I stretched my senses out, searching for Sydney—the person I knew better than anyone else on this earth. Finding someone asleep whom I knew only a little would've been easy. Finding *her*—if she were asleep—would've been effortless. But I made no contact and eventually let go of the magic. She either wasn't asleep or was still blocked from me. Defeated once again, I found a flask of vodka in my bag and settled in on it as I waited out the ride to Vista Azul.

I was pleasantly buzzed, cut off from my magic but not from my heartache, when I arrived at Amberwood Preparatory School. Classes had just finished for the afternoon, and students in stylish uniforms were moving back and forth between the buildings, off to study or make out or whatever it was high school kids did near the end of term. I walked to the girls' dorm and then waited outside for Jill Mastrano Dragomir to find me.

Whereas Rowena had only guessed at what was troubling me, Jill knew exactly what my problems were. This was because fifteen-year-old Jill had the "benefit" of being able to see into my mind. Last year, she'd been targeted by assassins wanting to dethrone her sister, who happened to be queen of the Moroi and a good friend of mine. Technically, those assassins had succeeded, but I'd brought Jill back through more of spirit's extraordinary abilities. That feat of healing had taken a huge toll on me and also forged a psychic bond that let Jill know my thoughts and feelings. I knew my recent bout of depression and binge drinking had been hard on her—though at least the drinking numbed out the bond some days. If Sydney had been around, she would've scolded me for being selfish and not thinking of Jill's feelings. But Sydney wasn't around. The weight of responsibility rested on me alone, and I wasn't strong enough to shoulder it, it seemed.

Three campus shuttle buses came and went, and Jill wasn't on any of them. This was our usual day of the week to get together, and I'd made sure to keep up with that, even if I couldn't keep up with anything else. I took out my phone and texted her: *Hey, I'm here. Everything okay?*

No answer came, and a prickle of worry started to go through me. After the assassination attempt, Jill had been sent here to hide among humans in Palm Springs because a desert was no place that either our kind or the Strigoi—evil, undead vampires—wanted to be. The Alchemists—a secret society of humans hell-bent on keeping humans and vampires away from each other—had sent Sydney as a liaison to make sure things went smoothly. The Alchemists had wanted to make sure the Moroi didn't plunge into civil war, and Sydney had done a good job of helping Jill through all sorts of ups and downs. Where Sydney had failed, however, was in getting romantically involved with a vampire. That kind of went against the Alchemists' operating procedure of humans and vampires keeping apart from each other, and the Alchemists had responded brutally and efficiently.

Even after Sydney had left and her stiff-faced replacement, Maura, had come, things had remained relatively calm for Jill. There'd been no sign of danger from any source, and we even had indications that she could return to mainstream Moroi society once her school year finished next month. This kind of disappearance was out of character, and when I didn't get a text response from her, I sent one to Eddie Castile.

Whereas Jill and I were Moroi, he was a dhampir—a race born of mixed human and vampire blood. His kind trained to be our defenders, and he was one of the best. Unfortunately, his formidable battle skills hadn't been enough when Sydney had tricked him into splitting up from her when the Alchemists had come after her. She'd done it to save him, sacrificing herself, and he couldn't get over that. That humiliation had killed the kindling romance between him and Jill because he no longer felt he was worthy of a Moroi princess. He still dutifully served as her bodyguard, however, and I knew that if anything had happened to her, he'd be the first to know.

But Eddie didn't answer my text either, and neither did the other two dhampirs serving undercover as her protectors. That was weird, but I tried to reassure myself that radio silence from all of them probably meant they'd gotten distracted together and were fine. Jill would show up soon.

The sun was bothering me again, so I walked around the building and found another bench that was out of the way and shaded by palm trees. I made myself comfortable on it and soon fell asleep, helped by both staying out late at the bar last night and by finishing off my vodka flask. A murmur of voices woke me later, and I saw that the sun had moved considerably in the sky above me. Also above me were Jill and Eddie's faces, along with our friends Angeline, Trey, and Neil.

"Hey," I croaked, managing to sit up. "Where were you?"

"Where were *you*?" Eddie asked pointedly.

Jill's green eyes softened as she looked at me. "It's okay. He's been here the whole time. He forgot. Understandable since . . . well, he's going through a tough time."

"Forgot what?" I asked, looking uneasily from face to face.

"It doesn't matter," said Jill evasively.

"What did I forget?" I exclaimed.

Angeline Dawes, one of Jill's dhampir protectors, proved as usual to be the voice of bluntness. "Jill's end-of-term expo."

I stared blankly, and then it all came back to me. One of Jill's extracurricular activities was a fashion design and sewing club. She'd started off modeling, but when that proved too public and dangerous in her position, she'd recently tried her hand at designing behind the scenes—and had found she was pretty good at it. She'd been talking for the last month about a big show and exhibit her club was doing as their end-of-term project, and it had been good to see her so excited about something again. I knew she was hurt over Sydney too, and with my transferred depression and her botched romance with Eddie, she'd lived under a cloud nearly as dark as my own. This show and the chance to display her work had been one bright spot for her—small in the grand scheme of things but monumentally important in the life of a teenage girl who needed some normality.

And I'd blown it off.

Bits of conversation came back to me now, her telling me the day and time, and me promising I'd come and support her. She'd even made a point to remind me the last time I'd seen her this week. I'd noted what she said and then went out to celebrate Tequila Tuesday at a bar near my apartment. Saying her show had slipped my mind was an understatement.

"Crap, I'm sorry, Jailbait. I tried texting. . . ." I lifted up my phone to show them, except it was the vodka flask I picked up instead. I hastily shoved it back in the bag.

"We had to turn our phones off during the show," explained Neil. He was the third dhampir in the group, a recent addition to Palm Springs. He'd grown on me over time, maybe because he was suffering from his own heartache. He was head over heels for a dhampir girl who'd dropped off the face of the earth, though unlike Sydney, Olive Sinclair's silence was most likely from personal baggage and not Alchemist abduction.

"Well . . . how it'd go then?" I attempted. "I bet your stuff was awesome, right?"

I felt so incredibly stupid, I could hardly stand it. Maybe I couldn't fight against what the Alchemists had done to Sydney. Maybe I couldn't prepare for an exam. But for God's sake, I should've at least been able to make it to one girl's fashion show! All I had to do was show up, sit there, and applaud. I'd failed at even that, and the weight of it was suddenly crushing. A black haze filled my mind, weighing me down, making me hate everything and everyone—myself most of all. It was no wonder I couldn't save Sydney. I couldn't even take care of myself.

You don't need to, Aunt Tatiana whispered in my mind. *I'll take care of you.*

A spark of compassion showed in Jill's eyes as she sensed the dark mood coming on. "It was great. Don't worry—we'll show you pictures. They had a professional photographer doing everything, and it'll go online."

I tried to swallow back that darkness and managed a tense smile. "Glad to hear it. Well, how about we all go out and celebrate then? Dinner's on me."

Jill's face fell. "Angeline and I are eating with a study group. I mean, maybe I could cancel. Exams are still a month away, so I could always—"

"Forget it," I said, getting to my feet. "Someone in this bond needs to be ready for exams. Go have fun. I'll catch you later."

No one tried to stop me, but Trey Juarez soon fell in step with me. He was perhaps the oddest member of our circle: a human who'd once been part of a group of vampire hunters. He'd broken ties with them, both because they were psycho and because he'd fallen—against all reason—for Angeline. Those two were the only ones in our little group with any semblance of a happy love life, and I knew they tried to downplay it for the rest of us miserable souls.

"And how exactly are you going to get home?" asked Trey.

"Who says I'm going home?" I retorted.

"Me. You have no business going out and partying. You look like crap."

"You're the second person to tell me that today."

"Well, then, maybe you'll start listening," he said, steering me toward the student parking lot. "Come on, I'll drive."

It was an easy offer for him to make because he was my roommate.

Things hadn't started out that way. He'd been a boarder at Amberwood, living at school with the others. His former group, the Warriors of Light, had the same hang-ups the Alchemists had about humans and vampires interacting. Whereas the Alchemists dealt with this by covering up the existence of vampires from ordinary humans, the Warriors took a much more savage approach and hunted vampires. They claimed they only went after Strigoi, but they were no friends to Moroi or dhampirs either.

When Trey's father had found out about Angeline, he'd taken a different approach than Sydney's father. Rather than kidnapping his son and making him disappear without a trace, Mr. Juarez had simply disowned Trey and cut off all his funding. Lucky for Trey, tuition had already been paid for through the end of the school year. Room and board had not, and so the Amberwood dorm had turned Trey out a few months ago. He'd shown up on my doorstep, offering to pay me rent with his meager coffee shop earnings so that he could finish high school at Amberwood. I'd welcomed him in and refused the money, knowing it was what Sydney would've wanted. My only condition had been that I had better never, ever come home and find him making out with Angeline on my couch.

"I suck," I said, after several minutes of uncomfortable silence into our drive.

"Is that some kind of vampire joke?" Trey asked.

I shot him a look. "You know what I mean. I screwed up. No one asks that much of me. Not anymore. All I had to do was remember to go to her fashion show, and I blew it."

"You've had a lot of crap going on," he said diplomatically.

"So has everyone else. Hell, look at you. Your whole family denies your existence and did their best to get you kicked out of school. You found a workaround, kept up your grades and sports, and managed to nab some scholarships in the process," I sighed. "Meanwhile, I may have failed an introductory art class. A few of them, actually, if I've got more exams coming this week—which seems likely. I don't even know."

"Yeah, but I've still got Angeline. And that makes it worth putting up with all the other crap. Whereas you . . ." Trey couldn't finish, and I saw pain flash over his tanned features.

My friends here in Palm Springs knew about Sydney and me. They were the only ones in the Moroi world (or the human world that shadowed the Moroi) who knew about our relationship. They felt bad for what had happened for my sake and also for hers. They'd loved Sydney too. Not like I did, of course, but she was the kind of person who was fiercely loyal and inspired deep bonds in her friends.

"I miss her too," Trey said softly.

"I should've done more," I said, slouching into my seat.

"You did plenty. More than I would've thought to do. And

not just the dream walking. I mean, you harassed her dad, pressured the Moroi, made life a living hell for that Maura girl . . . you exhausted everything."

"I *am* good at being annoying," I admitted.

"You've just run into a wall, that's all. They're just too good at keeping her prison a secret. But they'll crack, and you'll be there to find that crack. And I'll be right by your side. So will the rest of us."

The pep talk was unusual for him but didn't cheer me up any. "I don't know how I'm going to find that crack."

Trey's eyes went wide. "Marcus."

I shook my head. "He's exhausted his leads too. Haven't seen him in a month."

"No." Trey pointed as he pulled the car up to my apartment building. "There. Marcus."

Sure enough. There, sitting on the building's front step, was Marcus Finch, the rebel ex-Alchemist who'd encouraged Sydney to think for herself and who had been trying—futilely—to locate her for me. I had the door open before Trey even brought the car to a stop.

"He wouldn't be here in person if he didn't have news," I said excitedly. I jumped out of the car and sprinted across the grass, my earlier lethargy replaced with a new sense of purpose. This was it. Marcus had come through. Marcus had found answers.

"What is it?" I demanded. "Have you found her?"

"Not exactly." Marcus got to his feet and smoothed back his blond hair. "Let's go in and talk."

Trey was nearly as eager as me when we ushered Marcus inside to the living room. We faced him down with mirrored stances, arms crossed over our chests. "Well?" I asked.

"I got a list of locations that may have possibly been used as Alchemist re-education holding facilities," Marcus began, not looking nearly as enthusiastic as he should have for news like that. I clutched his arm.

"That's incredible! We'll start checking them out and—"

"There are thirty of them," he interrupted bluntly.

I dropped my hand. "Thirty?"

"Thirty," he repeated. "And we don't exactly know where they are."

"But you just said—"

Marcus held up a hand. "Let me explain it all first. Then you can talk. This list my sources got is from cities in the United States that the Alchemists were scouting for re-education and a few other operations centers. It's several years old, and while my sources confirm that they did build their current re-education facility in a city on the list, we don't know for sure which one they ended up picking—or even where in that location they chose. Are there ways of finding out? Sure, and I know people who can start digging around. But we'll have to do it on a city-by-city basis, and each one is going to take a while."

All the hope and enthusiasm I'd felt upon seeing Marcus shattered and blew away. "And let me guess: 'A while' is a few days?"

He grimaced. "It'll be a case-by-case basis, depending on the difficulties of researching each city. Might take a couple days to knock one off the list. Might take a few weeks."

I hadn't thought I could feel worse than I had over the exam and Jill, but apparently I was wrong. I threw myself down on the couch, defeated. "A few weeks times thirty. That could be over a year."

"Unless we get lucky and she's in one of the first cities we search." I could tell even he didn't think that was likely, though.

"Yeah, well, 'lucky' hasn't really been the way I'd describe how things have been going for us," I remarked. "Don't see why that should change now."

"It's better than nothing," said Trey. "It's the first real lead we've got."

"I need to find her dad," I muttered. "I need to find him and compel the hell out of him so that he tells me where she's at." All attempts at locating Jared Sage had proven unsuccessful. I *had* managed a phone call and been promptly hung up on. Compulsion didn't work so well over the phone.

"Even if you did, he probably wouldn't know," said Marcus. "They keep secrets from each other, for the very purpose of protecting against forced confessions."

"And so there we are." I stood up and headed for the kitchen, off to make a drink. "Stuck just like we were before. Come get me in a year when you're able to verify your list was a dead end."

"Adrian—" began Marcus, looking more at a loss than I'd ever seen him. He was usually the poster boy for cocky confidence.

Trey's response was more pragmatic. "No more drinks. You've had too much today, man."

"I'll be the judge of that," I snapped. Rather than actually making a drink, I ended up just grabbing two liquor bottles at random. No one tried to stop me as I went to my room and slammed the door.

Before I began my one-man party, I made another attempt to reach out to Sydney. It wasn't easy since some of this afternoon's vodka was still hanging around, but I managed a tentative grasp of spirit. As usual, there was nothing, but Marcus's certainty that she was in the United States had made me want to try. It was early evening on the East Coast, and I'd had to check, just in case she was calling it an early night. Apparently not.

I soon lost myself in the bottles, desperately needing to wipe away everything. School. Jill. Sydney. I hadn't thought it was possible to feel this low, to have my emotions so black and so deep that there was no way to raise them into any sort of constructive feeling. When things had ended with Rose, I thought no loss could be more terrible. I'd been wrong. She and I had never really had anything substantial. What I'd lost with her was *possibility*.

But with Sydney . . . with Sydney, I'd had it all—and lost it all. Love, understanding, respect. The sense that we'd both become better people because of each other and could take on anything so long as we were together. Only we weren't together anymore. They'd ripped us apart, and I didn't know what was going to happen now.

The center will hold. That was the line Sydney had coined from "The Second Coming," a poem by William Butler Yeats, for us. Sometimes, in my darkest moments, I worried the poem's original wording was more fitting: *Things fall apart; the center cannot hold*.

I drank myself into oblivion, only to wake up in the middle of the night with a raging headache. I felt nauseous too, but when I staggered to the bathroom, nothing came up. I just felt miserable. Maybe that was because Sydney's hairbrush was still in there, reminding me of her. Or maybe it was because I'd skipped dinner and couldn't remember the last time I'd had blood either. No wonder I was in such bad shape. My alcohol tolerance had built up so much over the years that I rarely felt ill from it, so I must've really screwed myself up this time. The smart thing would've been to start hydrating and drinking gallons of water, but instead, I welcomed the self-destructive behavior. I returned to my room for another drink and succeeded only in making myself feel worse.

My head and stomach calmed around dawn, and I managed some kind of fitful sleep back in my own bed. That was interrupted a few hours later by a knock at the door. I think it was actually pretty soft, but with the lingering remnants of my headache, it sounded like a sledgehammer.

"Go away," I said, peering bleary-eyed at the door.

Trey stuck his head in. "Adrian, there's someone here you need to talk to."

"I've already heard what Merry Marcus has to say," I shot back. "I'm done with him."

The door opened farther, and someone stepped past Trey. Even though the motion made my world spin, I was able to sit up and get a better look. I felt my jaw drop and wondered if I was hallucinating. It wouldn't have been the first time. Usually, I only imagined Aunt Tatiana, but this person was very much alive, beautiful as the morning sunlight illuminated her chiseled cheekbones and blond hair. But there was no way she could be here.

"Mom?" I croaked out.

"Adrian." She glided in and sat down beside me on the bed, gently touching my face. Her hand felt cool against my fevered skin. "Adrian, it's time to go home."

CHAPTER 3
SYDNEY

I COULD FORGIVE THE ALCHEMISTS their light-show shock tactics because once I was able to see reasonably well again, they offered me a shower.

The wall in my cell opened up, and I was greeted by a young woman who was maybe five years older than I was. She was dressed in the kind of smart suit that Alchemists love, with her black hair pulled back tightly in an elegant French twist. Her makeup was flawless, and she smelled like lavender. The golden lily on her cheek shone. My vision still wasn't at full capacity, but standing beside her, I became acutely aware of my current state, that I hadn't truly washed in ages and that my shift was little more than a rag you might use to scrub the floors.

"My name is Sheridan," she said coolly, not elaborating on whether that was her first or last name. I wondered if she might be one of the people behind the voice in my cell. I was pretty sure they'd worked in shifts, using some sort of computer program to synthesize it so it always sounded the same. "I'm the current director around here. Follow me, please."

She turned down the hall in her black leather heels, and I followed wordlessly, not trusting myself to say anything yet. Although I'd had some freedom of movement in my cell, I'd also had limitations and hadn't done a lot of walking. My stiff muscles protested against the changes, and I moved slowly behind her, one agonizing barefoot step at a time. We passed a number of unmarked doors along the way, and I wondered what they held. More dark cells and tinny voices? Nothing seemed to be marked as an exit, which was my immediate concern. There were also no windows or any other indication of how to get out of this place.

Sheridan made it to the elevator long before I did and waited patiently for me. When we were both in, we went up one floor and emerged into a similarly barren hall. One doorway led to what looked like a gym bathroom, with tiled floors and communal showers. Sheridan pointed to a stall that had been supplied with soap and shampoo.

"The water will last for five minutes once you turn it on," she warned. "So use it wisely. There'll be clothes waiting for you when you're done. I'll be in the hall."

She stepped outside the locker room, in a seeming show of offering privacy, but I knew without a doubt I was still being watched. I'd lost all illusions of modesty the moment I got here. I started to strip off the shift when I noticed a mirror on the wall to my side, and more importantly, who was looking back from it.

I'd known I was in bad shape, but seeing the reality of that face-to-face was an altogether different experience. The first thing that struck me was how much weight I'd lost—ironic considering my lifelong obsession with staying thin. I'd certainly met that goal, met and blown past it. I'd crossed from thin to malnourished, and it showed not just in the way the shift hung on my thin frame but also in the gauntness of my face. That hollow look was intensified by dark shadows under my eyes and a paleness in the rest of me from lack of sun. I looked like I'd just recovered from some life-threatening disease.

My hair was in bad shape too. Whatever decent job I thought I'd been doing at washing it in the dark was now proven a joke. The strands were limp and oily, hanging in sad, messy clumps. There was no doubt I was still a blonde, but the color was dull, made much darker now by the dirt and sweat that scrubbing with a washcloth just couldn't get off. Adrian had always said my hair was like gold and had teased me about having a halo. What would he say now?

Adrian doesn't love me for my hair, I thought, meeting my eyes. They were steady and brown. Still the same. *This is all exterior. My soul, my aura, my character . . . those are unchanged.*

Resolved, I started to turn from that reflection when I noticed something else. My hair was longer than the last time I'd seen it, a little over an inch longer. Although I'd been well aware my legs needed a good shaving, I'd had no sense in the cell of what the hair on my head was doing. Now, I tried to remember how fast hair grew. About a half inch a month? That suggested at least two months, maybe three if I took the poor diet into account. The shock of that was more horrifying than my appearance.

Three months! Three months they've taken from me, drugging me in the dark.

What had happened to Adrian? To Jill? To Eddie? A lifetime could've passed for them in three months. Were they safe and well? Were they still in Palm Springs? New panic rose in me, and I staunchly tried to push it down. Yes, a lot of time had passed, but I couldn't let the reality of that affect me. The Alchemists were already playing enough mind games with me without my helping them.

But still . . . three months.

I stripped off my poor excuses for clothes and stepped into the stall, pulling the curtain closed behind me. When I turned the water on and it came out hot, it was all I could do not to sink to the floor in ecstasy. I'd been so cold for the last three months, and now here it was, all the warmth I could want. Well, not *all* the warmth. As I turned the temperature up full blast, I secretly wished I had a bathtub and could just sink into this heat. Still, this shower alone was glorious, and I closed my eyes, sighing with the first contentment I'd experienced in a very long time.

Then, remembering Sheridan's warning, I opened my eyes and found the shampoo. I applied it to and rinsed my hair three times, hoping it was enough to get out the worst of the grime. It'd probably take a few more showers to ever be fully clean again. After that, I scrubbed my body with the soap until I was raw and pink and smelled vaguely antiseptic, then just gloried in standing under the steaming water until it turned off.

When I stepped outside, I found clothes folded neatly on a bench. They were basic scrubs, loose pants and a shirt like you'd find hospital workers or—more fittingly—prisoners wearing. Tan, of course, since the Alchemists still had taste levels to maintain. They'd also given me socks and a pair of brown shoes, kind of a cross between loafers and slippers, and I wasn't surprised to find they were exactly my size. A comb completed the gift set, nothing fancy, but enough to attempt some semblance of neatness. The reflection that peered back at me now still didn't look good, exactly, but it certainly looked improved.

"Feeling better?" asked Sheridan, with a smile that didn't meet her eyes. Whatever strides I'd made in appearance felt lame beside her stylish grooming, but I consoled myself with the thought that I still had my self-respect and ability to think for myself.

"Yes," I said. "Thank you."

"You'll want this too," she said, handing me a small plastic card. It had my name, a bar code, and a picture from much better days on it. A little plastic clip on its back allowed it to attach to my collar.

She led me back to the elevator. "We're so happy you've chosen the path to redemption. Truly. I look forward to helping you on your journey back to the light."

The elevator took us to another floor and a new room, this one with a tattooist and a table. Whatever comfort I'd taken from a hot shower and real clothes vanished. They were going to re-ink me? But of course they were. Why rely on physical and psychological torture alone when you could have the added element of magical control?

"We just want to do a little touchup," Sheridan explained cheerily. "Since it's been a while."

It had been less than a year, actually, but I knew what she and the others really wanted to do. The Alchemist tattoos contained ink with charmed vampire blood woven with compulsion spells to reinforce loyalty. Obviously, mine hadn't worked. Magical or not, compulsion was basically just a strong suggestion, one that could be overridden if the will was fierce enough. They were probably going to double their usual dose in the hopes of making me more compliant so that I'd accept whatever rhetoric they were now going to subject me to.

What they didn't know was that I'd taken steps to protect against this very thing. Before being taken, I'd created an ink of my own—one made with human magic, something equally appalling to the Alchemists. From all the data I'd gathered, that magic negated whatever compulsion was in this vampire-derived ink. The downside was, I hadn't had a chance to inject that ink into my tattoo and provide that extra layer of protection. What I was counting on was the claim from a witch I knew that the very act of practicing magic would protect me. According to her, wielding human magic infused my blood, and that would counteract the vampire blood in the Alchemist tattoo. Of course, I hadn't really had a chance to practice many spells in solitary confinement and could only hope what I'd done in the past had left its mark permanently on me.

"Become one of us again," said Sheridan, as the tattooist's needle pricked the side of my face. "Renounce your sins and seek atonement. Join us in our battle to keep humans free of the taint of vampires and dhampirs. They are dark creatures and have no part of the natural order."

I tensed, and it had nothing to do with the needle piercing my skin. What if what I'd been told was wrong? What if magic use wouldn't protect me? What if, even now, that ink was working its way through my body, using its insidious power to alter my thoughts? It was one of my greatest fears, having my mind tampered with. I suddenly had trouble breathing as that idea crippled me with terror, causing the tattooist to pause and ask if I was in pain. Swallowing, I shook my head and let him continue, trying to hide my panic.

When he finished, I didn't *think* I felt different. I still loved Adrian and my Moroi and dhampir friends. Was that enough? Or would the ink take time to work? And if my magic use hadn't protected me, would my own strength of will be enough to save me? Obviously, I'd overcome the previous round of re-inking. Could I do it again?

Sheridan escorted me out when the tattooist released me, chatting away as though I'd just been to a spa and not subjected to an attempt at mind control. "I always feel so refreshed after that, don't you?"

It was kind of unbelievable to me that she could act so casually, like we were friends out for a walk, when she and the others had left me starving and half-naked in a dark cell for months. Did she expect me to be so grateful for the shower and warm clothes that I could forgive everything else? Yes, I realized moments later, she likely did. There were probably plenty of people who emerged from that darkness and were willing to do anything and everything for a return to ordinary comforts.

As we journeyed up another floor, I noticed that my head felt clearer and my senses seemed sharper than they had in months. Probably with good reason. They wouldn't be subjecting me to that gas, not with Sheridan around, so this was likely the first pure air I'd breathed in a long time. Until now, I hadn't realized what a shocking difference there was. Adrian could probably reach me in dreams now, but that would have to wait. At the very least, I could practice my magic again, now that my system was no longer polluted, and hopefully fight off any of the tattoo's effects. Finding an unwatched moment to do that might be easier said than done, though.

The next corridor we entered had a series of identical rooms, doors open, revealing narrow beds inside. I continued keeping track of everything we passed, each floor and room, still searching for a way out that didn't seem to exist. Sheridan led me inside a bedroom with the number eight written outside.

"I've always thought eight was a lucky number," she told me. "Rhymes with 'great.'" She nodded toward one of the two beds in the room. "That's yours."

For a moment, I was too taken aback by the idea of a bed to recognize the larger implications. Not that it was very comfortable-looking—but still. It was leagues away from my cell floor, even with its hard mattress and thin sheets made of a material similar to my old shift. I could sleep in this bed, no question. I could sleep and dream of Adrian. . . .

"Do I have a roommate?" I asked, finally taking note of the other bed. It was hard to say if the room was occupied since there were no other signs of personal belongings.

"Yes. Her name is Emma. You could learn a lot from her. We're very proud of her progress." Sheridan stepped out of the room, so apparently we weren't lingering. "Come on—you can meet her now. And the others."

A hallway branching off of this one took us past what looked like empty classrooms. As we headed toward the corridor's end, I became aware of something my dulled senses hadn't experienced in a while: the scent of food. *Real* food. Sheridan was taking us to a cafeteria. Hunger I hadn't even known I possessed reared up in my stomach with an almost painful lurch. I'd adapted to my meager prison diet so much that I'd taken my body's deprived state as normal. Only now did I realize how much I craved something that wasn't lukewarm cereal.

The cafeteria, such as it was, was only a fraction of the size of Amberwood's. It had five tables, three of which were occupied with people in tan scrubs identical to mine. These, it seemed, were my fellow prisoners, all with golden lilies. There were twelve of them, which I supposed made me lucky thirteen. I wondered what Sheridan would think of that. The other detainees were of mixed age, gender, and race, though I was willing to bet all were American. In some prisons, making you feel like an outsider was part of the process. Since this one's goal was to bring us back to the fold, they would most likely put us with those of shared culture and language—those we could aspire to be like if we only tried hard enough. Watching them, I wondered what their stories were, if any of them might be allies.

"That's Baxter," said Sheridan, nodding toward a stern-faced man in white. He stood in a window that overlooked the dining area and was presumably where the food came from. "His food is delicious. I know you're going to love it. And that's Addison. She oversees lunchtime and your art class."

It would not have been clear to me that Addison was a "she," if not for that introduction. She was in her late forties or early fifties, wearing a suit just as prim if less stylish than Sheridan's, and was stationed against the side wall with sharp eyes. She kept her hair shaved close to her head and had a hard-angled face that seemed at odds with the fact that she was chewing gum. The golden lily was her only ornamentation. She was pretty much the last person I would've expected for an art teacher, which in turn led to another realization.

"I have an art class?"

"Yes, of course," said Sheridan. "Creativity is very therapeutic for healing the soul."

There'd been a very soft murmur of conversation when we'd entered, one that had come to a complete stop when the others had noticed us. All eyes, detainees and their supervisors alike, swiveled in my direction. And none of them looked friendly.

Sheridan cleared her throat, like we weren't already the center of attention. "Everyone? We have a new guest I'd like to introduce you to. This is Sydney. Sydney has just come from her reflection time and is eager to join the rest of you on your journeys to purification."

It took me a second to realize "reflection time" must be what they called my solitary confinement in the dark.

"I know it will be difficult for you to accept her," Sheridan continued sweetly. "And I don't blame you. Not only is she still very, very shrouded in darkness, but she has been tainted in the most unholy of ways: through intimate and romantic contact with vampires. I understand if you don't want to interact with her and risk that taint yourselves, but I hope you'll at least keep her in your prayers."

Sheridan turned that mechanical smile on me. "I'll see you later for communion time."

I'd been nervous and uneasy since getting out of my cell, but as she turned to leave, panic and fear of a new sort hit me. "Wait. What am I supposed to do?"

"Eat, of course." She looked me over from head to toe. "Unless you're worried about your weight. It's up to you."

She left me there in the silent cafeteria, with all those eyes staring. I'd stepped out of one hell and into another. I'd never felt so self-conscious in my life, put on display for these strangers and having my secrets revealed. Frantically, I tried to think of a course of action. Anything to get me away from the stares and one step closer to getting out of here and back to Adrian. *Eat*, Sheridan had said. How did I go about that? This wasn't like at Amberwood, where the front office assigned veteran students to help new ones. In fact, Sheridan had gone out of her way to all but discourage them from helping me. It was a brilliant tactic, I supposed, one meant to make me desperately try for the others' approval and perhaps see someone like Sheridan as my only "friend."

Thinking through the psychology of the Alchemists calmed me down. Logic and figuring out puzzles were things I could deal with. Okay. If they wanted me to fend for myself, so be it. I looked away from the other detainees and walked steadily up to the window, where chef Baxter still wore a grimace. I stood in front of him expectantly, hoping that would be enough. It wasn't.

"Um, excuse me," I said softly. "May I have . . ." What meal had Sheridan said this was? I'd lost all track of time in solitary. ". . . some lunch?"

He grunted by way of response and turned away, doing something out of my sight. When he came back to me, he handed over a modestly filled tray.

"Thank you," I said, taking it from him. As I did, my hand lightly brushed one of his gloved ones. He exclaimed in surprise, and a look of distaste crossed his features. Gingerly, he removed the glove I'd touched, threw it away, and replaced it with a new one.

I gaped for a few moments in surprise and then turned away

with my tray. I didn't even attempt to engage with the others and instead sat down at one of the empty tables. Many of them continued staring at me, but some resumed their meals and whisperings. I tried not to think about if they were talking about me and instead focused on my meal. There was a small portion of spaghetti with red sauce that looked like it had come from a can, a banana, and a pint of 2 percent milk. Before coming here, I would never have touched any of it in my daily life. I would've lectured on the fat content of the milk and how bananas were one of the highest-sugar fruits. I would've questioned the meat quality and preservatives in the red sauce.

All of those hang-ups were gone now. This was food. *Real* food, not mushy, tasteless cereal. I ate the banana first, barely pausing to breathe, and had to slow myself so I didn't finish the milk in one gulp. Something told me Baxter didn't give seconds. I was more cautious with the spaghetti, if only because logic warned me my stomach might not react too well to the abrupt change in diet. My stomach disagreed and wanted me to cram it all in and lick the tray. After what I'd been eating these last few months, that spaghetti tasted like it had come from some gourmet restaurant in Italy. I was saved the temptation of eating it all when soft chimes suddenly sounded five minutes later. Like one person, all the other detainees stood up and carried their trays over to a large bin monitored by Addison. They emptied the trays of remaining food and then stacked them neatly on a nearby cart. I scurried up to do the same and then trailed behind the others as they left the cafeteria.

After Baxter's reaction to touching my hand, I tried to save the other detainees the trouble of being near me and kept a respectful distance apart. We bottlenecked in the narrow hall, however, and the maneuvers some of them did to avoid bumping into me would've been comical in any other circumstances. Those not near me went out of their way to avoid eye contact and pretend I didn't exist. Those forced to avoid contact fixed me with icy glares, and I was shocked to hear one whisper, "Slut."

I'd braced myself for a lot of things and expected to be called any number of names, but that one caught me off guard. I was surprised by how much it stung.

I followed the crowd into a classroom and waited until all of them had sat down at desks, lest I choose the wrong one. When I finally selected an empty seat, the two people nearest me moved their desks away. They were probably twice my age, again giving it that twisted yet sad, comical quality. The suited Alchemist leading the class looked up sharply from his table when he heard the movement.

"Elsa, Stuart. Those aren't where your desks go."

Chagrined, the two of them slid their desks back to their neat rows as the Alchemist love of orderliness trumped its fear of evil. From the glares Elsa and Stuart gave me, though, it was clear they were now adding their reprimand to the list of sins I was guilty of.

The instructor's name was Harrison, again making me wonder if that was a first or a last. He was an older Alchemist with thinning white hair and a nasally voice whom I soon learned was here to teach us about current affairs. For a moment, I was excited, thinking I'd get some glimpse of the outside world. It soon became clear to me that this was a highly specialized look at current affairs.

"What are we looking at?" he asked as a gruesome image of two girls with their throats ripped open appeared on a giant screen at the front of the class. Several hands went up, and he called on the one that had gone up first. "Emma?"

"Strigoi attack, sir."

I'd known that and was more interested in Emma, my roommate. She was close to my age and sat so unnaturally straight in her desk that I was certain she was going to have back problems later on.

"Two girls killed outside of a nightclub in St. Petersburg," Harrison confirmed. "Neither of them even twenty." The image changed to another grisly scene, this of an older man who'd obviously been drained of blood. "Budapest." Then another image. "Caracas." Another still. "Nova Scotia." He turned the projector off and began pacing in front of the classroom. "I wish I could tell you these were from the last year. Or even the last month. But I'm afraid that's not true. Anyone want to hazard a guess when these were taken?"

Emma's hand shot up. "Last week, sir?"

"Correct, Emma. Studies show that Strigoi attacks have not decreased since this time last year. There's some evidence they might be increasing. Why do you think this is?"

"Because the guardians aren't truly hunting them down as they should be?" That, again, was from Emma. *Oh my God*, I thought. *I'm rooming with the Sydney Sage of re-education.*

"That's certainly one theory," said Harrison. "Guardians are much more interested in protecting Moroi passively than actively seeking out Strigoi for the good of us all. In fact, when suggestions have been made to increase their numbers by recruiting at younger ages, the Moroi have selfishly declined.

They apparently have enough to consider themselves safe and feel no need to help the rest of us."

I had to bite my tongue. I knew for a fact that wasn't true. The Moroi were suffering from low guardian numbers because there was a shortage of dhampirs. Dhampirs couldn't reproduce with other dhampirs. They had been born in an age when humans and Moroi freely mixed, and now their race was continued by Moroi mixing with dhampirs, which always resulted in dhampir children. It was a genetic mystery even to the Alchemists. I knew from my friends that guardian ages were a hot topic right now, one that the Moroi queen, Vasilisa, was passionate about. She was fighting to keep dhampirs from becoming full-fledged guardians until they were eighteen, not out of selfishness, but because she thought they deserved a chance at adolescence before going out and risking their lives.

I knew now wasn't the time to share my insight, though. Even if they knew it, no one wanted to hear it, and I couldn't risk telling it. I needed to toe the line and act like I was on the road to redemption in order to secure as many privileges as I could, no matter how painful it was to listen as Harrison continued his tirade.

"Another factor may be that the Moroi themselves are aiding the increase in the Strigoi population. If you ask them, most Moroi will *claim* they want nothing to do with Strigoi. But can we really trust that, when they can so easily turn into those vile monsters? It's practically a stage of development for the Moroi. They live 'normal' lives with children and jobs, then when age starts to catch up with them . . . well, how convenient to just drink a little longer from their 'willing' victims, claim it was an 'accident' . . . and poof!" The number of air quotes Harrison used as he spoke was truly mind-boggling to follow. "They turn Strigoi, immortal and untouchable. How could they not? The Moroi are not strong-willed creatures, not like humans. And certainly not strong-souled. How can such creatures resist the lure of eternal life?" Harrison shook his head in mock sadness. "This, I'm afraid, is why Strigoi populations aren't dropping. Our so-called allies aren't exactly helping us."

"Where's your proof?"

That voice of dissent was a shock to everyone in the room—especially when they realized it had come from me. I wanted to smack myself and take the words back. I'd barely been out of imprisonment for two hours! But it was too late, and the words were out there. My own personal interest in the Moroi aside, I couldn't stand when people posited speculation and sensationalism as facts. The Alchemists should've known better, having trained me in the arts of logic.

All those eyes fell on me again, and Harrison came to stand in front of my desk. "It's Sydney, correct? So charming to have you in class so fresh out of your reflection time. It's especially charming to hear you speak so soon after joining us. Most newcomers bide their time. Now . . . would you be so kind as to repeat what you just said?"

I swallowed, again hating myself for having spoken, but it was too late to change things. "I asked where your proof was, sir. Your points are compelling and even seem reasonable, but if we don't have proof to back them up, then we're nothing but monsters ourselves, spreading lies and propaganda."

There was a collective intake of breath from the rest of the detainees, and Harrison narrowed his eyes. "I see. Well then, do *you* have an explanation backed by 'proof'?" More air quotes.

Why, why, why couldn't I have just stayed quiet?

"Well, sir," I began slowly. "Even if there were as many dhampir guardians as Strigoi, they wouldn't be evenly matched. Strigoi are almost always stronger and faster, and while some guardians do make solo kills, often they need to hunt Strigoi in groups. When you look at the actual dhampir population, you see it's not a match for the Strigoi one. The dhampirs are outnumbered. They aren't able to reproduce as easily as Moroi and humans—or even Strigoi, if you want to call it that."

"Well, from what I understand," said Harrison, "you *are* an expert at reproduction with Moroi. Perhaps you'd be personally interested in helping increase those dhampir numbers yourself, yes?"

Snickers sounded from around the class, and I found myself blushing in spite of myself. "That wasn't my intent here at all, sir. I'm just saying, if we're going to critically analyze the reasons why—"

"Sydney," he interrupted, "I'm afraid *we* won't be analyzing anything, as it's obvious you aren't quite ready to participate with the rest of us."

My heart stopped. No. No, no, no. They couldn't send me back to the darkness, not when I'd only just gotten out.

"Sir—"

"I think," he continued, "that a little purging might make you better able to participate with the rest of us."

I had no idea what that meant, but two burly men in suits suddenly entered the classroom, which must have been under surveillance. I attempted another protest to Harrison, but the men swiftly escorted me out of the room before I could make much of a plea to my instructor. So I tried arguing with the henchmen instead, going on about how there was clearly some sort of misunderstanding and how if they'd just give me a second chance, we could work all of this out. They remained silent and stone-faced, however, and my stomach sank at the prospect of being locked away again. I'd been so condescending toward what I viewed as the Alchemists' mind games with creature comforts that I hadn't realized how dependent I'd already grown on them. The thought of being stripped of my dignity and basic needs again was almost too much to bear.

But they only took me down one floor this time, not back to the level with the cells. And the room they led me to was painfully well-lit, with a larger monitor at the front of the room and a huge armchair with manacles facing it. Sheridan stood nearby, looking serene as ever . . . and she was brandishing a needle.

It wasn't a tattooist's needle either. It was a big, wicked-looking thing, the kind you used for medical injections. "Sydney," she said sweetly, as the men strapped me down in the chair. "What a shame I have to see you again so soon."

CHAPTER 4

ADRIAN

I HAD SO MANY QUESTIONS for my mom that it was hard to know where to begin. Probably the most important one was what she was even doing here, since last I'd known she was serving time in a Moroi prison for perjury and interfering with a murder investigation.

"We'll have plenty of time to talk later," she insisted. "Right now we have a flight to catch. Human boy, can you find us a suitcase?"

"His name is Trey," I said. "And he's my roommate, not my valet." I staggered to my closet and pulled out the suitcase I'd brought when I first came to Palm Springs. My mom took it from me and began packing up my room's belongings as though I were eight again.

"You're leaving?" asked Trey, looking as dumbfounded as I felt.

"I guess I am." I thought about it a little more, and suddenly, it seemed like a great idea. Why was I still here, torturing myself in a desert? Sydney was gone. Jill was making rapid strides in learning to block me through the bond, thanks to my extreme behavior recently. Besides, she'd be leaving here in another month as well. "Yes," I said more confidently. "I'm definitely leaving. It's prepaid through fall. You can stay on."

I needed to be away from this place and its memories of Sydney. She was everywhere I looked, not just in this apartment but also at Amberwood and even Palm Springs at large. Every place brought up some image of her, and although I hadn't given up on finding her, I'd continue doing so in a place that didn't cause me so much pain. Maybe this was the fresh start I needed.

That . . . and my mom was back! I'd missed her deeply, in a different way from Sydney, and had almost as little contact. My mother hadn't wanted me to reach her in dreams, and my father wouldn't deliver any letters. I'd worried about how Daniella Ivashkov had survived in a prison, but watching her now, she seemed no worse for it. She seemed as elegant as ever, well-dressed and well-made-up, moving around my room with that single-minded authority and confidence that defined her—and had played a role in her arrest.

"Here," she said, handing me something from the dresser. "Keep these on you. You don't want to check them in your luggage."

I looked down and was met with a sparkling array of diamonds and rubies set in platinum. They'd been a gift from my Aunt Tatiana. She'd given them to me "for special occasions," as though I'd have all sorts of reasons to wear thousands of dollars on my sleeves. Maybe I would have if I'd stayed at Court. Mostly in Palm Springs, they'd been a temptation, one I'd nearly pawned in a desperate attempt to get some cash. I squeezed them tightly a few moments now, letting the sharp corners dig into my palms, and then slipped them into my pocket.

My mom finished the suitcase in less than ten minutes. When I pointed out she'd only packed a fraction of my belongings, she waved my concern off. "No time. We'll buy you new things at Court."

So. We were going to Court. I wasn't entirely surprised. My family had a few other guesthouses around the world, but the Moroi Court in the Pocono Mountains of Pennsylvania was their primary residence. Honestly, I didn't care where we were going as long as it was away from here.

In the living room, I found a watchful guardian waiting for us. My mom introduced him as Dale and said he'd also be our driver. I made an awkward farewell with Trey, who still seemed stunned by the abrupt turn of events. He asked if I wanted to send a message through him to Jill or the others, which gave me pause. At last, I shook my head.

"No need."

Jill would understand why I needed to leave, why I needed to get away from my memories and my failures. Anything I told her in words would pale to what she'd learn from the bond, and she could either tell the others or come up with a pretty story for me. Eddie would think I was running away, but staying here for three months had brought me closer to only misery, not Sydney. Maybe this change of venue was what I needed.

My mom had booked us first-class seats to Pennsylvania, with Dale sitting right across the aisle. After living a frugal college student's life for so long, that kind of expense made my mind reel a little, yet the more I sat with my mom, the more natural it became. A flight attendant came around offering drinks, but my pounding head made me abstain and stick to water. That, and I wanted my wits about me to hear what my mom had to say.

"I've been home for a week," she said, as though she'd been away on holiday. "Naturally, I've been busy getting things back in order there, but you were first and foremost on my mind."

"How did you know where to find me?" I asked. My location, being tied to Jill's, was a tightly guarded secret. No one would risk her by revealing me.

Her brow knit. "I received a puzzling message. Anonymous. Said you were 'going through a tough time' and needed me. It had your address and strict instructions not to share it, as you were conducting important business for the queen. A little of that's gotten around—about the work you've been doing to protect us from Strigoi. It's very impressive."

Going through a tough time. Those were the words Jill had used to defend me last night for forgetting her fashion show. I nearly groaned. No one would risk Jill's safety to tell my mom where I was—except Jill herself.

"Does anyone know you're here?" I asked.

"Of course not," said my mom, looking offended. "I'd never reveal secrets so important to the Moroi's future. If there's a way to eradicate the Strigoi, I'll do my part and help you in yours . . . though, I must admit, darling, you *do* seem a bit out of sorts."

If my mom thought we were just doing Strigoi research in Palm Springs, then so be it. She'd hopefully have no reason to give it a second thought now that she'd retrieved me.

"'Out of sorts' is putting it lightly," I told her.

She rested her hand on mine. "What's wrong? You were dealing so well. I understand you've been taking classes again? And doing this work for the queen?"

With a start, I realized I'd never checked on my other two classes. Did I have final exams in them? Culminating projects? Crap. I'd been so stunned over my mom's arrival and the chance to escape that I'd completely forgotten to follow up at Carlton. I may have blown my last attempt at college success. The pride in her voice touched me, though, and I couldn't bear to tell her that part of the truth.

"Yeah, I've been busy," I said vaguely.

"Then what's wrong?" she reiterated.

I met her eyes, seeing the rare compassion few saw. Before her imprisonment, most saw her as prim, aristocratic Daniella Ivashkov, cold and unconcerned with image. I knew her that way as well, but in these rare, shining moments, I also knew her as my mother. And suddenly, I found myself telling the truth . . . or at least a version of it.

"There . . . well, there was a girl, Mom."

She sighed. "Oh, Adrian. Is that all?"

"It's not all!" I exclaimed angrily. "She was *the* girl. The one who changed everything. The one who changed me."

"All right, all right," she said, trying to soothe me. "I'm sorry. What happened with her?"

I tried to find some way to accurately convey the truth. "Her family didn't approve of me."

Now my mother was angry, assuming, naturally, that I was talking about a Moroi girl. "That's ridiculous! You come from the finest Moroi bloodlines, on both the Tarus and Ivashkov sides. The queen herself couldn't ask for better lineage. If this girl's family has problems with you, then they're clearly deluded."

I almost smiled. "Well, that we can agree on."

"Then what's the problem? If she's an adult—oh, Adrian, please tell me she's an adult and not a minor."

"She's an adult."

Relief flooded my mother's features. "Then she's capable of making her own decisions and coming to you, regardless of what her family thinks. And if she stands with them, then she's not worth your time, and you're better off without her."

I wanted to tell her that it wasn't that simple, but she hadn't reacted well to me being involved with Rose. A dhampir was unforgiveable. A human was inconceivable.

"I think it had as much to do with me personally as my bloodline," I said instead.

My mother tsked in disapproval. "Well, we'll see if she comes around. Who wouldn't want my boy? In the meantime, I wish you wouldn't let these things hit you so hard. What is it with you and girls, dear? Why do they either mean nothing to you or everything? It's always an extreme."

"Because I don't do things in halves, Mom. Especially when it comes to love."

When we landed and I was able to turn on my cell phone, I found a text message waiting from Jill: *Yup, it was me. I know you came to Palm Springs for my sake, but I figured it was time for you to change things. When I heard from Lissa that your mom was back, I thought it'd be good for you to see her, so I helped get you two connected. Hope that was okay.*

You're the best, Jailbait, I wrote back.

Her response made me smile: *You don't know the half of it.*

Your other two classes required final projects, not exams. Trey and I dug around the apartment and found some of your rejected projects to turn in. Not sure if you'll pass, but some credit is better than no credit.

It figured. Jill had kept track of what was due in my classes when I hadn't. I started and stopped a lot of projects, so there was no telling what she'd turned in, but in my recent state, it was probably better than anything I would've attempted on purpose for those final grades. It was in fate's hands now.

One thing puzzled me, though, as Dale drove my mom and me to Court. My mom herself had said that she'd been back for a week. Jill had given my address to my mom, which certainly created greater impact with a personal visit, but had it been necessary? Although Jill's location was a secret, Lissa would have made sure my mom had a secure way to call me as soon as she was free, had my mom asked. Why hadn't she? It was almost as though my mom had been putting off contacting me, and it wasn't until Jill called her attention to the problems I was having that my mom had acted. Surely, even if everything was fine with me, my mom would've wanted to get in touch right away . . . right?

Or maybe I was overthinking things. I couldn't doubt my mom's love. Whatever her faults, she still cared about me, and seeing her alive and well drove home how worried I'd been about her while she was imprisoned. Whenever I tried to bring up her time away, though, she brushed the subject off.

"It's done," she said simply as we drove up to the Court's front security gates. "I've served my sentence, and that's all there is to it. The only thing you need to know is that it's made me reassess my priorities in life and what really matters."

She gently touched my cheek. "And you're at the top of those priorities, my darling."

The Moroi Royal Court was arranged like a university, with lots of old Gothic buildings set on sprawling grounds. In fact, in the human world, its cover story was that it was an academic institution, a private and elite one that was generally left alone. Government officials and certain royal Moroi had permanent lodging there, and there were also accommodations for guests and all sorts of services to make life bearable. It was, in a sense, its own little enclosed city.

I expected my mother to take us to our family townhouse, but instead, we ended up at one of the guest housing facilities. "After living on your own, I couldn't imagine you'd want to be holed up with your father and me," she explained. "We can work on something more permanent later, but in the meantime, the queen has allowed these arrangements for you."

I was surprised, but she was right about one thing—I didn't really want my father tracking my comings and goings. Or her, for that matter. Not that I intended on too many wild and crazy goings-on. I was here for a fresh start, resolved to use what resources I could to help Sydney. After she'd gone out of her way to find me, though, I'd assumed my mother would want to keep me under lock and key.

An attendant at the building's front desk set me up with a room, and my mother hugged me goodbye. "I have an appointment to get to, but let's get together tomorrow, shall we? We're having guests over for dinner. I'm sure your father would love to see you. Come by, and we'll catch up. You *will* be okay now, won't you?"

"Of course," I said. We'd lost a lot of the day owing to travel and time change. "Not much trouble left for me to get into. I'll probably call it an early night."

She hugged me again, and then I made my way up to my room, which was the kind of one-bedroom suite you'd find at any five-star hotel. Once I'd deposited my suitcase in the bedroom, I immediately made some phone calls and began setting up plans. With those in place, I took a quick shower (my first of the day) and promptly headed back out again. It wasn't for any wild time, though.

Of course, some might consider any get-together with Rose Hathaway and Lissa Dragomir a wild time.

Both lived inside what was dubbed the royal palace around here, though from the outside, it maintained that same university facade. Once indoors, the full weight of Moroi history came pressing down with Old World grandeur: crystal chandeliers, velvet drapes, oil paintings of monarchs past. The queen's rooms were pretty updated, however, having been decorated more for her personal tastes and less for her office. I was just glad she'd taken a set of rooms different from the ones my aunt had lived—and died—in. It was already surreal enough coming here sometimes without that memory to haunt me.

The girls were in Lissa's living room when I arrived. Lissa was sitting cross-legged on a couch surrounded by books, while Rose had managed to arrange herself upside down in an armchair, her long, dark hair dangling and fanning out on the ground. She leapt upright to her feet with dhampir skill and grace upon my entrance. Hurrying over, she gave me a quick, friendly embrace. "You're really here. I thought it was a joke at first. Figured you'd be staying with Jill."

"She doesn't need me right now," I said, going over to hug

Lissa as she rose up from her books. "School's wrapping up, and there's all sorts of things keeping her busy for now."

"Tell me about it," said Rose, rolling her eyes at Lissa. "Miss All-Study-and-No-Play here has been taking the fun out of everything."

Lissa smiled indulgently at her best friend. "Exams start tomorrow."

"Mine just ended," I said.

"How'd you do?" Lissa asked, settling back down.

I eyed her books. "Let's just say I didn't put nearly as much work into it as you."

"See?" grumbled Rose. She flounced back into her chair, arms crossed.

I found my own chair between them and reflected upon my sketchy chances of passing this semester. "I think Lissa's doing it the right way."

At eighteen, Lissa was the youngest queen in the history of the Moroi, elected in the chaos following my aunt's murder. No one would've faulted her for not going to college or for simply attempting to do it long distance. Lissa, however, had held true to her lifelong dreams of going to a big university and felt that as monarch, it was now doubly important for her to have a thorough education. She'd been attending Lehigh University, a few hours away, and had kept her GPA up while ruling a restless nation. She and Sydney would get on beautifully.

Lissa put her feet up on a coffee table, and I used spirit to briefly look at her aura. It was warm and content, as it should be, with the flashes of gold that marked another spirit user. "Then you'll understand if I have to keep this short. I've got to memorize some dates and places before I go to bed tonight, and then we're heading up to school early in the morning. We're going to actually stay on campus for the rest of exam week."

"I won't keep you," I said. "I just wanted to ask you about something."

Lissa looked mildly surprised at that, and I realized she'd thought this was just a social call.

"Have you looked any more into what happened to Sydney Sage?"

Mild surprise turned to extreme surprise. "That again?" asked Lissa. It sounded unkinder than I knew she intended. No one outside of the Palm Springs circle knew what Sydney meant to me, and Lissa didn't even have the connection of friendship to Sydney that someone like Rose did.

In fact, the mention of Sydney brought a frown to Rose's face. "She's still missing?"

Lissa glanced between us. "I don't know anything more since you asked me a few months ago. I made inquiries. They said she'd been reassigned and that the information was classified."

"That's a lie," I said hotly. "They kidnapped her and sent her to one of their goddamned re-education centers!"

"You told me that before, and unless things have changed, you also told me you don't have any proof," said Lissa calmly. "Without that, I can hardly accuse them of lying . . . and really, what right do I have to question what they do with their own people?"

"You have the right because what they're doing goes against basic rules of decency and respect for others. They're holding her and torturing her."

Lissa shook her head. "Again, not something I can interfere with. Guardians often seize dhampirs who run away from training and then punish them. What if the Alchemists tried to dictate how we do that? We'd say what I'm saying now: It's not in our jurisdiction. They have their people, we have ours. Now, if one of my own people were in danger from them, then yes, I'd have every right to throw my weight around with the Alchemists."

"But you won't—because she's human," I said flatly. All the high hopes I'd come here with were starting to teeter.

Rose, at least, looked more sympathetic. "Are they really torturing her?"

"Yes," I said. "Well, I mean, I haven't been in touch with her or anyone who's talked to her to say exactly what they're doing, but I know someone who knows about situations like hers."

Sadness—for me—shone in Lissa's light green eyes, so similar to Jill's. "Adrian, do you realize how convoluted it sounds?"

Outrage and anger burned within me, both because of my helplessness and because the Alchemists had fooled Lissa with their lies. "But it's the truth! Sydney got friendly with all of us. She stopped acting like an Alchemist who thought we were creatures of evil. She became our friend. Hell, she treated Jill like she was a sister—ironic, since Sydney's own sister's the one who betrayed her. Ask Eddie. He was there when she was taken."

"But not for what happened afterward," finished Lissa. "He didn't see if she was taken to be tortured like you say. He didn't see if maybe she was just reassigned somewhere else, somewhere far away from you guys. Maybe that's the only 'treatment' the Alchemists are giving her if they think you interfered with their ideologies."

"They've done more than that," I growled. "I feel it in my gut."

"Liss," began Rose uneasily. "There must be something you can do. . . ."

Hope returned to me. If Rose was on board, maybe we could get others to help us behind the scenes. "Look," I said. "What if we try a different approach? Instead of directly questioning the Alchemists again, you could maybe send a . . . I don't know . . . strike team to investigate some possible locations for where she's being held?" It seemed like a brilliant idea to me. Marcus had been tapped for resources to investigate his list, but maybe we could recruit the Moroi and other dhampirs.

Rose lit up. "I'd totally help with that. Sydney's my friend, and I've got experience with—"

"No!" exclaimed Lissa, standing up. "No, both of you! Do you even hear what you're saying? Asking me to send a 'strike team' to break into Alchemist facilities? That's like an act of war! Can you even imagine how that would sound reversed? If they were sending teams of humans to investigate us?"

"Considering their ethics," I said, "I wouldn't be surprised if they've already tried."

"No," Lissa repeated. "I can't do any more with this, not if it doesn't directly affect my own people. I wish I could help everyone in the world—yes, including Sydney. But right now, my responsibilities are to my own people. If I'm taking risks, it has to be for them."

I stood up, full of anger and disappointment and a whole bunch of other emotions I couldn't yet define. "I thought you were a different kind of leader. One championing what was right."

"Yes, I am," she said, forcing calm with what appeared to be a great deal of effort. "And I'm currently championing more freedom for dhampirs, supporting Moroi who want to defend themselves, and getting the age law amended so that my own sister can come out of hiding! Meanwhile, I'm doing all this while going to school and trying to ignore the very loud faction that keeps demanding my removal from power. And don't even ask me what time I have left over for a personal life. Is that enough to satisfy you, Adrian?"

"At least you have a personal life," I muttered. I headed for the door. "Sorry to have interrupted your studying. Good luck with exams."

Rose tried to summon me back, and I think she might have even tried to follow me, but then Lissa called her name. No one came after me, and I let myself out of the royal apartments and back down through the winding halls of the palace. Fury and frustration simmered within me. I'd been so certain if I appealed to Lissa face-to-face—sober, even!—and explained my case, she'd do something for Sydney. I understood if the Alchemists were blocking Lissa's official attempts, but surely she could have found a group of Rose Hathaways to do some snooping around! Lissa had let me down, claiming to be a crusader but ultimately proving as much a bureaucrat as any other politician.

Despair began winding its way through me, dark and insidious, telling me I'd been a fool to come here. How could I really believe anything would change? Rose had looked like she wanted to help, but could I get her to go behind her best friend's back? Probably not. Rose was stuck in the system. I was stuck in my inability to help Sydney. I was useless to her, useless to everyone and everything—

"Adrian?"

I'd just been about to walk out of the palace's front doors when I heard a voice behind me. I turned and saw a pretty Moroi girl with gray eyes and dark, curly hair hurrying up to me. For a moment, my earlier emotional storm clouded my recognition skills. Then it came back to me.

"Nina?"

Her face broke into a grin as she threw herself at me in an unexpected embrace. "It *is* you," she said happily. "I was worried you'd disappeared. You haven't answered any messages or calls."

"Don't take it personally," I assured her, holding the door open. "I've been neglecting everyone." It was true. I'd dropped off the face of the earth when Sydney had been taken.

Those remarkable gray eyes watched me with worry. "Everything okay?"

"Yeah, yeah. I mean, no. It's complicated."

"Well, I've got time," she said as we stepped into the warm summer night. "We could get some food and talk."

I hesitated, unsure if I wanted to unburden myself. I'd met Nina earlier this year, just after she'd helped her sister transform back from being a Strigoi. Nina was a spirit user like me and had helped a little when I'd fought to capture some of the power that went into restoring a Strigoi—power that we'd found could act as a vaccine to stop others from being forcibly turned against their will. Her sister, Olive, was also Neil's object d'amour, if you could go that far. The two had only met a few times and *maybe* had a brief fling, though when she dropped out of communication, he pined for her as though they'd been together for years.

"I'm a good listener," said Nina when I didn't respond.

I shot her a smile. "I'm sure you are. I just don't want to drag you down."

"Drag me down?" She gave a harsh laugh. "Good luck. First of all, spirit's already doing a great job at that, so you've got tough competition. Ever since I restored Olive, that . . . I don't know . . . do you get that? That kind of dark, dreary haze?"

"Yup," I said. "Sure do."

"Well, that seems to be a daily visitor now, which makes life *delightful*, as I'm sure you can imagine. Meanwhile, after going through all that for Olive, *she's* run off on some vision quest because she decided she needed some 'alone time' to think about everything that's happened! She somehow manages to keep ending our dreams before I get a chance to talk to her. I'd go try to look for her, but Sonya keeps insisting I stick around here to help with her spirit research. They put me up here in swanky accommodations, but I don't have any other means to live off of, so I had to take a part-time secretarial job at the palace. Let me tell you, doing 'customer service' for a bunch of self-absorbed royals? Well, it's like a new circle of hell." She paused, remembering whom she was talking to. "No offense."

I laughed, maybe the first time I'd genuinely done so in a while. "None taken, because I know exactly the types you're talking about. If you do talk to your sister, by the way, you should let her know she's breaking poor Neil's heart."

"Noted," said Nina. "I think he's one of the things she's reflecting on."

"Is that good or bad?" I asked.

"I have no idea," she laughed.

I started laughing too, and suddenly, I decided to take her up on her offer. "Okay. Let's get something to eat . . . though honestly, after the last twenty-four hours . . . I'd rather have a drink. I don't suppose you'd be into that?" It was probably a terrible idea, but that hadn't stopped me before.

Nina grabbed my hand and began leading me toward a building across the lawn. "Thank God," she said. "I thought you'd never ask."

CHAPTER 5

SYDNEY

FOR A MOMENT, WHEN I SAW Sheridan's syringe, I thought she was opting for some extreme form of tattoo refreshing. Like, instead of injecting my skin with small amounts of charmed ink, she was going to shoot me up with a monster dose to make me toe the line.

It won't matter, I tried to tell myself. *Magic use protects me, no matter how strong the amount they use.* The words sounded reasonable, but I just wasn't sure if they were true.

As it turned out, however, Sheridan had something entirely different in mind.

"Things seemed so promising for you after we last spoke," she told me after plunging the needle into my arm. "I can't believe you didn't last an hour on your own."

I nearly said, "Old habits dic hard," but remembered I needed to act contrite if I wanted any sort of advancement. "I'm sorry," I said. "It just slipped out. I'll apologize to Harrison if that'll—"

A strange feeling began to well up in my stomach, starting at first as just slight discomfort and then building and building until it was full-blown nausea, the kind that took over your whole body. My stomach felt like it had a tidal wave in it, and my head began to throb. I could sense my temperature rising as well and sweat breaking out everywhere.

"I'm going to be sick," I said. I wanted to put my head down, but the chair kept me locked in place.

"No," said Sheridan. "You won't be. Not yet. Enjoy the show."

Along with arm restraints, the chair's headrest also made sure I couldn't turn my head, thus forcing me to look straight ahead at the screen. It turned on, and I braced myself for horrific images. What I saw instead were . . . Moroi. Happy Moroi. Friendly Moroi. Moroi children. Moroi doing ordinary things, like sports and eating at restaurants.

I was too miserable to puzzle out these baffling pictures, though. All I could think about was how I wished I could throw up. It was that kind of sickness—the kind where you knew you'd feel better if you could just expel that poison. But somehow, Sheridan was right. I couldn't get my body to throw up, no matter how much I might've longed to, and I instead had to sit there as that terrible, corrupting nausea twisted my insides. Waves of agony swept me. It didn't seem possible that I could contain this much misery inside me. I groaned and closed my eyes, mostly to make my head feel better, but Sheridan read another motive into it.

"Don't," she said. "This is a pro tip: It'll go a lot easier on you if you watch of your own free will. We have ways of keeping your eyes open. You won't like them."

I blinked back tears and focused back on the screen. Through my suffering, my brain tried to figure out why she'd care if I was watching pictures of happy Moroi or not. What did that matter when my body felt like it was being turned inside out?

"You're trying to . . ." I gagged, and for a moment, I thought I might get that relief after all. I didn't. ". . . create some sort of Pavlovian response."

It was a classic conditioning technique. Show me the image and make me feel terrible while I look at it, with the goal being that I'd eventually come to associate the Moroi—harmless, happy Moroi—with extreme discomfort and suffering. There was just one problem.

"Y-you need repeat sessions for this to take effect," I realized aloud. One time wasn't going to make me instantaneously feel revulsion to images of Moroi.

The look Sheridan gave me spoke legions about what I could expect in the future.

My heart sank. Or maybe it was my stomach. Honestly, with the way my insides felt just then, I couldn't distinguish one part from another. I don't know how long they kept me in that state. Maybe an hour. I couldn't really focus on counting time when my goal was just surviving each rollicking wave of sickness. After what seemed like an eternity, Sheridan gave me another injection, and the screen went dark. Her henchmen undid the restraints, and someone handed me a bucket.

For a few seconds, I didn't understand. Then, whatever had been holding my body back from finding release no longer held. Everything from that meager lunch came back up, and even afterward, my stomach still kept trying. I was reduced to dry heaves and finally just gagging before I stopped altogether. It was a long, painful process, and I was beyond the point of caring that I'd just thrown up—excessively—in front of others. And yet, as awful as it had been, I still felt better, now that I'd finally managed to purge whatever had caused that nausea to churn and churn within me. One of the lackeys discreetly took the bucket from me, and Sheridan gave me the courtesy of a cup of water, as well as the chance to brush my teeth at a small sink on the room's side. It was next to a cabinet full of medical supplies, as well as a mirror that let me see how miserable I looked.

"Well, then," Sheridan said cheerily. "Looks like you're ready for art class."

Art class? I was ready to curl into a ball and fall asleep. My whole body was weak and shaky, and my stomach felt as though it had been turned inside out. No one seemed to notice or care about my debilitated state, however, and the henchmen escorted me out of the room. Sheridan waved goodbye and said she'd see me soon.

My escort took me upstairs to the classroom level, to what served as the detainee art studio. Addison, the stern and androgynous matron from the lunchroom, was just getting class started, issuing instructions on today's assignment, which appeared to be the continuation of painting a bowl of fruit. It figured an Alchemist art class would have the most boring project ever. Despite her speaking, all eyes swiveled toward me as I entered. Most of the expressions that met me were cold. Some were a little smug. Everyone knew what had happened to me.

One nice thing I'd picked up on in this class and the previous one was that in re-education, the prized seats were closest to the teachers, unlike at Amberwood. This allowed me to slink to an empty easel in the back of the room. Most of the eyes couldn't follow me there unless they blatantly turned and ignored Addison. No one was willing to do that. Most of my effort was focused on remaining standing, and I only listened to her speak with half an ear.

"Some of you made good progress yesterday. Emma, yours in particular is coming along nicely. Lacey, Stuart, you'll need to start over."

I peered around, trying to match the people to their easels, which I had a full view of from the back. I thought maybe my recent purging had addled my brain, because Addison's comments made no sense. But no, I was certain I had the people right. That was Emma, my alleged roommate, a girl who looked to be of Asian American heritage who wore her black hair in a bun so tight, I swore it stretched her skin. Her painting seemed like nothing special to me and was barely discernible as fruit. Stuart was one of the people who'd pushed their desks away from me in Harrison's class. He actually appeared to have some artistic talent, and I thought his painting was one of the best. It took me a moment to learn who Lacey was, and I figured it out when she swapped out her canvas for a blank one. Her painting wasn't as good as Stuart's, but it was leagues better than Emma's.

It's not about skill, I finally realized. *It's about accuracy.* Stuart's pears were perfect, but he'd added a couple more than were there in real life. He'd also altered the fruit's position and painted a blue bowl—which looked much better than the actual brown one being used. Emma, while having created a much more rudimentary work, had the correct number of fruit, had placed them perfectly, and had matched every color exactly. The Alchemists didn't want creativity or embellishment. This was about copying what you were told to do, no questions and no deviation.

No one made any effort to help or advise me, so I stood there stupidly for a little while and tried to pick up on what the others were doing. I knew the basics of painting with acrylics from being around Adrian but had no practical experience myself. There was a communal supply of brushes and paint tubes near the fruit, so I made my way there with some of the other students and tried to pick my initial colors. Everyone gave me a wide berth, and when I selected and rejected one paint color for not being a close enough match, the next person who picked it up made sure to wipe the tube clean before taking it to her station. I finally returned to mine with several tubes, and while I couldn't speak for my ability to mimic the fruit, I felt fairly confident my colors were spot-on. I could at least play that part of the Alchemist game.

Getting started was slow work, though. I still felt terrible and weak and had a hard time even squeezing out some of the paint. I hoped we weren't being graded on speed. Just when I finally thought I might attempt to put brush to canvas, the door to the room opened, and Sheridan entered with one of her henchmen. Each was holding a tray full of cups, and I didn't need her to say a word because I could identify the contents on smell alone.

Coffee.

"Sorry for the interruption," said Sheridan, wearing her big fake smile. "Everyone's been working so hard lately that we thought we'd offer up a little treat: vanilla lattes."

I swallowed and stared in disbelief as my fellow detainees swarmed toward her and each took a cup. Vanilla lattes. How many times had I dreamed of those in captivity, when I'd been half-starved on that lukewarm gruel? It didn't even matter if they were skinny or full of sugar. I'd been deprived of anything like that for so long, and my natural instinct was to run up with the others and grab a cup.

But I couldn't. Not after the purging I'd just been through. Both my stomach and throat were raw, and I knew if I ate or drank anything other than water, it would come right back up. The coffee's siren song was torture to my mind, but my poor, sensitive stomach knew better. I couldn't have handled the gruel right now, let alone something as acidic as that latte.

"Sydney?" asked Sheridan, fixing that smile on me. She held up her tray. "There's one cup left." I wordlessly shook my head, and she placed the cup on Addison's desk. "I'll just leave it here in case you change your mind, shall I?"

I couldn't take my eyes off that cup and wondered which Sheridan wanted more: to see me suffering and deprived, or to have me risk it all and throw up in front of my classmates.

"Favorite of yours?" a low voice asked.

I was so certain no one could be speaking to me directly that I didn't even look for the speaker right away. With great effort, I dragged my gaze from the longed-for latte and discovered it was my neighbor who'd spoken, a tall, nice-looking guy who was maybe five years older than me. He had a lanky frame and wore wire-rimmed glasses that added an intellectual air, not that Alchemists needed it.

"What makes you say that?" I asked quietly.

He smiled knowingly. "Because that's how it always is. When someone goes to their first purging, the rest of us get 'rewarded' with one of that person's favorite foods. Sorry about this, by the way." He paused to drink some of the latte. "But I haven't had coffee in ages."

72

I winced and looked away. "Knock yourself out."

"At least you resisted," he added. "Not everyone does. Addison doesn't like the risk of us spilling hot drinks in here, but she'd like it even less if someone got sick all over her studio."

I glanced up at our teacher, who was offering advice to a gray-haired detainee. "She doesn't seem to like a lot of things. Except gum."

The smell of coffee was stronger than ever in the room, both alluring and revolting. Trying desperately to block it out, I lifted my paintbrush and was about to attempt some grapes when I heard a click of disapproval beside me. I glanced back at the guy, who shook his head at me.

"You're just going to start like that? Come on, maybe you don't have the values of a good Alchemist, but you should still have the logic of one. Here." He offered me a pencil. "Sketch. At least start with quadrants to guide you."

"Aren't you afraid I'll taint your pencil?" The words were out before I could stop them.

He chuckled. "You can keep it."

I turned back to the blank canvas and stared at it for several moments. Gingerly, I divided my canvas into four parts and then did my best to make a rough sketch of the fruit bowl, paying careful attention to where each piece was in relation to the others. Partway through, I noticed the easel was too tall for me, further complicating things, but I couldn't figure out how to adjust it. Seeing my struggles, the guy beside me leaned over and deftly lowered my easel to a more suitable height before resuming his own work.

"Thanks," I said. The expectant canvas in front of me

diminished whatever pleasure I might have felt from the friendly gesture. I attempted to sketch again. "I've seen my boyfriend do this a hundred times. Never thought I'd be doing it as some sort of twisted 'therapy.'"

"Your boyfriend's an artist?"

"Yes," I said warily, uncertain if I wanted to engage in this topic. Thanks to Sheridan, it was no secret my boyfriend was a Moroi.

The guy gave a small snort of amusement. "Artistic, huh? Haven't heard that one before. Usually when I meet girls like you—who fall for guys like *them*—all I ever hear about is how cute they are."

"He *is* really cute," I admitted, curious as to how many girls like me this guy had met.

He shook his head in amusement as he worked on his painting. "Of course. I guess he'd have to be for you to risk so much, huh? Alchemists never fall for the Moroi who aren't cute and brooding."

"I never said he was brooding."

"He's a 'really cute' vampire who paints. Are you saying he *doesn't* brood?"

I felt my cheeks flush a little. "He broods a little. Okay . . . a lot."

My neighbor chuckled again, and we both painted in silence for some time. Then, out of the blue, he said, "I'm Duncan."

I was so startled, my hand jerked, causing my already bad banana to look even worse. In over three months, these were the first genuinely civil words anyone had spoken to me. "I . . . I'm Sydney," I said automatically.

"I know," he said. "And it's nice to meet you, Sydney."

My hand began to tremble, forcing me to set down the brush. I had made it through months of deprivation in the dark, endured the glares and name-calling from my peers, and somehow even survived being made medically ill without a tear. But this small act of kindness, this nice and ordinary gesture between two people . . . well, it almost broke me when nothing else had. It drove home how far away I was from everything—from Adrian, my friends, safety, sanity . . . it was all gone. I was here in this tightly regulated prison of a world, where my every move was governed by people who wanted to change the way I thought. And there was no sign of when I'd get out of here.

"Now, now," said Duncan brusquely. "None of that. They love it when you cry."

I blinked back my tears and gave a hasty nod as I retrieved my brush. I set it back on the canvas, barely aware of what I did. Duncan also continued painting, his eyes on his work as he spoke more.

"You'll probably be able to eat when dinner comes. But don't overdo it. Be smart about what you eat—and don't be surprised if you find another favorite of yours on the menu."

"They really know how to make a point, don't they?" I grumbled.

"Yes. Yes, they do." Even without looking at him, I could tell he was smiling, though his voice soon grew serious again. "You remind me of someone I used to know here. She was my friend. When the powers-that-be realized we were friends, she went away. Friends are armor, and they don't like that here. Do you understand what I'm saying to you?"

"I—I think so," I said.

"Good. Because I'd like us to be friends."

The chimes signaling the end of class sounded, and Duncan began gathering up his things. He started to walk away, and I found myself asking, "What was her name? Your friend who was taken?"

He paused, and the look of pain that crossed his face immediately made me regret asking. "Chantal," he said at last, his voice barely a whisper. "I haven't seen her in over a year." Something in his tone made me think she'd been more than a friend. But I couldn't think much about that when I processed the rest of what he'd said.

"A year . . ." I did a double take. "What did you do to get here?"

He simply gave me a sad smile. "Don't forget what I said, Sydney. About friends."

I didn't forget. And when he didn't speak to me for the rest of the day and instead hung out with the other glaring and snickering detainees, I understood. He couldn't show me any special treatment, not when our peers and the unseen eyes of superior Alchemists were always watching. But his words burned inside me, giving me strength. *Friends are armor. I'd like us to be friends.* I was trapped in this terrible place, full of torture and mind control . . . but I had a friend—one friend—even if no one else knew. It was empowering, and that knowledge helped carry me through another class full of Moroi propaganda and sustained me when a girl tripped me in the hall with a muttered, "Vamp whore."

Our last class wasn't really a class at all. It was a session called "communion time," and it took place in a room they called the sanctuary, where apparently Sunday church services were also held. I made note of that because it meant I'd have a way to mark time. It was a beautiful room, with high ceilings and wooden pews. No windows, though. Apparently they were serious about cutting off our escape options—or maybe it would've simply been too uplifting for us to see the sun and sky every once in a while.

One wall of the sanctuary was full of writing, and I lingered in front of it as my fellow detainees filed in. Here, on painted white bricks, was a record of all those who had come before me, written in their own hand. Some were short and to the point: *Forgive me, I have sinned.* Others were full-out paragraphs, detailing perceived crimes and how their authors longed for redemption. Some were signed, some were anonymous.

"We call this the Wall of Truth," said Sheridan, walking up beside me with a clipboard. "Sometimes people feel better after confessing their sins upon it. Perhaps you'd like to?"

"Maybe later," I said.

I followed her to a circle of chairs, set up away from the pews. Everyone settled down, and she made no comments when my nearest neighbors scooted their chairs a few inches away. Communion time, it seemed, was a type of group therapy, and Sheridan engaged the circle in what everyone had accomplished today. Emma was the first to speak up.

"I learned that although I have made progress in restoring my soul, I have a long way to go before I attain perfection. The greatest sin is to give up, and I'll keep going forward until I'm completely immersed in light."

Duncan, sitting beside her, said, "I made progress in art. When we started class today, I didn't think anything good would come of it. But I was wrong."

Whatever temptation that might've given me to smile was

cut short when the girl beside him said, "I learned today how glad I am to not be as bad as someone like Sydney. Questioning my orders was wrong, but at least I never let one of *them* lay their profane hands on me."

I flinched and expected Sheridan to laud the speaker for her virtue, but instead, Sheridan fixed cold eyes on the girl. "You think that's true, Hope? You think you have the right to declare who's better or worse among you? You're all here because you've committed grave crimes, make no mistake about it. *Your* insubordination may not have resulted in the same vile outcome as Sydney's, but it stemmed from a place just as dark. Failure to obey, failure to heed those who know best . . . that is the sin at hand, and you're just as guilty of it as her."

Hope had gone so white, it was a wonder someone didn't accuse her of being a Strigoi. "I—I didn't mean—that is—I—"

"It's clear you didn't learn as much as you thought you did today," said Sheridan. "I think you need to do some further learning." And through another unseen command, her henchmen showed up and hauled off a protesting Hope. I felt sick inside, and it had nothing to do with my earlier purging. I wondered if she'd face the same fate, though her fault here seemed to be pride, not defense of Moroi.

Sheridan turned to me now. "What about you, Sydney? What did you learn today?"

All those eyes turned on me. "I learned that I have a lot to learn."

"Indeed you do," she replied gravely. "Admitting that is a big step toward redemption. Would you like to share your history with the others? You may find it liberating."

I hesitated under the weight of those stares, unsure what

answer would get me in the most trouble. "I . . . I'd like to," I began slowly. "But I don't think I'm ready. I'm just still so overwhelmed by everything."

"That's understandable," she said, causing me to sag in relief. "But once you see how much everyone's grown here, I think you'll want to share. You can't overcome your sins if you keep them locked up inside."

There was a warning note in her voice that was impossible to miss, and I responded with a solemn nod. Mercifully, after that, she moved on to someone else, and I was spared. I spent the rest of the hour listening to them blather on about the amazing progress they'd all made in casting off the darkness in their souls. I wondered how many of them meant what they said and how many were just trying to get out of here like me. I also wondered: If they *had* made that much progress, then why were they still here?

After communion time, we were dismissed for dinner. Waiting in line, I heard the others chatting about how chicken parmesan had been replaced at the last minute by fettuccine alfredo. I also heard someone say fettuccine alfredo was Hope's favorite. When she joined the end of the line, pale and shaken— and shunned by the others—I realized what had happened. Chicken parmesan was a childhood favorite of mine—which the authorities here probably knew from my family—and had originally been on the menu to punish me and my purging-weakened stomach. Hope's act of insubordination had trumped mine, however, resulting in a last-minute dinner switch. The Alchemists really were serious about making a point.

Hope's miserable face confirmed as much when she sat alone at one of the empty tables and stared at her food without touching a thing. Although the sauce was too rich for me, I at least was at a point where I could stomach some of the milder sides and milk. Watching her then, ostracized like me, struck me deeply. Just earlier that day, I'd seen her in the thick of social life with the others. Now she was shunned, just like that. Seeing an opportunity, I started to stand up, intending to join her. Across the room, Duncan, who was sitting and chatting pleasantly with a group of others, caught my eye and gave a sharp headshake. I wavered a few moments and then sat down again, feeling ashamed and cowardly for not taking a stand with another pariah.

"She wouldn't have thanked you for it," he murmured to me after dinner. We were in the facility's small library, allowed to choose a book to take back for bedtime reading. All the books were nonfiction, reinforcing Alchemist principles. "This stuff happens, and she'll be back with the others tomorrow. You going to her would've drawn attention and maybe delayed that. Worse, if she did welcome you, the powers-that-be would've noticed and thought the troublemakers were ganging up."

He selected a book seemingly at random and walked away before I could respond. I wanted to ask him at what point I'd be accepted by the others—or if I'd ever be accepted. Surely everyone had gone through what I had at some point. And surely they'd eventually worked themselves into the detainees' social world.

Back in my room, Emma made it clear no breakthroughs were going to occur with her. "I'm making good progress," she told me primly. "I don't need you ruining it with your perversions. The only thing we do in this room is sleep. Don't talk to me. Don't interact with me. Don't even look at me if you can help it."

With that, she took her book and lay on the bed, purposely putting her back to me. I didn't care, though. It was no different than any other attitude I'd received today, and I now had a much bigger concern on my mind. I'd scarcely allowed myself to think about it until now. There'd been too many other trials and ordeals to get through, but now we were here. The end of the day. Bedtime. Once I was in pajamas (identical to my day scrubs) and had brushed my teeth, I got into bed with a barely constrained excitement.

I would sleep soon. And I would dream of Adrian.

The realization had swirled at the back of my mind, keeping me going through my low points. This was what I had worked for, why I had endured the day's indignities. I was out of my cell and free of the gas. Now I would sleep normally and dream of him . . . provided my eagerness didn't keep me awake.

As it turned out, that wasn't going to be an issue. After an hour of reading time, the chimes sounded, and the lights went out automatically. The room's door was a sliding pocket door that didn't quite hit flush against the wall, allowing a crack of light in from the hall that I was kind of happy to see after my months in pitch-blackness. I heard a click, like some kind of bolt coming out, that locked the door in place. I snuggled into the covers, filled with excitement . . . and suddenly began to feel tired. Very tired. One minute I was imagining what I'd say to Adrian; the next, I could barely keep my eyes open. I fought it, forcing my mind to stay focused, but it was as though a heavy fog was descending on me, weighing me down and clouding my mind. It was a sensation I was all too familiar with.

"No . . ." I managed to say. I wasn't free of the gas. They were still regulating our sleep, probably to make sure no afterhours collusion took place. I was too exhausted to think past that. Thick sleep soon wrapped around me, dragging me into a darkness that had no dreams.

And no chance for escape.

CHAPTER 6
ADRIAN

NINA WAS A GOOD DRINKING BUDDY and not just because she could hold her liquor.

Even when not actively wielding spirit, she had the same intuitiveness that we spirit users naturally possessed. She quickly picked up on when I wanted to talk about things and, most importantly, when I didn't. We started off in a quiet bar, and I was happy to let her do most of the talking. It didn't sound like she'd made many friends these last few months at Court, and with Olive gone, Nina had had little chance to unburden herself.

"I just don't understand," she said. "People almost seem afraid of me. I mean, they say they aren't, but I can tell. They avoid me."

"Spirit still freaks a lot of people out, that's all. And I can tell you this, after living around Moroi, dhampirs, and humans, it's a fact that people are afraid of what they don't understand." I emphasized my point with a drink stirrer. "And most are too lazy or ignorant to find out more."

Nina smiled but still looked wistful. "Yeah, but everyone seems to accept Dimitri and Sonya. And they actually *were* Strigoi. Seems like that would be a lot harder to get on board with than a girl who just helped restore one."

"Oh, there was plenty of freaking out going on when those two were first restored, believe me. But Dimitri's gallant reputation and heroic acts soon overshadowed that. Then Sonya got her own fame with all her 'Strigoi vaccine' work."

"Is that what it takes?" Nina asked. "Do I—and Olive—have to do great deeds to get people to forget about our pasts?"

"You don't have to do anything you don't want to," I said staunchly. "Is that why Olive left? Was it too hard being around others?"

Nina frowned and looked down at the edge of her glass. She was drinking cosmos, which were a little too fruity for my tastes. I spared a moment to idly wonder what Sydney would drink, if she ever allowed herself to indulge. Some girly cocktail like that? No, I instantly knew if Sydney ever drank, it would be wine, and she'd be one of those people who could tell you the year, region, and soil components the grapes were grown in, based on a sip alone. Me? I'd be lucky if I could tell the difference between boxed and bottled wine. The thought of her made me start to smile, and I quickly hid it, lest Nina see and think I was laughing at her.

"I don't know why Olive left," she said at last. "And that's almost as bad as her leaving in the first place. I'm her sister. I brought her back!" Nina jerked her head back up, and tears glittered in those gray eyes. "If something's bothering her, she should have come to me first. After everything I went through for her . . . does she think I wouldn't listen? Doesn't she know how much I love her? We share the same blood; that's a bond nothing and no one can ever break. I would do anything for her—anything—if she only asked, if she'd only trust me enough to ask. . . ."

She trembled, and there was a slightly unhinged quality to her voice, one I recognized. It happened to me when spirit started to make me feel unstable. "Maybe she feels like you've done too much for her already," I said, gently placing a hand over hers. "Have you reached out to her in dreams?"

Nina nodded, calming a little. "She always tells me she's fine and that she just needs more time."

"Well, there you go. My mom told me the same thing when she was locked up. Sometimes people need to work things out on their own."

"I guess," she said. "But I still hate the thought of her being alone. I wish she'd at least reached out to Neil or someone else."

"I think he wishes it too. But he'll be glad to know she's just figuring things out. He probably respects the whole solitary journey thing." I finished my drink and saw hers was getting low too.

"Another round?" she asked.

"Nah." I stood up and put some cash on the table. "Let's find a different scene. You said you wanted to meet more people, right?"

"Yes . . ." Her voice was wary as she stood with me. "Do you know where to find a party or something?"

"I'm Adrian Ivashkov," I declared. "The parties find me."

That was a slight exaggeration, as I actually did have to go seeking one . . . but I was right on my first try. A royal who'd been in my class at Alder, Vanessa Szelsky, used to always throw

weekend parties at her parents' Court accommodations, and I
had no reason to think things had changed in less than a year,
especially since I'd heard her parents still traveled excessively.
Vanessa and I had made out a few times over the years, enough
that she regarded me pretty favorably but not enough that she
would blink or get upset about me crashing her party with
another girl.

"Adrian?" she exclaimed, pushing her way through the
packed courtyard behind her parents' place. "Is that really you?"

"In the flesh." I kissed Vanessa's cheek. "Vanessa, this is
Nina. Nina, Vanessa."

Vanessa gave Nina a once-over and raised an eyebrow in
surprise. Vanessa was a society girl if ever there was one, and
although she would probably claim this was a "casual" party,
her dress had undoubtedly come from some famous designer's
spring collection. Getting her hair and makeup done for tonight
had probably cost more than Nina's whole outfit, which was
suitable for a secretarial job but was, at best, off the rack from
a midrange department store. It didn't bother me in the least,
but I could see Vanessa deliberating. Nina could see it too and
wrung her hands nervously. At last, Vanessa shrugged and gave
Nina a genuinely friendly smile.

"Nice to meet you. Any friend of Adrian's is welcome here—
especially since you managed to get him out." Vanessa put on a
pout she'd undoubtedly practiced a hundred times in the mirror
to make herself look extra adorable. "Where have you been? You
dropped off the face of the earth."

"Top secret government business," I said, trying to make my
voice sound sinister while still being heard above the music. "I
wish I could tell you lovely ladies more, but the less you know,

the better. For your own protection. Think of it as me looking out for you."

They both scoffed at that, but it earned my welcome, and Vanessa beckoned us forward. "Come on and get a drink. I know a lot of people who are going to be happy to see you."

Nina leaned toward me as we walked through the crowd. "I think I might be out of my league here."

I put an arm around her to steer her past a guy heedlessly waving his arms to tell some wild story. "You'll be fine. And really, these people are just like anyone else you know."

"The people I know don't casually eat shrimp off their best china in one hand while drinking champagne in the other."

"Technically," I said, "those are prawns, not shrimp, and I'm sure that's actually her mother's second-best china."

Nina rolled her eyes at me but didn't get a chance to say much more as word spread that Adrian Ivashkov was back. Nina and I found drinks and took up chairs near a koi pond, where people flocked to come talk to us. Some were friends I'd regularly partied with before leaving for Palm Springs. Many others were those drawn by the allure and secrecy of my long disappearance. I'd never had much trouble attracting friends, but a mysterious past suddenly raised my stock like nothing else I could've concocted.

I let it slip that Nina was a spirit user too and didn't stop others from drawing the conclusion that she was part of whatever clandestine business I'd been involved in. I made a point to particularly introduce her to some of the less-vapid royal kids I knew, in the hopes that she might walk out of here tonight with a few solid acquaintances. As for me, I took on a role I hadn't had in ages and practically felt like a king at my own court. One thing I'd learned over the years was that confidence had a powerful effect on others, and if you acted like you deserved their attention, they believed it. I joked and flirted in a way I hadn't in months and was surprised at how easily it all came back to me. The high of that attention was heady, but it, like everything else, felt empty without Sydney in my life. I soon found myself cutting back on the alcohol as the night wound down. As much as I loved the escape the drinks brought me, I was determined to search for Sydney again before I went to bed. I needed sobriety for that.

"Well, well, look who's back," an unwelcome voice suddenly said. "I wouldn't have thought you had the balls to show your face in public after last time."

Wesley Drozdov, asshole extraordinaire, came to a halt before me, flanked by his lackeys, Lars Zeklos and Brent Badica. I stayed seated and made a big show of looking around and behind me. "Are you talking to yourself? I don't see a mirror anywhere. And really, your performance wasn't *that* bad. You shouldn't get so down over a little embarrassment like that."

"Little?" asked Wesley. He took a step forward and clenched his fists, but I refused to move from where I was. He pitched his voice low. "Do you know how much trouble I got in? My dad had to hire a flock of lawyers to get me out of that! He was furious."

I put on a look of mock sympathy and spoke loudly, making him wince. "I would be too, if a human girl kicked my son's ass. Oh, wait. *I* was the one who kicked your ass."

We'd gathered quite an audience, as these things often did, and Vanessa soon came hurrying over. "Hey, hey," she demanded. "What's going on?"

"Oh, the usual," I said, giving her a lazy smile. "Catching up on old times, laughing at times past. And if I've learned one thing, it's that Wesley just makes me laugh and laugh."

"You know what makes me laugh?" snapped Wesley. He nodded toward Nina. "Your cheap date there. I've seen her before. She's the receptionist at my dad's office. You promise you'd get her a better job if she sleeps with you?"

I sensed Nina stiffening beside me, but I didn't dare shift my gaze from the guys standing over me. They'd started off as a nuisance, but now they were kindling a dark, uncharacteristic anger in me. Looking into Wesley's eyes brought back all the memories of that night with Sydney when he and his henchmen had planned on taking advantage of her. Thoughts of the harm they'd intended for her mingled with my fears of all the unknown danger she might be facing now. It became one and the same, making my chest clench in rage and fear.

Destroy them, Aunt Tatiana whispered in my mind. *Make them pay.*

I worked to ignore her and conceal my emotions as best I could. Still wearing a dumbass smile, I said, "Why, no. She's here with me by choice. I know that's probably a weird concept for you, considering your track record with girls. Vanessa, I think Wes was just about to tell that story when you walked up—about the 'flock' of lawyers his dad had to hire to cover up how he and his entourage here tried to dabble with a human that was a guest of the queen's?" I gestured grandly. "Please, go on. Tell us how it all worked out. And if they let you keep the drugs you were going to use on her. Might come in handy with some of the ladies around here, eh?"

I broke eye contact with Wesley long enough to give an

exaggerated wink to a group of horrified girls standing nearby. I was positive what Wesley had tried to do wasn't public knowledge, nor had he intended it to become so when he'd come up to me posturing about his past and dad's lawyers. Humans might be less in the eyes of many Moroi, but dabbling—the act of drugging a non-feeder human and drinking from them against their will—was a pretty ugly sin among our kind. Attractive humans were especially desirable to the lowlifes who tried that, and Sydney had caught Wesley's eye on her last visit. He and the others had tried to assault her, thinking I'd help. I'd ended up attacking them with a tree branch until guardians showed up on the scene.

I didn't need the gasps around us to confirm that story hadn't made local news. Wesley's angry face told me as much. "You son of a bitch—"

He charged me, but I'd been expecting it and had spirit at the ready. Telekinesis wasn't a spirit ability I utilized that much, but it was well within my range.

Destroy him! Destroy him! Aunt Tatiana insisted.

I opted for something a little less savage. With a thought, I sent one of those fine china platters Nina had commented on flying toward Wesley's face. It clipped him hard on the side of the head, showering him with prawns and achieving my dual goals of pain and humiliation.

"That's a cheap air user's trick!" he snarled, attempting to move toward me again. The attack lost some of its impact since he was still wiping prawns off.

"What about this?" I asked. With a flick of my hand, Wesley's advance came to a halt. The muscles in his body and face strained as he ordered his limbs to move, but the energy of spirit blocked them. It would've been difficult for an air user to manage that kind of complete immobility, and it sure as hell wasn't easy for me either, seeing as I was only barely sober and was using an ability unfamiliar to me. The effect it generated was worth the effort, judging from the looks of awe on everyone's faces. I mustered what remaining spirit I could to make myself appear extra charismatic to those gathered. It was impossible to compel a crowd, but spirit used correctly could make you much more endearing to others.

"Last time, you guys asked if I was a big, bad spirit user," I remarked. "The answer? Yes. And I really don't like it when assholes like you demean any girl—human or Moroi. So, if you want to move again, you'll first apologize to my beautiful friend here. Then you'll apologize to Vanessa for ruining her party, which was actually pretty amazing until you showed your disgusting faces and wasted her prawns."

It was a bluff. Using telekinesis to restrain an entire person took a ridiculous amount of spirit, and I was running out. Wesley didn't know that, however, and he was terrified at being immobilized.

Why stop there? demanded Aunt Tatiana. *Think what he did to Sydney!*

He didn't succeed, I reminded her.

It doesn't matter! He tried to hurt her. He has to pay! Don't just freeze him with spirit! Use it to crush his skull! He needs to suffer! He tried to hurt her!

For a moment, her words and that storm of emotion building in my chest threatened to overcome me. He *had* tried to hurt Sydney, and maybe I couldn't stop her current captors, but I could stop Wesley. I *could* make him pay, make him suffer for even thinking of hurting her, make sure he was never able to—

"I'm sorry," Wesley blurted out to Nina. "And to you too, Vanessa."

I hesitated a moment, torn between the desperate look on his face and Aunt Tatiana's urgings—urgings that a dark part of me secretly wanted to give in to. Soon, the decision was made for me. I couldn't have held out longer if I'd wanted to. My grasp on spirit vanished, and he collapsed to the ground in an ungraceful heap. He scurried to his feet and quickly backed away, with Brent and Lars shadowing him like the toadies they were. "This isn't over," Wesley warned, feeling brave once he'd put more distance between us. "You think you're untouchable, but you aren't."

You showed him weakness, Aunt Tatiana told me.

"Get out," ordered Vanessa. She gave a nod toward a couple of her larger male friends, who were more than happy to help Wesley to the door. "And don't ever come back to any of my parties again."

From the mutterings of others, Wesley and his cronies weren't going to be welcome at any parties for a long, long time. But me? Suddenly, I was even more of a star than I had been. Not only was I shrouded in secrets, I'd also just used the still little-understood power of spirit to put a would-be womanizer in his place. The girls at the party loved that. Even the guys did. I had more invitations and friends than I'd ever had in my life—and that was saying something.

But I was also exhausted. The sun was threatening to come up over the horizon, and I was still on a human schedule. I took the well wishes with as much humility as I could and attempted to make my way to the door, promising each person I'd be sure to hang out with them later. Here, Nina jumped in to help me, steering me through the crowd, just as I'd guided her earlier, and dropping hints about official business I supposedly had to deal with.

"The only business I want to have now is with my pillow," I told her with a yawn, once we'd broken free of the Szelsky home. "I'm nearly dead on my feet."

"That was some hardcore magic you did," she told me. "I didn't even notice you'd stopped drinking. Pretty impressive restraint."

"If I had my way, I'd live on a constant buzz of alcohol," I admitted. "But I try to sober up a couple of times a day. It's— it's hard to explain, and I can't really, but there's something I have to do that I need my wits and spirit for. It timed out lucky tonight that Wesley made his appearance when he did. I wouldn't have been so impressive if it had come down to a fist fight."

Nina grinned. "I have faith in you. I bet you would've been awesome."

"Thanks. I'm sorry for what he said to you."

"It's okay," she said with a shrug. "I'm used to it."

"That doesn't mean you have to like it," I said.

Something vulnerable in her eyes told me I'd hit the mark, that those comments stung her deeply. "Yeah . . . I mean, people don't usually say things *quite* that explicitly, but I've seen that attitude in the people I deal with at work. You were right about the party, though. Some of them weren't as bad as I thought." Her voice suddenly turned shy. "And thank you . . . thank you for standing up for me."

Her words and my small victory over Wesley gave me more

self-determination than I'd had in weeks. My mood, which had been wallowing in darkness and self-loathing for so long, swung up dramatically. I wasn't worthless after all. Maybe I hadn't been able to find Sydney yet, but I was still capable of little things. I couldn't give up the fight yet. Who knew? Maybe tonight my luck would change. I could barely wait to escort Nina back to her place so that I could get back to mine and search for Sydney.

When I did, though, it was clear my luck was staying the same on this front. No Sydney. That heady mood came crashing down, but at least I was so exhausted that I had little time to beat myself up over the failure. I fell asleep promptly thereafter and slept until almost the middle of the next vampiric day as my body continued figuring out what schedule I was on.

When I woke, my phone had a message from my mom, reminding me about dinner later on. When I checked the voice mail on the phone in my suite, I discovered about a million messages from my new "friends." My cell phone number wasn't widely known, but a bunch of the party goers had managed to find which guest building I was at and get messages through that way. I had social opportunities for months.

But today, I only had one that mattered. My parents'. I didn't care so much about my dad, but my mom had gone out of her way to come get me. She'd gone out of her way for me on so many things, really, and I owed it to her to be respectable in front of her friends tonight. I stayed sober throughout the day and did boring things like laundry instead of following up on any of the invitations I had—including one that came in from Nina. As much as I liked her, and as much as I'd had fun with her, an inner voice told me it was wiser to keep my distance.

I showed up at my parents' townhouse ten minutes before dinner started, wearing a freshly ironed suit and Aunt Tatiana's cufflinks, and was greeted by my father in his usual gruff way. "Well, Adrian, I assume whatever business the queen has you on back here, it must be important."

The comment took me aback until my mother rushed into the living room, looking glamorous in emerald green silk. "Now, Nathan, dear, don't try to get state secrets out of him." She rested a hand on my arm and gave a small, controlled laugh. "He's been on me about that ever since the queen let me escort you back to your business here. I told him I just wanted to catch up, but he's certain I know things he doesn't."

I finally caught on and shot her a grateful look when his attention was elsewhere. My mother hadn't told him she'd found me in a drunken stupor in California and saved me from myself and a downward spiral. She'd let him think it was just an impulsive motherly gesture to travel with me and had even used it as an opportunity to pad my reputation. I didn't necessarily feel the need to hide my shameful behaviors from my father, but I had to admit, life was certainly easier when he didn't have them to rub in my face. Saying he was proud of me might have been a stretch, but he certainly seemed satisfied for the time being, and that was enough to make the night passable.

The dinner guests were other royals I'd met off and on throughout the years, people I knew little about, save that my parents were concerned with impressing them. My mother, who I was pretty sure had never personally cooked a meal in her life, oversaw every detail of their chef's operation, making sure each course was perfect, be it in terms of wine pairing or simply how it was laid out on the plate. After a day of good behavior (and having checked for Sydney just before coming here), I let myself sample some of the wine, and even if I couldn't correctly identify the region and soil type, I could tell my parents hadn't been stingy.

I soon learned why: This was my parents' first real leap into society since my mother's return from incarceration. No one had invited them anywhere since she came back, so my parents were making the opening gesture, intent on showing the royal Moroi world that Nathan and Daniella Ivashkov were worthy company. That extended to me as well, since my parents went out of their way to keep bringing up the "important business" I was allegedly on. My relationship with Jill and her seclusion were top secret—not even my parents knew about those details—but Sonya's work with the vaccine was known, and everyone was curious to learn more.

I explained it as best I could, using layman's terms and avoiding state secrets. Everyone seemed impressed, particularly my parents, but I was glad when the attention shifted off me. Dinner wound down with some political talk, which I found mildly interesting, and society talk, which I didn't find interesting at all. That had never been my thing, even before the life-changing events in Palm Springs. I didn't care about golf scores or job promotions or upcoming formal gatherings. Still conscious of my role, I smiled politely through it all and contented myself by drinking more of the excellent wine. By the time the last of the guests left, I could tell that we'd successfully won them over and that Daniella Ivashkov would be welcomed back into that royal society she craved.

"Well," she said with a sigh, sinking into one of the formal living room's newly upholstered loveseats. "I daresay that was a success."

"You did well, Adrian," my father added. That was a big compliment, coming from him. "We have a few less problems to worry about now."

I finished off the port that had been served with dessert. "I wouldn't say not being invited to Charlene Badica's annual summer tea really constitutes a 'problem,' but if I could help, I'm glad to."

"You both helped repair damage you've caused to this family. Let's hope that continues." He stood up and stretched. "I'm going to my room. I'll see you both in the morning."

He'd been gone about thirty seconds when the full impact of his words penetrated my wine-soaked brain. "*His* room? Isn't that your room too?"

My mother, still looking beautiful after the long evening, elegantly crossed her hands in her lap. "Actually, dear, I'm sleeping in your old room now."

"My . . ." I struggled to string sense together. "Wait. Is that why you sent me to guest housing? I thought you said I needed my own space."

"Both, really. You do need your own space. And as for the other . . . well, since my return, your father and I have decided things run much more smoothly if we each live our own lives here . . . just under one roof."

Her tone was so easy and pleasant that it made it difficult to grasp the severity of the situation. "What's that mean? Are you getting divorced? Are you separated?"

She frowned. "Oh, Adrian, those are such ugly words. Besides, people like us don't get divorced."

"And married people don't sleep in separate bedrooms," I argued. "Whose idea was it?"

"It was mutual," she said. "Your father disapproves of what I did—and the embarrassment it caused all of us. He's decided he can't forgive that, and honestly, I don't mind sleeping on my own."

I was flabbergasted. "Then get a divorce, and truly be on your own! Because if he can't forgive you for acting impulsively to save your own son . . . well, I've never been married, but that just doesn't seem like good husband protocol. That's not how you treat someone you love. And I don't know how *you* can love someone who treats you like that."

"Darling," she said with a small laugh, "love doesn't have anything to do with this."

"It has everything to do with it!" I exclaimed. I promptly dropped my voice, fearing I'd inadvertently bring my dad back, and I wasn't quite ready for that. "Why else get married—or stay married—if not for love?"

"It's very complicated," she said in the kind of tone she had used on me as a child. "There's status to consider. It wouldn't look right if we split up. That, and . . . well, all of my finances are tied up with your father. We had paperwork drawn up when we married, and let's put it this way: If he and I divorced, I'd have no way to support myself."

I jumped to my feet. "*I'll* support you then."

She met my gaze levelly. "With what, dear? Your art classes? I know the queen doesn't pay you for your help—though goodness knows she should."

"I'll get some job. Any job. We might not have much to start with, but you'd at least have your self-respect! You don't have to stay here, tied to his money and his judgment, pretending this is love!"

"There's no pretending about it. This *is* as close to love as you get in marriage."

"I don't believe that," I told her. "I know what love is, Mom. I've had love that burns in every fiber of my being, that drives me to be a better person and empowers me through each moment of the day. If you'd ever had something like that, you'd hold on to it with every bit of strength you had."

"You only think that because you're young, and you don't know any better." She was so damnably calm, it almost made me more upset. "You think love is a reckless relationship with a dhampir, just because it's exciting. Or are you referring to the girl you were pining for on the plane? Where is she? If your love is so all-consuming and can triumph over everything, why aren't you together?"

Good question, said Aunt Tatiana.

"Because . . . it's not that easy," I told my mother through clenched teeth.

"It's not that easy because it's not real," she replied. "Young people mistake infatuation for 'true love' when there's no such thing. Love between a mother and child? Yes, that's real. But some romantic delusion that conquers all? Don't fool yourself. Your friends, who have such grand romances, will eventually see the truth. This girl of yours, wherever she is, isn't coming back. Stop chasing a dream and focus on someone you can build a stable life with. That's what your father and I have done. That's what we've always done . . . and I daresay it's served us well."

"Always?" I asked in a small voice. "You've always lived this sham?"

"Well," she admitted. "Some parts of our marriage have been more . . . amicable than others. But we've always been pragmatic about it."

"You've been cold and shallow about it," I said. "You told me when you got out of prison, you understood the things that matter. Apparently not, if you're willing to put up with this act—with a man who doesn't respect you—for image and money! No security is worth that. And I refuse to believe this is the best anyone can hope for in love. There's more to it than this. *I* will have more than this."

My mother's eyes almost appeared sad as she met mine. "Then where is she, dear? Where is your girl?"

I had no good answer for her. All I knew was that I could no longer stand being there. I stormed out of the townhouse, surprised to feel the sting of tears in my eyes. I had never thought of my parents as flowery, romantic types, but I'd believed that there'd still been some sort of strong affection in spite of—or perhaps because of—their prickly personalities. To be told that was a sham, that all love was a sham, couldn't have come at a worse time. I didn't believe it, of course. I knew there was real love out there. I'd experienced it firsthand . . . but my mother's words stung because I was vulnerable right now, because no matter how popular I was at Court or how good my intentions were, I was still no closer to finding Sydney. My brain didn't believe my mother, but my heart, so full of fear and doubt, worried there was truth to her words, and that dark, dreary pull of spirit only made things worse. It made me second-guess myself. Maybe I'd never find Sydney. Maybe I'd never find love at all. Maybe wanting something badly enough wasn't enough to make it happen.

The weather had cooled outside, and a brisk wind promised rain. I paused in my walk and tried to reach out to Sydney, but the wine from dinner clouded my powers. I gave up and took out my cell phone instead, opting for simpler means of communication. Nina answered on the second ring.

"Hey," she said. "When I didn't hear from you, I thought . . . well, never mind. How's it going?"

"It's been better. You want to do something tonight?"

"Sure. What'd you have in mind?"

"It doesn't matter," I said. "You can pick. I've got a million invites. We can have parties all night."

"Don't you need to take a break at some point?" she teased, not knowing how close she was to hitting a nerve. "I thought you said you try to sober up every once in a while."

I thought about my mom, trapped in a loveless marriage. I thought about me, trapped without options. And I thought about Sydney, who was simply trapped. It was all too much, too much for me to do anything about.

"Not tonight," I told Nina. "Not tonight."

CHAPTER 7

SYDNEY

IT TOOK ALMOST A WEEK for the other detainees to stop moving their desks away from me or cringing if we happened to touch. They were still nowhere near being friendly to me, but Duncan swore I was making remarkable progress.

"I've seen it take weeks or even months to reach this point," he told me in art class one day. "Before long, you'll get asked to sit with the cool kids at lunch."

"*You* could ask me," I pointed out.

He grinned as he touched up a leaf on today's still-life project: replicating the potted fern that lived on Addison's desk. "You know the rules, kiddo. Someone else besides me has to reach out to you. Hang in there. Someone'll get in trouble soon, and then your time will come. Jonah's in trouble a lot. So is Hope. You'll see."

Since that first day, Duncan had pretty much restricted our social interaction to this class, aside from the occasional wisecrack in the halls if no one was close enough to hear.

Consequently, I found myself craving art time. It was the only time anyone spoke to me like I was a real person. The other detainees ignored me throughout the day, and my instructors, whether it was in class or in purging, never failed to remind me of what a sinner I was. Duncan's friendship centered me, reminding me that there was hope beyond this place. He was still cautious—even in this class—with his conversation. Although he rarely mentioned Chantal, the friend—who I secretly believed had been more than a friend—that the Alchemists had taken away, I could tell that her loss haunted him. He'd chat and smile with the others during meals but made a point of not talking to any one person excessively there or in classes. I think he was too afraid of risking anyone to the Alchemists' wrath, even a casual acquaintance.

"You're pretty good at this," I said, noting the detail on his leaves. "Does that come from being here so long?"

"Nah, I used to paint as a hobby before coming here. I hate this still-life crap, though." He paused to stare at his fern. "I'd kill just to free paint something abstract. I'd love to paint the sky. Who am I kidding? I'd love to *see* the sky. I never painted many outdoor scenes when I was assigned in Manhattan. Thought I was too good for it and would save myself for some Arizona sunset."

"Manhattan? Wow. That's pretty intense."

"Intense," he agreed. "And busy and loud and noisy. I hated it . . . and now I'd do anything to be back there. That's where you and your broody boyfriend should end up."

"We always talked about going somewhere like Rome," I said.

Duncan scoffed. "Rome. Why deal with the language barrier

when you can get everything you want stateside? You guys can get some sketchy apartment that you work two jobs to afford while you take classes on anything imaginable and he hangs out with his unemployed artist friends in Bushwick. Come home at night to eat Korean food with your kooky neighbors, then make love on your shabby mattress on the floor. The next day, start all over again." He resumed painting. "Not a bad way of life."

"Not bad at all," I said, smiling in spite of myself. I could feel that smile fade as a pain lurched in my heart at the thought of any future with Adrian. What Duncan had described was as good as any of the "escape plans" Adrian and I used to concoct . . . and, at this moment, just as impossible. "Duncan . . . what did you mean when you said you'd do anything to be back there?"

"Don't," he warned.

"Don't what?"

"You know what. I was just using an expression."

"Yeah," I began, "but if there was a way you could get out of here and—"

"There's not," he said bluntly. "You're not the first to suggest it. You won't be the last. And if I can help it, you won't be thrown back into solitary for doing something stupid. I've told you, there's no way out."

I thought very carefully how to proceed. In the last year, he probably had seen others attempt to get out of here and, judging from his reaction, had watched them all fail. I'd asked him about exits a number of times, and like me, he'd never discovered where they were. I needed to find a different approach and gather other information that might lead to our freedom.

"Will you answer just two things for me?" I asked at last. "Not about exits?"

"If I can," he said warily, still not making eye contact.

"Do you know where we are?"

"No," he said promptly. "No one does, which is part of *their* plan. The only thing I'm sure of is that every level we ever go on is underground. That's why there are no windows or obvious exits out."

"Do you know how they get the gas in here? Don't act like you don't know what I mean," I added, seeing him start to scowl. "You had to notice it when you were in solitary confinement. And they're using it now to knock us out at night and keep us agitated and paranoid when we're awake."

"They don't need any drugs for that," he remarked. "Groupthink does a fine job of spreading that paranoia on its own."

"Don't dodge. Do you or do you not know where the gas comes from?"

"Come on, just because a fern's a vascular plant doesn't mean it's producing carbon dioxide any differently," he interrupted. I was taken aback, both by the weird subject change and the slight raising of his voice. "All the chemical reactions in basic photosynthesis are still there. It's just a question of using spores instead of seeds."

I was too lost to respond right away, and then I saw what he already had: Emma was standing near us, searching a drawer for colored pencils. And it was clear she was listening.

I swallowed and tried to string some semblance of words together. "I wasn't arguing that. I was just pointing out what the fossil record says about megaphylls and microphylls. You're the one who started getting bogged down with photosynthesis."

Emma found what she needed and walked away, causing

my knees to nearly give out from under me. "Oh my God," I said, once she was out of earshot.

"That," said Duncan, "is why you need to be more careful."

Class ended, and I spent the rest of the day nervously waiting for Emma to report me to some authority, who'd haul me off for purging or, worse, back to the darkness. Of all the people to overhear us! The other detainees might not be social with me yet, but I'd already been able to observe who were better or worse candidates for allies. And Emma? She was the worst. Some of the others would occasionally slip up, much like Hope had that first day, making a wayward comment that got them in trouble. But my too-good roommate never, ever deviated from perfect Alchemist rhetoric. In fact, she went out of her way to bust others who didn't fall in line. I honestly couldn't figure out why she was still here.

But no one came for me. Emma didn't so much as glance my way, and I dared hope that the only thing she'd heard was Duncan's hasty photosynthesis excuse.

Communion time came around, and we all filed into the chapel. Some sat down in the folded chairs while others wandered the room like me. Yesterday had been Sunday, and in place of communion time, we'd gathered here in the pews, along with all our instructors, while a hierophant came and gave us a bona fide church service and prayed for our souls. It was the only part of our routine that had changed. Otherwise, we had the same classes on weekends as we did on weekdays. But that one service was empowering, not because of its message but because it was another way to mark time. Every piece of information I could get in this place could only be used to help me . . . I hoped.

That was why I read the Wall of Truth each day before our meeting. There was a history here of detainees who had come before me, and I longed to learn something. Mostly, all I found were the same sort of messages, and today was no exception. *I have sinned against my kind and greatly regret it. Please take me back into the fold. The only salvation is human salvation.* Another message read: *Please let me out.* Seeing Sheridan walk into the room, I was about to join the others when I noticed something out of the corner of my eye. It was in a region of the wall I hadn't gotten to yet, in scrawling writing:

Carly, I'm sorry.—K. D.

I felt my jaw drop. Was it possible . . . could it really be . . . the more I stared at it, the more I was certain of what I was seeing: an apology to my sister Carly, from Keith Darnell, the guy who'd raped her. I supposed it could be a different Carly and someone else with the same initials . . . but my gut told me otherwise. I knew Keith had been in re-education. His crimes had been of a much different nature than mine, and he'd also been released recently—recently being more than five months ago. He'd also practically been like a zombie by the time he'd gotten out of here. It was surreal thinking that he'd walked these same halls, gone to these same classes, endured the same purging. It was even more disturbing to wonder if I might be like him when I got out of here.

"Sydney?" asked Sheridan pleasantly. "Won't you join us?"

Flushing, I realized I was the only one not sitting and hurried over to join the others. "Sorry," I murmured.

"The Wall of Truth can be a very inspiring place," said Sheridan. "Did you find something that spoke to your soul?"

I thought very carefully before answering and then

decided the truth wouldn't hurt me here. It might also help, since Sheridan was always trying to get me to talk. "Mostly I was surprised," I said. "I recognized the name of someone I knew . . . someone who was here before me."

"Did that person help corrupt you?" asked Lacey in innocent curiosity. It was one of the few times someone had shown semi-personal interest in me.

"Not exactly," I said. "I was actually the one who reported him—who got him sent here." Everyone looked interested, so I continued. "He was in business with a Moroi—an old, senile Moroi—and taking his blood. He told the Moroi it was being used for healing purposes, but he—this guy I knew—was actually selling it to a local tattooist who was in turn using it to sell performance-enhancing tattoos to human high school students. The blood in the ink would make them better at things, especially sports, but there were dangerous side effects."

"Did your friend know?" asked Hope wonderingly. "That it was hurting humans?"

"He wasn't my friend," I said sharply. "Even before this started. And yes, he knew. He didn't care, though. All he was focused on was the profit he was making."

The other detainees were enraptured, maybe because they'd never heard me speak so much or maybe because they'd never heard of a scandal like this. "I bet that Moroi knew," said Stuart darkly. "I bet he knew everything—what the tattoos were really being used for and how dangerous they were. He was probably just playing at being senile."

The old Sydney—that is, the Sydney who'd been here on her first day—would've been quick to defend Clarence and his innocence in Keith's scheme. This Sydney, who'd seen detainees punished for lesser comments and had endured two purgings this week, knew better. "It wasn't my job to judge the Moroi's behavior," I said. "They'll do what their natures tell them to do. But I knew no human should be subjecting other humans to the dangers my associate was. That was why I had to turn him in."

To my amazement, a round of nods met me, and even Sheridan regarded me with approval. Then, she spoke. "That's a very wise insight, Sydney. And yet something must have gone terribly wrong if you learned no lessons from that incident and ended up here yourself."

All those eyes swiveled from her to me, and for a moment, I couldn't breathe. I discussed Adrian occasionally with Duncan, but this was different. Duncan didn't judge or tear my romance apart. How could I bring up something so precious and powerful to me in front of this group, who would revile it and make it sound dirty? What I had with Adrian was beautiful. I didn't want to lay it out to be trampled here.

And yet, how could I not? If I didn't give them something, if I didn't play their games . . . then how long would I be here? A year—or more—like Duncan? I'd told myself, back in that dark cell, that I'd say anything to get me out of here. I had to make good on that. Lies told here wouldn't matter if they got me back to Adrian.

"I let my guard down," I said simply. "My assignment had me working around a lot of Moroi, and I stopped thinking of them as the creatures they are. I guess after my associate, the lines of good and evil got blurred for me."

I braced myself for Sheridan to start grilling me on the more intimate details of what had happened, but it was another girl, one named Amelia, who spoke up with something wholly unexpected. "That almost makes sense," she said. "I mean, I wouldn't have taken it to the, uh, extremes you did, but if you'd been around a corrupt human, it could maybe make you lose faith in your own kind and erroneously turn to the Moroi."

Another guy I'd rarely spoken to, Devin, nodded in agreement. "Some of them can almost seem deceptively nice."

Sheridan frowned slightly, and I thought those two might get in trouble for comments semi-favorable to the Moroi. She apparently decided to let it slide in favor of the progress I'd made today. "It's very easy to get confused, especially when you're out on assignment by yourself and things take unexpected turns. The important thing to remember is that we have an entire infrastructure in place to help you. If you have questions about right or wrong, don't turn to the Moroi. Turn to us, and we'll tell you what's right."

Because heaven forbid any of us think for ourselves, I thought bitterly. I was spared further romantic questioning as Sheridan turned her attention on the others to hear what kind of enlightenment they'd had that day. Not only was I off the hook, I'd apparently scored points with Sheridan and—as I saw when dinner came around—with some of my detainees.

When I took my tray from Baxter and started to walk toward an empty table, Amelia beckoned me to hers with a curt nod. I sat down beside her, and although no one actually made conversation with me for the meal, no one ordered me away or berated me. I ate wordlessly, instead taking in everything I heard around me. Most of their talk was typical of what I'd hear in Amberwood's cafeteria, comments about the school day or roommates that snored. But it gave me more and more insight into their personalities, and I again began gauging who might be an ally.

Duncan had been sitting with others at another table, but when we passed each other leaving the cafeteria, he murmured, "See? I told you you were making progress. Now don't screw it up."

I almost smiled but had learned my lesson earlier today about getting too comfortable. So I kept what I hoped was a solemn and diligent look on my face as we shuffled off to the library to select our boring reading choices for the night. I ended up over in the history section, hoping for something a little more interesting than what I'd checked out recently. Alchemist histories were still full of lessons on morals and good behaviors, but at least those lessons weren't explicitly directed at the reader, as most of the other self-help books were. I was debating over a couple of different medieval accounts when someone knelt beside me.

"Why did you want to know about the gas?" asked a quiet voice. I did a double take. It was Emma.

"I don't know what you're talking about," I said lightly. "Do you mean in art today? Duncan and I were discussing the ferns."

"Uh-huh." She pulled out a book of Renaissance-era diaries and flipped through the pages. "I'm not going to say a word to you in our room, you know. It's under surveillance. But if you want my help now, you've got about sixty seconds."

"Why would you help me?" I demanded. "Assuming I even want it? Are you trying to trap me into something so that you can make yourself look better?"

She snorted. "If I wanted to 'trap you into something,' I'd

have done it ages ago in our room, caught on video. Forty-five seconds. Why do you want to know about the gas?"

Anxiety crawled over me as I waffled on what to do. In my assessments of who might be an ally, Emma had never come up at all. And yet, here she was, offering the closest to sedition that anyone—even my friend Duncan—had presented so far. That made it all the more likely I was being set up, yet part of me just couldn't resist the opportunity.

"The gas keeps us here as much as the guards and walls," I said at last. "I just want to understand it." Hopefully that wasn't too incriminating.

Emma slipped the book back and selected another diary, this one with fancy embellishments. "The controls are in a workroom that's on the same level as purging. Each bedroom also has a small pipe feeding in from that system. It's right behind a ventilation panel near the ceiling."

"How do you know?" I asked.

"I walked by some repair guys doing maintenance in an empty room once."

"So it'd be easier to block it on a room-by-room basis than at the control level," I murmured.

She shook her head. "Not when it's right in line with the cameras in the bedrooms. The guards would be on you before you even had the panel off. Which you'd need a screwdriver for."

She started to set her book back, and I took it from her. Glittering inks decorated the cover, and the corner of each chapter was covered with a flat piece of metal. I ran my fingers over one. "A flathead screwdriver?" I asked, sizing up the thickness of the metal corner. If I could pull it off, it'd make an okay tool to undo a screw.

A slow smile spread over Emma's face. "As a matter of fact, yes. You get creativity points, I'll give you that." She studied me a few moments more. "Why do you want to block the gas? Seems like we've got a lot bigger problems—you know, the biggest one being that we're stuck here."

"You tell me something first," I said, still not sure if Emma was part of some great sting operation that was going to get me in even worse trouble. "You're pretty much the poster child for model Alchemist behavior. What did you do to get here?"

She hesitated before answering. "I sent away some guardians that had been assigned to help my Alchemist group in Kiev. There were some Moroi I knew that I thought needed the protection more than we did."

"I can see where that would upset the powers-that-be," I admitted. "But it seems like there are worse things, especially with how good you've been. Why are you still here?"

Her cocky smile shifted to something more bitter. "Because my sister isn't. She went through all of this too, was discharged, and then went even more rogue than before. No one knows where she is, and now, no matter how many strides I make, they're ensuring they don't make the same mistake twice in letting me go too soon. Bad blood in our family, I guess."

That would certainly explain things. She seemed sincere too, but she was also an Alchemist, and we were good at conning others. Another question popped into my head as my eyes darted across the room to where Duncan and a few others perused the sociology section. "Why has Duncan been here so long? He seems to be on good behavior. Bad blood in his family too?"

Emma followed my gaze. "My guess? Too good of behavior."

"Is that even possible?" I asked, startled.

She shrugged. "He's so docile, I think they're worried he won't be able to stand up to vampire influence, even if he wants to. So they're afraid to let him out just yet. But they don't want him to have too much of a spine because that kind of goes against the operating procedure here. I think he *wants* to be braver . . . but something holds him back—I mean, more than the usual stuff holding us all back."

Chantal, I thought. That was what held him back. He'd had enough of a spine to befriend me, but Emma's words explained why he was so cautious in even that. Losing Chantal had left its mark and made him too fearful to do anything else. Hoping I wasn't making a terrible mistake, I took a deep breath and turned back to Emma.

"If the gas is off, I can get a message to the outside. That's all I can tell you."

Her eyebrows rose at that. "Are you certain? Tonight?"

"Absolutely," I said. Adrian would be searching for me in dreams. He just needed a window of natural sleep.

"Hang on a minute," Emma said after a little more thought. She stood up and walked across the room, over to where Amelia was browsing. They conversed until the chimes rang, signaling it was time to return to our rooms. Emma hurried back to me. "Check out that book," she said, nodding to the embellished diary. "I won't say another word to you once we walk out that door. Go back to our room, count to sixty, and then go to town on whatever you need to do with the vent."

"But what about the camera—"

"You're on your own now," she said, and walked off without another word.

I gaped for a few moments and then scurried to join the others who were signing out books with the librarian. As I filed out with them, I tried to look natural and not like my heart might pound out of my chest. Was Emma serious? Or was this the ultimate setup? What could she have possibly done in one conversation that would suddenly make it okay to tamper with the ventilation system? Because when we got back to our room, I could see the small black camera that watched us was pointing straight in the direction of the vent in question. Anyone opening it would be easily spotted.

It had to be a setup, but Emma made it clear from her body language that she was going to have no further interaction with me as we got ready for bed. I silently counted and knew she must have as well because when I reached sixty, she spared me one sharp, meaningful look.

There are easier ways to set me up, I thought. *Easier ways with worse consequences.*

With a gulp, I pushed my bed over to the wall and used it to stand on, so that I had easy access to the vent panel. I'd pulled off a metal page corner from the book, and Emma's assessment had been correct. Its thickness was right on par with a flathead screwdriver. Of course, it was nowhere near as ergonomically easy to use as a screwdriver, but after a little fiddling, I finally got all four corners of the panel loosened enough to pull it off. My nerves and shaking hands weren't helping speed along the process, and I had no clue how long I might have to do this—or if Emma would warn me when time was up.

Inside, I found an ordinary ventilation shaft. It was too small to crawl through, so there'd be no movie-worthy escapes that way. As she'd told me, a small pipe was attached to the vent's side, opening just behind the panel's grates to feed its fumes into our room when the lights went out. Now I needed to block the pipe. I reached down to the bed, where I'd put an old sock retrieved from our room's laundry hamper earlier. I didn't put it past the Alchemists to take inventory of our clothing regularly, but I also knew when this was picked up, it was promptly dumped into a larger bin of clothes. If they noticed a missing sock, they wouldn't know whose room it had come from. And surely even Alchemist dryers ate socks sometimes.

I crammed the sock into the pipe as best I could, hoping it was enough to keep the worst of the gas out. Behind me, under her breath, I heard Emma mutter, "Hurry." My hands slick with sweat, I screwed the panel back into place and just barely remembered to move my bed before flouncing onto it with my book. The whole endeavor had taken less than five minutes, but was that enough?

Emma was fixated on her book and never so much as looked my way, but I caught the glimmer of a smile on her lips. Was that one of triumph over helping me achieve my goal? Or was she gloating at having tricked me into committing serious insubordination on camera?

If I had been busted, no one came for me that night. Our reading-time hour wound down, and before long, the lights went out and I heard the familiar click of the doors automatically locking. I snuggled into my sparsely made bed and waited for something else that had become familiar this last week: the artificially induced drowsiness brought on by the gas. It didn't come.

It didn't come.

I could hardly believe it. We'd pulled it off! I'd stopped the gas from getting into my room. The ironic part was, I could have used a little help in getting to sleep because I was so excited to talk to Adrian that I couldn't calm down. It was like Christmas Eve. I lay in the dark for what had to be two hours before natural exhaustion won out and put me to sleep. My body was in a perpetual state of fatigue around here, both from the mental stress and the fact that the sleep we were given was just barely adequate. I slept soundly until the morning wakeup chimes, and that was when I realized the awful truth.

There'd been no dreams. Adrian hadn't come.

CHAPTER 8

ADRIAN

I DIDN'T MEAN FOR THINGS to get so out of hand.

My intentions had been good when I came to Court, but after failing with Lissa and then learning about my parents, something snapped inside me. I threw myself back into my old life with a vengeance, losing all semblance of responsibility. I tried to tell myself that I was just having a little fun and finding a way to unwind while I was at Court. Sometimes I even told myself it was for Nina. Maybe that excuse would've worked in the first few days I was back, but after a week of almost nonstop revelry and parties, even she timidly offered a protest when I picked her up one night.

"Let's stay in," she said. "We'll take it easy and watch a movie. Or play cards. Anything you want."

Despite her words, she was still dressed to go out and live it up, looking very pretty in a periwinkle dress that made her gray eyes luminous. I gestured to it. "And waste this? Come on, I thought you wanted to meet new people."

"I do," she said. "I have. In fact, we're starting to see the same ones over and over. They've all seen me in this dress already."

"Is that the problem?" I asked. "I'll lend you money for another one."

She shook her head. "I can't even pay you back for this one."

After finding out about the lie my parents were living, I'd been tempted to make a statement and refuse the ample allowance my dad had regularly wired into my account. I didn't have the same bills here that I had in Palm Springs, and I'd liked the idea of showing Nathan Ivashkov that he couldn't buy off everyone in his family. But when Nina had casually remarked she felt underdressed at some of the royal parties we went to, I'd decided using my father's money to fund a secretary's wardrobe would be just as irritating. Admittedly, he didn't know about it yet, but I took a lot of personal satisfaction from it. Nina had only agreed to the arrangement if it was treated as a loan, not a gift, but even she'd been taken aback when she saw the amounts I was throwing around. A small voice of reason warned me I was in danger of falling into some of the bad spending habits I'd had in my low moments in Palm Springs, but I shushed it. After all, I'd get more from my dad soon, and most everyone was pouring my drinks for free these days anyway.

"Well, it looks great," I said. "It'd be a shame to hide such beauty away. Unless there's some other problem?"

"No," she said, flushing at my words. She looked me over, and I had the feeling she was reading my aura, which would have revealed—if other signs hadn't already—that I'd done a little pre-party imbibing already. She sighed. "Let's go."

She can't keep up with you, said Aunt Tatiana as we trekked across the Court's grounds. Sunset was causing shadows to lengthen around us. *But then, what girl can?*

Sydney could keep up with me, I thought. *Not in the partying sense. I mean . . . in life.*

Her words brought that terrible ache that no amount of revelry could ever chase away. Sydney. Without her, I simply felt like I was going through the motions of life, creating a dreary existence made worse by my inability to find her. All I could do was my fruitless and increasingly sporadic dream searching. I hadn't yet searched for her tonight and wondered if maybe I should heed Nina's suggestion, if only to buy some brief sobriety.

It's too early, warned Aunt Tatiana. *Check later. No human would be asleep yet in the United States. Besides, do you want* it *to come back?*

She had a point about the time. The thing was, I'd missed good times to check for Sydney all week, and it was starting to bother me. But she was also right about *it* coming back: that terrible, plunging darkness that threatened to consume my whole world. My depression had been bad in Palm Springs after Sydney's disappearance and had only worsened here after my failure to get Lissa's help. I knew my former psychiatrist and even Sydney would probably tell me that was a sign to go back on medication, but how could I, when I might be able to use spirit to help her? Admittedly, I wasn't of much use right now, but I still refused to let the magic go. And so, an increase in the self-soothing wonders of alcohol helped mute some of it, as did relying on phantom Aunt Tatiana's advice and presence—a presence that had become disconcertingly more frequent in the last week. I knew she wasn't real and that my psychiatrist would've had plenty to say about her too, but her delusion seemed to be creating a wall between the worst of my depression and me. At least she got me out of bed each morning.

That night's party was being hosted by a Conta guy I didn't know very well, but he seemed pleased that we'd shown up and welcomed us with a friendly wave across the room. Nina had become my accepted shadow at these events, and a lot of people who wanted to get in good with me thought cozying up to her was the way to do it. I could tell it flustered her, but I rather enjoyed the show of royals who'd normally treat her like furniture in the palace offices now sucking up as they tried to get on her good side.

Almost every party this time of year was held outdoors, weather permitting. We were schooled from such an early age to stay inside and hide from Strigoi that if an outdoor opportunity presented itself in a safe location—like Court—we could hardly refuse the opportunity. Young Lord Conta had gone out of his way to make this party particularly memorable, with all sorts of novelties to amuse and entertain. One of my favorites was a giant fountain sitting on a table, shooting up champagne in high arcs. Within the depths of the glass base, an array of colored lights shone through the sparkling liquid.

I filled glasses for Nina and me, admiring the lights as they went through a turn of colors. "Adrian," she said softly. "Look over there, on the other side of the pool."

I followed her gaze and saw Wesley Drozdov sipping from a martini glass and glaring daggers at me. I was kind of surprised to see him. He'd made himself noticeably scarce since our last run-in, and I wondered if he'd shown up tonight thinking I wouldn't be at a party where I didn't know the host well. *Trash,*

Aunt Tatiana murmured in my head. *He doesn't deserve a royal name.*

"What an aura," added Nina. "He *hates* you."

I'd already accepted a shot from a passing server on our way in and wasn't in the best position to read auras. I had no reason to doubt Nina and chuckled at the concern in her voice. "Don't worry. He's not going to start anything. See?"

Sure enough, Wesley set down his empty glass and slinked off into the shadows, much to my relief. I didn't want Aunt Tatiana to start ranting about him again. Nina still looked uneasy. "Don't ever let him get you alone."

I handed her a glass. "When would that ever happen, with you by my side?" I asked gallantly. "I've always got you to watch my back."

Her face lit up, far more than I would've expected from such an over-the-top comment. But if it made her happy, I was happy. Maybe I couldn't fix everything in my own life, but Nina was a nice girl who deserved good things after all she'd been through. That, and having her around at these parties made me feel a little less pathetic. Drinking alone was sad. Drinking with a companion could technically be justified as social interaction.

We went through our usual routine of drinking and mingling. I'd arrived with ideas about setting limits for myself but soon lost track. I can only assume that was what drove me to answer my cell phone when it rang. Usually, I checked the display before even considering answering, but tonight it didn't even occur to me.

"Hello?"

"Adrian?"

I winced. "Hi, Mom."

Nina stepped discreetly away, and I tried to move to a quieter spot. My mother was one of the main reasons I made sure to check my display these days, since she'd been calling me almost nonstop since our post-dinner altercation. Now there was no easy escape.

"Where are you, darling? I can hardly hear you."

"I'm at a party," I told her. "I can't talk long." That wasn't exactly true, since few in the crowd were paying attention to me just then, and Nina had found a group to talk with near the pool.

"This won't take long." Unless I was mistaken, there was an edge of nervousness in her voice. "I don't know if you received my messages. . . ." She trailed off meaningfully, perhaps hoping I'd provide a reassuring reason for ignoring her all week. I didn't.

"I got them," I said.

"Ah," she said. "Well, then, as you know, I'm not happy with the way we left things. I miss you, Adrian. I spent a lot of time thinking about you while I was away, and one of the things I most looked forward to was being with you when I was back."

I felt a spark of anger at that, recalling how she hadn't wanted to talk to me in prison when I'd visited her in dreams. I kept that sentiment to myself and let her continue.

"I'd like for us to try again, just you and me. Perhaps a quiet lunch, so I can explain things better. I'd like for you to understand—"

"Are you still living with him?" I interrupted. "Are you still taking his money?"

"Adrian . . ."

"Are you?" I pushed.

"Yes, but as I said—"

"Then I understand perfectly. You don't need to explain anything."

I expected apologies or cajoling, which I'd been getting a fair amount of in her many voice mail messages and could nearly recite myself. So it was a bit of a surprise when she shot back with more bite than usual. "Are *you*, Adrian? I see the accounts. I see he's still sending you money."

She's calling you a hypocrite, Aunt Tatiana whispered to me, venom in her voice. *Are you going to let her get away with that?*

"It's not the same," I said, feeling both angry and embarrassed. "I'm giving mine away."

"Are you really?" My mother's tone implied she didn't believe that for a second.

"Yes, I—"

My angry retort was interrupted by a scream and a splash. I looked over to where I'd last seen Nina. Some horseplay had broken out in the group she'd been standing with, and she and a couple others were now surfacing in the pool, coughing and wiping water out of their eyes.

"I've got to go, Mom," I said. "Thanks for calling, but until you get some self-respect, I'm just not interested." I knew it was mean, and I didn't give her a chance to respond before I disconnected and hurried over to the pool. I held out a hand to Nina as she dodged a tray of floating shot glasses and attempted to climb out. "Are you okay?"

"Yeah, yeah, fine." The curls that had been so cute and springy earlier now hung around her face in dark, dripping clumps. "Wish I could say the same for this dress."

Waiters hurried forward with towels, and I took one for Nina. "It'll dry."

She gave me a wry smile as she wrapped the towel around herself. "You don't do much laundry, do you? This is silk. It's not going to mix well with the chlorine and God knows what else was in that pool."

My mom's words were still fresh in my mind. "Then I'll make good on what I said earlier: We'll get you some new clothes."

"Adrian, I can't keep accepting your money. It's sweet, and I'm grateful, really. But I have to earn my own way."

A mix of feelings flooded through me. The first was pride. Here she was, embodying exactly what I'd just been chastising my mom about. On the other hand, there was no denying that while Nina was admirably trying to do things on her own, I was very much the hypocrite my mother had insinuated. That humiliation burned through me, compounded by the frustration I already felt over being unable to help Sydney.

"You will earn your own way," I said decisively. "We both will. Come on."

I took Nina's hand and led her out of the crowded yard, sparing little thought to the consequences of my impulse decision. We walked to nearly the opposite side of Court, far from the royal residences we spent so much time at. Here, among much more modest townhomes, I marched up the steps to an address I was proud to have remembered and knocked loudly on the door. Nina, still wrapped in her towel, shifted uncomfortably beside me.

"Adrian, where are we?" she asked. "Don't you realize—"

Her words were cut off as the door opened, revealing a very surprised Sonya Karp. She'd once been a high school biology teacher and a Strigoi (though not at the same time). Now, she was Moroi once more and a spirit user like Nina and me. Her red hair was tousled from sleep, and it wasn't until I noticed her pajamas that I had a moment of hesitation. The sun wasn't up quite yet, but the eastern sky was definitely more purple than black. Still prime Moroi time.

"Adrian, Nina," said Sonya, by way of greeting. She was remarkably calm, considering the unusual circumstances. "Are you two okay?"

"I . . . yeah." I suddenly felt kind of stupid but then pushed such feelings aside. We were already here. I might as well make my stand. "We need to talk to you about something. But if it's too late . . ." I frowned, trying to parse the time through my drink-addled brain. There was no reason she should be in bed. "Are you on a human schedule?"

"I'm on Mikhail's schedule," she replied, referring to her dhampir husband. "He's been working some odd shifts, so I've adjusted my sleep accordingly." She took in Nina's towel and stepped aside from the doorway. "No point stressing about it now. Come in, both of you."

Although the apartment had a kitchen and my suite didn't, the overall living space was much smaller than what I currently enjoyed over in guest housing. Sonya and Mikhail had decorated things nicely and certainly given the place a warm feel, but it still struck me as wrong that a visiting royal like me received more luxurious accommodations than a hard-working guardian who was constantly risking his life. Even worse, I knew this was one of the larger guardian homes since Mikhail was married. Single guardians lived in little more than dorms.

"Do you want anything to drink?" asked Sonya, gesturing to us to sit at her kitchen table.

"Water," said Nina quickly.

Sonya brought over two glasses and then sat down opposite us. "Now," she said. "What's so important?"

I pointed at Nina. "Her. She's been helping you with some of your vaccine work, right? She puts in time but doesn't get paid. That's not right."

Nina flushed, now that she realized what this was about. "Adrian, it's fine—"

"It's not," I insisted. "Nina and I have both done a lot for you with your spirit research but haven't seen any compensation."

Sonya arched an eyebrow. "I hadn't realized that was part of your requirements. I thought you were glad to be working against Strigoi for the sake of doing good."

"We are," said Nina, still looking mortified.

"*But,*" I added, "you can't ask us to take time out of our schedules and lives while still expecting us to find some way to survive and make ends meet. You want our help with this? Don't half-ass it. Hire a full-time spirit squad." I frowned, not liking the way that came out. "Or a spirit dream team. I don't know. I'm just saying, if you want to do it right, give us the compensation we deserve while also making sure you get the best help available. Nina has to juggle her office job while still helping you out."

Sonya's gaze rested on Nina, who squirmed and looked even more uncomfortable. "I know you work a lot of hours, and I *do* feel bad that I'm asking extra of you." Sonya turned to me and looked distinctly less sympathetic. "But remind me again what exactly it is you're doing these days, Adrian?"

Such nerve, said Aunt Tatiana.

"Well," I said obstinately, "I could be helping you mass produce your vaccine, if you'd hire me on full time."

Sonya gave a small, dry laugh. "I'd love that, except that there are two small problems. One is that I'm not mass producing anything."

"You aren't?" I asked. I glanced briefly at Nina, who seemed too embarrassed by this whole encounter to notice. "But I thought that was your top priority."

"It is," said Sonya. "But unfortunately, replicating the spirit in Neil's blood is proving very difficult. The spirit doesn't seem to be bound to the blood in a stable way, and I worry it's going to fade over a long enough time before we can crack its secrets. Having spirit users on hand to advise me *is* very useful, no question. But solving this also requires a biology background and understanding of blood at the cellular level, and unfortunately, there's only one person I know who meets that requirement. And that spirit user hasn't been able to solve this yet."

It took me a moment to realize Sonya was talking about herself. I knew Nina had been helping Sonya, but it was news to me—and Nina too, from her face—that the project was at a standstill. We'd made such huge strides in creating a Strigoi vaccine for Neil that it was maddening to think we were now in a position where we couldn't fully take advantage of that. I'd just assumed after all our hard work that Sonya was now creating her miracle elixir in a lab somewhere, ready to share it with the world.

"What's the second problem?" I asked, recalling her earlier statement.

"The second problem," said Sonya, "is that I'm in no position to pay you. Believe me, I would *love* a 'spirit dream team' dedicated to this task, but I don't even get paid for this. The queen and the council have money and grants set aside for scientific research, and I file requests for that to cover expenses for supplies and travel. But as for any other compensation? I see no more than you. Although . . . it might be an avenue worth considering. If the council truly wants this work to move forward, they should ensure those best suited to it are able to fully devote their time and resources."

Sonya sounded sincere about that, but I felt idiotic yet again. I'd come here demanding money as though she were some master treasurer when the truth was she was putting in even more work than we were—also for nothing. Even in the throes of alcohol, I could recognize what an ass I'd been.

"Sonya, I'm sorry," I said.

Ivashkovs don't apologize! snapped Aunt Tatiana.

"Don't be," said Sonya. "It's not an unreasonable request."

"I was unreasonable in the way I asked it," I said gruffly.

Will you stop doing that? demanded Aunt Tatiana.

Nina, though still flustered at the attention brought upon her, unknowingly took my imaginary aunt's side and rested a hand gently on my arm. "You didn't know. And you were doing it for me."

"I really will ask," Sonya added, glancing between us. "Who knows? Maybe a 'dream team' will help get things moving. Mostly I'd been waiting for school to end at Amberwood, so that we could have Neil back here with Jill. I'd hoped having him in person might illuminate the situation."

"Maybe if Neil comes back, Olive will too," said Nina. This whole encounter with Sonya had clearly upset her, but the thought of Olive cheered her a little.

"Maybe," I said, not feeling so confident based on everything

I'd heard recently from Nina. "Seems like you'd be a bigger draw than some guy she hardly knows."

"She fell for him pretty hard, though." Nina played with the edges of her towel a moment and then looked up to meet my eyes. "Falling in love with someone can make you do things the love of a relative can't."

I frowned as I studied her more closely and realized she was shivering. "Good God," I said, ashamed of my own obliviousness. "You must be freezing." The temperature outside, while pleasant, wasn't as sweltering as it had been earlier in the week, and making that long walk in a drenched party dress couldn't have been fun. I glanced at Sonya. "Do you have anything she can wear?"

Nina turned crimson. "I'm fine. Don't go to any trouble—"

"Of course," interjected Sonya, rising. She beckoned Nina up as well. "I've got a few things you can try."

Nina followed her reluctantly out of the room. Sonya returned a minute later and rejoined me at the table. "She's changing now."

I nodded, my mind still on our earlier conversation. "I hope she doesn't get too let down if Olive doesn't come back to Court. I think Olive's got a lot to process after—well, you understand."

"I do," said Sonya solemnly. "But to be too honest, I'm not worried about *Olive* letting Nina down."

I was sobering a little, only enough to give me a headache and not, apparently, enough to clear my mind. "What do you mean?"

Sonya sighed. "That's what I was afraid of. You have no idea that girl is crazy about you, do you?"

"Who . . . you mean Nina?" I shook my head. "No, she's not. We're just friends."

"You spend an awful lot of time together. And whenever she and I meet for work, you're all she talks about."

"I have no interest in her," I said firmly. "Not that way, at least."

Sonya gave me one of those knowing looks she excelled at. "I never said you did. In fact, it's perfectly clear to me you don't. But she's not aware of that. And it's cruel of you to lead her on."

"I'm not!" I protested. "We just hang out."

"She told me you bought her clothes."

"It's a *loan*," I said staunchly. "Because she doesn't make enough to live on."

"She was doing just fine until you started pushing her into the whirlwind of royal social life." Sonya met me directly in the eyes. "Look, you want my advice? If you care about her, back off. Without realizing it, you're sending her mixed messages, and eventually it's going to go bad when the one she finally gets isn't the one she was hoping for. It would be hard on anyone— but you of all people know how fragile we spirit users can be."

"Well, actually, I don't want your advice, and I'm not backing off anything because I'm not doing anything wrong. Nina's a smart girl. She knows we're just friends and likes what we have. Telling me to give her up is kind of premature."

"Give her up?" Sonya chuckled. "That's an addict's term. What is it exactly you're using her for? Or more importantly, should I ask, what—or whom—is she replacing?"

"Nothing. No one. Stop giving me the third degree! What's wrong with me just having a friend?"

Nina returned, wearing Sonya's borrowed sweatpants and

T-shirt, and ended the conversation. Oblivious to the tension she'd walked in on, Nina was effusive with her thanks to Sonya and made a few more inquiries about the vaccine status. As they spoke, my mind wandered, and I wondered if I'd been inadvertently lying to Sonya.

Not about anything romantic with Nina and me. There was no one I could even imagine being with besides Sydney. But when we left Sonya's and I walked Nina back to her place, I found myself wondering about the other part of Sonya's commentary.

What—or whom—is she replacing?

There was no replacement for Sydney, of course. There was no one like her in the world, no one who could even compare to her in my heart. Yet, when Sonya had suggested I back off from Nina, the first panicked thought that had raced through my mind was that I would be alone again. Because while grief and fear and anger had dominated my emotions in the wake of Sydney's disappearance, I couldn't deny that loneliness had been there as well. My relationship with Sydney had healed a lost part of me, a piece of my soul that had felt adrift in the world. When she'd vanished, I'd lost that tether and floated loose once more.

Nina, though not replacing Sydney romantically, had certainly done a lot to ground me. Not that I was exactly exhibiting model behavior these days. But Nina gave me someone to talk to—who didn't live inside my head—and at least provided some regularity to my partying lifestyle. Picking her up and getting her home on time each night ensured I wasn't completely running wild. And aside from the pleasure of secretly punishing my father by spending his money on her,

I also took satisfaction in taking care of someone. It made me feel a little less useless. I couldn't find Sydney, but by God, I could make sure Nina was dressed for royal nightlife.

But was Sonya right that I was taking advantage of Nina in the process?

I pondered this as we reached Nina's doorstep, over in another section of housing that was only slightly less barebones that Sonya's. Nina unlocked her door and then turned to face me. The sun was definitely up now, lighting her face with dawn's colors.

"Well, thanks as always for an interesting time," she said with a small laugh. "And thanks for what you tried to do with Sonya. You really didn't have to. But thanks." She was wringing her hands together, a nervous habit of hers I'd noticed before.

I shrugged. "You heard what she said. Maybe something'll come of it regardless."

"Maybe." A moment of silence hung between us before she asked, "Well . . . same time tomorrow?"

I hesitated, wondering if I was creating an unhealthy situation for myself. Wondering if I was creating one for her.

Are you going to let Sonya dictate your life? demanded Aunt Tatiana. *What does she know?*

I felt a flare of anger within me. Sonya was overreacting. What was wrong with me having a friend? What was wrong with me having someone to talk to? Was I expected to live in isolation, just because Sydney was gone? And furthermore, Nina was too intuitive to harbor any feelings for me. She had her own issues and wasn't going to get any crazy ideas about us.

"Same time," I assured her.

CHAPTER 9

SYDNEY

HOW COULD ADRIAN HAVE NOT come for me? Was it possible enough gas had gotten in to mess with my system after all? I knew there was no way he would give up on me. He had to be searching. If he hadn't come to my dreams that night, there was a good reason.

The problem was, he didn't come the night after that. Or the next.

Things had gotten worse when Emma had grilled me the morning after I'd disabled the gas, wanting to know if I'd had any luck in getting the outside help I'd promised. She'd been joined by Amelia, who, I learned, had been my distraction. Our rooms were apparently monitored from a control center with lots of screens. Upon Emma's instructions, Amelia had staged an argument with her roommate, saying incriminating things that had been picked up by the surveillance team. Amelia had been especially unruly, and, they told me, had occupied the full attention of those monitoring the rooms on camera so that they missed my little performance.

"I needed a big block of sleep for my plan to work," I had told them, after explaining that I hadn't been successful. "It took me a while to doze off last night, so maybe it was too short. It'll work better tonight."

Both Amelia and Emma had looked disappointed but also hopeful. They believed in me. They barely knew me, but both were convinced I had a way to help them.

That had been five days ago.

Now their looks of hope were gone—and replaced by ones of animosity.

I didn't know what was wrong. I didn't know why Adrian wasn't coming. Panic rose in me, that something had happened to him and that he was unable to walk in dreams anymore. Maybe he was still on his prescription . . . but no, I was certain that he would have gone off it an effort to try to find me. Was it possible the pills had caused permanent damage to his ability to use spirit? I couldn't ponder it for long because my life in re-education had taken a definite turn for the worst.

Emma and especially Amelia, who'd been sent to purging for her distraction, felt played. They didn't tell anyone else what had happened, lest it incriminate themselves, but they made it known through subtle group signals that I was on the outs. They ignored my pleas that help would come, and I soon found myself eating alone in the cafeteria. Others who'd started to warm up in their standoffish behavior resumed old habits with a fury, and everything I did was scrutinized and reported to our superiors—who sent me to purging twice more that week.

Only Duncan remained my friend, in his way, but even that was tainted a little. "I warned you," he said in art class one day.

"I warned you not to mess things up. I don't know what you did, but you've definitely undone all your progress."

"I had to," I said. "I had to take a chance on something, something that I know will pay off."

"Do you?" he asked sadly, in a voice that said he'd seen similar attempts many, many times.

"Yes," I said fiercely. "It'll pay off."

He gave me an amiable smile and returned to his painting, but I could tell he believed I was lying. The awful thing was, I didn't know if he was right.

All the while, I held out hope that I would connect to Adrian in the world of dreams. I didn't understand why it hadn't happened yet, but I never doubted for a moment that he was out there still loving me and looking for me. If something was truly interfering with our dreams, I was certain he'd find another way to get to me.

A week after I'd disabled the gas, the re-education status quo was shaken up when a newcomer joined us. "That's good news for you," Duncan told me in the hall. "The attention'll shift to her for a while, so don't get too friendly."

That was hard advice to follow, especially when I saw her sitting alone at a cafeteria table for breakfast. A warning look from Duncan reluctantly sent me to my own table, where I felt foolish and cowardly for letting both the new girl and me suffer being ostracized. Her name was Renee, and she appeared to be my age, if not a year or so younger. She also seemed to be someone I could've bonded with pretty easily since, like me, she was sent off to purging during our first class for talking back to the teacher.

Unlike me, however, Renee returned later looking pale and

ill—but not cowed. In some ways, I admired that. She was still worn from her time in solitary but carried a rebellious spark in her eyes that showed promising strength and courage. *Here's someone I can ally with*, I thought. When I mentioned this to Duncan in art class, he was quick to chastise me.

"Not yet," he murmured. "She's too new, too conspicuous. And she's not making things easy on herself."

He had a point. Although she'd apparently learned enough not to blatantly talk back anymore, she made no attempt to look contrite or act as though she had any intention of buying what the Alchemists were selling. She seemed to exalt in her exclusion from the others, ignoring me when I daringly offered a friendly smile in the halls. She sat sullenly through our classes, glaring with anger and defiance at both students and instructors alike.

"I'm kind of surprised she got out of reflection time already," Duncan added. "Somebody messed up."

"That's why she needs a friend more than ever," I insisted. "She needs someone to tell her, 'Look, it's okay to feel this way, but you've got to lay low for a while.' Otherwise, they're going to send her back."

He shook his head warningly. "Don't do it. Don't get mixed up in that, especially since her arrival means you'll move up soon. Besides, they're not going to send her back to her cell."

There was an ominous note in his voice he wouldn't explain, and against my better judgment, I kept my distance for the rest of the day. When morning came—still with no contact from Adrian—I resolved to sit with Renee and not give in to peer pressure. That plan was delayed when one of Duncan's regular tablemates invited me to join them. I stood there uncertainly, holding my tray as I glanced between Renee and Duncan's tables. Going to her seemed like the right thing to do, but how could I turn down the first chance at bonding with the others that I'd had in a while? Resisting my better instincts, I headed toward Duncan's table, vowing I'd remedy things with Renee later.

Later never came.

Apparently, after a day of letting her resentment seethe within her, Renee couldn't take it anymore and snapped during third period, going off on an even longer tirade than yesterday about our instructor's closed-minded propaganda. Security hauled her off, and I felt a wave of sympathy that she had to endure purging two days in a row so soon out of solitary. Duncan met my eyes as she was led from the room, with an *I told you so* look on his face.

When lunchtime came around, I expected a last-minute change to the menu to reflect one of Renee's favorite foods and add insult to the injury of her punishment. The posted menu showed the same thing that was listed this morning, however, and I wondered if she'd gotten off the hook or simply had the unfortunate luck to already have chicken strips as one of her favorite foods. But when Renee entered the cafeteria, long after the rest of us were seated and eating, I forgot all about the menu.

Gone was that defiant glint in her eyes. There was no sparkle to them at all as she stared around in confusion, looking as though she'd never seen this room, let alone any cafeteria, before. Her facial expression was equally bland, almost slack-jawed. She stood just inside the doorway, making no attempts to enter or get food, and no one bothered to help her.

Beside me, a detainee named Elsa caught her breath. "I thought that might happen."

"What?" I asked, totally lost. "Was it a bad purging?"

"Worse," said Elsa. "Re-inking."

I thought back to my own experiences, wondering how that could be worse, since we were all re-inked at some point here. "Wasn't she re-inked already when she got out of solitary?"

"A standard re-inking," said another of my tablemates, a guy named Jonah. "Obviously, that wasn't enough, so they super-sized it—maybe a little too much. It happens sometimes. It gets the message through to them, but it leaves them kind of dazed and forgetful about ordinary life for a while."

A feeling of horror crept over me. This was what I'd feared, why I'd worked to create a magical ink that would fight the effects of the Alchemists' compulsion. I'd seen that lifeless stare before—in Keith. When he'd been fresh out of re-education, he too had acted like a zombie, unable to do anything except parrot back the rhetoric the Alchemists had drilled into him. At least by that point, however, Keith had been able to handle the daily functions of life. Had he initially emerged that wiped? It was awful to behold. Even more awful was the fact that no one showed any sign of helping her.

I was out of my seat in a flash, ignoring the sharp intake of breath from Duncan behind me.

I hurried over to Renee and took hold of her arm, guiding her inside the room. "Come in," I said, focusing on her so that I wouldn't have to see I had the attention of every single person in the room. "Don't you want to get some food?"

Renee's gaze stared blankly ahead for several seconds and then slowly turned to me. "I don't know. Do you think I should?"

"Are you hungry?" I asked.

A small frown appeared between her eyebrows. "Do you think I am? If you don't think so . . ."

I steered her toward Baxter's window. "I think you should be whatever you want to be," I said firmly. She said nothing to the chef when we reached him, and as usual, he wasn't forthcoming, so it was on me. "Renee needs some lunch."

Baxter didn't respond immediately, and I almost wondered if he might not act unless she specifically asked for food. If so, we could be standing here for a while. But after a few more moments of indecision, he turned away and began making up a tray of chicken strips. I carried it to an empty table for her and pulled out a chair, gesturing to her to sit. She seemed to respond well to a command like that, even unspoken, but made no attempts to do anything on her own once I sat down opposite her.

"You can eat if you want," I said. When that elicited nothing, I changed my wording. "Eat your chicken, Renee."

She obediently picked up a chicken strip and began working her way through the tray while I looked on with a growing sense of dread. Dread—and anger. Did the Alchemists really think this was a better alternative than someone questioning authority? Even if the most severe of the effects wore off over time, it was still sickening that they could do this to another human being. When I'd discovered I was protected from re-inking, I'd thought I was home free in that regard. And it was true: *I* was. But everyone around me, whether they were friend or foe, was at risk if the Alchemists went overboard with their re-inking. It didn't matter if this extreme of an effect was a rarity. Even if it only happened one time, that was one time too many.

"Drink your milk," I ordered when I realized she'd finished the chicken and was just staring at her plate again. She was halfway through the carton when the chimes rang. "Time to go, Renee. That sound means we have to go somewhere else."

She stood as I did, and I looked up to see two of Sheridan's henchmen approaching. "You need to come with us," one of them told me.

I started to comply and then saw Renee's helpless expression. Ignoring my escort's urging, I turned to her and said, "Follow along and do what the others do. See how they're putting their trays away now? Do that, and then go with them to the next class." One of the guards tugged my arm to move, and I resisted until I saw Renee nod and join the others with her tray. Only then did I let the duo lead me out, and they didn't look pleased at all by my small act of defiance.

They led me to the elevator and then down one level, to the floor where purging took place. I wondered if not finishing my own lunch would make that experience more or less unpleasant. To my surprise, though, we walked past the usual door and kept going to the end of the hall, where I'd never been. We passed closets labeled respectively as kitchen and office supplies and then continued on to doors that were ominously unmarked. It was into one of these that they took me.

This new room looked like the usual purging ones, save that the chair had strange arms on it. They were larger than the ones I was used to but still had restraints on them, which was all that mattered. Maybe this was the new upgraded model from wherever they got their torture devices from. Sheridan was waiting in the room for us, holding a small remote control. The guards strapped me into the chair and then, at a nod from her, left us alone.

"Well, hello, Sydney," she said. "I must say, I'm disappointed to see you in trouble."

"Are you, ma'am? I've been in purging a few times this week," I replied, thinking of how the others had been incriminating me recently.

Sheridan made a dismissive gesture with her hand. "That? Come on, we both know it's just the others playing their games. You've actually been doing remarkably well—until now."

A spark of my earlier anger returned. Sheridan and the other authorities were well aware of when someone legitimately stepped out of line compared to when that person was simply being ganged up on. And she didn't care.

I swallowed my rage and put on a polite face. "What exactly did I do, ma'am?"

"Do you understand what happened to Renee today, Sydney?"

"I heard she was re-inked," I said carefully.

"The others told you that."

"Yes."

"And did they also tell you not to help her when she returned?"

I hesitated. "Not explicitly. But they made it clear in their actions they weren't going to."

"And don't you think you should have followed their lead?" she pushed.

"Begging your pardon, ma'am," I said, "but I thought my duty was to follow *your* instructions, not those of my fellow residents. Since neither you nor any other instructor told me not to help Renee, I didn't think I was doing anything wrong. In fact, I thought acting compassionately toward another human was something right. I apologize if I misunderstood."

She scrutinized me for a long time, and I met her gaze unblinkingly. "You say all the right things, but I wonder if you mean them. Well, then. Let's get started."

With a push of the button, the screen came on, showing a typical picture of happy Moroi.

"What do you see, Sydney?"

I frowned, realizing she'd forgotten to inject me with the nausea-inducing drug. I certainly wasn't going to call her attention to it, though. "Moroi, ma'am."

"Wrong. You see creatures of evil."

I didn't know how to respond to that, so I said nothing.

"You see creatures of evil," she repeated.

This new turn of events left me uncertain how to proceed. "I don't know. Maybe they are. I'd have to know more about these particular Moroi."

"You don't need to know anything except what I've told you. They are creatures of evil."

"If you say so, ma'am," I said cautiously.

Her face remained tranquil. "I need *you* to say so. Repeat after me: 'I see creatures of evil.'"

I stared at the Moroi in the picture. It showed two girls, close to my age, who looked like they might be sisters. They were smiling and holding ice cream cones. Nothing about them looked evil at all, unless they were about to force that ice cream on some diabetic children. As I mulled this over, the armrest on my right suddenly clicked. The top of it slid back, revealing a hollowed out compartment below that was filled with some sort of clear liquid.

"What's this?" I asked.

"Do you see creatures of evil?" Sheridan said by way of answer.

I must have taken too long to answer, and Sheridan pushed a button on the remote control. The restraints that held my arm in place suddenly began to move, lowering my arm down. It stopped just as the bottom of my arm grazed that liquid and then began raising my arm back up.

Grazing was all that was required, however. I cried out in pain and surprise as a burning sensation spread over where my skin had touched the liquid's surface. Whatever chemical was in it made it feel as though I'd just touched a pot of boiling water, searing my exposed flesh. Once my arm was away from the liquid, the pain began to slowly ebb away.

"Now then," said Sheridan, far too sweetly after what she'd just done. "Say 'I see creatures of evil.'"

She didn't even give me a chance to respond before repeating the same procedure, letting my arm stay down a bit longer than before. Despite that, I was more prepared and managed to bite my lip to stop from crying out. The pain was there all the same, and I exhaled in relief when after a few moments, she raised my arm up and allowed me a small recovery.

It was short-lived, and she soon said, "Now say—"

I didn't give her a chance to finish. "I see creatures of evil," I responded quickly.

Triumph lit her features. "Excellent. Now let's try a different one." A new image came, this one showing a group of Moroi schoolchildren. "What do you see?"

I was a fast learner. "I see creatures of evil," I said promptly. It was ridiculous, of course. There was nothing evil about these Moroi or the subsequent pictures she then began showing me.

I'd vowed to myself in solitary that I'd play whatever games it took to get me out of here, and if she needed me to parrot back this lie in order to make up for helping Renee, I'd gladly do it.

A Moroi couple, more children, an old man . . . on it went. Sheridan flipped through face after face, and I responded accordingly. "I see creatures of evil. I see creatures of evil. I see—"

My words fell short as I stared up at two more Moroi—two Moroi I knew.

Adrian and Jill.

I had no idea where she'd gotten the picture, and I didn't care. My heart leapt as I looked into their smiling faces, faces I loved and had missed so terribly. I'd imagined their faces countless times, but there was no substituting the actual image. I took in every detail: the way the light played off Adrian's hair, the way Jill's lips curved in a shy smile. I had to swallow back a wave of emotion welling up within me. Maybe Sheridan had meant to punish me by showing them, but it actually came off as more of a reward—until she spoke again.

"What do you see, Sydney?"

I opened my mouth, ready to recite that inane line, but I couldn't do it. Looking into those beloved faces, their eyes sparkling with happiness . . . I couldn't do it. Even telling myself it was lie, I couldn't bring myself to condemn Adrian and Jill.

Sheridan wasted no time in acting. The chair's device lowered my arm into the liquid, farther than it had before, so that my arm was immersed about halfway. The shock of it caught me off guard, and it was made worse by her leaving my arm there even longer than before. Whatever acid was in that concoction burned my skin, setting every nerve on fire. I yelped at the pain, and even after she raised my arm, I still found myself whimpering as the effects lingered.

"What do you see, Sydney?"

I blinked back tears of pain and focused on Adrian and Jill. *Just say it*, I told myself. *You need to get out of here. You need to get back to them.* At the same time, I suddenly wondered, *Is this how it starts? How I become like Keith?* Would I start off by telling myself that what I said was okay, so long as I knew it was a lie being used to avoid pain? Would that lie eventually become truth?

At my silence, Sheridan lowered my arm again, dipping it even more than before. "Say it," she said, her voice devoid of any human emotion. "Tell me what you see."

A low moan of pain escaped my lips, but that was it. Internally, I tried to give myself a pep talk: *I won't say it. I won't betray Adrian and Jill, even with empty words.* I thought if I could just withstand the pain a little longer, she'd give me a reprieve like before, but instead, she lowered my arm even farther so that it was completely immersed in the liquid. I screamed as I felt it sear my skin. Glancing down, I expected to see my flesh peeling away, but my arm and hand only looked pink. Whatever this compound was, it was designed to feel like it was causing more damage than it was.

"Tell me what you see, Sydney. Tell me what you see, and I'll end it."

I tried to fight against the pain, but it was impossible when I felt like I was being burned alive.

"Tell me what you see, Sydney."

The pain built and built the longer my arm stayed submerged, and finally, feeling like a traitor as I met the eyes of those I loved, I blurted out, "I see creatures of evil."

"I didn't hear that," she replied calmly. "Say it more loudly."

"I see creatures of evil!" I yelled.

She touched the remote, and my arm was lifted and released from its liquid torture. I started to breathe a sigh of relief, and then suddenly, without a word of warning, she dunked my arm again. I screamed at the pain, which lasted about ten more seconds until she brought my arm up again.

"What are you doing?" I exclaimed. "I thought you said—"

"That's the problem," she interrupted. Through some silent command, her henchmen returned and began unfastening my restraints. "You *thought*. Just like you thought it was okay to help Renee. The only thing you need to be doing is what you're told. Do you understand?"

I glanced down at my arm, which was a dark, angry pink but in no way showed the true extent of what I'd just undergone. I then looked back up at Adrian and Jill, feeling guilty for my weakness. "Yes, ma'am."

"Excellent," Sheridan said, setting the remote down. "Then let's get off to your next class, shall we?"

CHAPTER 10
ADRIAN

"ADRIAN?"

I opened my eyes and squinted into the face of a girl I didn't know. She was fully dressed, and I was fully dressed, so that at least was a promising sign. Seeing the confused expression on my face, she gave me a wry smile.

"I'm Ada. You crashed here last night. But you've got to go now before my parents get home."

I managed to sit up and saw I'd been lying on a hardwood floor, which explained the ache in my back and head. Glancing around, I saw a few other partygoers in similar shape, rustling themselves up and heading for the door. Satisfied I was on my way, Ada rose from her kneeling position and went to kick out the next unwelcome overnight guest.

"Thanks for letting me stay," I called after her. "Great party."

At least, I assumed it had been, if I'd crashed on the floor. An empty bottle of vermouth lay near where I'd slept, but I didn't know if it was mine or not. I hoped not. Getting drunk on vermouth was just sad. The last two weeks had been a blur of decadence and debauchery, but this was the first time I'd actually stayed over somewhere. Usually, Nina managed to see that I got back to my place. For a moment, I felt hurt that she hadn't been here to look after me again. Then, I vaguely remembered that it was Monday now, and she hadn't wanted to stay out late before her workweek started.

It looked to be about six in the morning when I stepped outside, and the rising sun was merciless on my hangover. Few people were out yet. On vampiric time, this was pretty late at night. People would be going to bed in the next few hours. Even the guardians had light patrols this time of the day, and I only passed a couple as I trudged back to guest housing. One did a double take when he saw me.

"Adrian?"

I thought maybe my reputation had preceded me, and then I saw it was Dimitri. "Oh, hey," I said. "Good morning. Or something."

"Looks like you've had better," he observed. "I'm just finishing my shift. You want to go get some breakfast?"

I considered, unsure of my last solid meal. "My stomach's pretty empty. I don't know how it'll react to that."

"The fact that you're unsure probably means you need food that much more," he said, which sounded like the weirdest logic I'd ever heard. "At least in my experience."

I wondered how much "experience" he had in these matters. I really didn't know what he did in his free time. Maybe there was more Russian vodka being consumed than I knew about. I always just figured when he wasn't working, he and Rose were off grappling on training mats, or whatever passed between those two as foreplay.

"You sure you don't want to go home and cuddle up with Rose?" I asked. "Wait . . . is she even back? Weren't they at Lehigh?"

"They've been back for a week," said Dimitri patiently. "Come on, my treat."

I followed along because really, it was hard to say no to Dimitri Belikov about anything. Plus, I was still processing the news that I'd lost enough time for Rose and Lissa to be back that long. "I can pay. Or, well," I added bitterly, "my dad can, since that's the only way my mother and I can apparently survive."

Dimitri's expression stayed neutral as we walked into a building that held a number of restaurants, most of which weren't open yet. "Is that why you've been living in such a pit of despair since you got back here?"

"I like to think of it as a lifestyle choice," I told him. "And how do you know what I've been doing?"

"Word gets around," he said mysteriously.

The restaurant he took us to was chock-full of guardians who must've just gotten off their shifts. It was also probably the safest place at Court, judging from their numbers.

"What I do is my own business," I said hotly.

"Of course it is," he agreed. "This just hasn't been your kind of business for a while. I'm surprised to see it come back."

The restaurant served buffet breakfast, and though my mother would've fainted at the thought of serving herself, I obligingly took a plate and followed Dimitri into the line. Once we had our trays, we settled into a small table in the corner. He didn't touch his food and instead leaned toward me with a look that meant all business.

"You're better than this, Adrian," he said. "Whatever the reason, you're better than it. Don't trick yourself into thinking you're weaker than you are."

It was so like what Sydney had told me in the past that it momentarily took me aback. Then, my anger returned. "Is that why you invited me here? To lecture? Don't even act like you know anything about me! We aren't that good of friends."

That comment seemed to surprise him. "That's too bad. I'd hoped we were. I'd hoped I knew the real you."

"You don't," I said, shoving my tray aside. "No one does." *Only Sydney*, I thought. *And she'd be ashamed of me.*

"There are a lot of people who care about you." Dimitri was still the picture of calm. "Don't turn away from them."

"Like they've turned away from me?" I demanded, thinking of Lissa's refusal to help. "I tried asking for help, and I was refused! No one can help me." I stood up abruptly. "I'm not hungry anymore. Thanks for the 'pep talk.'"

I left my untouched tray and stormed out on him. He didn't follow, for which I was glad, since he probably could have literally dragged me back with no effort. I left from anger—and also from humiliation. His words hurt, not just because they leveled judgment at me—judgment I'd already been giving myself—but because they again reminded me of Sydney. Sydney, who'd always said I was so much more. Well, I'd done a damned good job of proving her wrong. I'd failed her. Dimitri's words had driven that home, even if he didn't realize it.

I went back to my room and downed a couple shots of vodka before crashing into my bed and falling almost instantly asleep. I dreamed of Sydney, not in the spirit magic way I'd hoped, but in the normal way. I dreamed of her laughter and the exasperated—yet amused—way she'd say, "Oh, Adrian," when I did something ridiculous. I dreamed of sunlight turning her hair to molten gold and bringing out the glints of amber in her eyes. Sweetest of all, I dreamed of her arms around me, her lips pressed to mine and the way they could fill my body with desire and my heart with more love than I'd ever thought it capable of holding.

My dreaming and waking worlds shifted, and suddenly, there *were* arms wrapped tenderly around my waist and soft lips kissing me. I responded in kind, increasing the fervor in that kiss. I'd been so lonely for so long, so lost and adrift not just in the world but in my own head. Having Sydney here in bed grounded me and brought me back to myself in a way I hadn't known was possible. I could weather the storms in my world, the craziness in my family . . . all of it could be endured now that Sydney was here.

Except she wasn't here.

Sydney was gone, being kept far, far away from me . . . which meant it wasn't her arms around me or her lips I tasted. Struggling out of my sleepy haze, I opened my eyes and tried to make sense of my surroundings. The blinds filtered out most of the morning sun, but I could still see enough to realize the girl in bed with me had black hair, not gold. Her eyes were gray, not brown.

"Nina?"

I pushed her gently away and scooted as far from her as I could while still managing to stay in the bed. Amusement sparkled in her eyes, and she laughed at my surprise. "You were expecting someone else? Wait, don't answer that."

"No . . . but what are you doing here?" I blinked around the dim room. "How did you even get in here?"

"You gave me a key for emergencies, don't you remember?" I didn't, but it also didn't surprise me. She looked mildly disappointed that it had just been something I'd done on drunken impulse. "I got worried when I didn't hear from you this morning, so I headed over here to check on you when I went on my lunch break. I've got a weird late shift."

"Assaulting isn't really the same as checking on me," I said.

"'Assaulting' is kind of an exaggeration," she chastised. "Especially since *you* were the one who reached for me when I sat next you on the bed."

"I did?" Again, I couldn't say I was entirely surprised. "Well . . . I'm sorry. I was half-asleep and didn't know what I was doing. I was . . . dreaming."

"You seemed to know what you were doing to me," said Nina huskily. She reached toward me. "Were you dreaming of her?"

"Who?"

"You know who. Her. The girl who torments you. Don't deny it," she ordered, seeing me about to protest. "Don't you think I can tell? Oh, Adrian." It was jarring hearing her say it, after I'd just dreamed about Sydney uttering those very words. Nina lightly stroked my cheek. "I could tell as soon as you came back to Court someone had broken your heart. I've hated seeing you on the path you're on. It eats me up."

I shook my head but didn't remove her hand. "You don't understand. There's more to it than you know."

"I know that she's not here. And that you're miserable. Please . . ." She scooted back across the bed and leaned over me, her hair forming a curtain of dark curls around us. "I've been drawn to you since the moment we met. Let me make you feel better. . . ."

She leaned down to kiss me, and I held up a hand to stop her. "No . . . I can't."

"Why? Is she coming back?"

Nina's voice wasn't cruel, but there was certainly a challenge in it, and I found myself looking away. "I . . . I don't know. . . ."

"Then why fight this?" she asked beseechingly. "I know you like me. More importantly, I know you understand me. No one else gets what it's like, to be tossed around on the waves of spirit and endure what we do. Isn't that worth something? To just have someone around so you aren't alone?"

She tried to kiss me again, and I didn't stop her, largely because it was hard to argue against her point. I certainly didn't love her like I did Sydney, but we did get what the other was going through. She didn't judge me for what I did or try to get me to find better ways to handle my despair. And yes, she was right: It was nice not being alone.

Like that, my mother's words suddenly hit me like a slap in the face: *Stop chasing a dream and focus on someone you can build a stable life with. That's what your father and I have done.*

Was that what I was doing with Nina? Building a stable relationship with someone who shared my vices and need for escape—but whom I ultimately didn't love? It would certainly be easy. Nina made sure of that. We could spend a lifetime together, commiserating about how hard it was to be a spirit user, going to one party after another in the hopes of putting off the darkness a little longer. It would be a pleasant life. Stable, as my mother had said. But I would never try to better myself. I would never achieve greatness, the way Sydney had always made me feel I could. And I would never, ever have that euphoric, all-consuming love that had wrapped around me every moment I was with Sydney, that feeling of love that constantly made me think, *Yes, this is what it means to be alive.*

It would be easy, whispered Aunt Tatiana, fickle as usual. *She's here. Use her. Make the pain disappear. Your other girl is far away, but this one's right in front of you. Give in. Just say yes. Yes, yes, yes . . .*

"No," I said.

I broke the kiss with Nina and actually stood up this time, making sure she was out of reach. I'd been a fool. A weak, lazy fool. I'd let my depression over my parents and not having any leads on Sydney get the best of me. I hadn't just given up on Sydney. I'd given up on myself, getting lost in this decadent life of Court parties and pleasure because it was easy—much easier than both trying to find Sydney *and* staying strong when the options seemed hopeless.

"Nina, I'm sorry, but I can't do this," I said, putting as much strength into my words as I could. "I'm sorry if I led you on, but this isn't going to happen. I like hanging out with you, but I'm never going to feel any more for you than I do right now. And if I don't, then that's not acceptable for either of us. I'm sorry. We'll never, ever have a future together."

It was a bit excessive, largely because I was lecturing myself as well as her. She flinched, and I realized too late that maybe I should've found a gentler way to express my feelings—especially, knowing as I did, how sensitive spirit users were. Her earlier smile disappeared, and she actually recoiled as though I'd struck her. Blinking back tears, she stood up from the bed with as much dignity as she could muster.

"I see," she said. There was a tremor in her voice, and she was doing that hand-wringing thing, to the extent that her own nails were digging into her flesh. "Well, I'm sorry for wasting your time these last couple of weeks. I should've known clerical help wasn't good enough for Lord Adrian Ivashkov."

Now I winced. "Nina, it's not like that at all. And I really like having you as a friend. If you'd just let me explain—"

"Don't bother." She turned her back on me and headed for the bedroom door. "I don't want to waste any more of your time, and besides, I need to find something to eat before my lunch break's over. Sorry I woke you. I'm glad you're okay."

"Nina—" I tried. But she was gone before I could say anything more, her exit punctuated with a loud slamming of the front door.

I sank down on my bed, feeling like crap both physically and mentally. I hadn't meant to end things like that with her. I hadn't meant for a lot of things to happen. And as the overwhelming state of my life threatened to swallow me, I had to fight the urge to go make a drink.

"No," I said aloud. "I'm done with that."

Then and there, I was stopping cold turkey. I'd been deluding myself (even more than usual) thinking that I could drink sporadically throughout the day if I checked for Sydney every once in a while. Speaking of which . . . when was the last time I'd actually checked for her at night—the human night? When she'd first been taken, I'd searched for her nonstop. But recently . . . well, it was usually some half-hearted attempt after I woke up hungover. By the time darkness rolled around—the most likely time she'd be asleep, if she truly was still in the United States—I was usually a few drinks into my first party.

I'd let myself get sloppy, disheartened by my earlier failure and real-life distractions. I wouldn't make that mistake again, though. I needed to keep myself sober and full of spirit, so that I could regularly check throughout the day. It didn't matter how many times I'd failed. One day, one time, I'd catch her.

Despite my pounding headache, I shifted into the trance needed to embrace spirit and reach out to her. Nothing. That was okay, though. I slipped back to myself, vowing to try again later. I hopped in the shower and washed away last night's party. When I got out, I found I could stomach food a little better than earlier and ate a leftover donut I'd brought home the previous day. Or maybe the day before that. It was stale, but it did the trick.

As I munched on it, I made a mental to-do list of things that didn't include going to parties tonight. Apologies were first on my list. Along with Nina, I needed to fix things with Dimitri, after the asshole way I'd walked out on him. I also needed to talk to my mother. Just because she'd given up on herself was no reason for me to. I'd start with her first, seeing as she was the one I hadn't spoken to in the longest time. Before I did, though, I should probably stop by a feeder since I couldn't recall my last blood. It would help clear my head.

I was almost at my front door when I decided to search for Sydney. Maybe hourly searching was excessive, but it would keep me in practice and sober. It was important that I get in the habit of these new patterns if I was going to change my life. I closed my eyes and took a deep breath.

Tendrils of spirit shot out from me across the world of dreams, reaching for Sydney as they so often did . . .

. . . and this time, they connected.

I was dumbfounded. It'd been so long since I'd formed a successful dream connection that I almost didn't know what to do. I hadn't even gone in with a preplanned setting because I'd simply been running on autopilot, making the effort without expecting results. As the world shimmered around us and I felt her materialize in the dream, I quickly summoned up our old meeting place: the Getty Villa in Malibu. Columns and gardens appeared around us, surrounding the museum's focal point: an enormous pool and fountain. Sydney appeared on the other side of it. For several moments, I could only stare across the water at her, certain I was imagining this. Could I hallucinate in a dream I'd created? Surely this was too soon for any crazy alcohol-withdrawal symptoms.

"Adrian?"

Her voice was small, nearly lost in the dripping of water from the fountain. But the power it carried—and the effect it had on me—was monumental. I'd heard the expression "weak-kneed" before but had never lived it until now. My muscles didn't feel as though they could sustain me, and there was a great swelling in my chest, the result of a tangle of emotions I couldn't even begin to describe. Love. Joy. Relief. Disbelief. And mixed in with all of them were the emotions that I'd endured these last few months as well: despair, fear, sorrow. It spread out from my heart, and I felt tears form in my eyes. It wasn't possible that one person could make you experience so many emotions at once, that one person could trigger a universe of feelings, simply with the sound of your name.

I also knew then that they were wrong—all of them. My mom. My dad. Nina. Anyone who thought love could simply be built on shared goals alone had never, ever experienced anything like what I had with Sydney. I couldn't believe I'd almost lost this through my own ignorance. Until I looked into her eyes now, I didn't truly realize what a hollow life I'd been living.

"Sydney . . ."

It would take too long to walk around the fountain. I jumped up on the edge and then into the pool, wading through the water toward her. I would've done it even if I wasn't wearing dream clothes. No physical discomfort mattered. Only getting to her did. My entire world, my entire existence, became focused around her. The journey took seconds, but it felt as though I'd been traveling toward her for years. I reached the other side and stepped out, dripping water onto the sunlit stones. I hesitated only a moment and then wrapped my arms around her, half expecting her to vanish into thin air. But she was real. Real and solid (in that dream kind of way), and her whole body shuddered with a repressed sob as she buried her face against my chest.

"Oh, Adrian. Where have you been?"

It wasn't a chastisement, simply an expression of her own longing and fear. She couldn't have known about the demons I'd faced these last couple of weeks or how very close I'd come to missing this opportunity. I cupped her face in my hands and gazed into those brown eyes I loved so much, eyes that now glittered with unshed tears.

"I'm sorry," I whispered. "I'm so sorry. I looked for a long time . . . but I couldn't reach you. And then I—I slacked off. I know I shouldn't have. You wouldn't have. God, Sydney, I'm so sorry. If I'd tried harder and sooner—"

"No, no," she said softly, running her hand through my hair. "There was nothing you could have done—not until recently. They regulate our sleep here with some kind of gas. I've been too drugged for spirit to reach me." She began to tremble. "I was so afraid I'd never reach you—so afraid I'd never find a way out—"

"Shh. You found me now. Everything's going to be okay. Where are you?"

A remarkable transformation took place. She looked as though she wanted nothing more than to hold me and cry out all the fear and frustration she'd experienced over the last few months. I knew because I kind of felt the same way. But no matter her own longings, no matter what hell she'd endured, she still remained the strongest, most amazing woman I knew. Before my eyes, she pushed all those fears and insecurities aside, ignoring the part of her that only wanted comfort in my arms. She became the Sydney Sage I'd first met: efficient, strong, competent. Ready to make the tough choices in order to accomplish what needed to get done.

"Right," she said. She paused to wipe the tears from her eyes. "We might not have long to talk. I'm not sure how long I've been asleep. And . . . I don't know where I'm at. I haven't seen a window since I was taken. We're kept underground."

"Who's we?" I asked.

"There are twelve others—er, thirteen now, we just got someone new—all former Alchemists who got in trouble. They've been reprogrammed to varying degrees. Some are just playing along, I'm certain of it, but it's hard to tell. We get in big trouble for stepping out of line."

"What kind of trouble?" I asked. Although I'd been drinking up all her features since she appeared, I only now paused to truly study her. She was in some kind of horrible khaki outfit, and her golden hair looked longer than before. Both her face and body also seemed thinner, but I was uncertain how accurate that was. Unless the spirit user specifically altered the other person's appearance, that person usually showed up in the dream as a mix of what he or she looked like in reality and how that person perceived him or herself. Often, the two weren't the same. I made a mental note to ask her about her physical condition later.

"It doesn't matter," she said brusquely. "I'm fine, and I'm sure there are others like me, they're just too scared to act. Others have been completely reprogrammed, though. They're just like Keith. They're—" Her eyes widened. "Keith. That's it."

"Keith?" I repeated dumbly. I was still hung up on her evasiveness about getting in "big trouble" and didn't see where her former asshole colleague fit into this.

"He was there. Long before me. At the same facility." She clutched my sleeve in her excitement. "They have this wall where people write confessions, and he wrote one—well, an apology actually, to my sister Carly. The point is, he was there, and we know he left. Maybe he knows where the facility is. He had to go outside when he got out, right?"

"Didn't you say he was really out of it, though?" I asked. "Is he even going to have the sense to talk to us?"

Her expression darkened. "Yes . . . he was more than out of it. That's what happens when you're fresh off of re-inking. But in most cases, the worst of that wears off over time, and even if people are still compliant, they should eventually lose some of that brain-deadness. He might have some answers if you can find him."

"Finding him might be easier said than done," I murmured, thinking of the difficulties I'd had locating Sydney's father and Zoe. "The Alchemists aren't very forthcoming about their agents' assignments."

"Marcus can help you," she said decisively. "And don't look like that. He *can*. He has resources. I know you guys can put aside your differences and work together."

I'd grimaced at his name, and she'd misunderstood, not realizing that Marcus and I had been in contact extensively since her disappearance. Mostly I was reminded that he too was another person I hadn't parted well with, but that wasn't her problem.

"We'll make it work," I assured her. "Plus, he's got this list that—"

Her image began to fade before my eyes as the real world summoned her back. "Time to wake up," she said sadly.

I clutched at her, but she was losing substance. Panic filled me. There were so many things I still wanted to ask her, but I only had a few seconds to use. "I'll talk to Marcus, and I'll come find you again. Is this your usual sleeping time?"

"Yes. I love you."

"I love you too."

I don't know if she heard me because I was suddenly standing alone in the garden, with the fountain splashing behind me and Malibu sun shining all around. I stared at where she'd been a few moments longer and then let the dream dissolve, returning me to my suite in guest housing. I was still by the front door, where I'd been about to go see my mother. But now, everything had changed. I'd made contact with Sydney! I'd seen her face, and she was okay . . . relatively speaking, of course.

Thinking of my mom brought a pang to my heart, but I couldn't go to her. I didn't want to leave things badly with her—

or with Nina, Dimitri, Rose, and Lissa. But none of them could help me right now. They would have to wait. It was time for me to return to the people who could help me find Sydney.

I took out my cell phone and began looking up ticket prices to Palm Springs.

CHAPTER 11
SYDNEY

BEING RIPPED AWAY from Adrian was agonizing, but I still woke with a renewed sense of hope, feeling even more optimistic than I had when I'd disabled the gas. I saw Emma give me a double take as we got ready for the day, so my inner thoughts must have shown on my face. I quickly tried to rectify that and look subdued. She didn't dare say anything to me while we were under our room's surveillance, but I could see curiosity burning in her eyes. When we were in the crowded hall with the others, on the way to breakfast, I fell into step beside her.

"I did it," I murmured. "I got a message out."

It was a sign of the supernatural things we dealt with that she didn't ask for specifics. She took me at my word and focused on more pressing concerns. "So, what, help's on the way? Some knight in shining armor is going to come bust us all out?"

"Not exactly," I admitted. "Especially since I don't know where we're at . . . do you?"

She gave a frustrated sigh and rolled her eyes. "What do you think? We share a room. Do I have my own private window?" With that, she hurried off to join Amelia and some others.

I wasn't entirely surprised Emma didn't know where the facility was. Duncan hadn't either. That was a secret no detainee seemed able to crack but one that I would need to find out if I made contact with Adrian—no, *when* I made contact with Adrian.

Emma's brusque attitude didn't sting quite as much anymore because some attention had been taken off me, thanks to a shake-up in the veteran detainees. A guy named Jonah, who was around Duncan's age, had slipped up in our history class and gotten too vocal with his opinions recently—much more than I had my first day. It had earned him a trip to purging and obvious disapproval from our superiors. Some of the other detainees had also started shunning him, but Duncan and those at his table were still including him. I had recently been allowed to sit with them and was learning the whole story.

"I ruined it," Jonah muttered, lest one of the cafeteria supervisors overhear. "I was doing so good. I could've been out of here! But Harrison made me so mad when he started off with his so called historical facts about dhampirs and—"

"Hush," said Duncan. He had an easy smile on his face, no doubt for the benefit of those watching us. "Don't fixate on it. They can tell. You'll make things worse. Smile."

"How can I smile?" demanded Jonah. "I know what's coming. I'll be like Renee. They're going to re-ink my tattoo with stronger compulsion! They're going to try to force me to change my mind that way!"

"You don't know that," said Duncan. His expression, however, betrayed him.

"And it doesn't always take," added Elsa. She was one who'd moved her seat from me on that first day, but I'd since learned she wasn't that bad—just scared, like they all were. "None of us would be here if it did. You might power through it."

Jonah looked skeptical. "Depends on how heavy they dose me."

I thought of Keith and his automaton responsiveness when I'd last seen him. From what I'd gathered, that could only have been achieved by some pretty severe conditioning here, as well as strongly compelled ink like Renee's. Silence fell at the table, and I wrestled with a decision. Duncan had told me my acceptance with the group needed to be in baby steps and that although it was okay for me to sit with them now, it'd be better if I stayed quiet for a while and didn't act like I had too many opinions or attitude left. That was probably sound advice, yet I suddenly found myself speaking anyway.

"I might be able to help you," I said. Jonah's gaze locked on to me.

"How?" he asked.

"She's kidding," said Duncan, a warning note in his voice. "Aren't you, Sydney?"

I appreciated his help, but the fear in Jonah's face was too strong. If I could stop him from becoming another Keith, I would. *Are you sure?* an inner voice asked me. *You actually made progress in getting to Adrian. You need to lay low now until he talks to Marcus. Why risk everything by helping someone else?*

It was a valid question, but I knew the answer immediately: because it was the right thing to do.

"I'm not kidding," I said firmly. Duncan sighed in dismay

but let me continue. "I can make a compound that'll fight the effects of the compulsion."

Jonah's face fell a little. "I almost believe you. What I don't believe, not even for an instant, is that they give you access to the standard bank of Alchemist chemicals."

"I don't need them. I just need"—my eyes fell on the center of the table—"that saltshaker. Specifically, the salt. Do you think I could smuggle it out of here without them noticing?"

The others looked incredulous, but Elsa played along. "Yes . . . but I think they'd notice it was missing afterward and come asking questions."

She was probably right. With the Alchemist's efficiency, they probably counted every piece of silverware after we left. A missing saltshaker might make them think we were making weapons out of its plastic or something. I casually slid my napkin toward the center of the table and then reached for the saltshaker. As I lifted it over my tray to salt my scrambled eggs, I managed to unscrew the top with one hand. When I went to return it to its spot, the shaker slipped out of my hand and fell over on the table, spilling salt onto my napkin.

"Oops," I said, quickly reassembling the saltshaker. "The top was loose." I moved my napkin around like I was cleaning the table, but in actuality, I folded the napkin up as I worked, making a neat little pouch of salt. I then slid it back beside my tray. It would be easy enough to pocket the napkin when we left. Usually, they were thrown away with the trays. No one would count them.

"Deftly done," said Duncan, who still looked like he didn't approve. "That's all you need?"

"Mostly," I said. I wasn't close enough to any of them to

reveal that I'd be using magic for the rest of the key components. "It'd be better if I had some of the compounds that go into ink, but injecting you with a saline solution—once I've treated this salt—should work just as well." As soon as the words were out of my mouth, I spotted another problem and groaned. "I don't have anything to inject you with." Salt might be a common commodity, but needles generally weren't left lying around within our reach.

"Do you need a tattoo gun?" asked Jonah.

I speculated, based on what I knew of the Alchemist tattooing process and my own experiments. "Ideally, that'd be great. A full-fledged tattoo with solid ink would provide permanent protection. But we should be able to get fine short-term protection from a basic medical syringe—like they do for run-of-the-mill re-inkings."

Duncan arched an eyebrow. "Short-term?"

"It'll negate whatever they do to you in the near future," I said, feeling confident even with a makeshift solution. "Like, months at least. But for lifetime protection, you'd eventually need it tattooed in for real."

"I'll take months," said Jonah.

It was hard to keep the dismay off my face. "Yeah, but I can't give you that without a proper needle. That's the one thing I can't improvise on here. I . . . I'm sorry. I was too hasty with this plan."

"Like hell," he retorted. "There are plenty of needles like that in the purging room. They're in that cabinet by the sink. I'll just get myself sent there and swipe one."

Beside him, Lacey scoffed. "If you act out again so soon, they aren't sending you to purging. You're going for re-inking—

168

or worse." That threat hung heavily over us a moment. "I'll do it," she declared. "I'll do something in our next class."

"No," I said quickly. "I'll do it. I'll get the needle directly that way. It'll save time in getting it back to me, in case they send Jonah for re-inking sooner rather than later." There was truth to my point, but a large part of my motivation was that I wasn't going to let anyone else get sent to purging for one of my plans. Amelia still glared at me whenever we made eye contact. I wouldn't risk any more enemies. Purging was miserable, but it did eventually end, and so far, it wasn't having the desired effect, considering my first impulse upon seeing Adrian last night was to kiss him, not throw up.

The rest of my tablemates thought it was a heroic act, particularly Jonah. Others, like Duncan, thought I was on the verge of making a huge mistake, but none of them would intervene.

"Thank you," said Jonah. "I mean it. I owe you."

"We're in this together," I said simply.

That sentiment took a few of them by surprise, but the chimes signaling the end of breakfast prevented any further conversation. I successfully smuggled my salt out and slipped it into my shoe when I reached my next class, on the pretense that I was adjusting my sock. As the others filed into their seats, I decided it was best to get this plan going as soon as possible. I wouldn't let Lacey do my work for me, but I used her now as an accomplice as she sat down in a nearby desk.

"Look, Lacey," I said, as though we were continuing some conversation from the cafeteria, "I'm not saying you're wrong . . . just misguided. Until the Strigoi are eradicated, there's nothing wrong with being civil toward the Moroi."

To her credit, she caught on quickly and played along. "You weren't talking about being civil. You were talking about being *friendly*. And we all know that's a dangerous area with you and your history."

I put on an offended look. "So you're saying it's not even okay to have a casual meal with one of them?"

"If it's not for business, then no."

"You're being completely unreasonable!" I exclaimed.

Kennedy, our instructor, glanced up from her desk at the raised voices. "Ladies, is there a problem?"

Lacey pointed accusingly. "Sydney's trying to convince me it's okay to hang out with Moroi in a personal way outside of work."

"I never said personal! I'm just saying, if you're on assignment and have a contact, what's the harm in getting dinner or a movie?"

"It leads to trouble, that's what. You need to draw a line and keep things black and white."

"Only if you're stupid enough to think they're as dangerous as Strigoi. *I* know how to walk in that gray area," I retorted.

This was a particularly compelling point that Lacey had set up nicely because just yesterday, Kennedy had been using the black-and-white and gray areas metaphors. She tried to interject, but I wouldn't let her and kept ranting at Lacey. Ten minutes later, I found myself ushered into the purging room. Sheridan looked mildly surprised to see me.

"A little early, isn't it?" she asked. "That, and you've done so well this week."

"They always backslide," remarked one of her assistants.

She nodded in agreement and gestured me to the chair. "You know the drill."

I did. It was as awful as it always was—maybe a little more

so since breakfast was so fresh in my stomach. When I was able to throw it all up after the slide show, they sent me to the sink to brush my teeth. The disposable toothbrushes were right next to the cabinet holding syringes. I turned on the water and pretended to spit again, after first glancing back. The others weren't watching me directly, presumably because they didn't think there was much I could do in that small room. I started to reach for the toothbrush, planning on opening the cabinet in the same motion.

There was just one problem, and I had only a split second to solve it. How was I going to get the syringe out? My scrubs had no pockets. The syringe was in a plastic wrapper and had a cap over the needle, so I could theoretically slip it into my sock or even my bra without injury. That much motion might attract attention.

A commotion at the door startled me and the others, and we all turned to see two other security guys escorting someone in: Duncan.

He made the briefest of eye contact with me and then began to struggle. "Come on, I was just kidding! It was a joke, for God's sake." They tried to drag him toward the restraining chair, and he dug his feet in. "I'm sorry, I'll never do it again! Please don't make me do this. It's been ages."

I realized then that it was no coincidence he was there just as I was finishing up. Duncan had timed whatever "joke" he'd made so that he'd get carted off and could make a commotion here—a commotion I was wasting by staring stupidly. Quickly, I reached out and took both toothbrush and syringe, slipping the latter underneath my sock while the others were busy with Duncan. I then proceeded to brush my teeth and not act like a friend was about to endure something awful to help me.

Duncan was strapped into the chair by the time I was escorted away. Sheridan shook her head in exasperation. "What a morning."

When I joined the rest of the detainees in our next class, I saw Jonah and a few of the others from our breakfast table shooting me furtive, curious looks. I gave a curt nod, indicating success, and then spoke to him later when we were filing out of the class. "It's not ready yet, but I've got what I need."

"I don't want to rush you," he whispered back, keeping his eyes fixed straight ahead. "But I overheard Addison telling Harrison that with all the acting out lately, they should maybe consider taking 'drastic action' soon."

"Noted," I said.

Duncan showed up to our next class, Conscious and Moral Living, wearing the telltale signs of recent purging. He looked properly contrite, but I got the full story out of him on the way to lunch later.

"What happened to not doing anything stupid?" I asked.

"Hey, I didn't do anything stupid. I stopped *you* from doing something stupid. No way could you have stolen that syringe without being noticed. I saved you. Now I hear they're serving manicotti for lunch—my favorite." He gave a woeful sigh. "You're welcome."

"What was it you said to Lacey that got you in trouble?" I asked.

He almost smiled then remembered there were always eyes around. "Well, you'd just had your little spat, so I followed up on it and said maybe she shouldn't be so down on the idea of getting personal with Moroi. That maybe a little 'personal time' would make her less uptight."

I had to try not to laugh. "She does know you were acting, right?"

"She better. You and I kept her out of purging today. Hey, where are you going?"

We'd almost reached the cafeteria, but I had started to turn away. "The only place a girl can get some privacy. I'll join you soon."

I stepped into a nearby hall that contained restrooms. I was entitled to visit them on my lunch break, so long as I didn't linger and catch someone's attention. While there were cameras in the bathroom's main area (I think they were afraid someone might break a mirror and use it as a weapon), the individual stalls offered one of the few private areas in the facility. I shut the door to one and worked quickly, knowing I had limited time.

It had been months since I'd used magic, but I was surprised at how naturally and quickly it came back to me. I pulled out my precious packet of salt and carefully poured it into the syringe's main compartment, giving me a much better storage container as I began the charming process. First was earth. I'd purposely touched my teacher's potted plant in our last class, getting dirt on my fingers. From that, I was able to summon the essence of earth, murmuring the words that drew out its power and sending it to the salt. A rush of exhilaration seized me as the magic took hold, and I nearly gasped. I hadn't realized how much I'd missed it or how alive I felt using it. It was especially noticeable after living in a hellish place like this.

Summoning air was next, which was also easy, seeing as it was everywhere. Water was also easy, since I had a toilet right in front of me, and I didn't have any sanitation concerns since I was only calling on magical properties and not using any actual water in the compound—yet. Fire proved to be the most difficult, seeing as the Alchemists didn't exactly leave matches within our reach. That was no surprise since, as far as I could tell, this place was one enormous fire hazard. There was no easily accessible source for elemental fire, so I had to create my own.

Ms. Terwilliger had grilled me in casting fireball spells, and I had excellent control over them. With a few whispered words, I called on that spell now, summoning just a spark of flame in my palm, barely enough to be seen. Its essence was strong enough, however, for me to pull its elemental power into the rest of the salt compound. Once that was done, I made the mini-fireball disappear.

Carefully concealing the syringe in one hand, I flushed the toilet and stepped out of the stall.

As I washed my hands, I was surprised that I felt a little dizzy. Being out of practice had taken its toll, especially having to summon fire rather than just take it from the environment. Still, that weariness was juxtaposed with that early heady feeling of bliss that magic use brought. Enhancing it was the knowledge that I wasn't powerless, that I had the ability to help someone else and thwart the Alchemist agenda. That was a high in its own right.

When I reached the cafeteria and approached Duncan's table with my tray, everyone appeared to be in light, easy conversation. Once I sat down, I could sense the unspoken tension among them. They continued talking about some earlier topic from history, though I could tell none of them were really into it. At last, smiling as though we were just kids at a regular high school with ordinary concerns, Jonah said, "Addison told me as I was walking in here to skip art class. She said Sheridan was going to meet me outside the room."

A cloud fell over us at the subtext. "They didn't waste any time," muttered Lacey. Her eyes flicked to me. "Did this morning's shenanigans pay off?"

"Kind of," I said, pitching my voice low as I stirred up my manicotti. My stomach wasn't quite as bad as Duncan's, but I still decided to stick to the blander side dishes. "I got the syringe. The salt's in it, ready to go. I just don't have a purified source of water to mix the solution. It'd also be best if we could've boiled the salt in," I added, "but a brisk shaking should do it if we can get the water. The teachers always have bottled water. Maybe we can steal some of theirs."

"No time," said Jonah. "Give me the syringe. I'll fill it with tap in the bathroom if someone'll block me from the camera."

I winced. "You have to inject that into your skin. You don't want tap water."

"The stuff's drinkable," he countered. "And it can't be any worse than what they're planning on injecting me with. I'll take my chances."

My sanitary sensibilities still resisted. "I wish we had more time."

"We don't," he said bluntly. "You've done a lot, and I'm grateful. Now it's my turn to take the risks. Slip me the syringe on our way out of here. Is there anything special I need to do with it? Aside from the obvious?"

I shook my head, still frustrated but knowing he was right. "Inject small amounts into your tattoo, just like they do with re-inking. You don't have to be precise. There'll be enough of it in your system to negate what's in their compelled ink."

"What *is* in your solution?" asked Elsa.

"Don't answer that," warned Duncan. "The less we know, the better for all of us—especially Sydney."

When the meal ended, our tablemates purposely crowded around Jonah and me as we waited to return our trays, allowing me to make the syringe pass. After that, it was literally out of my hands. I had to trust that Jonah would find a way to mix the solution with water on his own and inject himself before they came for him.

The rest of the day crawled, especially art class. He didn't show up, and worry filled me as I wondered what brainwashing he was enduring. Duncan, who'd treated this as a joke and told me numerous times how foolish I was, shared my tension.

"Jonah's a good guy," he said. "I really do hope your plan works. I've seen what they can do to people. Some come back pretty bad."

Remembering Duncan's long tenure, I was hit by a startling revelation. "Did you ever know a guy named Keith here? With one eye?"

Duncan's expression darkened. "Yeah, I know him. We weren't that close when he was here. He was one of those . . . one who came back pretty bad."

Reflection time followed, and Jonah returned. He looked cowed and said nothing as our usual session ran its course. Sheridan left him alone and instead drew out the rest of us, who were nearly as subdued, our moods darkened by the knowledge of what had happened to him. I almost hoped she would force him to talk so that I could get a sense of where he was at, but she must have decided he'd more than done his time today.

He simply sat and listened with glazed eyes, his expression changing little. My heart sank.

When the session ended, and we were dismissed for dinner, his attitude didn't change. Duncan ordered him to sit at our table, just as I had when Renee had returned. Jonah said nothing as the rest of us chatted about things we didn't care about, all of us too nervous to ask what was truly on our minds. This behavior was right in line with what happened after a hardcore dose of compulsion re-inking. The question was, was Jonah faking or not? If he was, interacting with him might draw attention to him. If he wasn't, he might very well report us.

Dinner wound down quietly at our table, and Duncan finished the last of his dessert, a cherry crumble that looked like it had been microwaved. "That actually tasted better than I expected," he remarked, more to himself than us.

"You know what else is better than expected?"

All of us looked up, surprised to hear Jonah for the first time since his re-inking. Chimes sounded, signaling the end of dinner and spurring a collective rising of everyone in the room. Jonah stood as well, tray in hand.

"Me," he said in a soft voice. "I feel great. Not a bit different." He shot me a smile that was gone as quickly as it came. "You saved my life, Sydney. Thanks." He strutted past me to join the line by the garbage bins, leaving me gaping.

I followed a few moments later, still stunned. He didn't say anything to me for the rest of the night, but I'd seen that gleam in his eyes when he smiled. He was still there. His personality and mind were intact. They hadn't gotten to him—and my formula had helped protect him. That realization stayed with me for the rest of the night, empowering me. For months, my captors had scored victory after victory on me, making me feel as though I could never fight back. Tonight, I had. It was a small victory, but it was real, and I had pulled it off.

I was so proud of my own cunning that I wasn't paying attention to much else when I got ready for bed later on. I was in the girls' bathroom, with a handful of others, still patting myself on the back. I was too oblivious to see Emma coming or make any defense when she slammed me into a corner of the wall. For a moment, I couldn't believe she'd dare do it under surveillance. Then, I realized she'd positioned me under the camera, out of its view. Amelia and a couple of their other friends started talking loudly, drowning out Emma's low and menacing voice as she kept me pinned in the corner and leaned forward.

"Jonah was re-inked today," she said. "A major one—the kind that can make people forget their own name. And yet people are saying it didn't affect him. And they're saying it's because of something *you* did to him."

"I don't know what you're talking about," I snapped back. "He seemed out of it to me."

She pushed me harder than I expected her capable of since she was smaller than I was. "Did you or didn't you do something to him?"

I glared. "Why? So you can report me and get out early for good behavior?"

"No," she said. "Because I want you to do it to me too."

CHAPTER 12
ADRIAN

IT HAD ONLY BEEN A FEW WEEKS, but I felt like I'd been away from Palm Springs for months. I had no idea what to expect when I walked into my apartment and wondered if I'd find Angeline cohabitating with Trey. I should've known better, though. For all his swagger, Trey cracked down when push came to shove, and I found him sitting in the living room with textbooks spread out around him. It was so Sydney-like that for a moment, emotion threatened to overcome me. Then, my new resolve took hold, and I pushed any distracting feelings aside.

Trey looked up, surveying me and my suitcase. "You're back, huh? How was the vacation?"

"Illuminating," I said. "I got a lead on Sydney. Everyone's on their way."

His eyes widened. "You what?"

I didn't get a chance to answer because I was already halfway down the hall, headed toward my old bedroom. When I stepped inside, I saw that Trey had taken it over, which I supposed was his right in light of my abrupt departure. With a shrug, I toted my suitcase back out to the living room and tossed it in the corner. I was happy to take a spot on the couch for now—if I even ended up staying here. I didn't really know where the search for Sydney would lead me or how long I'd be hanging out here.

Ten minutes later, a knock at the door heralded the arrival of Jill, Eddie, Angeline, and Neil. They barreled into me with hugs—even stoic Neil—though Jill held on the longest. "I've been so worried about you," she said, looking up at me with shining eyes. "Everything at Court was so crazy—I could only follow half of it—"

"And now it's done," I said firmly. "*And* we've got a lead on Sydney."

"So you said," Trey remarked. "But you didn't really elaborate."

"That's because I—" Before I could say more, another knock sounded. I opened the door and let Marcus inside. I was so happy to see him that I astonished him with a hug too. "Right on time," I said.

He'd been the trickiest one to get a hold of. I'd called him as soon as I'd booked my ticket back here and had been relieved to find out he was still in California, up in his old stomping grounds of Santa Barbara. When I'd told him what I'd learned, he promised to drive back and meet me after my flight landed. It was early evening, and the extensive travel had made for a taxing day, but I strangely found myself energized. This was it. We were all together, the people who loved Sydney, and we were going to make this happen.

"Can you catch the rest of us up now?" Trey demanded,

once we were all sitting in a circle in the living room. "Where is Sydney? Is she okay?"

"I don't know, and I don't know," I admitted. "I mean, she was okay enough to talk to me in a dream, but she wasn't very forthcoming about what was going on in that place. She still seemed like herself, though."

Marcus nodded in approval. "She's strong-willed. That'll get her through a lot. The thing is, if that will becomes too noticeable, they'll try to do something about it. She's got a dangerous line to walk."

"She has for a long time now," I said, thinking of her time here in Palm Springs when she struggled with her friendship with us and the doctrine the others were feeding to her. She'd finally picked a side of the line to stand on—and now she was paying for it. "She doesn't know where she is either, but she does know that Keith was in the same place, so right now, he's become our biggest lead."

"A very difficult one to find," said Marcus. He leaned back against the couch and sighed. "Admittedly, I was only able to make a couple of calls, but he's even better hidden than usual for Alchemists. They watch their 'reformed' agents pretty closely and don't want him exposed to much yet. He's probably locked away behind a desk."

A dark cloud of dismay started to sweep over me, and I pushed it aside. "But you can keep looking."

Marcus nodded. "Of course. I've also asked some of my other contacts who were in re-education if they remember any details about when they got out, but so far, no hits. Most of them were in there a long time ago. Keith's the most recent one we know of, so hopefully his memory is the best. I'm asking my sources to look for him. Something may turn up in a few days. But . . . in the meantime, I've got a farfetched lead that *might* give us results sooner. I know where Carly Sage is."

Eddie frowned. "You think she'd know where Sydney is? I mean, I don't know much about her, but I thought she was pretty removed from Alchemist affairs."

"She is," I said, guessing where Marcus was headed. "But Keith has a, uh, connection to her." I'd told Marcus about the note Sydney had seen, about Keith telling Carly he was sorry. I hadn't elaborated on the sordid details of their past, only that he'd done something pretty terrible to her. "You think he might have gotten in touch with her?"

"I don't know, honestly," said Marcus. "I've never met either of them. But I do know that place plays on guilt and self-worth. If Keith feels like he wronged her, maybe he reached out when he was free."

"It'd be the first decent thing he's ever done," muttered Jill darkly. From her bond with me, she knew what he'd done to Carly.

"I figured it couldn't hurt to check it out," said Marcus. "Especially since we've got to wait on any more hits with Keith. She's pretty close. She's a student at Arizona State University." He shot me a wry smile. "Up for a road trip?"

"Absolutely. We can leave right now." I nearly stood then and there, but he waved me down.

"I'd rather we go in the morning—both for the daylight and so you can talk to Sydney again tonight. See if you can get something from her that we can use to get Carly to trust us. I have to imagine if a couple of strange guys showed up asking about your sister and the organization your family's sworn you to secrecy about, you might not be that forthcoming."

I relaxed a little. "That's a good plan. And so long as there's no more gas drugging her, we should be in sync now. Based on when she was woken up, I think she was in this time zone. I might be wrong, though. Who knows what schedule those freaks have her on?"

"Probably a typical human one, even if they're underground." Marcus rolled his eyes. "Heaven forbid they get on anything that might seem remotely vampiric."

Neil leaned forward. "Back up a moment. Did you say gas?"

Now that there was a tentative plan in place to find Carly Sage, I was able to calm down a little and tell the others exactly what I knew. My dream with Sydney had been short, but I gave what details I could, including how she'd been drugged and her vague references to punishment.

Angeline rested her head on Trey's shoulder. "They better not be hurting her. Otherwise, I'm going to hurt *them* when we all go in and bust her out."

"'We all?'" asked Marcus with amusement.

Eddie had on his fiercest mini-Dimitri expression. "You don't think we're letting you two do all this alone, do you?"

I tried not to smile. "I think school's still in session and that your first priority is to Jailbait."

"Only for another week or so," said Jill. "And we're just doing finals now. You should take one of the dhampirs. Two of them, actually. Angeline can stay with me."

"Hey," Angeline exclaimed. "How come *I* don't get to go kick Alchemist ass?"

"Because you're the only one of us who hasn't actually finished high school," Eddie told her.

"But *all* of you are assigned to protect Jill," I warned. "And you're staying with her, at least for now. Marcus and I don't need bodyguards to go visit some partying kids at ASU."

Conflict warred over Eddie's features. "But what happens after that? What about when you find where Sydney is?" I could guess his worries. He was torn. His assignment—and his heart—bound him to Jill. But Sydney was his friend too, and he still felt guilty for her loss in the first place.

"We don't know when that'll be. School might be done then, and we'll all be back at Court." I patted his shoulder. "Let us worry about Carly and even Keith. When we get to the next phase . . . well, we'll figure it out."

Eddie didn't look happy about that, but really, there was no outcome that he would've been okay with. If he came with us tomorrow, he would be eaten with guilt for abandoning Jill. No part of this situation was going to be easy on him.

Marcus left early, once he and I had our arrangements in place for the trip to Tempe. The others lingered, wanting to catch up and share what had happened over the last few weeks. I blurred the details on my descent into decadence at Court, too ashamed to let them know I'd nearly lost Sydney. Only Jill knew the truth, and she'd never give me up. She did, however, give up something else.

"Hey, Trey," she said, eyes full of mischief. "Maybe you should give Adrian that very important piece of mail."

A matching grin lit Trey's face as he jumped up and hurried to the kitchen. When he returned, he handed over a business-sized envelope that had been opened. It was from Carlton College, addressed to me.

"You opened my mail?" I exclaimed.

"I told him to," Jill said, as though she had some kind of authorization. "Check it out."

Puzzled, I lifted a single piece of paper and found myself staring at my first college report card. Even more amazing than that, I saw that I had passed all my classes. C, C-, and B-. That last one made me raise an eyebrow.

"How the hell did I pull off a B- in oils? What did you turn in for my final project?" I asked them incredulously.

"I picked it," Trey said proudly. "It was that tall one you had leaning in the corner, the kind of weird yellow-and-purple-cloud thing."

A lump formed in my throat. "Sydney's aura," I murmured. I set the report card down and hugged Jill and Trey. "You guys saved me. I wouldn't have passed without you."

"*You* saved you," Jill murmured in my ear. "And now you're going to save her."

She and the others left soon thereafter, as Amberwood's curfew loomed. Neil lingered after the rest had walked out the door and strolled back to me. "Adrian," he said, unable to meet my eyes, "I don't suppose Olive was at Court, was she?"

I was sympathetic to everyone in love, and my heart went out to him. "No, but Nina was. Olive's been out of touch with her too, but Nina's checked in dreams, and Olive's okay. She just wants some time on her own to think things through. It can't be easy having come back from being a Strigoi."

Relief flooded Neil's angular features. "Really? That's great. I mean . . . it's not great that she's troubled, but I thought it was something to do with me. We'd gotten along so well, stayed in touch . . . then nothing."

"Nope," I assured him. "Nina says Olive cut off everyone.

Give her time. She'll come around. From what I briefly saw, she was pretty crazy for you."

Neil actually turned red at that, and I laughingly sent him on to join the others. Trey returned to his homework, and I began regular checks of trying to find Sydney asleep. At one point, Trey offered to give me the bedroom back, but I told him I'd be up off and on anyway. Better for him to be rested for exams and his scholarship prospects.

That eventually left me alone in the living room, and around midnight, I finally connected to Sydney. We met in the Getty Villa, and I swept her to my arms, not fully realizing until that moment how afraid I'd been that last night's dream encounter had been a fluke. "Before I start kissing you and forget everything reasonable, tell me how long you've been asleep."

She rested her golden head against my chest. "I don't know. Less than an hour."

"Hmm." I brushed that beautiful hair back as I crunched numbers. "I thought you were on Pacific time, based on when you woke up. That would've been around, oh, five here. But that's not very much sleep. Six hours. Maybe seven."

"Actually, that's about perfect for them," she said. "It's one of the things they do to keep us on edge. We get enough sleep to function, but we never *quite* feel rested enough. It makes us agitated, more susceptible to what they do and tell us."

I nearly let the comment slide, but the word choice caught me. "What do you mean 'one of the things?'" I asked her. "What else do they do?"

"It doesn't matter," she said. "We have other—"

"It *does* matter," I insisted, leaning closer to her. I'd tried bringing this up before, and she kept evading the topic. "You said yourself that place pushed Keith over the edge, and I see the way Marcus looks whenever he talks about re-education."

"A little sleep deprivation is nothing," she said, still not directly addressing what I wanted.

"What else are they doing?" I demanded.

Fire flared briefly in her eyes. "What would you do if I told you? Would it make you work harder to find me?"

"I'm already—"

"Exactly," she interrupted. "So don't add on to your worries—especially when we're already short on time."

She and I stood there deadlocked for several tense moments. We'd rarely fought before she was taken, and it felt particularly weird to be doing it now, in light of all that had happened. I disagreed that what she was experiencing in re-education "didn't matter," but I hated seeing her so upset now. She was also right about our time crunch, so at last I gave a reluctant nod and switched subjects, telling her instead about my plan to visit Carly with Marcus.

"That's not a bad idea. Even if Keith didn't reach out to her, Carly's in an Alchemist family and might be able to find out something for you." Sydney was still holding on to me as she spoke, and while I certainly had no problem with that, I couldn't shake the feeling of anxiety that radiated around her, as though she were literally afraid to let go of me. She was putting on a brave face, but those bastards had done something to her, and I hated them for it. I tightened my hold.

"Got anything we can say that'll let her know we've spoken to you?" I asked.

Sydney considered a few moments and then smiled. "Ask her

if college has still made her set on adopting Cicero's philosophy on life."

"Okay," I said. It made no sense to me, but then, that was the point.

"And ask her . . ." Sydney's smile faded. "Ask her if she knows how Zoe's doing. If she's okay."

"I will," I promised, amazed that Sydney could care so much about a sister who'd betrayed her. "But now, what about you? Isn't there *anything* you can tell me about your life in that place? I worry about you."

Her anxiety rose, and I worried she'd get upset again, but she apparently decided to give me something. "I'm fine . . . really. And I may have even helped someone. I kind of finagled some of that magic salt ink together and used it to protect someone from Alchemist mind control."

I pulled back a little so that I could meet her in the eye. "You used magic in Alchemist re-education? Weren't you just saying you get in trouble for stepping out of line?"

"I didn't get caught," she said fiercely. "And it really did help someone."

I drew her to me again. "Worry about helping yourself."

"You sound like Duncan."

"Duncan?" I asked jealously.

She smiled. "No need to worry. He's just a friend, but he's always warning me about staying out of trouble. I can't stop myself, though. If I can help these people, you know I will."

I was on the verge of reminding her of the many conversations we'd had about me and spirit use, how I'd always insisted that the risk to myself was worth it if I could do good for others. Sydney had constantly argued that I had to look out for myself because if I wasn't careful, I wouldn't be able to help anyone.

But I didn't get a chance to lecture her now because she unexpectedly pulled me closer, tightening her hold and bringing our lips together. Warmth flooded me, along with a desire as real and as strong as I'd feel in the waking world. She trailed her lips to my cheek and then to my neck, giving me a brief moment to speak.

"No fair distracting me," I murmured.

"You want me to stop?" she asked.

Like I even had to think about that one. "Of course not."

Our lips met again in another hungry kiss, and I barely had enough presence of mind to shift our setting from the sunny courtyard to a bedroom at a mountain inn. Sydney paused again, laughing softly as she recognized the scene. "Memory lane," she teased. "Back to the first time. You've even got it snowing out there."

I eased her back onto the sumptuous bed. "Hey, Adrian Ivashkov offers full service."

"And a money-back guarantee?"

"I wouldn't know," I told her. "No one's ever been disappointed."

Her laughter dissolved into more kissing, and with a last touch of dream shaping, I transformed her ugly tan scrubs into a formfitting black and maroon dress I'd once seen her in. Her beauty astonished me just as much now as it had then, and I ran a hand along her waist, coming to rest on the curve of her hip. Her own hands, which had been wrapped around my neck, now traveled down and tugged off my T-shirt with a boldness I would've never imagined when we'd first met. The touch of her fingertips on my chest was delicate yet managed to convey a power and urgency that sent shockwaves through me. Something told me the passion that burned in her now was driven by more than just our usual attraction—there was a need in her, a need born of months of desperation and isolation. I tipped her head back so that I could better kiss her neck, tangling my free hand up in her hair. She made a small gasp of pleasure and surprise as I grazed her skin with my teeth, though I was careful to do no more than just that teasing.

Slowly, tauntingly, I slid the hand on her hip up her body, loving the way she felt and reacted at my touch. I finally made my way to the zipper at her back and tried tugging it down—something that was more difficult one-handed than I'd expected.

She opened her eyes to regard me with both amusement and desire. "You could just dream the dress away."

"Where's the fun in that?" I returned, feeling triumphant as the zipper caught. I slid it all the way down and began pulling the dress off.

"Oh, Adrian," she breathed. "You have no idea how much—"

I didn't need to ask what cut her off. I could sense it from the way she was losing substance beneath my hands: She was being woken up.

"Don't go," I told her futilely. It was less about physical fulfillment than a deep-seated fear I couldn't give voice to: *I'm afraid if you leave, I'll never see you again.* I could tell from her face, however, that she knew my fears.

"We'll be together soon. In real life. The center will hold." She was growing translucent before my eyes. "Get some sleep. Go find Carly and Keith."

"I will. And then I'll find you, I swear it."

She was nearly gone, and I could just barely make out tears sparkling in her eyes. "I know you will. I believe in you. I always have."

"I love you."

"I love you too."

She was gone.

I woke up on the couch, feeling an emptiness and dissatisfaction that went beyond physical longing. I needed her heart and mind as much as her body. I needed her, and her lack caused an ache in my chest as I drifted off to sleep. As I did, I wrapped my arms tightly around myself, pretending it was Sydney I held.

Marcus showed up bright and early the next morning, getting our road trip off to a good start—with one exception. We had a small disagreement on whose car to take.

"Yours is probably stolen," I said.

He rolled his eyes. "It's not stolen. And it's a Prius."

"Even more reason not to take it."

"We can get to Tempe without even stopping for gas, unlike yours."

"It's worth the extra stops to go in style," I argued back.

"Is it worth the extra delay to get answers that might help Sydney?" That was his trump card, and he knew it.

"Fine," I grumbled. "We'll take your lame yet highly fuel-efficient car."

Despite our rocky past—like when I'd tried to punch him the first time we met—Marcus and I had a pretty smooth drive to ASU. He didn't expect much in the way of conversation, which was fine by me. Most of my thoughts were with Sydney. Every once in a while, Marcus would field a call from one of his contacts, chasing some lead that was part of his clandestine affairs. Some were about Sydney and Keith; some were about other people and missions that all sounded very important when you were only listening to half the conversation.

"You've got all sorts of things going on," I remarked when we crossed the Arizona border. "It means a lot that you'd take time to help Sydney. Sounds like she's not the only one counting on you."

He smiled at that. "Sydney's special. I don't think she can know how many people she's helped with that ink she made. It's huge for them to know the Alchemists can't corrupt their minds—at least through the tattooing. I owe it to her to help her for that, and . . ."

"And what?" I asked, seeing his expression darken.

"Whenever anyone does something incredible, like she's done, and gets caught, like she has, I always think that it could've been me. In helping me, I see them as serving the time that I probably deserve."

"Sydney wouldn't see it that way," I told him, recalling her crackpot plans to help her fellow inmates. "She's happy to do it—thinks it's her own risk."

"I know," he said. "And that makes me that much happier to help."

We reached the university by midafternoon. It was in the thick of the academic day, but they were also running on summer session, so campus crowds were thinner than they might otherwise have been. Marcus's intelligence had told him that Carly attended year-round and was an RA in a coed dorm. No one challenged us during daylight hours, and we were able to go right up to her door, which was covered in posters for various bands and rallies. After meeting Zoe, I couldn't even begin to say what the third Sage sister was like, though I had formed vague ideas of someone quiet and meek, knowing what I did about how Carly wouldn't report Keith or let Sydney do it either.

The girl who answered wasn't what I expected. She was tall and athletic, with pixie-cut hair and a little garnet nose ring. But she had Sydney's hair and eye color, as well as enough family resemblance to let me know we'd found the right person. She wore an outgoing smile that dimmed somewhat when she did a double take at me. She might not be the family Alchemist, but she knew a Moroi when she saw one.

"Whatever it is, I don't want to be involved," she said.

"It's about Sydney," said Marcus.

"And she said to ask you if college made you want to take on Cicero's philosophy on life," I added helpfully.

Carly's eyebrows rose at that, and after a moment, she sighed and opened her door to admit us. Two other girls, looking freshman-aged, sat on her floor, and she gave them an apologetic look. "Hey, I've got to take care of something real quick. Can we finish planning tonight?"

As the girls stood and made parting comments, Marcus leaned toward me and whispered, "Are you sure you got Sydney's pass phrase right? Cicero was more of a statesman than a philosopher. Not that he didn't have some good moments."

I shrugged. "That's what she said. And Carly let us in, didn't she?"

Once the younger girls were gone, Carly sat on the edge of her bed and beckoned us to find spots on the floor. "Okay. So, to what do I owe the pleasure of a visit from a Moroi and a guy who's not an Alchemist but has a very suspiciously placed tattoo?"

"We need your help to locate Sydney," I said, finding no need to waste time.

Carly tilted her head in surprise at that. "Is she missing?"

Marcus and I exchanged looks. "Have you heard from her recently?" he asked.

"No . . . not in a very long time, actually. But that's not unheard of. Dad used to disappear for a while too. It's part of the job. He told all of us that she's just wrapped up in something top secret." When neither Marcus nor I responded, she glanced between the two of us. "Isn't that true? Is she okay?"

"She's okay," said Marcus slowly, and I could tell he was choosing his words carefully. "But she's not on assignment. She got in trouble for something, and we're trying to get to her before that trouble gets worse."

Carly shot him a fierce look. "Don't sugarcoat things. I know what getting in trouble means with Alchemists. They've locked her up somewhere, haven't they? Like they did Keith?"

"Have you talked to him?" I exclaimed. "In person?"

Her face filled with disgust. "In person and in email. He showed up out of the blue like you guys did, back in March, with this big sob story about how sorry he was and how he needed my forgiveness to go on and how I should turn him in to the authorities."

"Back up," I said. "Keith *told* you to turn him in? Did you?"

"No." She crossed her arms and put on a smug expression that seemed to be at odds with the topic. "And he didn't tell me so much as beg. He was terrified he'd be sent back into Alchemist custody one day and seemed to think he'd be safer in a regular prison. So I said no. Now he can live in constant fear, just like I used to."

It was such a bizarre twist of logic, I didn't really know how to respond. Marcus looked perplexed, and I remembered he didn't know the whole history. "She and Keith had a, uh, falling out," I said, hoping to gloss things over.

Carly met Marcus squarely in the eye. "Keith raped me while we were out on a date and made me think I'd led him on and that if I told anyone, they'd think it was my fault. I convinced myself of that too and let it eat me up inside. The only person I told was Sydney, and that was on conditions of secrecy. It took me years to realize what an idiot I had been. Now I make sure other girls don't go through that." She nodded toward more posters on her walls, and only now I realized they were all anti-rape culture. "If I can save even one person from going through that kind of shame and self-doubt . . . well, I'll feel like I've lived my life's purpose."

Marcus, who was not easily surprised, looked completely awestruck as he gazed at her. I'd seen plenty of girls fall at his feet, but this was the first time I'd seen him drool over one. "That's incredible that you've been able to do that," he said. "And very brave."

As amusing as it was to see him lovestruck, we had to stay on track. I snapped my fingers in front of his face. "Focus." I turned back to Carly. "But you still won't turn Keith in now?"

She shook her head. "It sounds crazy, I know, but he suffers more this way. He *wanted* me to do it. Was almost in tears when I wouldn't. I don't care about him, though. I care about Sydney. Tell me what I can do to help her and stop whatever those bastards have done."

"Do you know a way to help us find Keith?" I asked.

"I can do better than that," she said. She fished a phone out of her pocket, scrolled around, and handed it over. "Will this work?"

I took it and saw Keith's name, along with a phone number and address in Boise, Idaho, of all places.

"Boise?" I asked. "Hasn't he suffered enough?"

Marcus looked over my shoulder and grinned. "There's an Alchemist research center there. It's exactly the kind of place I'd expect him—desk job, no real fieldwork or dangerous situations. Are you sure he's still there?"

Carly rolled her eyes. "Positive. He emails me every month, asking for forgiveness and telling me to get in touch if I change my mind. If he moved, I'm certain he'd let me know a hundred times over."

Marcus copied the information into his own phone and handed hers back. "I don't think we should give him the benefit of a warning before we talk to him. You up for another road trip?"

My geography wasn't that great, but even I knew that was a much bigger undertaking than what we'd just done. "As long as we can stock up on snacks before we go."

"Will finding him really help Sydney?" Carly asked, face grave.

Marcus's expression softened as he regarded her, but I didn't know if that was because of his infatuation or because he had bad news. "We don't know for sure, but we hope so. We think Keith was held at the same place Sydney is. If we can find out where that is, we can go get her back."

Carly blanched. "The same place . . . you mean the place

that's so bad, Keith would rather be sent to jail than risk going back?"

"We'll get her back," said Marcus gallantly. "I swear it."

"I want to help," she insisted.

"You already have." He held up his phone. "This address may have done it. You don't need to risk yourself anymore."

Carly leapt to her feet, fists clenched at her sides in defiance. The resemblance between her and Sydney was particularly remarkable just then. "She's my sister! Of course I need to risk myself. You think she'd do any less for me?"

I felt a lump in my throat. "You're right. She wouldn't. But at the moment, we're still just gathering info. If we get a clear lead and you can help, we'll let you know."

"You better," she growled. "Here, I'll give you my phone number."

"I'll take that," said Marcus quickly.

While he got the info, I told her, "In the meantime, the biggest thing you can do is not tell anyone—especially anyone you're related to—that we were here."

She scoffed. "I assume you mean my dad and Zoe? No problem there. They hardly ever check on me, especially since the divorce."

"So it's final?" I asked. I'd been wondering, but Sydney and I hadn't exactly had a chance for small talk in our dream.

"It's final." Carly's face turned grim. "I did my best to help Mom's custody case, but in the end, Dad's 'evidence' was just too substantial. I wondered why Sydney didn't testify for either side . . . now I know. If she got in trouble with those people, probably not even Dad could get her off the hook."

Obviously, Carly wasn't aware just how substantial her dad's role had been in getting Sydney in trouble, and I wasn't about to stir up more family angst by telling her the truth. "Sydney would've been there if she could," I assured her. "I know she really wanted to support your mom."

Carly nodded. "I wish she could have. I mean, I get why the Alchemists do what they do, but sometimes . . . I don't know. It's like they go overboard and lose sight of the big picture. Now that Zoe's with Dad all the time, I worry it's just going to get worse for her. At least with Sydney—the last few times I talked to her, that is—she seemed to be getting more perspective on life. I don't know what was going on, but she seemed more balanced. Happier. I'd hoped she could do the same for Zoe, but I guess that's not possible anytime soon."

I don't know what was going on, but she seemed more balanced. Happier. Carly's words triggered a mix of emotions, and I couldn't muster a response. That change she'd observed had been my doing. Carly thought it had been for the better, and I liked to think so too—but there was no denying it was also what had gotten Sydney in trouble.

As we moved to the door, ready for the next leg of our trip, Marcus paused and looked back at her. I thought he was going to ask her out, but instead he said, "What's up with that Cicero quote? I studied a lot of Roman history and never heard anything about his philosophy on life."

Carly grinned. "Cicero's our family cat. Sydney and I used to joke that he'd figured out what life was really all about: eating, sleeping, and taking baths. She was so sad she didn't go to college too, and I tried to downplay it, telling her I probably wouldn't learn anything better than what Cicero taught me. When you mentioned it, I knew you were legit."

Maybe it was the family resemblance coming out in Carly's smile again or just the mention of Sydney's college longing, but I felt an ache in me begin to surface that I hadn't felt in a while. *Go away*, I told it. *Mourn for Sydney later. Focus now on getting her back.*

Marcus shook Carly's hand, holding it a little longer than he probably needed to. "Thank you again for your help," he said. "We won't let you down."

"Forget about me," she said. "Don't let Sydney down."

CHAPTER 13

SYDNEY

CHARMING SALT WHILE in re-education was certainly more convoluted than it had been as a free woman, but it wasn't impossible. It was just a slow and unwieldy process, smuggling out small amounts of salt and then getting private moments in the bathroom to infuse it with elements. What proved to be far more difficult was getting the syringes.

"Someone's in the purging room almost every day, either because it's routine or they did something," said Emma, when I told her that would be the hardest part to pull off. "We'll just put the word out that anyone who's in there needs to smuggle out a syringe and get it to you."

"Even if they're able to successfully do that, the supervisors are going to eventually notice that many syringes going missing," I pointed out. "And I'm not sure I want the 'word out' with everyone."

She shook her head. "I'm not stupid. I'm only letting in select people I know we can trust, others who value their minds

200

more than they do turning you in. They all know something went down with Jonah. They'll keep your secret for the chance at getting that same protection for themselves."

"That doesn't really make me feel better," I grumbled. My last encounter with Adrian had left me feeling optimistic for the future, but that didn't mean the present wasn't fraught with complications. "And it doesn't solve the syringe issue." We were almost at our next class, meaning this conversation was just about up.

"Too bad we can't reuse them," she mused.

I grimaced. "Ugh. This is already unsanitary enough, not having access to purified water."

"What we need is free access to those supply closets on the purging level. You know where they are."

"Yeah," I said, in agreement. "There's just the small problem of me never being able to get to them again, what with the massive security around here."

She shrugged and smiled. "I didn't say it was a perfect plan."

"It's no kind of plan."

But the suggestion stirred in my mind as I went through the motions of my Alchemist schooling that day. Having talked to Adrian had lifted my spirits, as did knowing he'd be speaking to Carly soon. I hoped desperately that Keith would give them some lead to where I was. From there, I didn't know exactly how they'd get me out, but I was already envisioning liberating the others here with me. If I could send them into the world free of mind control, it'd be a job well done.

I turned over Emma's words in my head, trying to solve the jumble of problems before me. What I really needed was unfettered access to the floor with the supply closets, the ones

Sheridan had made me organize. To get to them, I needed to move around unseen, which wasn't easy but was actually easier than getting out of my room in the first place. Those night locks were a huge problem.

Although Emma—and a couple others—watched me eagerly throughout the day and were the ones most anxious for results, it was Duncan I finally broached the topic with in art class. He never spoke extensively about his past, but I'd gleaned some things that were important to him. The mysterious Chantal was one, of course, and he occasionally expounded on artistic pursuits before coming here. One thing he didn't speak much about that I'd picked up on was his knack for mechanical devices. Someone had easel trouble on a daily basis, and Duncan was always the go-to person to adjust them. I'd even observed him helping our instructors, like the time Harrison's projector stopped working.

"Do you know how the locks on our room doors work?" I asked that day. Still life was done for now, though Duncan had assured me it was a popular assignment and would be back. Now we were on to the tedious task of molding clay bowls by hand.

"They lock," he said bluntly. "They stop the doors from opening."

I tried not to roll my eyes. "I know that. I mean, do you know how—"

"Yes, yes, I know what you mean," he interrupted. "And it isn't something you should be worried about. You're playing a dangerous enough game already."

I peered around, but no one was listening to us as we worked at our table. "It's not a game!" I hissed. "This is serious. I can stop others from being brainwashed. Like I did for Jonah."

"And get yourself sent back to reflection time in the process." A small frown between his eyebrows was the only outward sign of his discomfort. "I can't handle another friend disappearing, Sydney."

I had to take a moment to blink back tears as I remembered that he had been my first ally here, offering me friendship because of what he liked about me and not because of what I could potentially do for him.

"I won't disappear," I said, taking on a gentler tone. "But I need to get out of my room some night. Tonight, ideally. It's important. I can help a lot of people."

His bowl, much like his painting, was nearly perfect. I was beginning to wonder if that was some inherent skill or simply the result of having been here so long. "The locks are turned on by a central system each night," he said at last. "It's actually just a simple bolt shooting out from the door into the wall. It's touchy. If there's an obstacle, it won't work."

"Will it alert the central system that there's a problem?" I asked.

"Not unless they've changed it in the last year. About, oh, eight months ago, someone's door malfunctioned, and the powers-that-be never knew. They found out when one of the guys in the room made a break for it and tried to find an exit."

That was useful—but also dangerous. "Did they fix it?"

"That particular door? Yes. But as far as I know, the bolt's still touchy. Doesn't matter much since even if the surveillance didn't catch someone trying to block it, the cameras in the hall would detect—" Duncan suddenly shot me a pained look. "Please tell me you aren't going to try to actually escape."

"I'm staying here . . . for now." I glanced down and lightly touched the ID badge clipped to my shirt. It was a little thinner than a credit card. "Something like this would work nicely to block the bolt."

"Very nicely," he agreed. "But remember there's that tiny gap between the door and the wall, even when it's slid closed. You can't just stick that card in there."

"I need some kind of adhesive to hold it there." I racked my brain, trying to remember when I'd last seen glue around here. I hadn't. But as my eyes rested on Addison's desk, I found something even better. "Gum would work. I wouldn't even need to use my card . . . I could just stick a clump over the bolt's release, couldn't I?"

Duncan chuckled in spite of himself. "Juvenile, but yes, you could."

"Go ask her for help on something," I said, inspired. "I'll swipe the gum while you talk to her."

"Sydney." He pointed at my bowl and then his. "Which of you us do you think legitimately needs to ask her for help?"

I looked between them, noting that his could go straight in the kiln now and that half of mine was caving in on itself. "You don't approve of my plan. I can't ask you to steal the gum."

"I don't approve of illogical plans," he said. "And it's much more logical for you to go ask for help. Besides, I need another potter's needle. This one's dull."

"They're all dull," I reminded him. Even for the sake of therapeutic art, the Alchemists didn't leave anything around that might be used as a weapon. "But I'll go ask."

Addison always appeared annoyed at being asked questions, but at the same time, I could tell she kept track of who came and asked for help. I was one of a handful that would generally suffer great pains before seeking assistance from our superiors, and I knew some of them viewed us giving in and relying on them as a sign of us breaking down our resistance. So, although she still wore that perpetually unpleasant expression as she smacked her gum, she didn't hesitate to advise me on why my bowl kept collapsing, and I had a feeling there would be new notes added to my record later on. As I spoke to her, I saw Duncan move toward her desk out of the corner of my eye. I nearly stopped breathing, terrified she'd turn around and see him.

But she didn't, and five minutes later, when he and I reconvened at our table, he covertly slid me two sticks of gum. "Use it wisely," he warned. "Or at least don't do something completely stupid tonight. Please tell me you have a plan not to get caught once you're out of your room. You know there are cameras in the halls."

"I do have a plan," I said hesitantly. "But I can't tell you."

"Hey, that's good enough for me."

Despite my anxiety over my daunting task, I was still feeling triumphant over this small victory. I was riding on a high and was totally unprepared to be knocked down when Sheridan turned to me in communion time and said, "Sydney, don't you have something you'd like to tell us?"

I froze and could've sworn my heart skipped a few beats. My eyes darted around the circle of watching faces as I wondered which of them had betrayed me. "I beg your pardon, ma'am?"

"You've been with us for some time now," she explained. "Yet you've spoken very little about your past. Every day, the others open up about themselves, but you keep to yourself. That's not really fair, now is it?"

I wanted to tell her that it was really none of their business, but I knew I should be grateful I wasn't on the hook here for more immediate crimes. "What would you like to know, ma'am?"

"Why don't you tell us why you're here?"

"I . . ." My earlier cockiness dried up. Masterminding plans to break out of my room by sabotaging the lock so that I could then create magical protection for my fellow detainees didn't faze me nearly as much as the scrutiny of all those eyes. It didn't matter how friendly I'd gotten with a few of them. I didn't want to share my story.

But you have to play the game, Sydney, I reminded myself. *It doesn't matter what you do, so long as you win at the end.*

I focused back on Sheridan. "I broke some of the cardinal rules of the Alchemists. I went against our basic beliefs."

"How?" she prompted.

I took a deep breath. "Because I became romantically involved with a Moroi."

My gaze stayed on Sheridan. I was afraid to look at the others because even though we were all rebels of sorts, there were varying degrees of sin around here—and mine was pretty extreme.

"Why?" Sheridan asked.

I frowned. "Ma'am?"

"Why did you become romantically involved with such a foul creature? That doesn't just go against Alchemist beliefs. That goes against the rules of nature. Why would you do that?"

My heart had an answer ready, but I didn't let it cross my lips. *Because he's wonderful and sensitive and funny. Because we bring out the best in each other and are better people because of our love. Because when we're together, I feel like I understand my place in the world.*

"I don't know exactly," I said, trying to find a believable answer that she would want to hear. "Because I thought I was in love."

"With one of them?" she asked. The tone in her voice when she said *them* made me want to slap her.

"He didn't seem like one of them," I said instead. "He seemed very kind and very charming. He was . . . is very good at compulsion. I don't know if that's part of what happened to me. Maybe I was just weak."

"Don't you feel ashamed?" she prodded. "Don't you feel dirty and used up? Even if you graduate from here, do you think any of your own kind would ever want to touch you after letting yourself be used like that?"

That took me aback for a moment because it echoed so closely the fears Carly had once had when justifying why she couldn't tell anyone about what Keith had done to her. I should've given some contrite response, but instead I answered Sheridan with a variation of what I'd told Carly. "I'd hope that whomever I'm with next will see me and value me for the person I am inside. None of the rest will matter."

Sheridan's expression turned to one of pity. "I don't think you'll ever find anyone like that."

I already have, I thought. *And he's coming to get me out of here and away from you.*

Aloud, I said simply, "I don't know, ma'am." Admitting your own ignorance was always a safe bet around here.

"Well," she said, "let's hope you're less delusional about

vampires than you are about how you've sullied yourself. How do you feel about him now?"

I knew better than to even breathe the truth on that. "He betrayed me," I said simply. "He was supposed to meet me the night I was brought here, and he never showed. I was deceived."

It was a lie none of them could disprove. In fact, no Alchemist really knew entirely what I'd been doing the night I was taken. Let them think they'd thwarted some reunion with Adrian and me, thus helping turn me against him.

"That's what they do, Sydney," Sheridan said, looking very pleased. "They deceive."

When we disbanded, I noticed a few of my fellow detainees— some of whom I thought I'd made strides with—physically avoiding me as they had in the early days. "What's that about?" I muttered to Emma, who was walking near me.

"Sheridan helped remind them of how tainted you are," she explained.

My heart sank a little as I gazed after them. "Do they really believe that? I thought some of them . . ."

I couldn't finish, but Emma knew my thoughts. "Were just playing along to survive here? Some are, but even if they haven't been reprogrammed, they've learned enough to survive here. And part of survival is steering clear from people who'll get you in trouble. You crossed a line—no, you trampled it, and even if they think what you did is okay, they know they can't let Sheridan and the others think so."

"What do *you* think?" I asked.

She gave me a tight smile. "I think you and your ink are a good precaution in case they ever try to mess with my mind. But I'm also going to keep my distance. See you later."

She hurried off, and I spent the rest of the day formulating my plan, wishing it was more solid than it was. When I was in the bathroom that evening, I popped one of Addison's gum sticks into my mouth, chewing until I hoped I'd mustered up a sticky enough result. I kept it in my hand as I left and then brushed my hand against the door as I entered my room, right over the place the bolt entered. I hoped the system was as touchy as Duncan had claimed and that the one piece had been enough. I'd nearly used both but thought a second might be useful in the future. I slipped it into my sock.

Later, when the lights went out, I heard a click at the door but didn't know if it had been successful. I crept out of bed and tentatively approached the slit of light, waiting and listening to make sure no one was outside. They weren't. Gingerly, I tried to slide the door open a crack . . . and succeeded. The bolt hadn't worked! I exhaled a deep breath and braced myself for the next part of the task: getting out unseen.

I'd used invisibility spells in the past, once even to break into an Alchemist facility, which seemed ironic in my current situation. They weren't easy, otherwise—as Ms. Terwilliger had noted—everyone would use them. The best coverage required a lot of spell components and ideally an amulet. Even then, the spell would often be unraveled if someone knew to look for you. I had nothing to aid me here, only the knowledge of a small spell and my own power to pull it off. It would last thirty minutes at most and be susceptible to anyone searching for me or who looked me directly in the eye. It would protect me from cameras, however, and my big gamble was that the halls would be deserted this time of night, when our masters thought we were all locked in and drugged.

I didn't know what kind of shifts the Alchemists pulled, but I had to assume personnel would thin out later. So I sat back on my bed for a half hour, hoping by then that everyone would have settled down for a quiet night. Before returning to the door, I stuffed my pillow under the covers. Between that and the near darkness, I hoped it wouldn't be obvious that the bed was empty to anyone glancing at the surveillance screens. At the door, I murmured the incantation as quietly as I could, not wanting to tip Emma off to my true nature. Meaning and focus were more important than volume, and I felt another exhilarating surge of power course through me as I finished speaking. The spell, such as it was, had worked, and now the clock was ticking. After again making sure no one was in the hall, I slowly slid the door open, just enough to slip through, and then closed it again. That was one of the other difficult parts of invisibility spells: just because you were invisible, it didn't mean your actions were. Someone seeing a door open by itself would give me away just as much as bumping into a person, so I had to make sure all my movements were small and cautious, attracting as little attention as possible.

The dorm hall was empty, with only the cameras keeping sentry, and I hurried toward the nexus where other corridors intersected. There, I found my first Alchemist on guard duty, a hard-faced man I'd never seen before who was texting on his phone as he stood stationed in a spot that let him supervise all the halls. He never looked up as I moved quietly and slowly past him, turning down the hall that led to the elevators. It was still amazing to me that the only exit off the floor didn't even lead outside in an emergency, but I supposed the Alchemists felt it was better to risk our lives than give us more escape points.

When I reached the elevators, I realized they'd taken precautions there too—precautions that I'd completely let slip my mind. You couldn't even push the button for the elevator without first scanning your ID card. I'd seen our Alchemist jailers do it many times, but I'd left it out of my plan. The elevator was inaccessible to me, as was the similarly access-controlled stairwell next to it. Otherwise, we detainees would've constantly been trying to use them. As I stood staring, trying to find a work-around, a ding indicated the elevator's arrival and that the doors were about to open. I hastily stepped to the side and out of direct sight. A moment later, the elevator opened and Sheridan came out.

Without hesitation, I slipped in after her while the doors were still open, praying the elevator would still function from the last swipe of her ID card. If not, I might be stuck in it for a very long time. Luck was with me, and the button for the operations and purging floor lit up when I pushed it. I moved down a floor, and the doors opened to an empty corridor. I hurried out and tried not to think about how I was going to be able to use the elevator again.

I remembered where the supply closets were, but when I reached them, I discovered something I hadn't noticed before: They too required a keycard to open them. Sheridan must've unlocked them ahead of our visit before, but now I was out of luck. Time was slipping away on my spell, and I was getting nowhere fast. Sadly, I accepted that I'd probably have to return to my room and try again with a better plan tomorrow. At least I still had that second stick of gum.

Laughter jerked my attention from the medical supply closet, and I saw two Alchemists round the corner and come walking down the hall—in my direction. Panicked, I flattened myself against the wall. There were no nearby corners or nooks to duck into. If luck was on my side, the twosome wouldn't walk past me at all. If they did, I'd have to hope looking down would save me from eye contact and detection. For all I knew, that might not be enough.

The two of them stopped in front of the operations room, and I started to breathe a sigh of relief until an idea came to me and I realized I might be missing a golden opportunity. I sprinted toward the room they walked into and just managed to make it inside before the door—an automatic pocket one—slid closed. I froze and held my breath, terrified someone would notice me, but the two Alchemists I'd followed never even turned around. The only other person in there was a bored-looking guy in headphones, who was eating yogurt near a wall of monitors. The majority of the monitors were dark, and I realized those were the displays from our bedrooms. The other monitors showed classrooms and halls, most of which were empty.

Desks and computers filled the room, and I prowled around, again struck by a sense of déjà vu for the time I'd conducted similar activities in an Alchemist facility. Only then I'd had a much more reliable invisibility spell to fall back on. Still feeling determined, I searched around until I found what I'd hoped for. The guy eating the yogurt had taken off his suit coat and draped it on a chair. Clipped to the coat's pocket was his ID badge. I had no idea if some badges had more access than others, but at the very least, this would get me back on the elevator before my spell wore off. I pilfered the ID from his coat while his back was to me and slipped it into the waistband of my pants. I'd thought at first when I saw his headphones he was monitoring sound surveillance, but being that close to him, I realized he was actually listening to some kind of metal band. I wondered how that would fly with his superiors.

Regardless, it was good news for me, as was the fact that the two people I'd followed in were huddled over some computers and chatting loudly. I was pretty sure I could slip out, and no one would really notice the door opening. Before I could make my way back, however, I saw something new that made me hesitate and then walk the opposite direction. It was a touchscreen panel in the wall labeled sedation control. Current readouts indicated that the system was on nighttime settings, and every region of the detainee living quarters was listed: bedrooms, halls, cafeteria, and classrooms. All bedrooms were labeled 27 percent, with the rest of the rooms at 0 percent.

The gas levels, I realized. When I'd been in isolation, I'd gotten the impression they were controlling my cell manually, which made sense since they would knock me out instantly if the conversation wasn't going their way. From this display, however, it was clear the regular detainees were modulated by a central, automatic system that piped in the correct level to keep us heavily asleep each night. Three options at the bottom of the touchscreen suggested there was occasionally a need for manual intervention: OVERRIDE—STOP ALL SYSTEMS, RESET, AND EMERGENCY PROTOCOL—ALL REGIONS 42 PERCENT.

For a moment, it was simply the number that was staggering. If the normal 27 percent sedative concentration sent us into a heavy sleep, what would 42 percent do? I knew almost instantly. That much sedative piped in would knock us out in the blink of an eye. There'd be no drifting off into heavy slumber. We'd keel over where we were standing and practically be in comas—which would be very useful if there was ever any sort of mass escape.

I didn't know exactly what Adrian and Marcus might be able to pull off when they found me, but I knew this could cause some serious kinks in the plan. Disabling the gas in my own room wasn't going to be good enough. I need to kill it for the whole floor, and that was no small feat. Turning it off here was pointless when the touch of a finger would bring it right back. Somewhere, there had to be a more mechanical system I could interfere with.

That wasn't a problem I could focus on tonight, though. With a last lingering look at the panel, I hurried away and slipped out the door, unnoticed as I'd expected. From there, it was a hasty trip to the supply closets. Like all the other doors I'd encountered, I opened them as little as possible, allowing me to slip inside each one and gather what I needed where there was no surveillance. I soon had two bottles of purified water tucked into my waistband and a dozen wrapped and capped syringes hidden variously in my socks and bra. It wasn't exactly comfortable, but I needed everything to remain under my clothing to be covered by the spell. My surprise find of the night was that extra condiments were also kept in the food supply closet: ketchup, mustard, and—salt. I'd planned on smuggling out small amounts throughout the week, but one stolen shaker from the closet solved that problem.

Laden down with my stolen goods, I made my way back to the elevator. Having seen how relaxed the night surveillance was in the control room, I was no longer as worried about them noticing doors opening small amounts by themselves on-screen as I had been. When I reached the detainee living floor, however, the texting guard came walking down the hall when he heard the elevator and saw no one come out. I pressed against the wall again, frozen and looking down as he passed me. He stopped a few feet away from me and stared at the elevator with a frown while I held my breath. Even if he didn't make eye contact, my spell had to be on its last leg.

After several agonizing seconds, he finally shrugged and returned to his post. I moved passed him, mercifully unnoticed, and finally made it back to my room, where I nearly fainted in relief. There, I carefully concealed all my contraband in the pocket formed between my mattress and its sheet. They made us change our own bedding once a week, and we'd done it two days ago. That meant I had five days to use up all my supplies before running the risk of someone noticing syringes falling out of my mattress sheet on laundry day.

Weak with relief, I finally crawled into my covers. Despite feeling weary in body, my mind was worked up and agitated from tonight's sleuthing. It took me a while to fall asleep, and I knew Adrian would worry.

Sure enough, when I materialized in the Getty Villa's courtyard, I saw him pacing back and forth. He turned abruptly toward me when I said his name.

"Thank God, Sydney." He hurried over and swept me into his arms. "You have no idea how worried I was when you weren't here at the usual time."

"Sorry," I said, holding him tightly. "I had some errands to do."

He pulled back and gave me a knowing look. "What kind of errands?"

"Oh, you know, the kind that involve breaking and entering and magic use."

"Sydney," he groaned. "We're getting closer to finding you. You need to just lay low. Do you realize how dangerous it is to be off prowling on these 'errands' of yours?"

"I do," I said, thinking back to the gas control panel. "And so you're not going to be happy when I tell you that I'm going to have to do it again soon."

CHAPTER 14

ADRIAN

I WANTED TO BELIEVE SYDNEY when she told me she had everything under control, but it was hard, especially when she continued to stay vague on the details of what exactly it was she was doing in re-education. Rather than worrying, I tried to focus on the positives, like how I was able to talk to her at all and how ostensibly, despite her secretiveness about re-education, she seemed healthy and well.

Aunt Tatiana, sometimes my helper and sometimes devil's advocate, didn't make that easy.

Who knows what they're doing to her? she said in my mind. *She could be suffering now, screaming for you to help her, and here you are.*

Sydney's fine, I retorted firmly. *Obviously not in ideal conditions, but she's tough.*

Aunt Tatiana was relentless. *So she wants you to think, when secretly, she wishes you'd come to her.*

Anger kindled in me—and guilt. *I'm trying! I'd be there now if I could. Don't make me feel worse than I already do.*

"Adrian?"

That was Marcus, speaking out loud. He peered at me across a diner's table, drawing me out of the imaginary conversation.

"Where are you?" he asked. "I said your name three times."

"Sorry, just tired," I lied.

He nodded, taking me at my word. "You ready to go then?"

We'd grabbed a quick dinner after talking to Carly and were now ready to resume the journey to Boise. It was a longer drive than we could do that day, so we ended up spending the night on the outskirts of Las Vegas, in a plain motel nowhere near the excitement of the Strip I usually frequented when in the area. I hardly cared, though. My concern now was to make good time and find a decent place to sleep where I could make contact with Sydney. The following morning, after those goals were met, Marcus and I were back on the road, off to the Potato State.

"Gem State," Marcus corrected when he heard me call it that on our drive.

"What?"

"Idaho's the Gem State, not the Potato State."

"Are you sure?" I asked, making no attempt to hide my skepticism. "I hear about Idaho potatoes all the time. No one's ever like, 'Wow, my engagement ring has a rare Idaho diamond in it.'"

A smile played on his lips as he kept his eyes on the road. "Pretty sure," he said.

I wasn't masochistic enough to argue random trivia with a former Alchemist, but when we crossed the border into Idaho and started seeing license plates that said FAMOUS POTATOES, I felt pretty confident about who was in the right on this topic.

Talking about gems reminded me I was still carrying around Aunt Tatiana's cuff links—in the pocket of my jeans, no less. I'd originally done it so they wouldn't get lost on the plane, but now I was courting danger of a different kind, carrying around a fortune that might easily fall out if I was careless. I lifted one out now, admiring the way the sunlight played over the diamonds and rubies. Foolish or not, having them with me made me feel lucky, as though I had Aunt Tatiana herself helping me—the real Aunt Tatiana, that is. Not my phantom tormentor.

Marcus and I reached Boise around dinnertime, going to the address Carly had given us. It was a complex of modest apartments, and Keith's was a first-floor one with its own tiny porch that we made use of when no one answered the door. Darkness and lack of movement inside suggested he actually was out—and wasn't just hiding from us. It was a nice summer evening, pleasant for Moroi and human both, but I worried how long we'd be out there.

"How do we know he isn't working a night shift?" I asked Marcus.

Marcus propped his feet up on the porch's railing. "Because he's an Alchemist that got in trouble for breaking rules and stepping out of line. If he was an Alchemist who'd become so fascinated with vampires he was in danger of collaborating with Strigoi, they'd give him a night shift to keep an eye on him. But for general insubordination? He's probably on an eight-to-five schedule, just to remind him what normal human life is like—and to save those night shifts for the real risks."

Marcus was proven right ten minutes later when a Kia

Sorrento pulled up in the parking lot, and Keith came striding out toward the apartment. When he caught sight of us—specifically, me—he ground to a halt and grew visibly pale.

"No. *No*," he said. "You can't be here. Oh my God. What if it's too late? What if someone's seen you?" He looked around frantically, as though expecting an Alchemist SWAT team to leap out at him.

"Relax, Keith," I said, getting to my feet. "We just want to talk."

He shook his head vehemently. "I can't. I can't talk to your kind, unless it's business. And I'm not allowed to actually do business with your kind until I—"

"It's about Carly Sage," I interrupted.

That drew his rambling up short. He stared at us for several long moments, deliberation written all over his features. "Okay," he said at last. "You can come inside."

Nervously, Keith stepped forward and unlocked his door, continuing to cast anxious looks at both us and the rest of the parking lot. Once we were in, he drew all the curtains and then backed up as far away from us as possible, arms crossed defensively over his chest.

"What's going on?" he demanded. "Who is this guy? Is Carly okay?"

"This is my friend, uh, John," I said, realizing I probably shouldn't cite the first name of one of the Alchemists' most wanted renegades. As it was, he'd put on some sort of makeup to cover his indigo tattoo. "And Carly's totally fine. We just saw her yesterday."

Keith's demeanor softened a little. "You . . . you saw her? She's doing well?"

"Very well," said Marcus. "She's the one who gave us your address. She wanted us to come talk to you."

"S-she did?" Keith's eyes widened in wonder, which was actually kind of creepy, since one of his eyes was made of glass.

"Sydney's missing," I told him. "Carly wants you to help us find her."

Keith looked genuinely surprised to hear this, then his expression turned to one of wariness. "Missing where?"

"She's in re-education," I said bluntly.

"No," he groaned. "No. I knew I shouldn't have let you in. I can't have anything to do with this. I can't have anything to do with her, not if she's there." He closed his eyes and sank to the ground. "Oh, God. They'll find out you were here and send me back."

"No one will know," I said, hoping that was true. Until this moment, I never thought I'd feel pity for Keith. "We just need to know where Sydney is. She's at the same place you were. Where's it located?"

He opened his eyes and managed some kind of choking laugh. "You think they told us? They don't even let us see the sun! We're lucky to get light of any kind."

I frowned. "What do you mean?"

A haunted look crossed Keith's features. "It's what happens when you're in isolation."

"Sydney's not in isolation," I said, not entirely following. "She's with other people."

"That's its own kind of torture," he said bitterly. "You learn pretty quickly what to do and not do to make your life easier."

I was kind of itching to get more details, but Marcus pushed us back on track. "Okay, I get that they wouldn't tell you where you were, but you *did* leave eventually. You had to come outside that place to get here."

"Yes. Blindfolded," Keith said. "I wasn't allowed to see anything until I was far away from there. And don't ask me to gauge distances because I have no idea. I was in different cars and planes. . . . I lost track after a while. And honestly, getting back to that place was the last thing on my mind, so I wasn't really paying attention."

"But you were conscious," Marcus reminded him. "You couldn't see, but you had your other senses. Do you remember anything else? Sounds? Smells?"

Keith started to shake his head, but then I saw a spark of remembrance flash in his eye. He kept his mouth shut, the earlier wariness returning.

"I don't know if Carly will ever forgive you, even if you help us," I said quietly. "But I know for a fact she *won't* if you're sitting on information that could help her sister."

Keith looked as though I'd hit him. "I tried everything," he murmured. "I begged. I pleaded. I even got down on my knees."

I realized he was talking about Carly now, not re-education. "Why?" I asked, in spite of myself. "Why do you care now about her forgiveness? Where was your conscience all those years ago? Or any of the years since then?"

"Re-education did it," he said, staring down at his feet. "I'd never felt so helpless—so *hope*less—in my life as I did there. To be completely under someone's power, with no one to turn to for help, to make someone feel like they're at fault for you hurting them . . . I realized that was exactly what I'd done to Carly. That hangs over me every day."

Again, I felt bad for him in a way, though he had no

sympathy from me over what he'd done to her. Even I got turned down by girls, and when it happened, I dusted off my ego and moved on. I'd never considered doing what he did. He should've known it was wrong before the Alchemists threw him into some mind-control camp. It was all between him and Carly now, and although he did appear legitimately sorry, she would be well within her rights if she let him suffer for the rest of his life.

Spelling that out for him probably wasn't going to help me with my task here, so I more kindly said, "It's up to her now. But I know she'll be grateful if you can offer us anything that might help Sydney. Any detail you remember from when you left re-education."

Long silence fell, and that seemed to weigh on Keith nearly as much as our coaxing. Finally, he took a deep breath. "It was hot out," he said. "Hotter than I expected. Even in the middle of the day. I got out in late November and thought it'd be cold. But it wasn't. It was almost like I was still in Palm Springs."

I gasped, and Marcus gave me a sharp look before I could jump to some terrible conclusion. "She's not there. Palm Springs isn't on the list." He turned back to Keith. "But when you say it was like that, do you mean it was a dry heat? Desert-like? Not tropical or humid?"

Keith's brow furrowed. "Dry. For sure."

"How hot is hot?" pushed Marcus. "What was the temperature?"

"I didn't really have a thermometer to look at!" exclaimed Keith, growing frustrated.

Marcus was equally impatient. "Then take a guess. A hundred degrees?"

"No . . . not that. But hot for November—at least for me. I grew up in Boston. More like . . . I don't know. Eighties, I guess."

My attention was on Marcus now. I secretly hoped he'd suddenly say, "Aha!" and have all the answers. He didn't, but he did at least look as though this was useful information.

"Anything else you remember?" he asked.

"That's it," said Keith morosely. "Will you please go? I've been trying to forget that place. I don't want to go back for helping someone try to find it."

I met Marcus's eyes, and he nodded. "Hopefully this'll be enough," he said.

We thanked Keith and started toward the door. Considering his insistence on us leaving, I was kind of surprised when he was the one who suddenly said, "Wait. One more thing."

"Yeah?" I asked, hoping he meant he had one more useful fact about re-education to share.

"If you see Carly again . . . tell her I really am sorry."

"Do you still want her to turn you in to the police?" I asked.

Keith got that faraway look again. "It might be better. Certainly better than going back there. Maybe even better than this." He gestured around him. "Technically, I'm free, but they're always watching, always waiting for me to screw up. This isn't how I pictured my life."

When Marcus and I got into his car, I couldn't help but remark, "Two months. He was only there for two months. And look at him."

"That's what that place does to you," said Marcus grimly.

"Yeah, but Sydney's been there more than twice that long."

Those words settled heavily between us for a few moments,

and I had a feeling Marcus was trying to protect my feelings. "Did she seem that defeated?" he asked.

"No."

"She's stronger than Keith is."

My heart sank a little. "And that's also probably why she's still there." When he didn't respond, I tried to find a more optimistic topic. "Was any of that of use to you? The dry-heat stuff?"

"I think so. Here. Let's trade." He opened the driver's side door. "You drive, so we can get some hours in. I've got calls to make."

I swapped places with him but still couldn't help but ask, "Are you sure that's a good idea? Maybe we should stay put until we're able to figure out where she is. We could be going in the wrong direction."

"Not if what Keith said is true. She might not be in Palm Springs, but she's definitely south of us." He pulled out his phone as I drove us toward I-84. "I've studied this list of possible re-education locations so much, I've practically got it memorized. There aren't many places in the United States that would be in the eighties in November."

"There are tons," I argued, feeling like we were having the Potato State discussion again. "Hawaii, California, Florida, Texas. We were just in Las Vegas, and it was an oven!"

He shook his head. "Most of those aren't going to have dry heat. They have warm temperatures and rain in the winter. And a lot of the high-altitude dry places with desert climates—like Las Vegas—aren't that hot in November. From what I can tell from this list, Keith's info, and you being certain she's in this time zone . . . well, I think there are only two possible hits.

One's in Death Valley. The other's outside Tucson."

I nearly drove off the road in surprise. "California and Arizona? The two states we were just in within the last twenty-four hours?"

"They're big states," he said wryly. "But, yes, those are the ones."

My mind reeled. Either one of those places was less than a day's drive from Palm Springs. It wasn't possible that she'd been that close the entire time, that I'd suffered like I had missing her, and there'd only been hours between us! Marcus started to dial his phone but then seemed to notice my stricken expression.

"Hey, it's okay," he said. "You couldn't have known."

Is that true? demanded Aunt Tatiana in my mind. *She was so close! All this time. You could've practically reached out and touched her.*

I didn't need her censuring. I was doing plenty of that myself. A sick, heavy feeling of guilt and despair settled within me. So close! Sydney had been so close, and I'd failed her . . . just as I'd failed at everything. . . .

"I should have known," I whispered. "Somehow, I should have felt it in here." I patted my chest. "I should've known she was nearby."

Marcus sighed. "First of all, put both hands back on the wheel. Second, I'll give you credit for being a brooding vampire with phenomenal magical powers, but even you don't have that kind of sixth sense."

His words made no dent in the cloud of despair clinging to me. "It's not about magic. It's about her and me. If the Alchemists were twisted enough to keep her that close as some kind of weird extra torture, I should have sensed it. You can't understand." Marcus, like Jackie Terwilliger, was one of those people who'd never explicitly been told about what was going on with Sydney and me but had pretty much figured it out.

"It wasn't any weird extra torture," he insisted. "It's a sad, ironic coincidence. The Alchemists have one re-education center in this country, and it happens to be a few hours from where she was taken. From what Keith and others have said, though, it might as well have been light years from where she was taken. We're going to have our work cut out for us, even if we narrow down the location. Now, can you focus on the road, or do I need to take over?"

"Do what you got to do," I told him bleakly.

I stayed quiet as he made his calls to his shadow agents, asking them to drop whatever else they were working on in order to determine whether the facility was in Tucson or Death Valley. He also put out feelers to find out everything possible about the facility itself, to help us with our rescue, and he even made some disconcerting requests for tranquilizer guns and "other related supplies." All the while, that dark debilitating depression swirled within me, as did Aunt Tatiana's condemnation. When Marcus finally finished his last call, he explained to me that most of his intel on the place's logistics wouldn't come until after he had a hit on the location.

"Once we have a concrete place, we can dig up old records. Even the Alchemists can't build a place invisibly. They'll have it masked, of course, but there should be a public paper trail if we know what to look for. I've got a few people on the inside too who'll be able to help once we've got better search parameters."

I nodded in compliance and finally managed to shrug off my despair by replacing it with something else: anger. Not just anger. Rage. Fury at those who'd done this to Sydney. This kind of reconnaissance was Marcus's thing. Mine would be blasting open the doors and getting Sydney out of that hellhole. That's how I would make this right.

Yes, hissed Aunt Tatiana. *We will make them pay for what they've done.*

"How long until they find out which place it is?" I asked. "Before you said it could take as long as a week or two."

"That was when we were guessing blindly. Knowing it's definitely one of these helps a lot. If it's Death Valley, we might find out pretty quickly. There's not a lot out there. Tucson could take a little longer since there's more of a metropolitan area—and the outlying desert—to hide things. I've got people working on both places. Maybe we'll get lucky."

We stopped for the night in northern Nevada, getting a room in a hotel attached to one of the many casinos so ubiquitous in that state. It was hardly a luxury place but proved decent enough, especially for being in a no-name town. We had cable and internet, as well as a minibar I yearned to raid. Cutting myself off like I had after Court had been brutal, but my determination to stay in control of both my wits and my powers for Sydney was strong.

Once we were settled, I texted Jill, and before long, we had a video call set up with the gang back in Palm Springs on Marcus's laptop. "Did you find Sydney?" Eddie asked immediately. Jill knew all the day's details from the bond but hadn't yet had a chance to brief the others.

"We're on the verge of getting her location," said Marcus.

"And it's not going to be far from you guys. Death Valley or Tucson. We're waiting on confirmation."

Our friends shared my surprise at the realization that Sydney had been so close the entire time. "Let us know as soon as you find out, and we'll be right there," exclaimed Angeline.

For a moment, I wanted nothing more than to have them all at my back. But a few realities hit me—as did knowing that Sydney would never forgive me if her original mission failed. On the laptop screen, Jill grimaced as she sensed my thoughts.

"No," I said. "You guys are still in exam week. And Jill's not going off on any crazy escapades. Her life is still in danger."

"There's only two more days of exams," she protested. "And I'm practically out of danger. Didn't you hear when you were at Court? Lissa expects a vote within the month to rewrite the law about how a monarch needs a living family member. Once that's changed and I don't matter, she's going to bring me back. I'm only staying on in Amberwood's summer program until that's resolved."

I hadn't heard that, likely because my time at Court had been spent in a drunken haze. "You always matter, Jailbait. And you just spelled it out yourself—that law hasn't been passed yet. You're still the key to the throne, and you're not going to be leaving the safe haven everyone worked so hard to create. And don't ask for the dhampirs to go," I added, remembering how she'd used that argument in our last meeting. "You need their protection."

"I'm not a dhampir," said Trey. "And I'm under no orders. Tell me where to go, and I'll be there."

I hesitated but then slowly nodded. He was right. He didn't have the same obligations as the others, and he was good in a fight. Angeline gave him a punch in the arm that looked painful but probably only endeared her to him more.

"No fair," she said. "I want to help."

"We all do," said Neil.

"You can take one dhampir," said Jill calmly. "I'll be okay with two, especially if I just stay on campus the whole time. Take Eddie."

He turned to her in surprise. "You don't . . . want me to guard you?"

The smile she gave him was very queenly, almost a mirror of something I'd seen Lissa do. "Of course I do. There's no one I trust more than you. But you *need* to do this. And you know he's one of the best, Adrian."

I doubt any of them, not even Eddie, realized the magnitude of what Jill was offering. I couldn't read her mind, but I knew her well enough to understand she very much wanted to be a part of any mission to free Sydney. I also knew that she realized no one was going to let that happen. Rather than fight it, she was sinking her energy into getting me to accept Eddie . . . not just because he was an asset but because her words were absolutely true: He *needed* to do this. I'd observed him since Sydney's capture and seen how it had eaten him up in a way different from what I suffered. My feelings over her loss were all about loneliness and feeling helpless to find her. His were about guilt—he still felt responsible for her being taken in the first place. She'd tricked him, sacrificing herself to save him, and he couldn't get over that. Jill, always wiser than anyone gave her credit for, understood that—and understood that saving Sydney might very well be the only thing that would let Eddie feel redeemed. Jill understood it because she was observant and wise.

Also because she loved him.

Eddie didn't realize this, though, and mostly felt conflicted. "I'd be breaking my orders . . . my promise to protect you."

"I'm freeing you from them," she said. "And I have that right, both because those promises are to me *and* because I'm part of the ruling family. As crown princess, I'm asking you to go and rescue Sydney. And then come back to me."

I'd never heard Jill invoke her royal status, let alone her title as crown princess. That was the whole point of the family law. If something happened to the ruling monarch and an emergency ensued that the Moroi Council couldn't handle, one of the former monarch's family members could be made interim ruler until a new one was elected. That law hadn't been invoked when Aunt Tatiana had died. The Council had managed things, but to keep the government running smoothly, the old laws still required one living family member, just in case.

Eddie gazed at her in adoration as she spoke, not fully grasping that she was speaking to him as someone who loved him and not actually as a commanding princess. But it worked. "I will," he told her. "I'll get her back. And then I'll come back to protect you, I swear it."

Marcus, not fully following the drama within the drama, nodded. "I'm fine with that. I'd never turn down a dhampir or two fighting with me."

The "or two" made Angeline and Neil look hopeful, and I quickly dashed their dreams. "You guys stay with Jill. Don't let your guard down, and *don't* get any crazy ideas about bringing her along so you all can help. The fact that this law might be over could also mean her enemies are redoubling their efforts to get to her while it still matters."

That sobered them all, and Neil and Angeline nodded in grim acceptance. Marcus's phone rang, and he stepped aside to answer it. While he conferred with one of his contacts, Trey said, "Oh, hey. I meant to tell you. Some girl stopped by yesterday looking for you and Sydney."

"Both of us?" I asked in surprise. There weren't many people who treated us as a duo.

"She mostly seemed interested in Sydney but would've accepted you too. She was human," he added, guessing my next question. "Blonde. Glasses. No one I'd ever seen."

It was no one I could think of either. The only human who might have an interest in both Sydney and me was Rowena, and she had teal hair (last I knew), not to mention my phone number if she really needed to get in touch. "She didn't say anything else?" I asked. "Why she wanted us? Who she was?"

"Nope. She just said she was an old friend who wanted to catch up. When I told her I didn't know where you were, she looked so disappointed that I offered to pass on a message if I heard from you. She said no, used the bathroom, and left with hardly another word."

"No lily tattoo?" I asked pointedly.

Trey scoffed. "You think I didn't look? I would've noticed that for sure. If she had one, it was covered up."

I had no answers about the mystery visitor, and Marcus's return soon pulled my mind elsewhere. Excitement practically radiated off him. "Remember when I said we might get lucky?" he asked. "We did. Death Valley. I got it confirmed. I mean, the actual location within that area still has to be verified, but it looks like we know where we're headed tomorrow."

"Trey and I will meet you there," said Eddie swiftly.

"You can finish your exams," Marcus told him. "It'll take a couple of days to plan and get all our intel. Like I said, we have to find the place, let alone figure out how to get into it."

Death Valley. Less than five hours from Palm Springs. I knew Marcus was right—that there really was no way I could've known Sydney was there—but it was still a hard thing to accept. *So close*, I thought. *So close this entire time.* Equally maddening was that although this was a huge leap in information for us, we were still powerless to act yet. The best we could do was finish coordinating with Eddie and Trey before Amberwood's curfew split the guys and girls up for the night. When we finally logged off, Marcus made a couple more calls and then stifled a yawn.

"I've got to get some rest," he said, heading for one of the double beds in the room. "Keep the TV on if you want. I can sleep through anything. I've learned to take advantage of solid sleeping conditions when I get them."

I didn't doubt it after his years on the run, but I still turned the volume off and just watched the pictures as I sprawled out on my own bed and tried to make contact with Sydney. It was past the time she normally went to sleep, but I didn't reach her, presumably because she was off on whatever other secret errand she'd wanted to take care of tonight. TV without sound turned out to be pretty boring, and I nearly drifted off twice before finding a channel with closed captions that I could read along with. I watched it for a good part of the night, fighting sleep as I continued to make periodic checks for Sydney. The last thing I remembered was a talk show around four in the morning . . .

. . . and then I was waking to sunlight streaming in the room as Marcus emerged from the bathroom.

"Good morning," he said. "Ready to hit the road?"

"I . . ." I stared around stupidly, trying to piece together what had happened. "I fell asleep."

He raised an eyebrow. "Before you talked to Sydney?"

"Yeah, but I mean, it wasn't for lack of trying. . . . I tried a dozen times to connect to her. It didn't work."

"Maybe she went to bed late," he said.

"After four?" Even with the previous night's secret errand, I'd finally connected with her before one. "I'm worried she never went to sleep."

"Is that a problem?"

"Actually, no," I said. "At least if it was by choice because she was doing her errands. What would be a problem is if she was asleep . . . and blocked from me again."

CHAPTER 15
SYDNEY

TIME WOULDN'T ALLOW ME to charm all the syringes at once, seeing as I could only do it in my rare moments of privacy. I managed five at first and distributed them to Emma and the select few Emma thought we could trust.

I felt emboldened after Adrian had told me he'd gotten Keith's address from Carly, and I couldn't wait to talk to him tonight about further progress. Knowing he and Marcus were advancing toward their goals drove home the importance of dealing with the "emergency protocol" situation as soon as possible. Equally pressing was knowing I would make the most progress if my stolen ID card was still working. For all I knew, once that guy reported he'd lost it, the Alchemists would disable it, and sabotaging an entire system was going to be difficult if I couldn't even use the elevator. I needed to act fast.

Emma was impressed to hear I'd been in the operations room but had little help to offer with the larger problem. "The gas controls weren't there?"

"The controls were," I said. "Including the power to render us all unconscious at once, anytime and anyplace. But I need access to its more basic parts—like where the gas comes from in the first place. How it gets into those pipes in the ventilation system."

She shook her head, looking legitimately sorry she couldn't help. "I have no idea. I don't know anyone who would."

I did, and I brought it up with Duncan later in art class. Whereas Emma had been perplexed by my inquiries, Duncan was shocked. "No, Sydney, stop. This is crazy. Bad enough you disabled it in your room! The entire floor? That's madness."

We were still working on clay bowls, our assignment now being to make a set of identical ones, which went right along with the Alchemist ideology of conformity. "What's madness is that with a push of a button, they can knock us all out within seconds."

"So?" he asked. "They'd only do that if there was a revolt or something. No one's that stupid." When I said nothing, his eyes widened. "Sydney!"

"What, are you saying you want to stay here forever?" I demanded.

He shook his head. "Just play the game, and you can get out. It's a lot easier and a lot less trouble than staging some ill-fated prank."

"Get out like *you* did?" My retort made him flinch, but I only felt a little bad.

"I would if I could," he muttered.

"I don't believe that," I said. "You've been here so long, you should know the game better than anyone else. You should be able to say and do exactly what it takes to get your walking papers, but instead, you do exactly what it takes to stay put! You're afraid to act."

The first glint of anger I'd ever seen in him flashed in his eyes. "To act on what? What is it exactly you expect me to do, Sydney? What's out there for me? There'd be no security. They track re-educated Alchemists forever. To not get sent back here, I'd have to either push all my morals about Moroi aside or constantly watch my back to hide my true feelings. There's no winning for us. We're screwed. We were born into a system we don't agree with, and we got caught. Here, out there, it doesn't matter. There's nothing left for us."

"What about Chantal?" I asked quietly. "Isn't she out there?"

His hands, which had been so deftly working the clay, faltered and dropped to his side. "I don't know where she is. Maybe she went to re-education in some other country. Maybe she killed herself rather than live a lie. Maybe she went on to some worse punishment. You think solitary confinement and monotonous art projects are the only weapons they have? There are worse things they can do to us. Worse things than purging and public ridicule. Being bold sounds great in theory, but it comes with a cost."

"Chantal was bold, wasn't she? And that's why you're afraid." The grief on his face was so intense, I wanted to hug him . . . yet at the same time, I wanted to shake him for cowardice too. "You're so afraid of acting! Of ending up like her!"

Swallowing, he returned to work on his bowl. "You don't understand."

"Then help me to."

He stayed silent.

"Fine," I snapped. "I'll figure out the gas control system

myself and won't bother you anymore. I suppose you might as well go ahead and throw this away too."

I knelt down as though I'd dropped something and swiftly transferred a capped syringe from my sock to his, neatly covering it with his pant leg before anyone saw. "What's that?" he hissed.

"The last of my current stock of syringes with the ink-repelling solution in them. I'd saved this one for you, but you'll probably be happier not using it. In fact, maybe you should just go ask them for an extra-strong re-inking so you don't have to think for yourself anymore."

Chimes signaled the end of class, and I turned to go, leaving him gaping. That evening, while getting ready for bed in the bathroom, I was able to charm a few more syringes that I smuggled back to my room. I also did the gum trick again, sticking it in place in the door to disable the lock after lights out. I might not know exactly where the main gas controls were, but based on the explorations I'd done, I could make some educated guesses. Emma noticed when I stuck the gum in the door's side and said, her voice barely audible, "You're serious about this?"

I gave her a sharp nod and settled into my bed with a book for our prescribed reading time. When the lights went out later, I again waited long enough for the Alchemists on guard to fall into their shifts before I sprang into action. I rearranged my bed and pillow, murmured the invisibility incantation, and then tucked my stolen ID into my shirt before quietly slipping through the unlocked door. In the corridor outside, I was faced with a scenario similar to yesterday's: little activity and the same guard stationed in the hallway nexus.

I crept down to the elevator and stairs, swiping my ID over

the door to the latter. Its security panel turned green, and I breathed a sigh of relief that I still had access. Although the stairwell door wasn't perfectly silent, I was able to carefully open it and slip through much more quietly than when I used the elevator with its telltale ding. I just had to be cautious in opening it the minimum amount needed for me to fit through. Once in the stairwell, I noticed something I'd also observed in the elevator. There was no way up. The only way to go was down.

How do *we get out of here?* I wondered for the hundredth time. It was the question I'd been mulling over since getting here. We had to have gotten in somehow, and obviously, the Alchemists who worked here got in and out. Duncan had explained to me that they had their own quarters elsewhere and lived there for months-long shifts until staff rotations replaced them. How did that happen? It was a puzzle for later, however, and for now I focused on heading to the operations and purging floor. I checked every door I reasonably could and found nothing matching the kind of mechanical room I'd been hoping for. Conscious of the time, I returned to the stairwell and reinforced the invisibility spell, buying me an extra half hour. I wouldn't be able to do it all night, not with the energy it required, but it would at least allow me to check out the next floor down.

I hadn't been on this floor in almost three weeks, and for a moment, I stood frozen as I stepped out into the hallway. This was the floor my cell had been on, where they'd kept me in darkness for three months. I hadn't thought much about it since joining the others, but now, as I stood and stared at the identical doors, it all came back to me. I shivered at the memory of how cold I'd been, how cramped my muscles had grown sleeping on that rough floor. The memory of that darkness was chilling, and I was kind of amazed at what a difference the crack of light from the pocket door in my current room made. It took a surge of willpower to shake off those old memories and walk down the hall, remembering my goal.

I hadn't noticed this when released, but each door was marked with the letter *R* and a number. Was the *R* for reflection? There were twenty of them in total, but I had no indication if they were all occupied. I didn't dare scan my ID card and try to open one. Some gut instinct told me only someone with high clearance could open them to begin with, and besides, if they were monitored, any crack of light would instantly show up on a surveillance screen. So, I simply walked past them all, despite feeling sick inside that others might be only a few feet from me, suffering as I had.

Once I cleared those rooms, I came to stand in front of a set of double doors labeled REFLECTION CONTROL. Many administrative and operations doors had glass windows, but this one offered no indication of what might lie behind it. I was wavering on whether I should try to scan my card and slip in when the doors suddenly swung open, and two Alchemists emerged from within. I quickly moved out of their line of vision, and thankfully, they headed the opposite direction from me at a brisk pace. The heavy doors swung shut too quickly for me to get in, but I managed a good look inside before they closed with a *clang*.

Several Alchemists sat in little booths with their backs to me, facing dark monitors and wearing headphones. Large microphones were embedded in their desks along with a control panel I couldn't read. This was where the solitary prisoners were monitored, I realized. Each prisoner must always have a watcher, with that microphone masking their voice and the panel allowing control of the gas and lights. I'd suspected they rotated personnel, and here was my proof. I hadn't had time to get a full count, especially with part of the room blocked from my view, but I'd seen at least five watchers.

What I had also seen, with absolutely clarity, was an exit sign. It had been on the far side of the room, past the watchers and monitors, but there'd been no mistaking those glowing red letters. My heart rate sped up. This was it, the way in and out! For a few seconds, I wondered how easy it would be to slip in and stroll right out of this place. Not that easy, I soon admitted. For one thing, this wasn't a simple room to infiltrate. Those doors didn't allow for darting in and out, and they made enough noise when opened that someone would likely notice them opening by themselves. Even with no Alchemist directly monitoring them, some personnel were sitting far too close for my comfort.

There was also the likely fact that no one could just "walk out" of that exit. I wouldn't have been surprised if there were real guards, more card readers, and probably numerical codes for exit and entry. The Alchemists had already set up a considerable fire hazard in having so few exits to begin with. If they felt so strongly about prisoner security that they were willing to take that risk, they certainly weren't going to leave that exit exposed.

Still, it was hard to walk away from that door, knowing what lay beyond it. *Soon*, I told myself. *Soon*. A further scan of the hall revealed nothing else of note, and I headed back toward the stairwell. As I did, its door opened, and Sheridan stepped out. I immediately flattened myself against the wall, averting my eyes downward. In my periphery, I could see her pause as though she were searching for something, and then she began walking again. When she was past me, I lifted my head and watched as she continued down the corridor, almost at a leisurely pace. At last, she reached the end, stood there a few moments, and then doubled back to the control room doors, which she soon disappeared through. I hurried into the stairwell before she came back, taking the last option left to me: down to the last level.

The elevators went no farther than this level, and the stairs ended here as well. This was the only level I'd never been on, and I couldn't imagine what happened down here. What else was there for them to do? The doors I found offered no answer. They looked identical to the reflection time ones, and I almost wondered if I'd simply found another set of solitary cells. These were labeled with the letter *P* and numbers, however, and I found no corresponding control room to illuminate what that letter stood for. What I did find were three doors labeled MECHANICAL 1, MECHANICAL 2, and MECHANICAL 3. Behind them, I could hear the buzz of generators and other equipment. They had no card readers but did require an old-fashioned mechanical key.

Racking my brain, I recalled a key spell I'd once copied for Ms. Terwilliger, one that would open an ordinary lock. I murmured the Latin words, calling on the magic within me, hoping there was nothing too unusual about this lock. Power surged through me, and a moment later, I heard a click. Dizziness briefly swept me, and I ignored it as I began my exploration, unlocking the other doors as needed.

The first door revealed a room with a furnace and other HVAC equipment but nothing like what I expected for gas controls. The second room was where I struck gold. Along with a generator and some plumbing systems, I discovered an enormous tank labeled with a chemical formula that read very much like a sedative to me. Four pipes fed off it, each one labeled with a floor number. Each also had a manual valve that could be adjusted. All of them were currently in the "on" position.

I saw no sign that there was any sort of sensor to alert tampering at this level. Taking a chance, I turned the valve for the detainee floor to "off." No alarms or lights went off. Emboldened, I nearly considered turning off the others but then realized I'd be exposing what I'd done. Maybe there were no sensors here, but the Alchemists would immediately notice if the gas was shut off on the level with the solitary cells. They controlled the gas there manually and were able to observe instant results. Turning off the gas on the detainee level would affect sleep right now, and that wouldn't be readily obvious to the Alchemists. It might not even be noticeable to the detainees. They didn't let us get eight hours of sleep anyway; it was unlikely anyone had much trouble falling asleep at night.

It was a hard call to make, abandoning the prisoners in reflection time, but there was nothing I could do for them right now. The status quo had to go on for them, and I needed that gas off on my floor as long as I could manage. Judging from the tank size, it probably went a while between refills, but eventually someone would come for a maintenance run and discover the valve. That was the timeline I had to worry about.

In the same room, I discovered another tank with a

chemical formula I wasn't entirely sure of, but I was betting it was a different substance, one I'd occasionally felt in my cell that made me agitated and paranoid. They didn't employ it with the same regularity as the sedative, but I turned this valve off for my floor too, just in case. We didn't need any extra incentive to be suspicious of one another.

With that work done, I hurried out and ignored my curiosity about the third mechanical room and P-marked doors. I'd achieved my goal tonight and needed to get back to my room before my spell wore off. That, and I knew Adrian would worry if I was very late. I took the stairs back up to the detainee living level and peered out the door's window before opening it. No one was visible. I opened it a crack, so as not to attract attention on cameras, and squeezed my way out . . .

. . . and ran right into Sheridan.

She'd been purposely hiding in the indentation in the wall made by the elevator doors, out of visual range when I looked through the window. I'd been searching for people moving with purpose on their shifts—not someone looking for me. And she was clearly looking for me—or someone like me. We made eye contact, and there was no mistaking the recognition on her face. The spell was over.

"Sydney," she exclaimed. That was the last thing I heard before I saw what looked like a taser in her hand. Then, I felt a jolt of pain, and everything went black.

When I woke up, everything was still black. For the space of a heartbeat, I thought I was back in my solitary cell. But no, this was different. There was no rough stone floor here, and I still had my scrubs on. Instead, I was lying down on a cool metal table, with my arms, legs, and head restrained.

"Well, Sydney," a familiar voice said. "I'm sorry to see you here."

"I know it's you, Sheridan," I said through gritted teeth. I gave my restraints an experimental tug. No luck. "You don't have to hide in the dark."

A tiny canister light in the ceiling turned on, shining down just enough to illuminate her lovely but cruel face. "That's not what the darkness is for. You're in darkness because your soul is also shrouded in darkness. You don't deserve the light."

"Then why am I here and not back in my cell?"

"The cell is to reflect on your sins and see the error of your ways," she said. "You've put on a good show but clearly haven't learned anything. Your chance at reflection and redemption is past. That, and we need some answers about your recent activities." She held up my pilfered ID card. "When and how did you get this?"

"I found it on the ground," I said promptly. "You guys should be more careful."

Sheridan gave a dramatic sigh. "Don't lie to me, Sydney. I don't like it. Now let's try again. Where did you get the card?"

"I already told you."

Pain suddenly shot through every part of my body. It was a strange mixture of things, crawling all over my skin and setting my nerve endings ablaze. If you could somehow combine the discomfort of electric shocks, bee stings, and paper cuts, it would feel kind of like what I experienced. It only lasted a few seconds, but I found myself screaming out in pain nonetheless.

The light on Sheridan turned off, plunging us into darkness, but when she spoke again, it was clear she hadn't moved. "That was the lowest setting and only a taste at that. Please don't make me do it again. I want to know how you got the ID card and what you were out looking for."

This time, I didn't lie to her. I simply stayed silent.

The pain returned at the same intensity, but it lasted much longer this time. I couldn't form any coherent thought while it was happening. Every particular of my being was too fixated on that terrible, excruciating agony. One of the things I'd loved about getting intimate with Adrian—aside from the obvious, like that he was insanely sexy and good at what he did—was that it often proved to be a rare moment when my always-thinking brain took a break, allowing me to become all about the physical experience at hand. That was kind of what was happening now, except the physical experience in question was pretty much as far from what I'd had with Adrian as one could get. My brain couldn't think of anything. All there was just then was my body and its pain.

I had tears in my eyes when the pain stopped, and I barely heard Sheridan rattling off her questions again. She also added a couple more, like, "How did you avoid detection?" and "How did you get out of your room?" I barely had time to answer, even if I'd wanted to, before the pain resumed. When it ended an eternity later, she came back at me with the questions. Then the cycle repeated.

During one of the brief respites, I managed enough coherent thought to understand her process. She was throwing different questions at me in the hopes I'd be so pushed to a breaking point from the pain that I'd blurt out an answer to something— anything. It probably didn't matter to them at first. Getting me started talking was their goal, and I had a feeling that prisoners in my situation didn't stop talking once those floodgates were opened. There'd be a strong urge to tell everything to make the pain go away. I was certainly feeling that urge now, and I had to physically bite my lip to keep from telling her whatever she wanted. I also tried to mentally focus on the faces of those I loved, Adrian and my friends. That worked a little during the lulls, but once the torture started again, no thought or image could stay in my mind.

"I'm going to be sick," I said at one point. I didn't know how long it had been. Seconds, hours, days. Sheridan didn't seem to believe me until I actually started coughing and retching. It was a different kind of sick from the purging, which was medically induced. This was my body's response to more than it could physically handle. Someone came to me from the opposite side of the room from her and undid enough of my restraints to turn me on my side, where I choked up what little was in my stomach. I didn't know if they were fast enough to have a receptacle to catch it in and really didn't care. That was their problem.

As the worst of the vomiting subsided, I could barely make out Sheridan speaking quietly with someone else across the room.

"Go get an 'assistant' to help us," she said.

A male voice sounded skeptical. "There's no love between any of them."

"I've seen her type. What she won't give up for herself, she might for someone else."

The sound of a door indicated her colleague left, and as I was re-restrained and wiped clean, her words triggered an awful realization. *Someone betrayed me!* Sheridan had been specifically looking for me, which was how the spell had been unraveled. I'd been foolish to think making the salt ink would create some kind of bond between the others and me. The only upside to this was that I'd disabled the gas, as planned, but now what would the cost be?

That was as far as I could speculate because the torture began anew—and incredibly, it was worse. I didn't get sick, maybe because my body couldn't muster the effort, but I couldn't stop my screams from filling the room. I hated myself for showing them that weakness, for admitting that they were getting to me . . . but it was all I could do not to tell them every secret I had during those pauses. *I will not talk*, I vowed. *If I'm going down for this, then I'll do it with them knowing they're not as powerful as they think.*

"Why do you make us keep doing this, Sydney?" Sheridan asked in that mock sad tone of hers. "I don't like it any more than you do."

"I sincerely doubt that," I gasped out.

"And here I thought you were making such progress. I was nearly ready to reward you for your good behavior. Maybe a visit from your family. Maybe this."

The tiny spotlight appeared on her again, and something in her hand shimmered. It was my cross, the little wooden one Adrian had made me, painted with morning glories. They'd tried to bribe me with it when I first arrived, as though one material object was all it would take to break me. Seeing it now made my chest ache—though that could've possibly been an aftereffect from the torture—and my eyes blurred with tears of sadness now, not pain.

"You could have it now," she said congenially. "You could have it, and we could stop the pain. All you need to do is tell us what we want to know. It really is a lovely piece." She held it up admiringly and then, to my complete and utter horror, she put it around her own neck. "If you don't want it, I might as well keep it."

I nearly told her it was made by a vampire but worried that might make her destroy it. So I stayed silent, letting my rage seethe within me—at least until the torture started again, and only agony seethed within me.

I lost track of time again until her colleague returned. This brought a reprieve from the pain, and a few new spotlights went on, including one shining uncomfortably in my face. The light also revealed the man hadn't come back alone.

"Look, Sydney," Sheridan said. "We brought you a friend."

The man dragged someone up to my table. Emma. I nearly accused her of betrayal then and there. After all, she was the perfect candidate. She had her sister's crimes to overcompensate for as well as her own. She'd gotten the salt ink from me already and had nothing to lose by turning me in, especially if she could convince them of her own innocence. She was also the only person who'd known for sure that I was out roaming the facility last night.

And yet . . . there was a terror in her eyes that kept me from making any accusations. Maybe she was the likeliest traitor, but on the off chance she wasn't, I couldn't insinuate she might be privy to any of my plans. "Who said she's my friend?" I asked instead.

"Well, she's about to share your experience," said Sheridan. "If that's not a basis for friendship, I don't know what is." She gave a curt nod, and Emma was dragged off out of my line of sight. Another assistant came forward, helping me to sit up so that I'd have a better view of what was taking place: They were restraining Emma on to a table just like mine.

"P-please," she stammered, as helpless in her struggles as I had been. "I don't know anything. I don't know what this is about."

"She's right," I said. "She doesn't know anything. You're wasting your time."

"We don't care what she knows," said Sheridan cheerfully. "We still want to know what *you* know. And if the methods of persuasion we've used on you don't work, perhaps you'll be more forthcoming seeing them on others."

"Persuasion," I said in disgust. "That's what the *P* on the doors stands for. We're on the lowest level."

"Indeed," said Sheridan. "You went on quite the little tour last night, judging from all the doors you used that card on. Tell us why you did it and how you didn't show up on any cameras, or else . . ."

She gave another nod, and in the split second before Emma started screaming, I understood what had happened. She hadn't betrayed me. No one had. I'd screwed up on my own. I'd worried the guy whose card I had might report it missing and get it disabled. No doubt he had reported it, but rather than deactivate it, they'd waited to see if anyone used it. Their system would have recorded every instance it had been scanned. I'd been an idiot, laying out the perfect trail for them to follow, with only the invisibility spell saving me from immediate capture. I'd hopefully checked enough places to obscure my intentions, especially since the mechanical rooms hadn't required card access. The odds were good no one knew what I'd pulled off.

But that didn't save Emma from being subjected to the same torture I had been. My skin crawled, watching that pain wrack her body, and I felt ill in an entirely new way.

"She's an innocent in this!" I exclaimed when they took their break. "How sick do you have to be to do this?"

Sheridan chuckled. "No one's truly innocent—at least not around here. But if you do believe she is, it makes it that much sadder that you're letting her suffer like this."

I stared at Emma and felt torn with indecision. How could I give up all my plans? And yet, how could I let this go on? My deliberation was read as defiance, and they resumed the procedure. I couldn't handle watching it, and when the next break came, I blurted out, "What do you think I was doing? I was looking for the way out!"

Sheridan held up her hand to halt whatever unseen torturer wielded the controls. "Did you succeed?"

"Do you think I'd be here if I had?" I snapped. "The only thing I saw was in your reflection control room, and you've got that pretty well guarded."

"How did you move around without being seen?" she demanded.

"I evaded your cameras," I said.

At Sheridan's nod, Emma was subjected to more pain, her body flailing like a ragdoll's as it tried to cope with the waves of agony coursing through her.

"I answered!" I exclaimed.

"You lied," Sheridan returned coolly. "There's no way you could have avoided all of them. No one noticed anything on camera at the time, but after extensive review, we found one small clip that shows what looks like a stairway door opening—

just barely—by itself. We almost missed it and only noticed on later replays. Explain."

I stayed silent, thinking I could endure watching Emma be tortured again. But I couldn't. Not when it was because of my actions. Her screams seemed to fill every part of the room, and she bucked against the restraints in a desperate effort to alleviate the pain. I tried reasoning with myself as those shrieks went on and on, that this was only a temporary discomfort, that Emma had known what she was signing up for when she started helping me. Surely the greater good was worth one person's suffering?

That cold logic almost had me convinced until I finally saw tears streaming from her eyes. I cracked.

"Magic!" I yelled, trying to make myself heard above her cries. "I did it with magic." Sheridan signaled for the torture to stop and looked at me expectantly. "I moved around with magic. Human magic. And if you think torturing her will get me to tell you more about that, you're wrong. You can torture her and everyone else in this place, and I won't say another word. Talking about it involves people on the outside, and next to them, the people here mean nothing."

It was kind of a bluff. I didn't know if I could truly stand against mass torture of the other detainees, but Sheridan either believed me or had bigger concerns.

"I didn't think it'd happen again," she muttered.

"It always happens. Eventually," said her colleague. He gestured one of the assistants in the darkness forward to Emma. "Get her up and back to her floor. There's no telling what kind of damaging propaganda's been spread. We're going to have to do a mass re-inking."

My heart sank. I'd only gotten to about half the detainees! The rest of the ink was still hidden in my bed.

"I didn't convert anyone if that's what you're worried about," I said.

"I told you, there are no innocents here," said Sheridan. "Get Emma back to her level, and get Sydney back on the table."

"I've told you everything I'm going to tell you," I protested as the assistants came forward. Emma was dragged away. "Your torture didn't work on me before."

Sheridan gave a low throaty laugh, and all the lights went out again. "Oh, Sydney. Now that I know what you are, I don't feel bad in the least about *really* turning up the intensity. We don't know everything about human magic users, but there is one thing we've learned over the years: They're remarkably resilient. So let's get started."

CHAPTER 16

ADRIAN

WHEN A SECOND NIGHT WENT BY with no contact from Sydney, I knew something had definitely gone wrong. I could tell Marcus was worried too, but he did his best to try to put me at ease.

"Look, she said there was some gas in her room that knocked them out, right? Maybe the Alchemists discovered it was off and just fixed it again. She lived that way for three months and wasn't in trouble—I mean, not in more than the usual trouble of re-education."

"Maybe," I allowed. "But even if that's true, don't you think they'd wonder how it got broken in the first place? She could be punished by association."

Marcus's phone rang before he could respond to me, and I waved him off to answer. He'd been on the phone nearly nonstop since we'd gotten the hit on Death Valley, always coordinating with some agent or another. We'd arrived in the area yesterday, discovering that there was really no place to stay in Death

Valley itself, which kind of made sense. Our base of operation had therefore become a motel in a rundown town fifteen miles away from the state park. There were no restaurants, so we got all our food from a convenience store across the street that was run by a kindly woman named Mavis, who constantly worried about me because of my complexion. "You need more sun, darlin'," she kept saying.

What you need is blood, Aunt Tatiana had remarked at the time. *Not from her, of course. We have standards.* She'd been right on the first count. It had been a few days since I'd had blood at Court, and although I could go a few more before noticing any major physical discomfort, it was a problem I'd need to eventually remedy.

As Marcus spoke on the phone now, I wandered to the window of our room, which overlooked Main Street and the convenience store, as well as a gas station. By the motel's standards, it was the best view in the place. To my surprise, a familiar car suddenly pulled up into the motel's parking lot, its sunny color a bright contrast to this otherwise dreary town. Without saying a word to Marcus, I headed out of our room and down the stairs.

Eddie and Trey were getting out of my Mustang when I stepped outside. Even this early in the day, the heat was rising considerably, creating shimmering mirages on the asphalt. "Survive exams?" I asked.

"For the second time in my life, yes," said Eddie.

"They're actually still going on today," said Trey. "But Ms. T pulled some strings with the other teachers so that we could finish up yesterday. She sent this—for when we get Sydney back."

I accepted a small tote bag that was filled with all sorts of witchy accoutrements—herbs, amulets, and a book that meant nothing to me but that would probably elate Sydney. *When we get Sydney back.* Trey had spoken with such confidence, and I hoped it was warranted. These last two nights of silence had been rough on me.

"And I brought this," said Eddie, with a wry smile. He handed over Hopper, whom I'd left at the apartment, still immortalized in gold. I touched the finely carved scales and then slipped the little dragon into the tote bag with the other magical items. "Any updates on Sydney?"

I beckoned them forward. "Come on up to HQ and out of the heat."

Marcus was off the phone when we returned to the room, and he greeted the newcomers with friendly nods. "Just confirmed we've got three guys—well, one's a girl—coming to help us tomorrow. Two of them used to be in re-education. They had no idea it was here, of course, but as you can imagine, they're kind of holding a grudge. They've got some intel on what the layout's like inside, though not nearly as much as I'd like. Meanwhile, we've finally got some hard data on the exterior. If you can believe it, they actually mask themselves as a desert research facility. They're outside the park proper too, probably about twelve miles from where we are now. This is actually the closest town to them. I wouldn't be surprised if Alchemists stopped here for gas on their way to work."

It was all good data, but it suddenly seemed lacking when Eddie asked, "Have you heard from Sydney?"

Marcus's face, which had momentarily seemed upbeat, fell again. "No. We've been out of contact for two nights."

"We don't need to make contact to raid the place, though,

right?" asked Trey. "We can just show up and bust her out."

"Sure," Marcus agreed, "but it would be nice to have a contact on the inside as this goes down."

I slumped down onto one of the room's narrow beds, which creaked under my weight. "And it would just be nice to know she's okay."

"Too bad there's no one else we can contact," said Eddie. "You don't have any leads on other prisoners there?"

Marcus shook his head as he explained what they knew, and the old familiar despair started to settle over me. Plunging into sobriety and using spirit daily was a deadly combination for my mood swings, and I'd been fighting them constantly. Sydney's latest disappearance had sort of shattered whatever fine control I'd held on to until this point. It'd be a wonder if my sanity lasted until we got her back.

Sanity's overrated, my darling, I heard Aunt Tatiana say.

I squeezed my eyes shut. *Go away,* I silently told her. *I need to listen to them.*

What's the use? she asked.

I need to focus. I need to get in touch with Sydney to make sure she's okay and get info about what's going on inside.

Your human girl has already given you info, the phantom Aunt Tatiana said. *You just haven't heeded it.*

I suddenly opened my eyes. "Duncan," I said out loud. My three friends looked in me in astonishment.

"Are you okay?" asked Eddie, who'd occasionally seen some of my worse sides.

"Duncan," I repeated. "One of the times I talked to Sydney, she mentioned a friend she'd made there named Duncan, someone who'd been there a while. If we can find out his name, get a picture . . . it'd be enough for me to form a dream bond. Assuming the gas is out for him too." I wasn't clear on the logistics of what Sydney had disabled. "Regardless, it's not a common name. Could you pull up anything?"

Marcus frowned. "Maybe . . . depending on how long 'a while' is, one of the ex-prisoners joining us tomorrow might even know him."

"Then call them," I said sternly. "Now."

"If Sydney's not in touch because that gas is back on, you won't be able to get to him either," warned Marcus.

I held up my hands in exasperation. "What other choice do we have?"

I could tell he thought it was a long shot, but a few phone calls soon yielded results from one of his guys—the one who was a girl. "She said when she was being held last year, there was a guy named Duncan Mortimer there," Marcus told us a little while later. He was already on his laptop, typing as he spoke. "No guarantee it's the same guy, but the odds seem good. Mortimer's a well-known name. I wonder . . ."

He didn't elaborate on what he was wondering and soon found a file on Duncan, including a picture and a few brief stats. Most spirit users wouldn't have been able to form a dream bond to someone they'd never met, and I again felt that occasional flash of pride at being able to do something worthwhile. When I was satisfied I had all the data I needed on him, we switched gears and spent the rest of the day poring over Marcus's intel about the facility itself. I didn't have the tactical mind the others had, but I did have the considerable power of spirit on my side and was able to advise on where I thought that would be useful.

When night—and what I termed "re-education bedtime"—

came around, I first tried reaching out to Sydney and again had no luck. That put us at plan B, and I pulled Marcus into the dream. He'd gone to sleep earlier for this very reason. As the mastermind of our break-in, it was essential he speak to Duncan. Marcus materialized by the Getty Villa fountain, examining his arms and hands as though he'd never seen them.

"It never gets old," he remarked. "You sure you can pull this guy in?"

"One way to find out."

I'd spent the day memorizing Duncan's picture and now summoned that image in my mind as I used spirit to reach out to him across the world of dreams, along with what little I knew about him. *Duncan Mortimer, age 26, originally from Akron, asleep twelve miles from here.* Over and over, I repeated that improvised mantra and concentrated on his face. Nothing happened immediately, and at first, I doubted my own abilities before accepting he might just be blocked as Sydney had been. Then, moments later, a third person materialized with us.

Tall and lanky, his face was a definite match for the picture I'd seen. That, and he was wearing that same horrendous tan outfit Sydney kept appearing in. He looked around with the kind of quizzical expression most people had when I summoned them for the first time, when they didn't fully grasp that this wasn't an ordinary dream.

"Huh," he said. "Been a while since I dreamed."

"This isn't a dream," I said, striding toward him. "At least, not the kind you're thinking of. I created it out of spirit. Adrian Ivashkov." I extended my hand to him. "I'm here to talk to you about Sydney Sage."

Duncan's expression still looked slightly amused, like this

might all be some weird trick of his subconscious, when my words finally sunk in. "Oh, man. You're him. The cute and brooding vampire boyfriend."

"She said I was cute and brooding?" I asked. "Never mind. Why can't I reach her? Where is she?"

"Some place I've never known anyone to came back from," he said darkly. "A place I never knew actually existed until Emma saw it."

"Who's Emma?" asked Marcus, joining us.

Duncan looked a little surprised at seeing another person here but then seemed to write it off as part of this odd experience. "Sydney's roommate. Ex-roommate, since Sydney has new accommodations."

I was on the verge of a million more questions and then decided to go straight to the source. "Can you picture her? This Emma girl? Like, visualize her in your head and think about all you know about her."

"Okay . . ." he said, a small frown appearing between his eyebrows.

If someone I'd brought into a dream could picture someone I'd never met, I could use spirit to reach out and use that visualization as the anchor to bring in the new person. It was no harder than pulling in someone I'd never met, so long as my subject's mental focus was spot-on. Duncan's must have been because a few moments later, a slim girl in those same khakis appeared beside him. We quickly caught her up, explaining what kind of dream she was in, which seemed to unnerve her more than it did him. Even liberal Alchemists had problems with vampire magic. But soon, her curiosity won out.

"That's how Sydney did it," Emma said. "She was in contact

with you through spirit. That's why she needed the gas shut off."

"It must be off for all of us, if I'm here," said Duncan. "I didn't think she could do it."

Emma nodded grimly. "That's where she was the night she was caught. I mean, I don't think she was *there*. When I saw her, they didn't seem to know what she'd been doing."

"Okay, kids," I said. "You need to back up right now and fill in a lot more details."

Between the two of them, they pieced together a story about how Sydney had been making anti-Alchemist ink on the sly and then expanded her operations to shutting down an emergency system that could render the entire place unconscious. I could tell Marcus approved of that strategy, but even he looked aghast when Emma told us what the cost had been of Sydney getting caught.

"It was awful," Emma said with a shudder, paling. "I don't know how they did it. It must have been built into the table. I also don't know how Sydney didn't just confess when they did it to her. I would've spilled everything, but she stayed tight-lipped . . . at least until she saw them do it to me. She told them she was using magic. It saved me . . . and got her in worse trouble."

My heart sank. "Because that's how she is. You don't know where she's at now?"

"Still on that fourth level, I suppose," said Emma. "Unless they moved her back to solitary."

Marcus sighed. "Well, at least that answers what those levels are used for." He looked both of the prisoners over, sizing them up before he delivered his bombshell. "We're coming to break her out soon. All of you, actually."

The difference in response was remarkable. Emma lit up. Duncan threw up his hands in disgust and walked away. "Duncan," she exclaimed. "Come back."

He stopped and turned. "Why? I don't want to hear this. It's futile."

"You haven't even heard the plan," said Marcus, almost sounding hurt.

"It doesn't matter," said Duncan. "You can't get in there. You can't get us out. Even if you can, what's next? Where do we go? You don't think they'll look for us?"

"I know they will," returned Marcus evenly. "And I'll make sure you're hidden."

Duncan still looked skeptical, but Emma was clearly on board. "What do you need from us?"

"As much detail about the inside as you can tell us," said Marcus. "Ideally where the main door lets in. No one who has been there has ever seen the exit."

"Sydney has," said Emma. "I overheard. It's on the floor with the solitary cells, in their control room. She made it sound like there were lots of people in there, though."

"I'd imagine so," said Marcus. "If that's their only way in and out. That place sounds like a fire hazard waiting to happen."

"It is," agreed Duncan, almost reluctantly. "That's why there are so many sprinklers and fire alarms in the place."

"Has there ever actually been a fire?" I asked. I wanted to participate in the plan but was having a hard time getting over the idea of Sydney locked up and tortured somewhere. "Any reason to evacuate you guys?"

Emma looked to Duncan for an answer. He shook his head. "No. I think there was a fire in the kitchen once, a couple years back, but they acted pretty quickly to nix that. It'd have to be pretty serious to get us all out of there."

I could see the wheels in Marcus's head turning. "Any way you could start a fire? Get access to something flammable?" he asked.

"Sydney could light that whole place up if she was free," I muttered.

"They go out of their way to minimize our exposure to flammable things," said Emma. Something small shifted in Duncan's expression, and she noticed it too. "What, do you know something I don't?"

He shrugged. "It doesn't matter."

"Yes, it does!" She marched up to him and pounded on his chest with her fists. "If you know something that can help them, tell us! Stop being a coward. Dare to hope there might be away out of this! If you hadn't been so afraid of helping Sydney find those gas controls, maybe she wouldn't have been caught!"

Duncan flinched as though he'd been hit in the face. "There was nothing I could've done! They were already on to her."

"Then make what she did worthwhile," cried Emma. "Do you really want to live the rest of your life like this? Because I don't. I want to get out. I don't care if I'm on the run. It's better than living in that trapped existence. You should feel the same way."

"You don't think I do?" he countered angrily.

She threw up her hands. "Honestly? No. All I see is that you're too spineless, even for our captors."

He gave a harsh laugh. "You think that's why I'm there?"

"You never step out of line. Why else would they keep you there so long?" she demanded.

He didn't answer, but Marcus did. "Because he's Gordon and Sheila Mortimer's son."

Emma's eyes widened slightly. "Really?"

"Who?" I asked, feeling lost.

"I realized it when I pulled up your full name," continued Marcus. "They're very powerful Alchemist leaders, Adrian."

"Ones who can't risk the rest of the world knowing how their son broke the rules to help some Moroi while he was on assignment," added Duncan bitterly. He turned to Emma. "That's why I've been held so long—and why they'll keep holding me. Even if I'm the most well-behaved detainee there, my parents can't risk the embarrassment of their son's past coming back to haunt them."

"Then don't let them win!" exclaimed Emma. "Fight back. Don't let them toss you aside like that. Help us with this. For yourself. For Chantal, when you find her."

The name meant nothing to me, but it hit Duncan hard. "There's no way to find her," he said glumly.

"*I* can find her," interrupted Marcus. "Whoever she is, I've got contacts all around the world—lots of them tied to the Alchemists. It might take a while, but we'll find her. We found Sydney, didn't we?"

Duncan still looked uncertain, and Emma clutched his hand. "Please, Duncan. Do this. Take a chance. Start living. Don't let them take everything away from you."

Duncan closed his eyes and took a few steadying breaths. Despite how anxious I was to save Sydney, I couldn't help but feel a little sorry for him. Alchemists, even asshole ones like Keith, were generally bright and competent people. Duncan no doubt had been equally capable—and probably still was. It was terrible that people like him could be worn down like this, and I prayed we could get to Sydney before it was too late.

"Yes," he said at last, opening his eyes. "Yes, I know how to start a fire."

We spent the rest of the night making plans with them. Marcus and the prisoners got to sleep the entire time, but I was exhausted by the time the dream ended, just before sunrise. My body had been awake all night, and my eyes, when I saw them in the mirror, were bloodshot enough to be Strigoi. Eddie and Trey had slept and were anxious to hear what had transpired overnight.

"Get some sleep," Marcus told me. "I'll brief them over coffee and make arrangements with the others. This is happening today."

I lay on the cheap bed after the three of them left, certain I'd never sleep being so close to freeing Sydney. It was all my mind could think about. My body knew better, however, and it only felt like minutes had passed when I later found Marcus waking me up. "Rise and shine," he said. "The cavalry's here."

I squinted against the afternoon light and nodded my way through introductions with Marcus's backup, a threesome named Sheila, Grif, and Wayne. They'd all made considerable plans as I slept, letting me rest as long as possible. Marcus got me up to speed with the newcomers, letting me better explain my role to them as I in turn took in the little adjustments that had been made throughout the day. There hadn't been many, though more details had certainly finalized, and Marcus's team had done a good deal of recon around the actual site. Once everything was hashed out, we found ourselves on the road, and I had to accept the impossible reality that I was finally going after Sydney.

Between my friends and Marcus's recruits, we had a veritable caravan. He'd had one of his guys bring a van, with the plan being that it would be used for the bulk of the detainees. After seeing Duncan's reticence, I'd questioned whether we could even get them to go with us, but Emma had assured us we could. When Sydney had been taken, Emma had found the rest of the salt ink in their room and used it to buy the loyalty of some of the other detainees. "They'll do what we say," she'd told me with a smirk. "And they'll make sure that everyone else does too."

A mile from the facility, our caravan split in two. Marcus, in my car of all things, and his associates in the van went off to a location they could park at just outside the facility's perimeter, where they would then approach on foot. Eddie, Trey, and I were going straight into the Alchemists' front door, with golden lilies on our cheeks that Sheila had painstakingly painted on us to look indistinguishable from the real thing. This part of the plan had been a bit controversial, as Marcus would have been the ideal choice to come in and play at being an Alchemist. His face was so widely known, however, that we couldn't risk it, and I didn't have the magical ability to alter both his and my appearance. Maybe if I only needed to look like a Moroi who didn't resemble Adrian Ivashkov, I could have obscured both of us, but I had to completely change my race. Under no normal conditions would any Moroi come to a re-education building.

We were in Marcus's Prius ("It's a totally Alchemist thing to drive," he'd assured us) and drove straight up the driveway to a checkpoint manned by a guy in a booth. He checked the fake Alchemist IDs Marcus had had made for us and then waved us through. This was all according to plan. Marcus had explained that a gate guard wouldn't electronically match our IDs to anything in their database. That was going to come when we actually walked in the building.

"You seriously cannot imagine the déjà vu I'm feeling now," Eddie remarked, once we'd parked in the lot. It had a handful of other sensible, fuel-efficient vehicles. "This is weirdly similar to when Rose, Lissa, and I broke out Victor Dashkov. It's kind of unsettling."

"The exception being that he was a hardened criminal who deserved his fate," I said. "What we're doing now is on the side of justice, rescuing those in need."

"Oh, I know," he said. "I'm just thinking how that escapade wasn't without its hitches, and we only broke out one person— not a dozen."

"It almost makes it easier," said Trey cheerfully. "I mean, it's all or nothing. You don't have to rely on the same subtlety you would getting out just one person. We're breaking this place open."

"That's what I'm worried about," Eddie said.

The front lobby of the alleged desert research facility certainly looked impressive and scientific. All the architecture was glass and metal, with framed pictures of sandy landscapes that were supposedly key to the place's function. One glass door led off to the left, to a wing where Marcus's intel had told us the Alchemists who worked on site lived. A young woman sat at the front desk, with a more sinister and unmarked door behind her that we'd been told should be the one entrance into the re-education lair. She looked up at our entrance, startled.

"My goodness," she said. "I didn't even see you walking in on the security cameras."

267

"Sorry about that," I said, oozing spirit-induced charisma. "Hope we didn't startle you." One of Marcus's merry men had been out on the grounds early and found a way to get the exterior cameras to loop on themselves, thus hiding everyone's approach. This was good for me, since my spirit disguise wouldn't hold up on camera, and good for Marcus, whose posse wasn't even attempting subterfuge.

"No, not at all." The girl smiled at us, showing me my illusion was holding up. "What can I do for you?"

"We're here to see Grace Sheridan," I said, flashing my ID. Eddie and Trey did the same. Getting that Sheridan person's first name had been another gem gleaned from Duncan.

The receptionist's eyebrows knit as she took our IDs to scan. "I wasn't told of any appointment. Let me call her."

Her murmured phone conversation was about what we'd expected, as was her surprise when she scanned our IDs and her computer told her we didn't exist.

"Our department's a bit—how shall I put this—clandestine," explained Trey. "There's no record of us because we generally don't like to advertise what it is we investigate. However, we understand there's been a resurgence of it here, and that Miss Sheridan's been at the center of the case."

The receptionist relayed this enigmatic message through the phone and hung up a few moments later. "She'll see you. Right through this door, please."

I stepped through, not sure what to expect. From the stories, barbed wire and chains on the walls wouldn't have surprised me. The Alchemists were still keeping it "business casual" on the ground floor, however, as the room we entered looked very much in line with the lobby's style—with one exception.

Six men stood guard in the room, ranged strategically around two doors: an elevator and a stairwell. The men wore suits and had golden lilies on their cheeks and were among the biggest and bulkiest I'd ever seen among the Alchemists. Their HR department must've searched pretty extensively to find the beefiest specimens in their gene pool. Most intimidating of all, however, was that each man visibly had a gun—a real gun that could kill, not the sleek little tranquilizing kind that Marcus had covertly armed Trey and Eddie with. Marcus had said the fallout would be big enough without us leaving fatalities behind and also worried about innocents getting injured in the fray. (It went without saying that no one had suggested giving me a weapon.)

I kept a cool smile on my face, like it was totally normal for me to see a bunch of armed guys there to keep a group of bedraggled prisoners from escaping or having free thought. The elevator chimed, and a smartly dressed young woman stepped out. She was pretty in the kind of way that said she'd run a dagger through your heart and still keep smiling the whole time. She maintained that smile as we made introductions.

"I'm afraid you've caught me off guard here," she said. She leaned forward a little bit to read my ID tag. "I wasn't expecting you. I wasn't even aware there was a Department of Occult and Arcane Transgressions."

"OAT doesn't make very many appearances—certainly not many public ones," I said sternly. "But when a debacle of this magnitude reaches my desk, we have no choice but to intervene."

"Debacle?" Sheridan asked. "That's kind of an exaggeration. We have things under control."

"Are you saying one of your detainees didn't use illicit

magical resources to escape your control and conduct affairs you *still* don't fully understand?" I demanded. "I'd hardly call that under control."

She flushed. Seriously, I deserved an Oscar for this stuff. "How do you know about that?"

"We have eyes and ears you can't even dream about," I told her. "Now. Are you going to cooperate with our investigation, or do I need to call both of our superiors?"

Sheridan wavered and then cast a self-conscious glance at the stoic guards. "Let's talk in here," she said, gesturing us to what looked like a small office adjacent to the room. We followed, and she shut the door as soon as we were all in. "Look, I don't know who's been telling you stories, but we really do have everything well in—"

The shriek of a fire alarm in the corner of the room cut her off. It was followed by a crackling sound, and a voice suddenly came from a small walkie-talkie attached to her belt. "Sheridan? This is Kendall. We have a situation."

Sheridan lifted out the walkie-talkie. "Yes, I can hear the alarms. Where is it?"

"Multiple locations on level two."

Sheridan winced at the word "multiple." "How big are they?" she shouted back. "The sprinklers should be able to contain them." She glanced up at the ceiling and looked surprised. "Are yours on? They should be set off universally for multiple fires. This whole place should be under water."

"No, nothing's come on yet," the voice replied. "Should we wait? Or do you want us to evacuate?"

Sheridan stared at her walkie-talkie in disbelief and then back at the inactive sprinkler in the ceiling. Duncan had said there were few situations that would actually cause them to evacuate the entire facility, so we'd gone out of our way to create one. Apparently, their art teacher was fighting a smoking habit, and along with a massive gum stash, she kept cigarettes and matches in her desk. Between those and a supply of paint remover, he'd made arrangements with other detainees to start fires simultaneously on their living floor. That was dangerous enough in those conditions, but one of Marcus's comrades had found exterior control of the facility's water system and had sabotaged it to delay the sprinklers coming on.

The walkie-talkie crackled again. "Sheridan, do you copy? Do you want us to evacuate?"

It was clear from Sheridan's face she'd never, ever expected to make a decision like this. After a few seconds, she finally responded. "Yes—you have my authorization. Evacuate." She gave us a brief glance as she lunged for the door. "Excuse me, we have an emergency."

In the other room, the guards were on full alert from the screaming of the fire alarms. "We have a Code Orange," she yelled to them. "Be ready. You two usher the detainees over there for holding. The rest of you, keep your weapons drawn, and watch for—"

The walkie-talkie went off again, this time with a male voice. "Sheridan, are you there?"

She frowned. "Kendall?"

"No, this is Baxter. Something's wrong. The detainees—they're taking over—resisting our orders—"

Sheridan blanched. "Have the control center initiate the gas shutdown. Knock everyone out. We'll get masks and send people down to pull you out and—"

"We already tried! The system seems to be disabled."

"Disabled?" exclaimed Sheridan. "That's—"

The door leading from the lobby suddenly burst open, and Marcus and his associates rushed in, wielding those little dart guns. They might not have been as lethal as the real guns, but they were still effective, especially when paired with the element of surprise. Eddie and Trey had theirs out in a flash, and within seconds, the Alchemist guards were down for the count. Only two of them managed to get off shots—shots that went wide—before collapsing from the tranquilizers. Marcus shoved a terrified receptionist into the room and assessed the situation. He ordered Grif and Wayne to pile the unconscious bodies in the office while Sheila stood guard over Sheridan and the receptionist. I let my spirit disguise drop, and both Alchemist women gasped upon realizing they'd been chummy with a Moroi. That shock increased when Sheridan did a double take and realized who Marcus was.

"You!" she spit out.

She didn't get a chance to elaborate. Moments later, the door to the stairs opened, and that's when the real chaos started. A mix of khaki-clad detainees came spilling out alongside more formally dressed Alchemist staff. Some of the detainees looked scared and unwilling to be there and were literally being dragged along by their colleagues, reminding me of how Emma had said they'd make sure everyone got out. Marcus quickly initiated a system that was the opposite of what Sheridan had intended in the evacuation. Detainees and Alchemists were split up as they emerged, with the latter—and very shocked—group being put under heavy guard. I watched it all anxiously, my jaw clenched so tightly that it was beginning to hurt. No one I knew was with the initial group coming up, but that was to be expected. When they began to thin out, my nervousness really increased.

This is it, I thought. *Any minute now, Sydney's going to come out with Emma and Duncan.*

And then, Emma and Duncan did emerge—without Sydney.

"What the hell?" I exclaimed. "Where is she? You said you'd get her!"

"We tried," cried Emma. She threw four ID cards on the ground. "None of these would open the doors on the fourth floor. They must not have had access . . . even though I've seen some of them going to that floor in the past."

I turned on Sheridan in a rage. "Why wouldn't the fourth-floor doors open?" I yelled. "Who has access?"

Sheridan took a step back from me. "Those are our most dangerous prisoners," she said, mustering what dignity she could. "The system automatically locks them in for an event like this. Normal card access is disabled. They're too dangerous to let escape."

The full implication of her words hit me. "So you just leave them there to die? What kind of sick bastards are you?"

Her eyes were wide with fear, but whether that was because of my outrage or her own conscience, I couldn't say. "It's a risk we take—it's a risk my own people take. Two of them are locked down there as well, one with each prisoner."

"You guys are even more screwed up than I imagined," growled Marcus. "Someone's ID must work. Does yours?" When she nodded reluctantly, he ripped it off her jacket. "The sprinklers should be coming on. Once they do, we'll go down and get them. It's unlikely the fire's spread to that level, but the stairs are going to be—"

"Uh, Marcus," said Grif uneasily. "The sprinklers should've come on by now. I didn't set the delay for that long."

Marcus gaped. "What the hell are you saying? Did you permanently sabotage them?"

"Not intentionally! It was just supposed to be long enough to instigate the investigation."

"Then get out there and take another look!" cried Marcus. "And bring the gate guard back with you." Grif scurried out.

I'd heard enough. More than enough. Sydney was down there, trapped in a room while a fire raged three floors above her and could be on its way. I strode over to Marcus and took Sheridan's ID from him before turning back to her. "How many are down there? You said two prisoners and two personnel. Anyone else?"

She did a quick count of the huddled Alchemists. "All m-my people are here," she stammered.

"We're all here too," said Emma. "Plus six we took from the solitary floor. We checked every cell."

"Fine," I said. I stormed over to the stairwell door and flung it open. While it wasn't exactly smoky, there was a faint haze in the air that didn't bode well for the fire's progress. "I'm going in for the last four. Anyone coming with me?"

I immediately felt Eddie by my side. "Do you even have to ask?"

CHAPTER 17
SYDNEY

IT TOOK ME A WHILE to realize the fire alarm was going off. At first, I thought it was some kind of new spin on the torture.

Unlike reflection time, when the Alchemists flaunted their power by putting us to sleep at will, those running the so-called persuasion floor had a big emphasis on keeping us awake. The scholar in me, who vaguely recalled reading articles on interrogation and torture techniques, understood this. The more sleep-deprived you were, the more likely you were to slip up and say something you didn't intend. In reflection, and even while living with the other detainees, I'd never felt fully rested, but what I experienced now was on a completely different level.

When I wasn't being tortured and asked the same questions over and over, I was subjected to blinding light and irritating noises to make sure I couldn't lapse into any sort of real rest. There was no need for gas to keep from dreaming; I never got close enough to REM for it to be an issue. I soon lost track of time again, and even the erratic meals (more lukewarm gruel) and bathroom breaks didn't help with that.

I'd actually remained remarkably resilient, despite how excruciating the experience was. I stuck to my story that I'd been looking for a way out the night I was caught, and I refused to tell them any details about how long I'd been practicing magic or who had taught me. It didn't seem likely they'd do anything to Ms. Terwilliger, but there was no way I could take a chance. I'd let them rip me apart before I ever uttered her name to them.

When the shrieking alarm and small strobe light in the room's corner went off, it jerked me out of a fragile dozing state I'd been enjoying. Those times were rare, and I was sad to see it end, especially since I knew what was probably coming. Aside from the alarm's light, the room was in pitch darkness, so I had no idea how many people were there until I heard a man speaking into a phone or radio. His name was Grayson, and he'd been a constant companion of mine in running torture and interrogation sessions—when Sheridan wasn't doing it personally.

"Hello?" he said. "This is Grayson in P2. Is anyone there? Is this a drill?"

If there was any response, I didn't hear it. After a few more attempts, I heard him over by the door, like he was trying to open it.

"Something not going according to Alchemist plans?" I asked. I wasn't sure if he heard me over the noise, especially since I couldn't actually manage to put much volume in my voice. But when he spoke again, he was right next to me.

"Quiet," he ordered. "And say your prayers that we actually walk out of here. Not that I expect yours to work."

The tension in his voice told me more than his words, and I struggled to snap my addled brain into focus and assess what was going on. Whatever was happening, this definitely wasn't part of any plan, and Alchemists *hated* it when their plans went awry. The question was: Was this to my advantage or not? Things were so regimented in re-education that it would take something extraordinary to really throw them off . . . and Adrian was the most extraordinary person I knew.

After Grayson failed at outside communication a couple more times, I dared speak again. "Is there really a fire?"

A few of those annoying spotlights came on, one illuminating him, the other shining right in my eyes. "Very likely. And if so, we are also very likely going to die in it," he said. I could see sweat on his brow, and there was an edge of unease in his voice, despite the cold delivery. Noticing my scrutiny—and that I'd observed his weakness—he scowled. "Who knows? Maybe in fire, your soul will finally be purged of its—"

A click at the door preceded its opening, and Grayson spun around in surprise, mercifully ending his tirade. I couldn't see his face, but I kind of wished I could have when I heard a familiar voice say, "Sydney?"

My heart leapt, and a hope I hadn't felt in ages filled me anew. "Adrian?"

Immediately, my hope dimmed. Suspicion born of weeks living in paranoia kicked in. This was a trick! It had to be a trick. I'd lost contact with Adrian. He couldn't have found me already. He couldn't have broken in here. This was probably the latest in a long line of Alchemist tricks to try to mess with my mind . . . and yet, when I heard his voice again, I was certain it was him.

"What the hell have you done to her?"

I wanted to see him, but the restraints wouldn't allow it. What I did see was Grayson pull what looked like a gun from his side and aim. That was as far as he got before the gun literally flew out of his hand and landed across the room. He gaped in disbelief. "What evil is—"

Someone who looked very much like Eddie came barreling into the dark room, knocking Grayson off his feet. They fell out of my line of sight, and suddenly, my vision was filled with the most beautiful image I could have hoped for: Adrian.

For a few seconds, that doubt plagued me again, that this was just one more deception on the Alchemists' part. But no, there he was before me. Adrian. My Adrian, gazing down with those piercing green eyes. I felt an ache in my chest as emotion momentarily overcame me. Adrian. Adrian was here, and I fumbled to find something to say, some way to convey all the love and hope and fear that had built within me these last few months.

"Are you in a suit?" I managed at last, my voice choking up. "You didn't have to dress up for me."

"Quiet, Sage," he said. "I'll make the hilarious one-liners during this daring rescue." His eyes, warm and full of love, held mine for a moment, and I thought I would melt. Then they narrowed with determination as he focused on the various restraints holding me. "What in God's name is this? Something from the Middle Ages? Does it need a key?" Meanwhile, in the background, Eddie and Grayson continued throwing each other around.

"I've never seen them use one," I told Adrian.

It took him a few tries, but he finally figured out how to undo one restraint. Once he had the knack, the rest soon followed, and I was free. Adrian carefully helped me sit up, and I was just in time to see Eddie pin Grayson to the floor in one of the spotlights. Eddie pointed a gun at the back of his head, which surprised me at first, but even in the poor lighting, I could tell there was something unusual about that gun.

"Get up," said Eddie, rising off his victim. "Slowly. And put your hands on your head."

"I'd rather die a fiery death than be the prisoner of some evil creature of hell!" retorted Grayson, though he still complied.

"Rest easy, we're not taking you prisoner," said Adrian. "We're saving your dumb ass so that you can go join the rest of your lame colleagues."

Eddie peered around. "Think there are any kind of restraints for him around here?"

"I'm sure of it," I said. I started to get off the table, but a wave of dizziness hit me. I turned to Adrian. "Check the sides of the room. That's where the supplies will be."

Adrian hurried off to look and first found something equally useful: a master control switch that turned on lights throughout the room. It made me squint after so long in the dark, but the added visibility soon allowed him to find shelves full of supplies, including some zip-ties that he used on Grayson. Various chemicals and controls were also on the shelves, along with chairs and night vision goggles so that other Alchemists could watch the torture show when the lights were off. It disgusted me, and I had to avert my eyes.

"Can you walk?" Adrian asked me.

"Eventually," I said.

He slid an arm around me, and my legs threatened to give

out. His strength, both physically and mentally, empowered me, and I was able to make slow progress out of the room with his help. Eddie moved ahead of us, marching Grayson at a brisker pace. When we reached the halls, which also had alarms but no sign of a fire, Eddie turned to his prisoner.

"Which is the other occupied room?" When Grayson didn't respond, Eddie glared and got into his face. "Come on! We're trying to save your colleague here."

"I'd rather die than forsake my duty or ask for your help," snarled Grayson.

Eddie sighed and handed Adrian his gun. "Keep it on him while I check the rooms out."

I was pretty sure Adrian had never used any sort of gun in his life, but he managed to look pretty convincing as he kept this one trained on Grayson. I leaned against the wall and watched as Eddie scanned an ID badge at each door, opened it, and looked inside. On his third attempt, I saw him lunge into a room. I couldn't see what happened but could hear the sounds of altercation.

Adrian glanced down at me, a frown creasing his forehead as he assessed my worn appearance more closely. Whatever strides I'd made after leaving solitary confinement had probably been diminished with my recent captivity. "You haven't been telling the truth. All those times I asked what else they were doing to you—"

"I wasn't lying," I said, averting my eyes.

"You just didn't tell me," he said. "When was the last time you ate?"

I was spared an answer when Eddie came out with another Alchemist at gunpoint. This time, Eddie definitely had a real gun, so I assumed he'd disarmed the guy in the room.

"Zip-tie this guy," Eddie told Adrian, "and go release the girl in there since you're a pro at those tables. I couldn't make heads or tails of it."

I gave an encouraging nod to Adrian, who looked reluctant to leave me. After binding the second Alchemist, Adrian disappeared into the room. I glanced at Eddie. "Are you sure there's not a fire? The alarms are still going off."

"Oh, yeah," said Eddie, "there's definitely a fire. We're just counting on it not reaching us since it's a few floors up. At least, it was."

I turned his words over in my head, making sure I truly understood them and wasn't just mishearing things in my bedraggled state. I was actually pretty sure I could smell smoke but wasn't certain if that was just my imagination. A minute or so later, Adrian came out of the room supporting a girl a little older than me, dressed in the same tan scrubs. My first thought when I saw her was: *Do I look that bad?* No, I decided, there was no way. I looked pretty bad, I knew, but something about her told me she'd been there much, much longer than I had. Her face was gaunt and pale beneath what looked like normally tanned skin. Her scrubs were a size too big, suggesting she'd lost considerable weight since first getting them, and her black hair was limp and in bad need of a thorough scrubbing and a haircut. She reminded me of how I'd looked coming out of solitary, only ten times worse. I hadn't been on this level for long and had enjoyed the benefit of food and sleep for the last few weeks.

Compassion flashed over Eddie's face, and then his hardened nature took over. "Let's go. Can you help both of them?"

I straightened up from the wall and waved Adrian off. "Help her. I can walk, just slowly."

Adrian looked uncertain, but it was clear this other girl needed him more than me. I walked beside her as our strange party moved down the hall and found myself trying to reassure her about a situation I knew nothing about. "It's okay," I said. "Everything's going to be okay. We're going to get you out of here. What's your name?"

Her dark eyes stared blankly ahead, and I wondered if she even heard me. Maybe she'd survived being in torture for so long by tuning out human voices. "Ch-chantal," she said. Her voice was barely a whisper, and I wouldn't have been able to hear it over the alarm if I hadn't been leaning close to her.

"Chantal . . ." I gasped. "I think I know you. I mean, I know of you. I know Duncan. He's my friend."

A tiny, barely perceptible spark of life appeared in her eyes. "Duncan? Duncan's here?"

"Yeah, he's waiting for us." I glanced questioningly at Adrian as I spoke, and he nodded in confirmation, emboldening me. "You'll see him soon. He's going to be so happy to see you. He's missed you a lot. He had no idea you've been here this whole time."

A chill ran through me at my own words. *This whole time.* Duncan had said the Alchemists had taken her away a year ago. Had she been in the "persuasion" area that long? It was horrifying. No wonder she looked like she did. And yet, the fact that she'd survived that and was apparently still enough of a threat to stay locked up spoke legions about her character. Maybe she and I should've been flattered to be in that exclusive club.

Eddie led us to the stairwell, and everything seemed clear until we opened the door and stepped out on the solitary floor. A wall of smoke hit us, thick and noxious, blocking the way between us and the control center that held the exit. He scowled. "I didn't expect it to spread down here so fast—especially if it's not in the stairwell."

None of us spoke right away, uncertain of what to do. It was a surprise when Chantal was the first to comment.

"It's the way the vents are set up," she murmured. "Where is the fire?"

"The living floor," said Adrian.

She frowned in thought and seemed to be coming more and more to life with each passing second. "Then this is probably just smoke. Of course . . . I shouldn't say 'just.' People often erroneously think only the fire itself is dangerous, when smoke proves just as lethal."

"You really are an Alchemist," said Adrian, with a wry smile. It was cut short as the smoke drifted closer and he began to cough.

I stepped forward, still unsteady on my feet but unwilling to do any less than what my friends had done for me today. Not so long ago, I'd worked invisibility and elemental charm spells . . . but that had been after a few weeks of moderate rest and acceptable diet. Could I do what I wanted to do now, after being in such a physically damaged state? Once again, I had no spell components to help me with the magic. It was all my will and words. Thinking back on my work summoning air for the salt ink, I called to that element now and lifted my hand. A very, very faint breeze came forth and slowly began to push the smoke away from us. It was a painstaking process since I didn't dare summon anything stronger, lest it feed an unseen fire on this floor. It was also much more exhausting than I'd expected. Even before I was halfway through, my legs began to shake, and I had to use my other hand to support me against the wall. The two Alchemists watched me in disgust and probably would've made the sign against evil if their hands weren't bound.

At last, the smoke was pushed back, opening our path to the control room. Adrian ignored my pleas that I was fine and caught hold of me with one arm, while he continued supporting Chantal with the other. Eddie looked like he wanted to help but didn't dare drop his guard on the two bound Alchemists. He ordered them into the room and then to the mysterious doorway I'd glimpsed in my nighttime investigation. Another stairwell took us up . . .

. . . and I saw sunlight for the first time in four months.

I was so stunned that I stopped walking, causing poor Adrian to stumble. On his other side, Chantal's eyes were equally wide as she too stared at the sunlight coming through the room's one small window. Gold and orange hues suggested it was nearing sunset.

"Beautiful," I murmured.

"I agree," Adrian said, and I saw his eyes were on me.

I gave him a smile, wishing I could say more, but the room was too full of other concerns. Like the entire Alchemist re-education staff huddled into a corner, with Marcus, Trey, and another guy standing over them.

"Where is everyone?" asked Eddie.

"Where's Duncan?" asked Chantal.

"I had Sheila take them to the safe house," said Marcus. "Thought it best to get them out of here." He flashed me his movie star smile. "Nice to see you in real life, Sydney." Despite his sunny grin, I'd caught a fleeting glint of anger in his eyes. Like Adrian, he too had noticed my bedraggled appearance.

"Safe house?" hissed Sheridan. I hadn't noticed her right away. "Do you really think there's any safe place you can go where we won't—"

Her threats were interrupted when a shrieking Chantal suddenly pulled away from Adrian and tried to attack Sheridan. "You!" screamed Chantal. "You did this to me! It was always you, no matter who was doing it. You giving the orders!" There was a desperate, animalistic nature to her, and I felt a pang in my chest as I wondered if I might have become the same way if I'd been locked away that long.

Her attack didn't get very far, as other Alchemists closed rank around Sheridan. I hurried forward, still weak, and tried to pull Chantal back as gently as I could. "It's over," I said. "Let it go."

"You know what she did!" The hate and pain in Chantal's face was a mirror to some of my own dark emotion I too had locked inside me but had yet to release. "You know what a monster she is!"

"We aren't the monsters in this world," hissed Sheridan. "We're fighting them, and you betrayed your own kind."

Chantal lunged again, and this time, Adrian helped me over. "It's done," I insisted. "She can't hurt you anymore."

"Is that what you think, Sydney?" A sneer marred Sheridan's lovely features. "Do you really think you can walk away from all of this? There's no place you can go. There's no place any of you can go, but *you* especially, Sydney. This is your fault, and no Alchemist will rest until we've hunted you down and—"

Once again, her dramatic moment was interrupted, this

time by the fire alarms silencing and the sprinkler system coming on. "Well, well," said Marcus, as water drenched us all. "I guess Grif got it to work."

"We should get out of here," said the ex-Alchemist I didn't know. "Even if their reinforcements are miles away, odds are good someone got a cell phone call out."

Marcus nodded in agreement. "Let's just make sure this lot's contained."

"Here," said Adrian. He emptied out his jacket pocket of a couple dozen zip-ties. "I thought some extras might come in handy."

Trey and Marcus's associate bound up all the Alchemists, and Marcus himself collected all the weapons he could find. "No way am I leaving these here. We'll take them and destroy them." He surveyed his team's handiwork and nodded in satisfaction. "Let's hit the road."

I turned to follow, but Sheridan's voice gave me pause. "There's nowhere you can go!" she called. "You can't just walk away from this!"

I glanced back, but before I could answer, something small caught my eye. In the tussle with Chantal, the top two buttons of Sheridan's shirt had come undone. I strode forward and reached my hand out toward her, making her recoil. No doubt she thought I was going to cast a spell on her. Instead, I ripped Adrian's necklace from her neck.

"This," I said, "is mine."

"You don't deserve it," she hissed. "Don't think this is over. You've just replaced Marcus Finch as the Alchemist's most wanted."

I made no response and simply fastened the cross around

my own neck. With that, I turned and followed my friends out without a backward glance.

Sunset or not, it was scorching outside, and our wet clothes suddenly became a blessing. "Where are we?" I asked.

"Death Valley," said Marcus. "You can't say the Alchemists don't have a flair for the dramatic."

"That, or the land was cheap," I said.

Trey astonished me by suddenly engulfing me in a giant hug. "You have no idea how much I've missed you, Melbourne."

I felt my eyes brim with tears. "I've missed you too. Thank you . . . thank you for this. I don't know how to repay you."

"No repayment needed." A small frown crossed his features as he looked me over. "Except to maybe rest and get something to eat."

Another hug swallowed me as Marcus took his turn. "Overachiever," he said, grinning down at me. "Replacing me on their list."

I smiled back, hiding just how much Sheridan's words had truly hit home with me. "Thank you, Marcus. I'm sorry for when I said you just talk and don't act." I gestured around us. "This . . . this was some pretty big acting."

"Yeah, well, you've been more than a little inspiring to me and to others," he said. "And probably to that lot we pulled out of this place too."

Eddie came last, and as we sized each other up, the tears hovering in my eyes finally spilled. "Eddie, I'm so sorry I lied to you that night."

He shook his head and pulled me to him. I heard tears choke up his voice. "I'm sorry I couldn't stop them. I'm sorry I wasn't protection enough."

"Oh, Eddie," I said, sniffling. "You're the *best* protection. No one could have a better guardian than you. Or a better friend."

Even Marcus looked touched. "You guys, I hate to break this up, but we need to get out of here. We can laugh and cry at the rendezvous spot."

I wiped my eyes and gave Eddie one last, quick hug. "Do me a favor," I told him. "Go back to Jill."

"Of course," he said. "I will as soon as everyone's safe. She's my duty."

"I don't mean go back to her because of your assignment. Go back to her because you love her."

His jaw nearly dropped. I don't think anyone had ever come out and called him on it like that, but after what I'd been through, niceties and dancing around the truth suddenly seemed like a waste of valuable time. I stepped back to join Adrian, and the one named Grif held up a set of keys.

"I brought the Mustang around while I was out. Who's driving it?"

"We are," I said, surprising everyone. I took the keys from him. "That is . . . you have another car?"

"A Prius," said Adrian dismally.

I did a mental headcount, verifying they'd all fit, and then put on what I hoped was a lovesick smile. "Is it okay if Adrian and I drive separately and meet the rest of you there? I . . . I'd like some alone time."

"There's going to be no legroom in that thing," exclaimed Trey. But then he looked at me, and his expression softened. "But far be it from me to stand in the way of true love. I'll suffer for your happiness, Melbourne. Like always."

Adrian got a bag out of the Prius and then gave the keys

to Marcus. In return, Marcus gifted me with something unexpected. "I had these made up for you a while ago," he explained. "Take them now, just in case. I'm going to get some for the other detainees too."

He handed me two driver's licenses. One was my original from Utah, which I'd hardly used in Palm Springs while living as Sydney Melrose. I was amazed he'd managed to get a hold of a copy from the DMV. But that wasn't nearly as startling as the second license, a fake one from Maryland with a most unexpected alias.

"Really?" I asked. "Misty Steele?"

Marcus shrugged. "It was Adrian's suggestion."

"It's badass," insisted Adrian.

I gave Marcus a quick hug of thanks. One thing we'd learned among the Alchemists was that when trying to blend in with the modern world, identification was critical. Good fake IDs were hard to find, but the work on the Misty Steele one was flawless. He and the others piled into the car, and Eddie shot me one last parting smile that nearly choked me up again.

"I never thought I'd see Castile brought to tears," said Adrian as he started up the Mustang. "This really hit him hard. Hell, it hit all of us hard, but he really beat himself up for it. He never forgave himself for you giving him the slip."

"Let's hope he can," I said, putting my seatbelt on. "Because it's about to happen again. We aren't meeting them at the safe house."

CHAPTER 18
ADRIAN

FOR A MOMENT, there was a part of me that was a little more in love with her than ever. You had to admire a woman who'd just walked out of incredible, horrific conditions and had wielded magic without missing a beat, not to mention standing strong in the face of her tormentors. Someone else might've broken down or immediately started expounding on their terrible experiences. But, no. Sydney was not only ready for action, she was also ready to defy carefully made, well-reasoned, and safe plans.

It was admirable. Also, out of the question.

"Sydney, no. Marcus has this under control. What we did back there? The planning that involved? Hell, Eddie and I were good backup, but most of the work there . . . that was all Marcus, all his foresight. He's looked into this place we're meeting at. It's safe until he can find a way to hide all of us out there in the world." When she still looked stubborn, I added, "This is what he does. He's hidden others. He's hidden himself! He knows what he's doing."

"He's hidden a few people at a time, Adrian," she said calmly. "Never more than a dozen. That's not going to be easy, and it'll be a while before he can split them up. Those people fresh from solitary can't be on their own! They need guidance, not just a place to hide. He's got his work cut out for them, and *I'm* a liability."

Across the parking lot, I saw the Prius pull out. I knew where the rendezvous spot was, but we needed to follow soon. "Sydney, you're not a liability. You're the main reason he pulled off this whole operation and rescued them."

"And now I'm endangering them." She looked at me, her brown eyes so earnest as the setting sun illuminated her. "Adrian, you heard Sheridan. I'm their target now. If they get even a hint of my whereabouts, the Alchemists are going to throw everything they've got at me—and that'll put the others at risk if I'm with them. It's safer for them if you and I head out on our own. We'll have an easier time disappearing if it's just you and me anyway."

Now that was a compelling argument, far more than the safety of the others. That wasn't to say I was a cold-hearted bastard who didn't care about them—because I did. I hated what they'd been through. But my first and most important priority had always been Sydney, and there was something to be said for two people disappearing instead of twenty. The question was, did having a sound plan offset the numbers? Because right now, a plan was the one thing we were missing.

"Where do you propose we go?" I asked at last.

"I don't know," she admitted. "First we just need to put some distance between us and this hellhole. I'll have to think on where the safest place would be—inside or outside of the

United States. And I'm not saying we won't ever get Marcus's help again. We might very well need it. But splitting off might mean the Alchemists chase us instead of him."

"You want that?" I asked incredulously.

"No, of course not. I don't want them to follow any of us. But if they do, I have faith that you and I can lose them easier than the others." She frowned in thought. "Okay, you get us on the road, and let me see your phone." I handed it over and pulled out onto the road, more than glad to be getting away from this place. "Where was he taking them?" she asked.

"South. Toward Mexico, though we planned to meet up with each other again about an hour from Death Valley. He didn't know if he was going to cross the border or not, but there was a place near it he was going to hide out."

She nodded and scanned a few things on my phone before setting it down. "Okay, then we go north. Northeast, actually." I couldn't see her with my eyes on the road, but I could hear a smile in her voice. "You still any good at poker?"

"Why? Are you finally going to play strip poker with me? I've only asked like a hundred times."

"No such luck. Yet. But we're going to need some cash, and Nevada's right around the corner. I bet there are casinos as soon as we cross the border."

"I know there are," I told her. "I've driven through it twice this week. I don't have much to offer up as a bet, so if you're hoping for an overnight fortune, I can't help."

"I'll settle for a hotel room, dinner, and a change of clothes."

"That I can do. Although . . ." I gave her a sidelong look. "I thought you didn't approve of me using spirit to play cards?" I couldn't actually read people's minds, of course, but seeing auras was almost as good. I could always tell who was bluffing and who was telling the truth.

She sighed and leaned back into her seat. "I don't. Or of you using spirit for anything. But these are kind of unusual circumstances we're facing. Maybe once this is all over, and we're settled, you can go back on your pills."

"You wouldn't be with me now if I'd stayed on those pills," I said quietly.

"I know . . . and you know I'm grateful. The spirit issue is one we'll have to deal with again sometime, but . . ."

"Right now we have bigger problems?" I finished.

"Nothing's bigger to me than you," she said firmly. "How have you been feeling? You said in one of our dreams that you stopped the pills as soon as I was gone. How has that been? You seem like you're doing well, like you have the mood swings under control."

There was a note of hope in her voice, and I couldn't bear to tell her that the reason I had the mood swings under control was because they'd been replaced instead by a delusion of my dead aunt.

"I'm alive and well here, aren't I?" I said glibly. "Don't try to change the subject. *You've* gone through a hell of a lot more than me."

"We don't need to talk about it now," she said.

We fell into silence, both of us keeping our own secrets of what we'd suffered in the other's absence. I wondered if we were trying to protect each other or simply didn't want to admit to our own fears and weaknesses. Not that I thought Sydney was weak in the least. But I'd seen her aura when we were back at the re-education center, around the other Alchemists, and there was definitely an edge of fear surrounding her and the other detainees. I knew she probably thought that was a failing.

"Well," I said, trying to cheer her up. "At least open your presents."

"You got me a 'congratulations on getting out of re-education' gift?" she asked.

"Not exactly. Just check the bag that's over there."

She did, exclaiming in surprise as she opened it. "My God! If I'd had these amulets in re-education, it would've made things a heck of a lot—Hopper!"

Out of the corner of my eye, I saw her lift the little golden dragon. When she spoke again, I thought she might start crying.

"Oh, Hopper. I've thought about him, you know. I wondered what had happened to him and what he must be going through. . . ." She started to speak the words of a spell and then stopped. "He'll be hungry. Let's wait until we get some food. I wouldn't mind a real meal myself."

"That I can accommodate even without hitting the poker tables," I told her. "What are you in the mood for? Steak? Sushi? Name it, and it's yours."

She laughed. "Nothing that fancy for me. I don't think my stomach could take it just yet after—" Her laughter faded.

"After what?" I asked quietly.

"Later," she said. "We'll talk about it later."

I sighed. "So we keep saying. When is later going to be?"

"When we're more than a few minutes out from the Alchemist holding facility," she returned. "We need to focus on this escape."

She had a point, but that didn't mean I liked it. In fact, it troubled me more and more as the drive continued, not knowing the full extent of what she'd been through. She was quick to tell me she loved me and had missed me and that nothing made her happier than being with me again. I believed all of that, but it didn't mean I could so easily let the past go.

Aunt Tatiana whispered: *Are you sure that's true? Maybe you don't actually want to know what happened to her. You saw a glimpse of what it was like in there. Do you want confirmation of the atrocities she suffered?*

If Sydney was able to endure it, then the least I can do is handle hearing about it, I silently retorted. And yet . . . I wondered if my phantom aunt had a point.

We crossed into Nevada about an hour and a half later, with no sign of pursuit. We did, however, get a call from Marcus just as we were pulling into a small hotel with an adjacent casino.

"Did you get lost?" asked Marcus. He didn't sound mad exactly, but something in his tone told me he knew perfectly well that we had not, in fact, gotten lost.

"More like we took a detour," I said cheerfully.

He groaned. "Adrian, we hashed this out! Everything's gone perfectly until now. Why would you even think about deviating from the plan?"

"Um, because that's how we roll?"

Sydney took the phone from me before I could offer any more compelling explanations. She used the same arguments she'd made with me, though Marcus wasn't as swayed by her beautiful eyes as I was. It was clear he wasn't won over by the end of the call, and Sydney finally ended it with a vague, "We'll be in touch."

I offered to take her out for a nice dinner, but she didn't even want to go to the hotel's front desk in her khaki clothes, let alone a public meal. I checked us in and discovered I had enough cash for a small suite. It wasn't anything glamorous—certainly nowhere near as posh as the place she and I had stayed when snowed in in Pennsylvania—but it had a separate bedroom and larger bathroom than the hotel's regular rooms. Maybe I didn't know all the details of what she'd gone through, but I knew enough to say she deserved an upgrade.

The look on her face when she sat on the bed confirmed as much. It was just average to me, but from her delighted sigh, you'd think it was made of angel wing feathers. She stretched out on it and closed her eyes.

"This. Is. Glorious," she stated. I stretched out beside her and felt my chest swell with joy. Once, I'd thought that if I was in bed with her, there was only one activity I'd want, but honestly, right now? I was pretty sure there was no greater contentment than just seeing her safe and happy and within arm's reach. After so much time apart, her very presence was a miracle.

"There's a shopping center across the street," I said. "I'll grab us some stuff . . . unless you want to come with me? I'm worried about leaving you alone. . . ."

She shook her head. "I'll be fine. Besides, there's an amulet in Ms. Terwilliger's bag that could blow a hole open in that wall. Just hurry back."

I fully intended to. I sprinted across the street, only realizing halfway through that I was violating basic rules of Moroi safety by going outside at night alone in a strange area. Hell, we were taught at a young age that being out alone at night in known areas was dangerous. I'd never imagined I'd reach a point in my life where Strigoi were no longer my first priority when it came to personal safety.

I'd undressed Sydney enough to know her size and bought her some basic clothes and toiletries. At a neighboring deli, I opted for turkey sandwiches and a variety of small snacks, hoping that'd be bland enough after whatever her stomach had been through. I cut myself off there, since I still needed money for poker stakes. The whole round trip took about twenty minutes, but when I got back to the hotel, Sydney wasn't in the suite's living room or bedroom. My heart stopped. I felt like someone in a fairy tale, who'd just woken up to realize everything he thought he'd won was just a dream, falling apart to stardust before his eyes.

I noticed then that the bathroom door wasn't quite closed and that the light was on. I hesitated outside. "Sydney?"

"Come in," she said.

I opened the door and was nearly knocked over with the cloying scent of jasmine. Sydney was in the tub, nearly up to her neck in bubbles, and the room felt like a sauna. "How hot is that bath?" I asked, eyeing the steam hovering in the air.

She laughed. "As hot as I could make it. You don't know how long it's been since I was really, truly warm." A slender arm reached out and picked up a small plastic bottle with the hotel's logo on it. "Or just smelled something . . . pretty. Everything was so sterile in re-education, almost medicinal smelling. I kind of went crazy with this stuff and used the whole bottle."

"We'll have them send up more if you like it that much." I lifted up the bottle and read the label. It was just a cheap bath gel. "Or get you some real jasmine perfume when I have my poker winnings in hand."

"You don't understand," she said, sinking a little deeper into the suds. "After what I've been through . . . this stuff *is* the height of luxury. I don't need anything fancier."

"Maybe we could talk about what you've been through," I suggested. "You can help me understand."

"Another time," she said evasively. "If you brought food back, I'd rather have that right now."

"And leave your boiling cauldron behind?"

"There'll be more baths," she said simply. "And I already managed to shave my legs, which was half my goal. Four months. Ugh."

She then stood up without warning, treating me to a view of her body, naked except for a few clinging suds and wisps of steam. It warmed my heart—and my blood—that things had stayed the same enough for her to not feel self-conscious around me. I had to work to keep my shock off my face, though. I had noticed she'd lost weight when we got her out of the facility, but I hadn't realized the extent of it until now. I could practically count her ribs, and even she, with her history of obsessive weight control, had to know that she'd far exceeded healthy limitations.

"Not what you expected, huh?" she asked in a sad voice.

I wrapped a towel around her and drew her close to me. "I expected to see the most beautiful woman in the world, to feel my heart skip a beat in her presence, and to want to carry her off to bed for a night neither of us will forget. So to answer your question, I got exactly what I expected."

A smile split her face, and she leaned into me. "Oh, Adrian."

In the other room, I showed her my purchases, and she laughed as she sifted through them, pausing to lift up a fuchsia T-shirt. "Have you ever seen me wear this color?"

"No," I said. "And it's about time, especially after those." I pointed at the pile of khakis on the floor. "Which we're going to burn."

She laughed again, and it was the most exquisite sound I'd ever heard. She went with the fuchsia shirt and a pair of white shorts. "You're the best," she told me.

I soon found out I wasn't the only one in her heart, however, when we settled down to eat our dinner. She summoned Hopper out of his inert state, and tears spilled from her eyes when he transformed from a rigid glittering statue to a dull-scaled, weak little creature that was nearly as skinny as she was. She cradled him to her chest and rocked him, telling him the kinds of nonsensical things people do to comfort pets and small children. She told him over and over that everything would be okay now, and I almost wondered if she were comforting herself as much as him. She kept breaking off little bites of her turkey sandwich for him and was halfway through when I finally realized what was happening.

"Hey, hey," I said. "Save some for yourself."

"He's so hungry," she said. "He can't even make that little pathetic mewling sound he usually does when he wants food."

"And that extra-small T-shirt is still too big on you. Finish your sandwich, and he can have my crusts."

She reluctantly handed him over, and I swore Hopper glared at me for depriving him of her attention. I loved the little guy too, but there was no way he was getting preferential treatment over Sydney. She ate the rest of her sandwich under my watchful eye but wouldn't touch any of the assorted candy bars I'd bought, no matter my urging. I honestly would've liked to have seen her eat them all but knew better than to point out how much she needed sugar and fat.

Hopper fell asleep after that, and I thought Sydney would too. Instead, she invited me to the bedroom and drew me on to the bed with her. "You sure you don't need some rest?" I asked.

She wrapped her arms around my neck. "I need you."

Our lips met in our first real kiss since she'd been taken away. It set me aflame, reminding me just how agonizingly much I'd missed her. I'd meant what I told her: It didn't matter how thin she'd become. She was still the most beautiful woman in the world to me, and there was no one else I wanted more. Not only that, there was no one else whose presence I felt more *right* in. Even in the midst of our escape from Death Valley and getting situated in these uncertain conditions, there was a comfortable certainty that just in being with her, there was nothing that couldn't be accomplished.

I trailed kisses down her neck and mentally took back what I'd said about the bath gel being cheap. The jasmine mingled with her own natural scent was intoxicating, far better than any perfume I'd ever gotten her. Her legs felt like silk under my touch, and I was astonished at how quickly my desire ramped up—even more astonished at how hers did too. I worried it might be too much too soon, but when I tried to dissuade her again, she only pulled me closer.

"You don't understand," she murmured, running one of her hands through my hair. "You don't understand how much I need this, how much I need you and to remember I'm alive and in love. They try to take that from you in that place, but I never forgot. I never forgot you, Adrian, and now that you're here, I . . ."

She couldn't finish, and she didn't have to. I knew exactly what she meant. We kissed again, the kind of kiss that bound us in way that was so much more than physical. I was trying to pull her shirt off when she suddenly paused and asked breathlessly, "You *did* get something at the store, right?"

My brain was too addled with lust and thoughts of her to fully process what she was saying. "Huh? I got lots of things."

"Protection," she said meaningfully. "Wasn't there a drugstore across the street? Bigger selection there than the other place."

"I—oh. That kind of thing. Uh, no, I didn't. I guess I forgot."

Before Sydney had been taken, she'd been on the pill, and I'd never really had to think about birth control. I think she preferred it that way, not really trusting anyone but herself to handle such important matters. I sighed.

"Don't I get points for being more concerned about feeding you and dressing you in bright colors than I was about getting you into bed?"

She placed a light kiss against my lips and smiled. "You get lots of points. But unfortunately, you don't get this."

I leaned over her and brushed golden strands of hair from her face. "Do you know how torn I am right now? I mean, I'm disappointed, obviously . . . but at the same time, I'm kind of in love with you even more for still being your meticulously careful self, in spite of everything that's happened."

"Really?" She shifted so that I could rest my head on her chest. "My meticulous and careful nature is what you love?"

"There're so many things to love, Sage. Who can keep track?"

As frustrating as it was to be unexpectedly denied that physical consummation, I still found myself basking in that earlier sense of bliss that just came from being near her. Did

I want sex? Sure, but I wanted her more—her presence, her laughter, her spirit. The churning hormones in my body soon quieted, and I found more than enough ecstasy just lying in her arms. And when she dozed off soon thereafter, I had a feeling my oversight in not going to the drugstore might have been for the best, no matter what she'd said. Getting her back to full health was most important right now, and I was pretty sure rest and candy bars were the best way to help.

As for me, I was too restless. Part of it was just the day's excitement and being with her. Another part was that it was still earlier than I was used to going to sleep. I loved being entwined with her, but after a while, I cautiously slipped out of bed and tucked the covers around her. I studied her fondly a few moments before turning off the lights and creeping out to the living room, careful to close the door behind me so as not to disturb her.

I settled onto the couch with a candy bar and watched TV at a low volume, needing to settle my spinning mind. I knew Sydney would undoubtedly have all sorts of plans and deductions that were better than mine, but it was hard not to think about the future. Where could we go? Was there a safe place? And whether it was with Marcus or on our own, what exactly was it we were going to do with our lives? So much energy had just been spent on being together—itself a daunting task—that we'd hardly ever paused to discuss what we'd truly do. One of our outlandish escape plans? College for her? An obscure life in the middle of nowhere? Fighting for the freedom of Moroi and ex-Alchemists?

There will be no peace for you, whispered Aunt Tatiana, in one of her more antagonistic moods. *No peace for you and your human girl. This was a mistake.*

No, I told her. *We'll make this work. We have to.*

How then? she demanded.

I had no answers after staring at the TV for over an hour and was considering going to bed when I heard screams from the bedroom. In a flash, I was off the couch, hurtling toward the bedroom. I ripped the door open and flung on the light, drawing spirit's power to me to attack the raging band of Alchemists I expected to see coming through the window. But there was no one—only Sydney, sitting up in bed, her screams piercing the night. I let go of spirit and hurried to the bed, pulling her to me. To my astonishment, she struck out against me.

"No! No! Don't touch me!"

"Sydney, it's me," I said, trying to catch hold of her hands before she did real damage. Even half-asleep, she'd apparently retained lessons from our old self-defense instructor, Malachi Wolfe. "It's okay. You're okay. Everything's okay."

She struggled against me a bit more, and in the poor lighting, I could see a frantic, terrified look in her eyes. At last, her thrashing stilled, and recognition lit her features. She buried her face in my chest and began to cry—not the wistful tears of love from her reunion with Eddie or the mournful ones for Hopper's sad state. These were full-on sobs that wracked her body and rendered her incoherent, no matter how much I tried to comfort her or ask what was wrong. I could do nothing but hold her and stroke her hair, waiting for her to calm down. When she did, intermittent sobs still occasionally broke up her speech.

"I . . . I thought I was back there, Adrian. In re-education. When I woke up. It was so dark there—I mean, until I joined the others. But when I was in that cell, there was no light. They literally kept me in the dark. It hurt when I got out—looking at the light. Three months, Adrian. Three months I was in a cell smaller than our bathroom here, in the dark. I thought I could handle it . . . I thought I was stronger than it . . . but when I woke up, and you were gone, and I couldn't see anything . . ."

She broke down in tears again, and it was all I could do to get a grip on my own emotions. I was sad for her, of course. Sad and hurt that she'd had to suffer like she had. But at the same time I was angry, so angry that if I'd known any of this back at the re-education center, I would've been right by Chantal's side—to help her, not pull her back. I wasn't given to violence or even anger that much, but a rage burned in me that the Alchemists could've done this to someone so bright and brilliant, who'd served them so faithfully and would've continued that service if there'd only been a way for her to do so while being true to her own heart. They'd tried to break her—not just her thoughts but her very self. Equally appalling was the realization that it might not be over yet, that getting her out of that place wasn't enough. What kind of mental damage had they done? Was this going to haunt us the rest of our lives, even if she was free? The implications were staggering, and in that moment, I hated the Alchemists as I'd never hated anyone else.

Destroy them! Aunt Tatiana said. *We'll find them and rip them limb from limb!*

"You're not there anymore," I told Sydney, squeezing her tightly. "You're with me, and I'm not going to let anything happen to you ever again."

She clung to me and stammered out, "I don't want to sleep with the lights out."

"You don't ever have to sleep in the dark again," I swore to her.

I stayed in bed with her this time, lights on as promised. It took her a little longer than it had before to calm down and fall asleep, but when she did, I could tell it was a deep and much-needed sleep. My own sleep wasn't quite as solid, both because of the lights and because I kept waking to check on her. It was worth my own discomfort, though, to know she was safe and secure.

She woke up bright and refreshed, giving no sign that last night's breakdown had ever happened. Best of all, she had an appetite. "I don't know what to order," she said, scanning the room service menu with Hopper on her lap. "Obviously, I'm going to get coffee—you have no idea how badly I want that—but I'm torn between the farmer's omelet and the blueberry pancakes."

I leaned down and kissed the top of her head. "Get both."

"How's our money?" she asked wryly.

"About to get better. I'll head downstairs to the casino today. You want to come and be my good luck charm?"

She shook her head. "I'd rather stay here and eat. Don't you want something?"

"They'll give me coffee down there. That's all I need for now."

That, and I could've used some blood, which was another issue we hadn't taken into consideration when we'd started this plan. Like so many things, though, that was for later. I wasn't in dire straits yet, but it would have to be dealt with.

After last night, I thought Sydney might have an issue with me leaving, but she was fearless with sunlight and Jackie's bag of tricks around. She showered with me—which was both a delight and a torment—and sent me off when her giant breakfast showed up. "Don't give it all to Hopper," I warned. She grinned and waved goodbye.

Down in the casino, things were quieter than they would've been at night but still pretty active. That was the beauty of Nevada. No matter the time of day, people always wanted to try their luck. I found a table with four other players with easy-to-read auras and settled down to business. Even though I had a considerable edge, I couldn't flaunt it, lest I attract the attention of those running the casino. So, while I won the majority of the time, I made sure to lose every so often too, to allay suspicion. I also offered to buy a round of morning Bloody Marys, which went a long way to further goodwill and worsen the others' game play.

I was nowhere near retirement, but after a couple hours, I'd built up a decent enough amount to take back to Sydney. I planned on doing a couple more hands first, and as I did a quick aura check when the bet came around, something caught my attention. It had actually caught my attention earlier, but I hadn't given it much thought. When I used spirit to look at my competitors' auras, I inadvertently caught sight of everyone else's around me. What was odd today was that there were a lot of people with yellow in their auras. Yellow—and occasionally orange, which I was also seeing a lot of—was a thinking person's aura, an academic's aura. Sydney's aura had a lot of yellow. It wasn't something you generally saw a lot of chronic gamblers with, certainly not this time of day. Those who only gambled for occasional fun and novelty came out at night, not early mornings. This was the hardcore lot, the desperate lot . . . and their auras should've reflected as much.

I pondered this as I made my bet and played out the hand. I

ended up splitting the pot with the guy next to me, much to his delight. As the next hand was dealt, I checked the auras around me again and was once more struck by the overabundance of yellow. I also noticed something else. No one with a yellow aura was directly looking at me, but they were arranged around me pretty symmetrically in the room. Just me. When I looked past them, the colors of other patrons shifted back to what I would have expected in a casino.

Yellow. A thinking person's color.

An Alchemist's color.

When the next hand started, I waved myself out and took out my cell phone, wishing I'd thought to pick up a prepaid one for Sydney. That would have to be our next priority for sure. Trying not to look panicked, I typed out a text to Marcus.

Call the Silver Springs Hotel in West Side, NV, and ask for room 301. Tell Sydney to pack right now and meet me at the car.

I was about to hit "send" when an explosion from somewhere outside rocked the casino. People gasped, and glasses rattled.

"Never mind," I muttered, deleting the message and heading for the door.

CHAPTER 19

SYDNEY

I ATE AND ATE, AND it was wonderful. I hadn't thought I'd be able to so soon, but after a real night of good rest, my body seemed ready to start accepting what it needed. Hopper shared my giant breakfast, of course, and I was pleased to see he too looked a lot better.

I put on another of Adrian's brightly colored shirt choices (teal this time) and debated going down to the casino to cheer him on. I knew he'd like seeing me out and about, but each time I thought about facing the crowd downstairs, something tensed within me. I longed to reenter the normal world, but I just wasn't quite ready for some things. It was overwhelming enough to turn on the news and hear references to big events that had happened while I was in re-education. Journalists spoke about them like they were common knowledge to everyone—which they probably were, if you hadn't just had four months of your life taken away.

I made catching up on the modern world my new goal,

308

and after packing everything up, I settled on the couch with Hopper while I also pondered our next step. After this, we'd have to keep moving, and as much as I hated to admit it, our next task would have to be trading the Mustang for something less conspicuous. From there, we had to make the same choice that Moroi always made in strategizing how best to stay away from Strigoi: Go somewhere heavily populated or totally deserted? Each had its own pros and cons.

A knock at the door made me jump. Immediately, my eyes darted to the knob, verifying that the "Do Not Disturb" sign was gone. We'd hung it outside last night. I stayed frozen and waited to see if the knocker would recognize their error and go away. A few moments later, another knock came, this time with, "Housekeeping." That sealed it. Room service would knock, despite the sign, if you'd placed an order, but hotel housekeeping almost never did. Nervously, I crept up to the chained door and dared a peek out the eyeglass. A young woman stood out there, smiling pleasantly and wearing a hotel uniform. She certainly looked innocuous, and I wondered if perhaps our sign had fallen down.

Just then, something in my peripheral vision caught my attention. A shadow off to her side—that didn't belong to her. It shifted slightly, and I realized there was another person standing near her, out of the eyeglass's site. Maybe more than one person. Quietly, I backed away and murmured the spell that turned Hopper into a statue before putting him into the shopping bag that held our clothes. I slung it and Ms. Terwilliger's bag over my shoulder and began assessing my escape routes. The bedroom window wasn't big enough to escape out of. The living room had a small glass sliding door that opened up to a Juliet balcony . . . on the third floor.

I stepped outside onto it and surveyed my options. There weren't many. Our room overlooked the parking lot, and there was nothing on the ground to break my fall. Directly under my balcony was another, and I wondered if I was physically up to managing that climb. Six months ago, I would have said yes. Now, I wasn't so sure. Before I could decide, a large black SUV pulled up, and two men in sunglasses got out, stationing themselves so that they could watch me. I could just barely make out an earpiece on one of them, and he looked like he was speaking softly.

It must have been to the group outside my room, because the knocking suddenly took on a much greater intensity. They also gave up on any pretenses of housekeeping: "Sydney, we know you're in there. Don't make this any harder than it is." This was followed by the sound of a hotel keycard sliding in the lock, but when they tried to open the door, the chain caught it. I stepped back inside and saw an eye appear in the crack formed by the chain. "You have nowhere to go, Sydney."

"Tell your guys outside they're going to want to clear away from their car pretty quickly!" I yelled to her.

I stepped back to the balcony and took out one of the amulets Ms. Terwilliger had given me. With most of the work having gone into the amulet's creation, it only required a small spell to activate. I spoke the words and hurled it toward the SUV, following up with a secondary air spell that propelled the amulet farther than I could on my own. Whether they realized the impending danger or had gotten a heads-up from their colleague, the men in sunglasses ran away, diving to the ground as the SUV exploded. I ducked as well, wincing at the heat and glad there was no one else out there who might have been injured.

Once the initial explosion passed, I wasted no time in getting up and climbing over the balcony's edge. The bars and scrollwork in it provided lots of hand- and footholds, and I had no difficulty clinging to the outside. It was when I tried to climb down and swing myself onto my neighbor's balcony that the results of four months of minimal physical activity showed. My upper body strength was nowhere near what it had been, and it suddenly became overwhelming to hang there, let alone swing myself onto the other balcony. I managed to climb down as far as I could, until my hands held the bottom parts of the balcony and my feet dangled only a few inches from the other one's railing. Touching it would be easy if I dropped. Falling inside—instead of outside—would not be. The muscles in my arms screamed, and my grip started to slip.

"Sydney!"

I recognized Adrian's voice but couldn't see him. I could only tell that he was somewhere behind me, possibly near the SUV.

"Let go!" he yelled.

"I'll fall," I called back.

"No you won't!"

I released my hold, and for half a heartbeat, there was nothing to stop me from falling to the ground. Then, an unseen force pushed me hard on the back, and I went tumbling over the balcony's edge, landing ungracefully—but safely—in it. I was confused about what had saved me until I turned toward Adrian, where he stood in the parking lot a healthy distance from the burning SUV. The Alchemists in sunglasses were coming toward him, and he fixed his gaze on them, knocking them over with an invisible wall of power, just like he'd used on me. I winced at that kind of telekinetic work, knowing it took an incredible amount of spirit and that he couldn't do it all day.

"Is the door open?" he called.

I tried it and nodded.

"Meet me at the place I forgot to go last night. Go!"

The Alchemists were starting to get to their feet, and he took off into the parking lot, running behind the flaming car. Sirens sounded in the distance, and gawkers were starting to come out. I hurried into the hotel room I'd landed outside of, relieved to see it was unoccupied. I cut through it and emerged into a second floor hallway and pondered my next move. *Meet me at the place I forgot to go last night.*

It made sense we wouldn't go to the car. The Alchemists undoubtedly had that staked out. But where did he mean? A moment later, I knew. To one side, the hall led to an emergency exit. To the other, the stairs and elevator led down to the lobby and casino. I tried to think like an Alchemist and went with the stairs to the lobby. An obscure back exit would be monitored for sure.

Downstairs, on the main floor, I found chaos, which was just what I needed. Everyone had heard the car outside, but no one knew exactly what had happened. Some people were trying to evacuate, while others, hearing the fire was outside, wanted to stay in. Hotel security seemed to be waffling on what to do, though one guard finally decided it would be safe to let people out of an exit door on the side opposite the SUV fire. I quickly joined the people gathering there and tried to determine if there were any Alchemists to look out for. I'd have no idea who they were if they were in hotel uniforms or even regular clothes. My biggest clue that someone was safe was if they were pushing past me, far more concerned with themselves than me.

I'd nearly reached the door when I made eye contact with a man in a tropical-print shirt who was definitely more interested in me. He began pushing his way through to me, and I had the good fortune of a security guard standing nearby, overseeing the evacuation. "My room faces the SUV that blew up," I told the guard. "And I saw that man there by it just before it happened!"

A claim like that might have normally been discounted, except that I think details of what had happened were still so fresh that me specifically mentioning the SUV lent credibility. Plus, the guard was young and had the eager look of someone who wanted to distinguish himself. He stepped past me, blocking the man in the Hawaiian shirt, who was only a couple people away now.

"Sir," said the guard, "can I talk to you?"

The man, impatient and fixated on me, made the mistake of trying to get past the guard, who shoved him back and began calling for backup.

"Let go of me!" yelled the Alchemist. "I need to get through!"

"Sir, get down on the ground!"

I didn't stick around to see what happened. I let them fight it out and finally slipped through the door. There, another well-meaning guard was trying to keep all the evacuees in an orderly group. I ignored him and immediately broke off from the others, trying to get my bearings. We'd actually come out near the front of the hotel, and across a busy boulevard, I could see the shopping center Adrian had been to last night. I began running toward it, wishing we were in a much busier city—like

Las Vegas—where I'd have a crowd to lose myself in. As it was, I was pretty conspicuous, and I soon heard shouts. Glancing back, I saw two more people in sunglasses charging toward me. I was more exhausted from my earlier climb than I'd expected, and that type of physical exhaustion translated to difficulty with magic use.

I was nearing a crosswalk that would take me across to the shopping center, and I began to slow down. Frantically, I wondered what on earth they really expected to do. We were in public, in broad daylight. Did they think they could just grab me off the street? Yes, I realized, that's exactly what they'd do, and they'd find a way to justify it later and write it off to any witnesses. They did it all the time with supernatural phenomena. How much harder could it be with a human abduction?

The light changed, and I sprinted across the street, moving as fast as my out-of-shape muscles would carry me. It wasn't enough, though. The Alchemists were gaining. I reached the shopping complex's parking lot and headed straight into the superstore my clothes had come from. Without looking back to see how close my pursuers were, I darted straight into an aisle of stationery and murmured the weak invisibility spell. I felt the magic settle around me, and then I hurried out into another aisle in case they'd seen my original destination. No one immediately came after me, and I took a roundabout way through some other aisles to finally circle back and get a vantage on the store's entrance. One of the Alchemists was stationed at the door, and I had to assume the other was searching the store. With them actively looking and expecting to see me, the spell wouldn't hold if we crossed paths. There was a much more powerful invisibility amulet in my bag, but I hated to waste it when I was so close to meeting up with Adrian. I either had to find another way out of here—without running into the roaming Alchemist—or distract the one by the door.

Continually ducking and looking all around me, I zigzagged toward a display of bathing suits that looked like they were made of pretty flammable material. Lighting a fire wasn't a problem for me. I could do a fireball in my sleep. The problem was, I didn't want to attract attention right away. As soon as my fire was noticed, all attention—including the Alchemists'—would head that way, which was what I wanted. But I needed to be well away from there when it happened.

I closed my eyes and summoned up the smallest of sparks in my hand. It was difficult keeping it from growing because my work with Ms. Terwilliger had focused on making the biggest, baddest fireballs imaginable. This one, though, needed to be just a kindling, like I'd made in re-education. Once I had it sustained, I set it on top of a khaki pair of swim trunks—out of principle—and then backed up as quickly as possible, crouching near some carts. Although I could see tendrils of smoke, the swimsuit didn't actually ignite as quickly as I'd expected, and long, agonizing moments went by as I waited for people to notice it. The Alchemist at the door held his position, and then to my horror, I saw the second one approaching, obliviously unaware that he was headed straight toward me. I was trying to figure out how to get out of his line of sight when someone shouted by the display, and finally, true flames erupted from the cheap material.

The Alchemist headed toward me stopped and stared at the fire while the one at the door gaped as well. With their attention diverted, I was able to slip past them and run three stores down the strip mall to a drugstore. Outside it, an idling tour bus marked LAS VEGAS was loading up senior citizens, and in my haste, I ran into one of them. He blinked in surprise as we made eye contact. I must have appeared out of nowhere for him, but as so often happened when humans encountered the unexplained, he shook his head and turned back toward the bus.

I headed straight to the back of the store, toward the pharmacy, and found Adrian in the contraceptive aisle, as I'd known I would.

"Hope you picked out something good," I said.

"Thank God," he breathed, wrapping me in a huge embrace. "I hated leaving you but thought our odds were better if we split up first. I knew you were smart enough to get over here."

"To the place you forgot to go last night?" I asked with a smile. "Yeah, I figured it out, but I had a couple of tagalongs. They're down at the megastore . . . which is also about to be visited by a fire truck, I think. Wish I'd found something less conspicuous."

"Can't be worse than me," he said. "When I heard the explosion in the casino, I used spirit to throw a whole bunch of Alchemists around in order to get out. I don't think it was obvious that I was the one responsible, but those places are packed with cameras that are now probably going to have some very questionable footage."

"Actually," I said, "the Alchemists most likely disabled all the cameras or put them on a loop before infiltrating the place. They wouldn't want their activities recorded any more than yours."

Adrian looked relieved. "Well, that's something. But now what's the plan? Should we call Marcus for help?"

"No," I said. "I don't want him coming back here and risking himself when this town is crawling with Alchemists."

"How do you think they tracked us? The car?"

I sighed, feeling foolish over something that had occurred to me earlier. "Honestly, I'm guessing they had eyes and ears in all the nearest towns to the re-education center, in the very event of something like this happening. They probably put our descriptions out, and someone reported back. Maybe a hotel employee. I should've considered that and gone a lot farther before we stopped for the night. This is my fault."

"The only ones at fault are those freaks who lock people up in dark cells in Death Valley," said Adrian. "So stop beating yourself up, Sage, and use that beautiful brain I know and love."

I swallowed and nodded, steeling myself. "Okay. We need to get out of this town fast, and I think I know how."

"Does it involve hotwiring a car?" he asked hopefully. "I disapprove on moral grounds, but Rose and Dimitri did a lot of that, and it *is* kind of badass."

I grabbed his hand and led him out of the store. "My plan is much less badass."

We stepped outside, and sure enough, there was a fire truck and growing crowd farther down the strip mall. Not waiting to see if there were Alchemists in the crowd, I hurried forward and stepped onto the tour bus that had just finished loading. The driver looked us over warily.

"You guys aren't in this group," he said.

Adrian glanced back at the seats on the bus, noting all the white and gray hair. "Very observant," he muttered.

I nudged him. "Were you lucky at the casino earlier?"

Adrian took the hint and pulled out his wallet. "We would like to join this group," he declared.

The driver shook his head. "It doesn't work that way. This is all arranged through a tour company, who then contracts with my boss to—" His eyes bugged as Adrian handed over a couple of hundred-dollar bills. After a moment's wavering, the driver snatched them and tucked them into his coat. "Come on in. I think there are still some seats in the back."

The bus's regular customers stared at us in astonishment as we moved past them and settled into the last seat. Moments later, the door shut, and the driver pulled out of the parking lot. Adrian slung an arm around me and sighed happily.

"Ah, I can't wait to tell our kids about this. 'Hey, honey, remember the time we bribed our way aboard a senior citizen tour bus going to Las Vegas?'"

I laughed in spite of myself. "Big romance there. I'm sure they'll be impressed."

The amusement stayed on his face, but it was tinged with sadness. "Actually, after what I've observed in marriage recently, this is big romance."

"What are you talking about?"

The last of his smile disappeared. "Nothing worth getting into. Let's just say I found out my parents' marriage is a sham, and my mother is fine living with a man who thinks poorly of her, so long as he keeps paying her bills."

"Adrian," I exclaimed, resting my hand on his. "Why didn't you tell me any of this?"

His smile returned, though this time it was wry. "Well, I kind of had some other things to worry about."

He leaned over and kissed me on my forehead, but his words brought up something I'd kept on the edge of my mind: my own parents. "You saw Carly," I began. "Do you know what happened to my family?"

The drive to Las Vegas was another hour and a half, and Adrian recapped what he'd learned about my family and the divorce. My heart sank. I wasn't entirely surprised to hear that my dad had won custody of Zoe, even though I'd held out hope that my mom might prevail.

"It doesn't mean she's a lost cause," I said to Adrian, trying to convince myself as much as him. "Zoe might still break free of all this."

"She might," he agreed, but I could tell he didn't believe it.

When we reached Las Vegas, we learned the bus was taking its occupants to the Tropicana. We unloaded in front of that hotel, where the tour company's guide was waiting for her charges and the next leg of their journey. She looked startled when we stepped off, and Adrian waved at her obligingly as we walked passed her, like it was totally normal for us to be there. She was too stunned to say or do anything to stop us.

Unfortunately, we then discovered we had someone waiting for us too.

"Adrian," I said warningly.

He followed my gaze to where a man and a woman standing by the hotel's door were staring straight at us. "Son of a bitch," said Adrian, coming to a halt.

I nearly expected a repeat of what we'd left behind, with those Alchemists charging straight toward us. Instead, the woman touched the arm of another man whose back was to us. He turned, revealing himself to be a security guard. She said something to him and pointed at us. Immediately, he strode over, with the two Alchemists in tow. I looked around, trying to see if we could run somewhere or at least catch a taxi.

"That's them," the woman was saying. "I told you."

"Excuse me," said the guard. "I need to bring you inside and ask you some questions. I understand you may be involved in something of interest to the authorities."

"Adrian," I said through gritted teeth. "We can't go with them." I knew how these things worked. If we ended up in police or even this hotel's custody, the Alchemists would simply work a little paperwork magic to get us turned over to them.

Adrian met the guard squarely in the eyes. "There's been some mistake," said Adrian amiably. There was a warm, honeyed quality to his voice that even drew me in. "We're just here to have a good time, spend lots of money in the casino. These two are the ones causing trouble. They're trying to distract you from what they're really up to."

The guard's brow furrowed as the compulsion poured over him. I shivered, both impressed and a little disquieted at just how powerful Adrian was. The Alchemists realized what was going on too. "He's lying," the man snapped. "Seize them, and bring them in. We'll help restrain them."

"'Seize them?' Really?" asked Adrian. "I knew you guys were into the Middle Ages. I just didn't realize you were still trying to live in them." He focused his energy back on the guard. "Let us go. That's our taxi that just pulled up. And don't let them stop us."

"Of course," said the guard.

Adrian steered me toward a taxi that had, in fact, pulled up. The two Alchemists tried to come after us, but the guard, still under Adrian's influence, blocked their way. The guy actually went so far as to punch the guard, allowing his female colleague to hurry over to the cab. By that time, Adrian and I had gotten inside, and he slammed the door and locked it as she pounded on the window.

"Drive," he told the driver. "Now."

The driver looked more than a little alarmed at the woman beating on his cab, especially when the male Alchemist joined him. "Go!" I urged.

The driver hit the gas. "Where to?"

For a moment, neither of us spoke. Then, I said, "The Witching Hour."

Adrian gave me a sharp look. "You sure that's a good idea?" he asked in a low voice, as the driver pulled into traffic. "The Moroi cooperate with the Alchemists."

"I'm playing a hunch." Seeing his surprised look, I said, "Well, it *is* Las Vegas."

The taxi took us midway down the Strip, and as we pulled up, I warned Adrian, "There'll likely be an Alchemist or two here waiting for us. Don't search around for them or act like you notice one if you see them. Just walk straight inside and head for the restroom. I'll do the same. When you come out, don't wait for me. Go play cards or something. I'll find you."

That brought a frown to his face, but he didn't argue as we paid and got out of the cab. The Witching Hour was no place I'd ever been, but it was well known in Alchemist circles. It was a Moroi-run casino and hotel, and while plenty of humans patronized it, its owners made sure it was chock-full of lots of things that catered to Moroi needs. We walked straight inside, and a Moroi bellman politely held the door open for us. Inside, it was like any other Las Vegas establishment: an array of lights and noise and far-ranging emotions. Adrian followed orders perfectly, going straight for the restrooms to the side of the lobby. I ducked inside the women's room and into a stall.

There, I took out Ms. Terwilliger's invisibility amulet and put it around my neck, casting the spell that activated it. Even with the amulet to help, it still required a lot of power, but the results were equally powerful. It would last much longer than what I'd cast in re-education, and now I could look people in the eye. Only those who knew Sydney Sage was standing there invisible, right in front of them, would be able to see through the spell's magic. With my camouflage in place, I headed out of the bathroom, waiting for another patron to open the door first.

Outside, Adrian was just leaving the men's room. I trailed behind him as he ordered a drink at the bar and then sought out a poker table. The drink was nonalcoholic, but did contain blood, which was an added bonus of this stop since I knew he hadn't had any in a while. Once he was seated and dealt in, I came up behind him and whispered in his ear, "Do *not* turn around. I'm here with you, invisible. If you look at me, it'll probably break the spell. Nod if you understand."

He nodded.

I scanned around and leaned back to him. "I think I've spotted one Alchemist in the room so far, watching you. Keep playing a few rounds. No one'll grab you yet. I wouldn't be surprised if another one or two showed up soon."

I took a quick walk around, made note that the main security and managerial offices were on the first floor, and then returned to Adrian. I continued monitoring the room, while still pausing occasionally to appreciate how he played. He was pretty good at it, making me glad I'd never caved to his strip poker requests. I was actually good at it too, but my gameplay came from statistical analysis. That couldn't stand up to the ability to read the truth in other players.

A second Alchemist soon appeared on the game floor. "Okay," I murmured to Adrian. "Finish this hand, and then go get a room. Check in under your own name, it's fine, and make sure you repeat the room number loudly. Then go to it. They'll follow you. When they do, don't hesitate to get in a loud, showy fight with them—but make sure they attack first. I'll take care of everything else. And when the authorities question you, make sure you make a big deal about who you are and how wronged you are."

He complied without missing a beat, and I carefully followed him to the front desk, staying out of his line of vision. The Alchemists followed as well, hovering within earshot. When he got his room key, he said, "Room 707, huh? Sounds like a lucky number." The two Alchemists exchanged glances and headed for the elevator. Adrian caught the next one up. As for me, I headed down an out-of-the-way corridor on the first floor and picked up an in-house phone, making sure no one was around to see the phone hovering in the air. I dialed security.

"Please help!" I exclaimed. "There's a man being attacked in the seventh-floor hallway!"

After that, I had to hope my gamble had paid off. I went back to where I'd seen the main security office and waited near it. Ten minutes later, four hotel security guards came downstairs with Adrian and the two Alchemists. The group entered the security office, and I slipped in after them, careful to stay out of Adrian's line of sight. We were soon joined by the day manager.

"What's going on?" he demanded.

A guard started to speak, but Adrian cut him off. "I'll tell you what happened! I was minding my own business, when *these two*"—he pointed at each of the Alchemists in turn—"jumped me for no reason! Do you have any idea who I am? I'm Adrian Ivashkov. Maybe you've heard of my late aunt, her royal majesty Queen Tatiana Ivashkov? And maybe you know one of my best friends, the current queen?"

That got the manager's attention, and he looked the Alchemists over. It was clear he knew who and what they were. "We don't see many of you around here."

"This man is a criminal," protested one of the Alchemists. "He and a human girl destroyed one of our facilities! It's our right to bring them in."

"Them?" asked the manager. "I only see one."

"She's here somewhere," insisted the other Alchemist.

One of the guards gestured to a large monitor. "We've got footage from the casino, sir. Lord Ivashkov was alone." He played a feed of Adrian at the poker table, and I prayed no one thought to check footage of us entering outside. "And here's the attack."

New footage showed the two Alchemists lying in wait on the seventh floor when Adrian got out of the elevator. They clearly made the first move, trying to grab and subdue him with a tranquilizer gun of their own. Adrian fought back gallantly, not just with spirit—which I'd expected—but by actually throwing a punch at one of them. Wolfe would've been so pleased. Other patrons emerged from their rooms, and soon the guards arrived, breaking everything up.

"This is unacceptable," said the manager angrily. "You can't walk into my hotel and try to assault a Moroi! I don't care who you are. You have no right to do that to us."

"He's guilty of all sorts of crimes," the first Alchemist said. "*You* have no right to keep us from bringing him in for questioning."

"Where's your proof?" asked the manager. "And where's your mystery girl? You've clearly made a mistake." He turned to another of the guards. "Escort them out."

"They've been following me all day," said Adrian. "How do we know they won't come back?"

"No one is going to intimidate our citizens," growled the manager. "Alert the rest of your staff. Scour this place for all signs of Alchemists, as well as the periphery and tunnels. Remove any of them from our property and put in a call to Court. You're safe as long as you stay here, Lord Ivashkov."

"Thank you," said Adrian gravely. He stood up. "If this is finished, I'm going to go to my room and make some calls of my own to Court."

The protesting Alchemists were led off, and the manager walked Adrian out, offering all sort of apologies and compensation for what had happened. When Adrian was finally alone in the elevator, I moved behind him and spoke.

"Don't turn around again. We need me off camera."

"Did everything go according to plan?" he asked.

"And then some."

He held his hotel room door open extra long so that I could slip in. Once it shut, I stepped in front of him and said, "Here I am." The spell unraveled, and he wrapped me in a giant hug that lifted me off my feet.

"That," he said, "was brilliant. How'd you know what would happen?"

"I didn't," I said. "Not for sure." He set me down and

took a seat on the couch. "But I felt pretty confident the Moroi management wouldn't let them haul off one of their own without proof—which there's no way they have. Marcus would've disabled the cameras in Death Valley. The Alchemists could only accuse you based on eyewitnesses, and I knew that wouldn't stand up here. Alchemist officials would have to file formal complaints with the queen. Me . . . well, that's a different story. They might have handed me over. The Moroi have no reason to protect me—hence the invisibility."

Adrian sat beside me and kissed my cheek. "I've said it before, and I'll say it again: You're a genius, Sage. I keep finding new reasons to love you, and I didn't think that was possible."

"I'm no genius," I said, slumping back into the seat. Tears formed in my eyes, and I hated it. I hated that the Alchemists had done this to me. I'd never been so emotional before! I was all about logic when problems came, not tears, yet right now, I just wanted to curl up in a ball and sob. The stress of re-education and now this attack was wearing on me. "I should've let us go with Marcus. I don't know if we can outpace the Alchemists! You think I'm clever, but where do you think I learned it from? Do you see the scope of what they can do? They had agents waiting outside in towns neighboring Death Valley. Then they must've seen us get on that tour bus, found out where it was going, and met us at the Tropicana. The Alchemists there either got our cab's license plate tracked here, or else there were already agents waiting, since this was a likely place to go." I met Adrian's gaze firmly. "How do we outrun that? How do we get away from a group that has eyes and ears everywhere? Who can protect us? We can't use invisibility and compulsion for the rest of our lives! We can't hide in this hotel forever!"

I knew I sounded hysterical, and Adrian's calmness only drove that home. "I think I have an idea," he said. "An idea that'll get us some hardcore protection . . . but I don't know how you'll feel about it."

"I'm open to anything," I assured him.

He hesitated a moment and gave a decisive nod. Then, to my complete and utter astonishment, he got down on his knees before me and clasped my hands in his. "Sydney Katherine Sage," he said, his green eyes full of love and earnestness. "Would you do a brooding, deadbeat Moroi the honor of being his wife?"

CHAPTER 20
ADRIAN

I EXPECTED A LOT OF different reactions to my proposal. Crying wasn't one of them.

"Okay," I said cautiously. "Probably this would've been better with a ring, right?"

She shook her head, furiously wiping tears from her eyes. "No, no . . . it was great. I mean, I just don't know. I don't know why I'm crying. I don't know what's wrong with me."

I knew what was wrong. She'd been locked away for four months, most of which had been in the dark, subjected to psychological and physiological torture, and told everything she believed was wrong and twisted—that *she* was wrong and twisted. Add to that the stress of the escape—multiple escapes—we'd just gone through, and it was no wonder she was breaking down. Even the strongest person would have a hard time recovering. She needed a break, time to heal mentally and physically, and those goddamned Alchemists wouldn't give it to her.

"Okay, go ahead," she said, a few moments later. I could see her toughening up, working hard to put all those emotions away because she thought that's what it meant to be strong. I wanted to tell her that strength wasn't about hiding your feelings, that it was okay for her to feel this way after what she'd been through. "Explain to me how me being a nineteen-year-old bride will solve our problems."

I stayed on my knees. "I know it wasn't part of your plan," I said. "Not yet, at least. I know, ideally, you'd be going to college right now, with marriage down the road."

She nodded. "You're right. And it's not for lack of love for you, believe me. I can't even imagine marrying anyone else. But we're still so young. . . ."

"I know." I squeezed her hands more tightly. "Here's my thinking, though. It came to me when you said you knew the Moroi would protect me as one of their own. If we get married, if you're my wife, then the Moroi will have to protect you too."

Sydney's earlier words had reminded me of something that Lissa had said, back when I'd asked her to help Sydney: *If one of my own people were in danger from them, then yes, I'd have every right to throw my weight around with the Alchemists.* I had no doubt I'd be safe if I went running back to Court. Lissa would protect me, even if I wasn't a good friend. Sydney was right that she could expect no such guarantees, and even the hotel manager had insinuated as much. But if she was Mrs. Ivashkov . . .

Sydney's brow furrowed. "You're thinking like how a person gets citizenship when they marry someone from a different country. I don't think it works that way with the Moroi and the humans. I don't automatically become a Moroi by marrying you. Your people aren't going to accept me as one of their own. Your people are going to freak out."

"True," I admitted. "But that doesn't mean they'll let my wife be punished. We go to Court, and we're golden." She didn't answer right away, and that silence unnerved me. I began to worry and find other problems, ones that had nothing to do with my plan's questionable logic. "But if you're not sure about us . . ."

She focused back in on me. "Oh, Adrian, no. That's not it at all. I mean, it's like I said. I never expected to get married so young, but I can't imagine spending my life with anyone but you. I figured it would happen someday. This is just kind of a shock. And think also about what our life would be like. If we're getting sanctuary with the Moroi, does that mean we have to stay at Court forever? Will I ever get to see my family again?"

That caught me off guard. The biggest complications I'd foreseen would've been reactions from my family—and others, say, like Nina. There would be problems there, yes, but what Sydney and I faced now was too important. I was prepared to deal with whatever fallout my people might present, but I honestly hadn't thought far enough to consider Sydney's side of it. I didn't have easy answers for that but responded confidently, as though I did: "It'll be short-term. I mean, I don't know how long 'short-term' is, but eventually, this'll pass, and we'll be free to go wherever we want and see whomever we want."

Her wry expression told me she was skeptical. "How do you know that?"

"Because I just do. And I believe no matter what conditions we're in, we'll be okay as long as we're together."

"Okay," she said after a little more deliberation. "One more thing. Putting aside the whole issue of getting sanctuary with the Moroi, do you think we're strong enough for it? Marriage isn't just a piece of paper."

I got up and sat next to her. "I know it isn't," I said. "And I know it would be hard—for all sorts of reasons. But I think we can handle whatever comes our way, so long as we keep loving each other like this." I thought of my parents and their sham marriage. That seemed like more of a joke than anything hasty Sydney and I might do.

"How do you propose we pull it off then?" she asked. "I'm sure this hotel has a wedding chapel, but there's no way we could do it here."

"No," I agreed. No Moroi minister was going to bless this union. "Right now, no Alchemists are getting near this place. We have a tiny window to get out. We can just go down to the courthouse and—what's wrong?" She was starting to tear up again.

"Nothing, nothing," she said. "It's just . . . no. Never mind."

"Tell me," I urged.

"It's just . . ." She sighed. "Every other plan I've had has gone out the window. College, my family . . . and now moving up my wedding by several years. And with that, even the wedding has changed. I always thought that when it happened, we'd have our friends there, a dress, the full deal. I know none of that matters, and I mean it: I'll gladly marry you in a teal T-shirt. It's just all so different. I just need a minute to adapt to all these changes."

I stroked the side of her face. "No, you don't. Not on this, at least. Give me a second."

I stood up and took out my cell phone, looking up a few

things while she watched me curiously. Within minutes, I had a plan. I just hoped it didn't cause us more trouble than it solved.

"Okay, we're getting out now, while the Alchemists are blocked from this hotel. They'll eventually find a way back in— if only with makeup-covered tattoos. Do you have any more invisibility amulets?"

She shook her head. "I can cast a minor invisibility spell . . . but it won't work well in a crowded place like this. Too many people to run into."

"I'll cover us then. Come on." I held out my hand. "We've got to get out of here now."

We went back downstairs, and I cast a wave of spirit around us that made us unmemorable and obscured our features to anyone who got too close. I knew it was working when we walked right past one of the guards who'd brought me in earlier, and he didn't give me a second glance. It wouldn't work for anyone seeing us from a distance, though. I couldn't affect minds that far away, which was why acting now before the Alchemists could get spies out was essential. I led Sydney down through the underground tunnels that existed underneath the Witching Hour and extended to certain prominent points on the Strip. There were a number of exits, and I didn't doubt the Alchemists would soon have them all monitored. I just hoped we were ahead of them and that the one I picked wasn't watched yet.

When we emerged, it was into a major hotel on the Strip. Neither of us saw any signs of being followed, so I relaxed the spirit magic as we walked through the establishment. I spent no time there and simply went straight to the taxi stand outside. We caught a cab and soon were on our way to the nearest office that would give us a marriage license. The first good luck we'd had in a while was on our side, and we arrived to find a minimal line, probably thanks to it being a weekday afternoon. We each offered up our IDs when our turn came, and I shot Sydney a grin as the clerk processed our paperwork.

"Getting married as yourself, huh? Not Misty Steele?"

"That would be safer, absolutely," she said with a wry smile. "But if we're going to try to claim asylum with the Moroi, we need this to be as legal as possible. You're marrying Sydney Sage, whether you want to or not."

I kissed her forehead. "It's the only thing I want."

No Alchemists assaulted us during this errand, which I took as a good sign. Once we had our license, we took a cab back to the Strip, to yet another hotel, this one adjacent to a huge underground shopping complex. I double-checked an address on my phone and then guided Sydney to the place I'd looked up earlier: a business whose sole purpose was to prepare people for quick Vegas weddings. The part we walked into was filled with wedding dresses, and beyond it, I could see a salon area. A consultant stepped out as soon as we entered.

"You look like a happy couple," she said. I wondered if that was true, since we were both pretty tense about being followed. "How can I help you?"

"We're getting married," I declared. "And you have two hours to give her anything she wants and needs to get ready."

Even Sydney looked startled at that. "Adrian . . ." she began nervously.

"You do hair and makeup here?" I asked, pointing at the salon. "Get her in there, and also help her find a dress. A good dress—not just one of these." I nodded toward a rack we were standing by, marked BARGAIN DRESSES.

RICHELLE MEAD

"Adrian . . ." said Sydney again.

"I'll need a tux too," I said. I pulled out a piece of paper from my pocket and plucked the pen the sales consultant was holding from her hand. "Here are my measurements. Get one that goes with her. I trust your judgment. And then anything else she wants."

"Are you leaving?" asked Sydney in sudden realization.

"I have some errands to run. But I'll be back in two hours." She and the consultant still looked dumbfounded. "Ah," I said. "I suppose we need to talk about money. How silly of me." I took the pen again and wrote an amount—a very large amount—next to my measurements. "Will this cover everything?" Sydney gasped when she saw it. The consultant merely raised an eyebrow.

"Yes, sir. Considerably. I don't suppose you actually *have* any of that money up front?"

"Nope," I said. "But I don't need it. I have an honest face, and you trust me to come pay my bills." I turned the compulsion on full blast, and after a moment's wavering, the consultant nodded in acceptance. The ironic thing was, I could've compelled her enough to give us everything for free. I knew Sydney would never forgive me starting our marriage with that kind of deception, though, not to mention it'd likely get the poor woman fired. I kissed Sydney on the cheek. "Have fun. I'll be back soon."

Sydney hurried after me and caught my arm. "Adrian, what are you going to do? Even you can't get that kind of money in two hours."

I kissed her again. "I'm going to make one dream of yours come true, Sage. Have faith. And if the Alchemists show up . . ."

It was a downer, and it seemed unlikely, but we had to prepare. "Do whatever you have to do to escape. We'll meet up in a dream or through Marcus."

"Be careful," she said, still looking understandably concerned.

"Always," I lied.

I headed out, back into the shopping complex, trying to hide how uneasy I felt. The smart, safe thing would've been to use this window to escape Vegas and get married in some other place. But aside from the fact that this city was built around fast weddings, I really meant it about wanting to make one of her dreams come true. I just hoped it wouldn't cost us in the end. My phone chimed with a text message, and I glanced down, expecting some ominous warning from Marcus. Instead, I saw a message from Jill:

This is the most romantic thing ever. I feel like I'm watching a made-for-TV movie.

Thanks, I wrote back. *Any tips?*

No, you're doing just fine. Eddie's furious you guys took off. Maybe this'll make him feel better.

It was a relief to know he was back with her, and no harm had been done in borrowing him for the rescue. I wrote: *Keep it secret for now. Then be ready for the fallout. Provided I can even get us out of here.*

I might be able to help with that part, she responded. I didn't see how she could, but she sent no other messages, and I soon grew lost in my other tasks.

It didn't take me long to reach my destination: a jewelry shop that both bought and sold items. It wasn't exactly as seedy as a straight-up pawnshop, but their operating principle was similar. This was Las Vegas, after all. An older, white-haired man greeted me as I entered, asking how he could help. With a deep breath, I did the unthinkable and took out one of Aunt Tatiana's cufflinks.

"What'll you give me for this?"

His breath caught as he took and looked it over with a jeweler's glass.

How can you do this to me? cried Aunt Tatiana. *How can you throw away my jewels?*

I'm not throwing them away, I told her. *This is important. This is for the future.*

A future with a human!

A future with the woman I love, I responded. *I love you, Aunt Tatiana, but you're gone. Sydney is here, and my place is with her. These cufflinks do no one any good just lying around.*

Phantom Aunt Tatiana was still outraged. *You're betraying me!*

I felt a little sick inside but still resolved. Once, I'd taken a ruby from these cufflinks to a pawnshop, with the intent of buying it back. I had gotten it back—barely—and that experience had been more than a little traumatic. Now, there was no going back. Not only was I giving up an entire cufflink, I was giving it up for good. With our time constraints, I wouldn't be able to win enough and come back here to buy it out. This was my sacrifice for Sydney's dream.

The amount he named was low, of course, and we haggled our way around various numbers. We'd almost settled at a price (though it was still less than the cufflink's worth) when I played my next move and took out the second cufflink. "Give me that amount," I said. "And I'll cut you this deal. I want these stones set into an engagement ring—white gold's fine. Then I need two plain wedding bands. You keep the platinum as payment. It's worth a hell of a lot more than what you'll be giving me in return. Oh, and I need it done in an hour."

We haggled some more details, but he knew he was getting a good deal out of all this and wanted it. We finally settled, and he showed me an assortment of rings. I didn't have much time and chose a simple engagement style that would hold the rectangular diamond with smaller rectangular rubies on each side. I'd planned on just getting plain bands, but he showed me a set of matching white gold rings with tiny rubies scattered throughout them that appealed to me. They seemed like a tribute to the cufflink that had been sacrificed on behalf of this crazy scheme. I signed off on everything, took my cash, and reminded him he had an hour.

From there, it was a trip to the nearest casino with a high-stakes poker room—with a very important phone call made along the way. Playing with that kind of money was a bit daunting, especially knowing I had such little time and that so much was riding on it. If I lost it, there'd be no time to win it back, and a lot of plans would fall through. I stayed calm and refused to panic, treating this as a casual game and relying on my usual trick of reading auras. The players here were no different than the others I'd played against, I told myself. They were just throwing around much bigger bets.

An hour later, I left the table with enough to cover all the wedding expenses I racked up, as well as a way out of Las Vegas. I headed back up to the jeweler, who'd come through with what he promised. I pocketed the rings and placed another phone call as I made two stops: one at drugstore and one at a wine store. With a sigh of relief, I realized I'd completed the last of my tasks, short of the wedding itself. I headed back to the bridal shop, amazed to find that I was right on schedule.

The last two hours had been so frenetic, so anxiety-producing, that I felt as though my world had been put on fast forward, with everything needing to be done *now now now*. And so, it was more than a little surreal when I stepped into the store and saw Sydney . . .

. . . and time as I knew it suddenly froze.

I'd meant it when I'd told her to get whatever she wanted. I didn't care. She really could've shown up at the altar in a teal T-shirt, and I would've married her with my heart full of love. That being said, I'd had a few ideas of what kind of dress she'd go with. Something modest, say with long lace sleeves, was my biggest guess. Or maybe one of those simple kinds with a short-sleeved top that had no extra embellishment. She was Sydney, after all. I expected pragmatism from her.

What I didn't expect was old Hollywood glamor. The dress wrapped around her snuggly, showing a body that in no way looked too skinny, with folds of organza and crystal beaded embellishment. Just below her hips, it flared out mermaid style in a burst of tulle that was also decorated with scattered embellishment. Only one delicate lace-and-crystal strap rested on her shoulder; the other shoulder was bare. Her hair, with its new extra length, had been swept into a simple updo with a crystal comb holding it into place at the back of her head, with a long, sheer veil trailing from it. Sparkling, dangling earrings were her only jewelry, and some masterful makeup artist had covered up all signs of her recent fatigue—and her golden lily—without making it look excessive. It was perfect.

She was perfect. Radiant. Glorious. A vision.

"I feel like I should be on my knees again," I said in a small voice.

She gave me a nervous smile and ran a hand over the glittering dress. "Just tell me you can afford all this, because I might take back what I said about going with the T-shirt."

"I can afford it," I said, still awestruck by her beauty.

She gave me a small nudge. "Then you'd better get dressed."

The consultant was happy to show me to a dressing room, happier still when she saw my money. The tux they'd picked out was classic and elegant, double-breasted and black. The consultant made sure I wanted to buy it, rather than rent it, and I reassured her I did. Renting would've required a credit card, and I wanted to use mine as little as possible, since that provided a trail. The more I could do in cash, the better.

Sydney's eyes shone when I stepped out of the dressing room. I felt paltry next to her brilliance, but she assured me I looked amazing. The consultant helped pin a white peony to my jacket, and I noticed Sydney was carrying a small bouquet of pink ones in one hand. In her other hand, she held the two bags we'd been juggling since coming to Nevada, and now I had more to add to the collection. We managed to consolidate them all into one bag before leaving the store, and she gave the wine-store bag a puzzled glance.

"What's that for?"

"Our honeymoon," I said.

"I figured that's what the drugstore bag was for," she remarked.

"That too," I promised.

We finished up the last of our payment and then walked

RICHELLE MEAD

out hand in hand, completing the last bit of our journey by foot.
Our destination was the Firenze, a new hotel with an Italian
theme that this shopping complex connected to. I could tell
Sydney was a little self-conscious walking through the crowds
in her wedding finery, but that was by no means an uncommon
sight in Las Vegas. People smiled as we passed, and many
congratulated us. It did, perhaps, attract more attention than
we wanted, but I kind of liked pretending all the people we
passed were guests attending our wedding. That, and I was
more than a little proud to show off the gorgeous bride at my
side.

Just as we reached the Firenze's entrance, a new text came
in from Jill. I read it and found a big smile spreading over my
face. "What is it?" asked Sydney.

"Wait and see," I said. "We just got a major wedding present."

The Firenze, like most big Las Vegas resorts, had a section
of wedding chapels, and I led Sydney to them through the
casino. A nervous-looking man in a hotel uniform paced the
wing and came to a halt when he saw us.

"Are you Adrian?" he asked.

"I sure am."

He looked relieved. "Okay, you've got ten minutes to get in
and out before I'm in big trouble. There's a big party that's got
this reserved, and they'll start showing up soon."

"That's all the time we need," I told him, handing over a
stack of cash.

"Right this way," he said, beckoning us to a door marked
TUSCAN CHAPEL. He opened it for us.

Sydney gave me an amazed look. "You bribed our way into
a wedding?"

340

"The good places book up in advance, even in Las Vegas." I gestured her inside. "This was the only way I could get you to Italy."

She stepped inside and laughed, looking around with delight. The chapel was small, designed to hold about fifty people, and was painted with an American idea of Italian grandeur. Murals on the walls depicted fields of grapes, while the domed ceiling was covered in angels. An abundance of gold trim throughout the room questioned good taste, but I could tell from her shining eyes that it didn't matter.

At the front of the room was a podium decked with flowers. An officiant stood behind it, with one of the hotel's staff photographers hovering nearby. I owed them money too. The guy who'd let us in worked for the wedding reservation desk, and I'd essentially had to do some fast talking over the phone earlier today, promising to make this illicit affair worth his while if he could get us a room and the appropriate personnel. We set our bags on an empty pew and started to approach the official when I remembered something.

"Oh, hang on. You need this first."

I caught hold of her hand and slipped on the newly made engagement ring. Sydney's breath caught at the glittering array, and then she looked up at me in alarm, finally realizing where the funding for this adventure had come from. "Adrian, those are your aunt's."

I led her forward. "And now they're yours."

The officiant knew about our time constraints and kept the service pretty basic, mostly sticking to what was legally required in the state of Nevada. He did add one part that was his own design, words that burned into me and repeated in my brain later when I slipped the little glittering circle of rubies onto Sydney's finger: "Until now, you have always lived your life alone. Every decision you've made has been for you and you alone. Now, and for the rest of your days, your life will be tied to another's. Every decision you make will be for both of you. What one does affects the other. You are a family, a team . . . inseparable and unbreakable."

They were powerful words for someone like me to hear, someone who'd indeed lived a pretty selfish existence. But as I met Sydney's shining eyes and saw the hope and joy radiating from her, I felt up to them. I was ready to take that selfless step with her, to know that everything we did now was about the two of us and, eventually, our family. This was the biggest decision I'd made in my life . . . and the one I did most happily.

When the vows were said and the rings were on, the officiant pronounced us husband and wife. I drew Sydney to me and kissed her, full of love and life and the happiness of what we had in store for us. When we finally pulled apart, the minister added, "I'm very pleased to introduce the world to Adrian and Sydney Ivashkov."

Sydney's smile turned a little wry at that, and I couldn't help but groan. "Oh no. What?"

She laughed. "Nothing, nothing. I just always figured I'd keep my own name. Or at least hyphenate."

"Really, woman?" I said. "You bring that up now? You owe me another kiss for that."

I drew her back to me and actually got two kisses. We signed the paperwork with the officiant, and then I paid him and the photographer their bonuses. I also bought the memory card out of the photographer's camera then and there, despite his protests about how he normally touched up the photos and uploaded them for online viewing. "No time," I said, waving the magic wad of cash around. It was nearly as good as compulsion.

With everything done, we gathered up our things and said farewell to our tiny slice of Italy. "What now?" asked Sydney, as we moved toward the door hand in hand.

"Now, we get out of here, and believe me, we're going in style."

The reservations guy held the door open for us, more than relieved his little escapade was over. I thanked him again and stepped out into the main hallway . . .

. . . where a group of Alchemists was waiting for us.

CHAPTER 21

SYDNEY

AN UNSEEN FORCE suddenly sent the Alchemists flying against the walls, and I didn't have to ask to know that was Adrian's handiwork. I felt his hand on my back, pushing me forward. "Come on."

We tore off down the hall, not looking back, both of us knowing the Alchemists wouldn't stay down for long. "We just have to make it to the Blue Lagoon," he told me.

"Is that a pool here or something?" I asked. My shoes and dress made it harder to keep up with him, and he grabbed my hand to pull me along.

"It's a new hotel. South end of the Strip."

"South end . . ." I pulled up my mental map of Las Vegas Boulevard. "That's at least a mile or more away!"

"Sorry," he said. "It couldn't be helped. We have some pretty specific parameters, and they were one of the few places that fit the bill."

I didn't ask for elaboration as we emerged onto the gaming

floor. Normally, I would've welcomed a congested area to get lost in, but Adrian and I didn't exactly blend in wearing our wedding finery. The fact that we were tearing through the crowd and bumping into people kind of made us stand out too.

"Sorry," I called back, when Adrian accidentally bumped into a waitress carrying a tray of drinks. They spilled on some very surprised people at a blackjack table, but there was no time for further apologies or amends. A quick glance back didn't reveal the Alchemists, but I could see signs of commotion in the crowd, making me think our pursuers were hot on our trail.

The casino floor was like a maze to me, but Adrian seemed to have a sense of purpose. Before long, we emerged out the front door, to the Firenze's circular drive, which was abuzz with a whole different type of chaos. Evening had fallen, and the number of people moving in and around us had increased significantly, as pleasure-seekers came out for gambling, shows, and other diversions. The Alchemists hadn't followed us out yet, and we both peered around for our next move.

"Where are the taxis?" exclaimed Adrian.

A large group of young women, dressed to impress, stood near us. One of them wore a "bride-to-be" sash and a rhinestone tiara, and the vibe surrounding them suggested they'd already had more than one drink in her honor tonight. They ooh'ed and ahh'ed when they saw us. "We're waiting for a taxi too," said the girl nearest me. She giggled. "A few of them, actually."

"Are you in some kind of trouble?" asked another.

"Yes," I said, thinking swiftly. "We eloped, and my dad doesn't approve. He and some of my family are right behind us, trying to get us to annul."

It wasn't *that* much of a stretch of the truth, and they gasped and exclaimed in dismay. Adrian swept his gaze over all of them and said in a honey-like voice, "It'd be really great if you could let us have this next cab." I looked up and saw a yellow taxi approaching where we all stood.

Mass suggestion was difficult, but drinking had made this group weak-willed. And honestly, they might have helped anyway in the name of romance. They started chattering about true love, and the bride-to-be waved us toward the taxi. "Take it, take it!"

As Adrian and I were getting in, the Alchemists appeared at the bank of glass doors and pushed them open. "Hey," I called to the girls, waving my bouquet. "Get some early practice!" I chucked it toward them, purposely aiming over and past them—right to the Alchemists coming out the doors. The girls screamed in delight, turning into a rabid pack as they all went after the bouquet and collided right with our startled pursuers. I didn't see how it resolved, because by that time, I was in the car, and Adrian was giving orders to the Blue Lagoon. The cab pulled out.

"Let's hope this is as simple as getting a ride down the street," said Adrian grimly. "How did they find us?"

"Hard to say. Could've been as simple as their eyes and ears catching sight of us somewhere." I sighed in dismay. "This is my fault. If I hadn't gotten so silly about a 'real' wedding, we would've been out of this city a long time ago."

He slipped an arm around me. "No way," he said. "I'm glad we did this. They've taken so much from us already. They can't take this day from us too."

"At the very least," I said wryly, "I should've anticipated something like this happening and picked a dress that was

346

easier to move in. This mermaid style does *not* have a lot of leg mobility, but that lady assured me if she laced it up correctly in the back, she could make it look like I have more of a figure than I do."

"Your figure looks pretty good from where I'm sitting," he said, running his fingers along the beads on my shoulder strap.

I smiled up at him and then glanced around as I noticed something. "Why aren't we moving?"

The driver gestured irritably at his windshield. "Typical this time of night. Everyone's going somewhere. You kids aren't trying to get to a chapel appointment are you?"

"Already been," said Adrian.

"Good thing," said the driver as we inched forward. I saw his eyes look up to the rearview mirror. "Because you may be waiting here a little bit. Only way to get around all this is on a motorcycle, like those nuts."

Adrian and I peered behind us. All I could see at first was a sea of headlights on the crowded road, but then a ways back, I spotted four individual headlights moving and weaving in and around the stopped and idling cars. Adrian, his vision superior to mine at night, grimaced. "Sydney, I've got a bad feeling about that."

"We need to get out," I said decisively. "Now."

Adrian didn't question me and simply handed over money to cover our current fare, much to the driver's astonishment. "Are you crazy? You're in the middle of a million cars!"

That became obvious when we got out and tried to cross to the nearest side of the road. Horns blared at us as we darted across Las Vegas Boulevard, but at least most of them were stopped, so we weren't posing too much of a risk. In fact, the only vehicles that seemed to be getting anywhere were the four motorcycles. They kept moving on their earlier trajectory, simply trying to get farther down the road, and I thought maybe we'd eluded them. But then, just as we reached the curb and stepped up on the sidewalk, I saw one of the motorcycles turn sharply in our direction. The others soon followed suit.

The sidewalk was packed with people, and like the road, no one seemed to be moving. "They won't mow down a bunch of pedestrians with their bikes, will they?" asked Adrian as we hurried through the crowd as fast as they could.

"Not likely," I said, "but they'll probably gain on us pretty fast once they get on foot. And they won't have qualms about just abandoning the motorcycles." We halted as a knot of camera-snapping tourists refused to part, forcing us to make a wide circle around them. "Why is everyone just standing around?"

"Because we're in front of the Bellagio," said Adrian, staring up at a sprawling hotel. "Their fountains are probably about to come on. Pretty sure there's a tram or monorail here that'll get us up the Strip if we can get to it."

"Beats running," I said. I was fully aware that not only my dress but also my shoes were slowing our pace. I'd at least had the sense to decline the five-inch-heeled "to die for" shoes that the consultant had initially recommended, but even these little kitten-heeled ones were starting to pinch and take their toll.

Adrian and I made the Bellagio's main door our goal, a journey complicated by the excited crowds growing thicker as we neared the fountains. We had to go considerably around them to make any sort of progress, which also took us away from the most direct route to the door. We'd just made it to the far side of the fountains from the road when I glanced back and saw the foursome running toward us, much more uncaring of whom they pushed aside than we had been.

"I didn't know the Alchemists had such buff recruits," remarked Adrian.

"Sometimes they outsource extra security forces for—"

My words were cut off by exclamations of delight as the fountains suddenly sprang to life. Streams of water shot hundreds of feet in the air, and the opening bars of "Viva Las Vegas" sounded. Adrian started to run again, but I held him back. "Hang on," I said.

The Alchemists had pushed their way as close to the fountains as possible, much to the outrage of those who'd been waiting for a while. The foursome scanned around, using the somewhat clear vantage point to search for us. I made eye contact with one, and he gestured his colleagues toward me. I summoned my magic, drawing on long hours of practice with channeling the elements to call upon the essence of the water near us. The Alchemists only managed to take a few steps in our direction when I made one of the streams from the fountain bend down, almost like an arm, toward them. My extensive elemental practice made reaching out to a pure element easier than it might once have been, but I was no Moroi water user. My control of the stream was sloppy, inadvertently spraying most of the people within twenty feet of the Alchemists. I gritted my teeth and poured all my magic and energy into giving the stream as much solidity as I could as it swept toward the Alchemists. It wrapped around the four of them and lifted them into the air, eliciting cries of astonishment and a lot of camera flashes. At this point, the feat was too much for my powers, but it achieved as much of my goal as I needed. I had the Alchemists over the fountain's lake by this point, and I released the magic—which in turn released them from their suspension. They dropped into the water with a splash.

"Wow," someone near me said. "They didn't have that in the show the last time I was here!"

As Adrian and I continued our run to the hotel, the ex-Alchemist in me couldn't help but wince at the public display of the supernatural I'd just made—especially with so many recording devices on hand. It went against every principle I'd been taught about hiding the paranormal world from ordinary people, and I tried to console myself with the knowledge that at least no one would be able to pinpoint how exactly the fountain had done what it did. And if the Alchemists were truly concerned with the public reaction, I had no doubt they'd find a way to spin it in the news.

We made it into the Bellagio unchallenged, and I had only a moment to admire the lobby's beautiful glass flowers as Adrian asked a worker for directions to the tram station. The way was straightforward, but it required leaving the hotel again. We didn't dare slow down and made the journey at a half jog, which was itself conspicuous. All the Alchemists would have to do when they eventually made their way out of the water was ask if anyone had seen a bride and groom running through there. I could only hope security would detain them and that there'd be a tram right at the station when we arrived.

There wasn't, but we only had a five-minute wait, and no one showed up in that time. We got on board and sank into a couple of seats, both of us exhausted. "Catch your breath," said Adrian. "We're going to the end of the line."

I nodded, weary from both the sprint and intense magic

use. I crossed my legs and pulled off one of my shoes so that I could massage my sore foot. A woman sitting across from me in electric blue Skechers studied my shoes admiringly.

"Those are great," she said.

"What size do you wear?" I asked.

"Seven."

"Me too. You want to trade?"

Her eyes went wide. "Are you serious?"

"I need something blue to complete the look." I held up one white shoe, glittering with crystal embellishment. "They're Kate Spade."

Her friend elbowed her. "Do it!" she said in a stage whisper.

A little while later, I was suited up in new shoes. They couldn't save me from the blisters I'd already accrued, but when we reached our stop and I stood, my feet certainly thanked me for the change in support. The tulle at the bottom of the dress settled over them, and no one was any the wiser about what lay beneath. No pursuers awaited us when we stepped out of the tram, and we had an almost leisurely one-block walk to the Blue Lagoon. I entertained a five-minute fantasy that we were here for our honeymoon, out enjoying the sights like any other normal couple. That pleasant daydream was shattered when we stepped into the Blue Lagoon's lobby and spotted a suited woman leaning against a wall. When she saw us, she immediately straightened up and spoke into an earpiece.

"She's getting backup," I said, noting that she only watched us but didn't move. "They've had all afternoon to set up spies in every major hotel out here while I shopped."

Adrian was undaunted. "Ignore her. We're home free now. They'll never get enough people here in time to stop us." He went straight to the front desk and asked, "Excuse me, could you direct us to your helicopter landing pad?"

I was nearly as surprised to hear those words as the desk attendant was. "Do you have authorization to access it? It's in a very secure area, not open to general hotel guests." He looked us over dubiously. "*Are* you even guests?"

"No," said Adrian. "But we're expecting a, uh, ride up there. There should be a helicopter coming in from Olga Dobrova Academy any minute now." That was another surprise. Olga Dobrova was a small, newish Moroi school up near the border of California and northern Nevada.

The attendant typed something into his computer. "What are your names?" We told him, and he shook his head. "Sorry. You aren't on the authorized list to go up there."

"Can you even tell us if it's arrived?" exclaimed Adrian. "We're the whole reason it's here!"

The man shook his head. "I'm sorry, I can't help you unless you get authorization. Next, please."

Adrian fixed his gaze squarely on him. "No, you're going to—"

"He said he can't help you."

An impatient man in an Elvis T-shirt shouldered his way in front of Adrian, followed by a similarly dressed woman and a group of kids. They immediately began talking at once, launching into a tale of woe about how their air conditioning didn't work. We stepped out of the way in dismay, and I noted that the watching Alchemist was gone.

"What's going on?" I asked.

"Best laid plans going awry," muttered Adrian. "This was Jill's wedding gift: our escape plan out of Vegas. She convinced

Lissa that I was in serious danger and got her to order the helicopter sent here to take us back to Dobrova and then catch one of their private planes back to Court. Long journey with all the refueling, but it'd avoid public places and no more chance run-ins with Alchemists. Jill said the helicopter was set to come here, but I guess no one realized that for us to even get to it, there needed to be some kind of paperwork done on this end."

Although he kept using "us," I wondered if Lissa knew I was with him or if Jill had simply convinced her to use royal resources based on a story—albeit a true one—about Adrian's safety.

Adrian soon rallied. "Okay. No problem. We have cash and compulsion. As soon as the Elvis family leaves, we'll just go back to that guy and—" His eyes searched the lobby, following various employees as they went about their duties. "Scratch that. We don't need him. Someone around here will crack and tell us the way to that helicopter pad. Doesn't matter if the hotel doesn't think we should be there. If we're there and that helicopter takes us, that's all that matters."

Two employees looked completely clueless when he asked, but an off-duty concierge hesitated long enough for Adrian to jump in and seize the opportunity. "You don't have to do anything," Adrian assured him. "Just tell us where it is, and there's a hundred bucks cash in it for you."

The man wavered and then shook his head. "You'll never get to the pad. The elevator won't even go to that floor on the Starlight Tower without the right card access, and hardly anyone has it. But . . ."

"Yes?" prompted Adrian. He wasn't exactly using compulsion, but he certainly seemed very appealing. Or maybe I was just biased.

"An ordinary guest key will get you to the top of the Aurora Tower. From there, go down the west corridor, and there's a door that goes out on the roof. At that point, you could theoretically walk over the maintenance bridge and climb the ladder up to the heliport." He eyed my dress skeptically. "Theoretically."

"Theoretical's good enough for us," said Adrian. "But we aren't guests. I'll give you another hundred if you can get us a generic guest room access key."

"Easy," said the guy. "But I can't get you one that'll unlock the door to the roof."

"We'll deal with it," I said, hoping that was true.

The concierge held true to his word, and a few minutes later, he supplied us with a guest keycard. Adrian gave him the cash, and we headed for the Aurora Tower elevator bank.

"How much cash do we have left?" I asked.

"Not much," Adrian admitted. "A couple hundred. But once we're on the flight back to Court, it won't matter."

The directions and keycard were both good, and before long, we found ourselves at the door leading out to the roof. It was a heavy glass door, split vertically with two panes of glass, and it had a warning sign that said an alarm would go off if it was opened.

"If it's opened," I murmured. "I wonder what'll happen if we remove a pane of glass? We should be able to fit through."

"You thinking of breaking it?" Adrian asked. "Hopper's in statue form, right? Maybe we could smash him into the glass."

"I had a more elegant solution in mind."

From among Ms. Terwilliger's supplies, I found a small pouch of bitter-smelling herbs. I sprinkled them on the larger, lower pane of glass and then double-checked a spell from the book she'd provided. After having been forced to wield so much improvised magic, having a standard spell and components seemed almost luxurious. I waved my hands over the glass and chanted the Greek words. Moments later, the glass in the pane began to melt like ice, dripping until it formed a puddle on the floor. That puddle soon solidified, but the lower half of the door was now wide open and exposed to the air outside. Best of all, no alarm went off.

"No question," said Adrian. "I definitely married up."

We each ducked through the opening and crossed the roof, which was full of vents and various maintenance signs. The walkway connecting this tower to the taller Starlight one was solid and steady, thankfully, but the ladder on the side of the building was a much more intimidating matter. It required climbing three floors, which wasn't an enormous distance in a hotel that was already twenty stories high, but being in a dress certainly complicated matters, no matter how sensible my shoes were.

Any fears I might have had were dashed as we recognized the loud, telltale signs of a helicopter nearby. We exchanged excited looks.

"You go first," said Adrian, as we stood at the bottom of the ladder and he took the bag from me. "If something happens, I'll use spirit to keep you up."

I shook my head. "No, you first. There'll be guardians in the helicopter. Better if they see a Moroi first. I should be able to summon enough air magic to help me if I slip."

"Should?" he asked pointedly.

"I don't plan on slipping."

Adrian kissed me and began the climb. Wind whipped

around me as I watched with bated breath, every part of me tense as he made the painstaking journey one step at a time. But he never slipped or seemed to falter even a little. In no time, he made it to the top and stood firmly on the upper roof. He waved at me and then took a few steps away that put him out of my sight. The helicopter had gotten louder, and I hoped he was there clearing things up with the Dobrova guardians.

Then it was my turn. My new shoes had good grip, and the dress's limitations didn't matter so much since the ladder's rungs were close together and easy to stand on. This ladder wasn't meant to be a deterrent. It was there for maintenance workers, designed to be as easy for them as possible. My difficulties came from other things, like the way my dress and veil were tossed in the wind—and the disorientation I got when I made the mistake of glancing over the side. Las Vegas sprawled out before me, in a glittering nighttime display of lights that was both breathtaking and terrifying when I realized how far below me it was.

But I didn't slip either, and after what felt like three hours, I was making my way onto the roof as well and getting my first glimpse of the helicopter and landing pad.

And that's when things went bad.

There was a helicopter, yes, but it couldn't land because two Alchemists—or Alchemist subcontractors—stood blocking the helipad. Two more Alchemists stood closer to my position, with guns pointed at me. That actually wasn't what made my blood freeze, though. What made my heart want to leap out of my chest was the sight of Adrian, on the opposite side of the roof from where the Alchemists stood aiming at me, on his knees. A gun was pointed at him too, so close it touched his head . . .

. . . and Sheridan was the one wielding it.

"I'm disappointed," she said, having to yell to be heard over the roar of the hovering helicopter. Its churning blades whipped all of us into disarray. "If I were you, I'd have been ten states away by now. Instead, I find you only a few hours from where I last saw you."

I couldn't formulate a response or even any coherent thought right away. All I could fixate on was the sight of Adrian, with that gun next to his head. No torture I'd faced in these last few months came close to matching the terror I felt at the thought of losing him. Everything I'd fought for, every challenge, every victory . . . all of it was empty if anything happened to him. Without him, I wouldn't have had the courage to become the person I was. Without him, I wouldn't have realized what it truly was to live and love life. *Centrum permanebit.* He was my center, and there was nothing I wouldn't do, nothing I wouldn't give up, to keep him safe.

Meeting his eyes, I knew he felt exactly the same away.

In my silence, Sheridan continued her taunts. "I admit, the whole Vegas wedding thing gets points for romance. You also get points for stupidity, I'm afraid, especially for applying for your license in your real names. We monitored local government offices as a precaution, but I didn't actually think you'd give yourselves up like that. Reserving a chapel off the record was pretty smart, though. We had to call nearly every one of them in town, claiming to have a 'surprise wedding gift' for you. They nearly claimed ignorance at the Firenze, and then one of their coordinators remembered a coworker talking to your 'husband' there."

"Let him go," I called. "You came here for me, not him."

"Sure," she replied. Her face looked more ghastly than

pretty in the weird interplay of lighting and shadows up here, brought on by a mix of the helicopter's spotlight and smaller lights embedded on the roof. "Walk over and surrender to one of my agents, and I'll let him go."

"Her aura's full of lies, Sydney," Adrian yelled. Sheridan pressed the gun more closely against him and ordered him to be silent.

I knew lying was part of her nature, but it was hard to say if she was lying about hurting him. There would be consequences for killing any Moroi like this, let alone a royal one—especially when she had witnesses. In the doorway of the hovering helicopter, I could see a dark, muscled figure, undoubtedly some guardian from Olga Dobrova Academy. It had to be hard for him to know what was going on down here, but I had no doubt that if he did, he'd be right by my side fighting to save Adrian. I wouldn't have minded an asset like that, but the guardian wasn't in a position to help in a way I could be certain wouldn't end up hurting Adrian if Sheridan got trigger happy. There were too many unknowns right now, and I needed to take control of the situation fast.

More elemental magic flared up in me, and I mixed what I knew of the fireball spell with some improvisation of my own. A wall of flame erupted from the ground, spreading out until it made an enormous, oblong enclosure around the two Alchemists nearest me and the two blocking the landing pad. The amount of magic required to summon it, let alone sustain it, was staggering, and I fought to keep my face cold and hidden of all stress.

"What are you doing?" exclaimed Sheridan.

"Offering you a deal," I said. "Give me Adrian, and you can have your four agents back. Alive."

Sheridan didn't move—neither did her gun—but there was definite fear on her face as her eyes darted to the Alchemists trapped in fire. They were even more terrified and no longer had their guns aimed. In fact, they'd backed up toward each other, trying to keep away from the fire. The ones on the landing pad actually stepped off it in their fear, moving until they were nearly back-to-back with their colleagues. This allowed me to narrow the enclosure and free up the pad, though the helicopter didn't attempt a landing yet with the flames still relatively close.

"They know the risks," Sheridan called back. "They would rather die than let darkness triumph in this world. They're prepared."

"Are you?" I demanded. "Are you prepared to watch this?"

With a quick motion of my hand, the circle of flame grew smaller and smaller, forcing the Alchemists to huddle together. The tighter circle helped me, but it was still excruciatingly difficult to maintain the fire at its current level, keeping it close enough so that the Alchemists would feel the heat but not actually be harmed. Hearing their cries of terror made my stomach twist. It brought back too many memories of what I'd endured in re-education. For four months, my life had been filled with fear and intimidation. I was so, so tired of it. I wanted it to end. I wanted us to be at peace. I didn't want to hurt these people. I didn't even want to scare them. Sheridan had pushed me to this point, and I hated her for it, hated her for making me act like this type of violent person.

And possibly making me become this violent of a person.

"You kill them, and I'll kill him," she told me.

"And then there'll be nothing to stop me from turning the fire on you," I retorted. "In every scenario, I walk free. Are you willing to pick the one that results in you and your colleagues burning alive?"

"You won't do it," she said, but even with all the noise and chaos around us, I could sense her uncertainty.

"Wouldn't I?" I couldn't bring the flames any closer to the trapped Alchemists without causing them injury, but I was able to make the fiery walls stretch higher. Sheridan's eyes widened, and it took a lot of resolve to act like I didn't hear or care the pitiful cries of those trapped within. "Test me, Sheridan! Test me, and see what I'm capable of! See what I wouldn't do for him!"

With another wave of my hand, the walls of flame grew taller once more, eliciting new screams. The exertion of this kind of magic had me dizzy on my feet, but I kept my gaze fixed and stony as I stared at Sheridan. She believed I was a black-hearted evildoer who had turned her back on humankind. She also believed I was deeply, madly in love with a vampire I'd do anything for. Only one of those profiles was true, but I needed to convince her of both.

"Test me!" I screamed again.

"Okay, calm down, Sydney." Sheridan looked between me and the other Alchemists, of whom only their fiery prison could be seen. "What do you want me to do?" she cried at last.

"Give Adrian the gun," I said.

The tension grew impossibly thick around us as she considered this. I was about to lose my control on the magic and was worried her indecision would call my bluff. But then finally she lowered the gun from his head and handed it to him. He took it and wasted no time scurrying to my side, his face pale and worried.

"Keep it aimed at her," I told him. To her, I said, "When I

drop the fire, order them to put their weapons on the ground and hands on their heads."

With a relief that nearly made me keel over, I released the magic. The walls of fire disappeared, and Sheridan immediately shouted the commands I'd given her. The Alchemists complied, and once they were unarmed, I ordered them over to the far side of the roof where she stood. Beyond all of us, the helicopter was finally attempting to land, now that the fire was gone.

"All of you, lay down on the ground," I told Sheridan and the other Alchemists. "And nobody even thinks of moving until that helicopter's long gone. Let's go, Adrian."

He and I slowly made our way across the roof to the helicopter, angling ourselves in a way that let us watch the Alchemists. Adrian admirably kept the gun pointed in their direction, even though I was pretty sure there was zero chance he could have actually hit one with any accuracy, even if he'd wanted to. A guardian I didn't know stood beside the helicopter's doorway, looking understandably confused.

"Am I glad to see you," Adrian told him.

"Glad I could help," the other man said uneasily. He glanced over at the Alchemists on the ground. "Though I feel like I should have done more. What's going on?"

"Never mind, you're doing plenty," said Adrian. "Can we go now?"

The guardian gestured to the helicopter. "After you, Lord Ivashkov." He hesitated. "You *are* Adrian Ivashkov, right?"

"Sure am," said Adrian. He beckoned me forward. "And this is my wife."

CHAPTER 22

ADRIAN

I DON'T THINK SYDNEY OR I truly relaxed until we were on Olga Dobrova's private jet hours later, up in the air and on our way to Court on the other side of the country. We'd been warned we'd have to stop for refueling on such a small plane, but I wasn't worried. They'd do it in discreet places, and besides, the Alchemists wouldn't dare attack a Moroi-owned plane under royal orders.

Two guardians were flying back with us, but otherwise, we had the jet to ourselves. The guardians sat near the front, while I occupied a cushy seat in the back, with my feet propped up on a large table. Sydney had disappeared into the bathroom shortly after takeoff, wanting to redo her hair after the helicopter and wind had disheveled it. "It's my wedding day," she'd explained earlier. "I need some dignity."

When she emerged, I saw that she'd actually managed to repair it to a fair approximation of what the stylists had done earlier, not that I cared. I thought she'd been beautiful with

362

it wild and windswept. The guardians nodded politely at her as she walked past, both obviously tense and uncertain in her presence. No one had briefed them that I was bringing a human bride back with me, and it was clear that while their training had prepared them for many a dire situation, this scenario was nothing they had any experience with.

I patted my lap as she approached. "Come here, Mrs. Ivashkov."

She rolled her eyes. "You know how I feel about that," she warned. But to my delight, she did actually sit in my lap, though maybe that was just because a recently roused Hopper had curled up and fallen asleep in the chair opposite me at the table.

I put an arm around her slim waist and held up my purchase from the wine store with my other hand. "Look what I opened for us to celebrate," I said. "Champagne."

Sydney peered at the label. "It says it's a sparkling Riesling from California."

"Close enough," I said. "It popped when I opened the cork, and the guy at the store gave me these plastic champagne flutes for free. He said something about a citrus bouquet and a late harvest. I didn't follow it all, but it seemed celebratory to me."

"Alcohol dulls human and Moroi magic," she warned.

"And this is still our wedding day," I countered. "Not to mention the only time we're probably going to get to do this. Once we get to Court, we'll want to stay clearheaded . . . not that I expect it to be anything like what we just went through. Compared to that, life at Court's going to be a breeze."

I expected another protest, but to my surprise, she accepted and let me pour us two flutes, which I deftly managed while still keeping her on my lap. I offered some to the guardians, but that actually only succeeded in making them look more uncomfortable than they already did.

"You know," said Sydney, after a sip. "I kind of can taste some citrus in this. Just barely. Like a hint of orange. And it's sweeter than I thought, but that'd make sense if the guy said it was a late harvest varietal. Grapes retain more sugar the longer they stay on the vine."

"I knew it," I said triumphantly. "I knew this was exactly what would happen if I ever got you to drink."

She tilted her head, puzzled. "What?"

"Never mind." I brushed a kiss over her lips and then studied her face, finally daring to believe that this beautiful, brave woman was really my wife. Her face was lovely in the ambient glow of the jet's interior, and I hoped I could remember exactly how she looked right now for the rest of my life. "Huh. Look at that."

"Look at what?" she asked.

I touched her cheek. The majority of her makeup had stayed on flawlessly, but some of the covering on her tattoo had rubbed off in places, revealing bits of the lily. "It's turning silver," I said.

"Is it?" She looked startled. "Marcus's did, but that took years after he sealed it."

"It hasn't completely changed," I said. "It's still mostly gold. But there's definitely silver starting to show here and there. Little shadows edging the gold." I trailed my fingers down along her neck, to her exquisitely bare shoulder. "It's beautiful. Don't worry."

"I'm not worried, just surprised."

"Maybe everything you've done recently has expedited the process."

"Maybe," she agreed. She took another sip and leaned back into me with a content sigh. "I don't suppose when we get to Court, they're going to just leave us alone and let us have our wedding night in some posh honeymoon suite?"

I shrugged, not wanting to worry her. "We'll probably have to answer a few boring questions, that's all. All the more reason to enjoy life now."

"I'm okay with boring," she said, her brown eyes staring off. "I'd like peace for a while. No drama. No life-threatening situations. I'm so tired of it all, Adrian. Maybe they didn't break me, but the Alchemists definitely wore me down in re-education. I'm sick of pain and violence. I want to help put an end to it with others . . . but first, I just need a break myself."

"We'll get it." My heart ached for her as I thought back to those awful moments on the rooftop when she'd faced down Sheridan, standing there in that glittering dress and wielding flame like some sort of avenging goddess. She'd been beautiful and terrible to behold, exactly as she'd needed to be to make Sheridan cave. Only I understood what it had cost Sydney to be put in that position, and if I could help it, she'd never go through anything like that again.

"I'm proud of you," she added unexpectedly. "You've used so much spirit throughout all of this and managed to keep in control of yourself. That doesn't mean I approve of it becoming a regular thing, but you've really shown you can master it without any dire side effects."

Yes, agreed Aunt Tatiana. *We certainly have.*

Indecision burned through me. I longed to tell Sydney everything—she was my wife, after all—but admitting I was tormented by a figment of my imagination was just too much.

Besides, once this was all resolved, I'd find a way to get rid of Aunt Tatiana, and none of this would matter.

Good luck with that, she whispered in my mind.

To Sydney, I said, "Just part of our new life. Like I said, it's going to be all smooth sailing from here on out."

I topped off our glasses, but rather than bring about any wild festivities, the extra drinking just added on to what was pretty severe exhaustion for both of us. We'd drained ourselves mentally, physically, and magically today, and we both eventually dozed off, with her still curled up on my lap and head resting against my shoulder. Her last words before sleep were, "I wish I'd kept my bouquet."

"You made some girl's night," I told her, stifling a yawn. "And I'll get you peonies on every anniversary, for the rest of our lives."

The next thing I knew, one of the uncomfortable guardians was waking us up, and the jet was on the ground. Peering out the window, I saw that we'd actually landed at Court, a privilege only given to a few. Most visitors landed at a nearby regional airport or rented a car at some major airport, like Philadelphia. It paid to be about the queen's business, I supposed. I noted also that it looked to be about noon outside, which was a time most Moroi on vampiric schedules were fast asleep. I hoped it meant we really would get shoved to some room for a while until everyone was up and about.

No such luck.

We were immediately escorted straight from the plane to the palace, where we were told Lissa "and others" wanted to speak to us immediately. We didn't even get a chance to change, and though I would never get tired of Sydney in that gorgeous dress, I knew both of us were at a point where jeans and a T-shirt would've been welcome. If that wasn't going to be an option, though, I decided to play up what I had. I retied my bow tie and put the tuxedo jacket back on.

"Let's do this," I said to the waiting guardians.

We were taken to a room of the palace I didn't get to very often, since most of my meetings with Lissa—and, in the past, my aunt—had been of a casual nature. The room we went to now was used for much more formal occasions, when Lissa actually had to have state meetings and conduct royal business. There was even a throne for her to sit on—albeit a modest and tasteful oak one without any extra embellishment. Her clothes were nice but nothing fancy, and her only nod to her title was a tiny tiara sitting atop her unbound hair. Silent guardians ringed the room's walls, but I paid no more attention to them than I did furniture. I was much more interested in those Lissa was speaking with: a motley assortment of people who both sat and stood, all seeming edgy, as though they were waiting for something. Us, I realized.

Rose, Dimitri, and Christian were there, which came as no surprise. Lissa wouldn't be without her confidantes, especially when it came to me. Marie Conta, an older Moroi who was an advisor of a more official nature, also hovered nearby. She'd stood by Lissa and helped her through her controversial rule, so it made sense Marie would come for something like this. It wasn't even *that* unexpected to see my parents on hand.

What did take me aback—and Sydney too, judging by the stiffening of her hand in mine—was that there were Alchemists here already. Not only that, they were very notable Alchemists: Sydney's father, her sister Zoe, and a guy it took me a moment to place. Ian, that was it. A guy who'd once had a pretty hardcore crush on Sydney.

This was the mess we strolled into, all dolled up in our wedding finery.

I'd been responsible for a lot of shenanigans in my life, but this was the first time I'd ever actually rendered an entire room speechless. Eyes widened. Jaws dropped. Even a few of the stone-faced guardians standing along the walls looked astonished.

"Don't all speak at once," I said.

Sydney's father got to his feet, face flushed with anger. "What in the world is this abomination?"

Lissa, only slightly more tactful, asked, "Adrian, is this some kind of joke?"

"What's a joke is waking everyone up for this," I said glibly. "I mean, I know you're all excited to see us, but there was no need to—"

"I demand you turn her over to our custody immediately," exclaimed Sydney's father. "So that we can stop this farce before it goes any farther. We'll take it from here."

"Mr. Sage says Sydney's committed terrible crimes among the Alchemists," said Lissa. "They claim you did too, Adrian, but they're willing to overlook yours if we give her to them, since you're one of my subjects."

I stood my ground. "The only crime we committed was getting her and a bunch of other poor wretches out of that freak show of a rehabilitation center—one they were going to abandon her to burn in. And you know what crimes she and the other prisoners committed? Treating dhampirs and Moroi like real people. Imagine that."

"According to them," said Lissa calmly, "Sydney tried to burn some of their people last night."

"It was a bluff," I stated. "They're still alive, aren't they?"

"This is irrelevant," snapped Ian. He stayed sitting, and judging from his proximity to Zoe, it looked like he'd shifted his affections from one Sage sister to another. "It's not for you to judge our people. We'll handle this."

This was it, the moment I dropped the real blow on them. "Well, that's the thing, your majesty. Sydney *is* one of your subjects, now that she's my wife. You said you wouldn't give me to them because I'm under your protection, right? Are you saying you'd abandon my wife to any less?"

That drew the room to silence again until Lissa found her voice. "Adrian . . . is that was *this* is about?" She gestured to Sydney and me in our formal wear when she said *this* but couldn't articulate anything more precise. "Why you did, um, this? You think it gets her Moroi citizenship or something? That's not how it works. Not at all. I know you care about her—"

"Care about her?" I exclaimed. I realized then that none of them really and truly got it. All the times I'd harassed Lissa to help Sydney over these last few months, Lissa had assumed it was out of my feelings of friendship for Sydney. And now, she and the others from Court thought that this was just some crazy stunt I'd pulled off to get my way. Only the Alchemists had an inkling of the sincerity of my feelings, but those feelings were twisted and wrong in their eyes. "Lissa, I *love* her. I didn't marry her as some sort of joke! I married her because I love her and want to spend the rest of my life with her. And I'd hoped, as my sovereign, you'd stand by me to protect me and my loved ones—especially since I'm guessing this lot has no hard proof of the crimes we're being accused of. You told me last month that you couldn't take risks for anyone but your subjects. Well, I know she's not technically your subject or Moroi, but *I* am, and if the promises you've made to me, as one of your people, truly mean anything, they will extend to her. We're married. She's my family now. We're bound together for the rest of our lives, and if you're going to let them haul her off, you might as well cast me out now too."

Lissa looked taken aback, but Jared Sage—my father-in-law now, I realized—showed nothing but contempt. "This is ridiculous. Humans and Moroi can't be married. That's your way, as well as ours. This isn't a real marriage."

"Not according to the state of Nevada," I said cheerfully. "We've got the paperwork to prove it. Get us a laptop, and we can all look at the wedding pictures together."

Rose's expression was hard to read. I was positive she was as shocked by these new developments as everyone else, but something told me she'd take on an attitude similar to what our friends in Palm Springs eventually had: acceptance and support.

"Liss," she said, "let them stay. Don't hand over Sydney."

Marie Conta, standing near Lissa's throne, leaned over and murmured something into her queen's ear. Judging from Marie's expression, I was guessing it was pretty much the opposite of what Rose had just advocated.

This time, Ian did get to his feet. "This isn't a decision you get to make!" he said incredulously. "Sydney Sage's fate isn't in your hands. You have no right to—"

"Ivashkov," interrupted Sydney. It was the first she'd spoken since we entered the room.

Ian turned his outraged expression from the throne to her. "I beg your pardon?"

"Ivashkov," she repeated, her face the picture of serenity. Only I could tell from the sweating of her hand how high her anxiety was running. The Alchemists had dealt her a low blow sending these three. "My name is Sydney Ivashkov now, Ian."

"The hell it is!" exclaimed her father, face filled with fury. "I'm done with this nonsense. I'll haul you out of here myself, if that's what it takes to save your soul from this filth."

He lunged toward Sydney and me, and in the blink of an eye, Dimitri swooped and put himself between us. "Mr. Sage," he said calmly. "No one will be hauling anyone out of here—unless her majesty the queen requests it."

All eyes swiveled toward Lissa. Her face was lofty and composed, but her aura betrayed her. We had put her in a position no Moroi monarch had probably ever been put in. I did feel a little bad about that, seeing as we were friends, but I stood by my decision. I meant every word of my marriage vows and would do whatever it took to keep Sydney safe.

"Adrian Ivashkov is my subject," Lissa declared at last. "And as such, he is entitled to all the rights and privileges of that position. His wife has come here seeking sanctuary—and I am granting it to her. They are both under my protection now, and so long as they are here at Court, you have no jurisdiction over them. I will not release them to your custody, especially since I truly haven't seen any evidence of their so-called crimes."

"Their crime is that they're standing right there in front of you, with no shame whatsoever!" exclaimed Ian.

Sydney's father clearly agreed. "This is an outrage! If you do this, you'll have the wrath of the entire Alchemist organization to contend with! You think you can get away with half the things you do now? We cover up for you! Without us, you're nothing. How do you think you'll exist in this society without us to help? If you don't have us—"

"Then the whole world will know vampires exist," said Sydney coolly. "Are you going to let that happen, Dad? Aren't you worried other weak humans might fall prey to their agenda if the Alchemists don't help hide them?"

Her father's expression grew even darker, and he looked as though he wanted to say any number of things to her. Instead, he took a deep breath and turned back to Lissa. "The Alchemists have been very powerful allies to you. You don't want to see what kind of enemy we'd be."

"Thank you for the advice." Lissa looked undaunted, though I saw her aura waver. "Glen?" she asked, directing her attention to one of the guardians at the door. "Would you and your people make sure Mr. Sage and the others are safely escorted off of Court property?"

The guardian swept her a bow and then strode forward, beckoning five other guardians to join of him. "Of course, your majesty."

The guardians led the protesting Alchemists out of the room, though we could continue to hear them make threats until they were well down the hall. At least, two of them did. Zoe hadn't said a single word the entire time and had simply watched her sister with wide, troubled eyes. Whether Zoe felt guilty over her role in Sydney's trip to re-education or was simply in shock over these new developments, I couldn't say. Beside me, Sydney was shaking. It couldn't have been easy to see her family hauled out like that. Still holding her hand, I stepped forward as more uneasy silence started to fall.

"Thank you, Lissa. You have no idea—"

Lissa held up her hand to stop me, a hand she then used to rub her forehead, as though she had a headache. "No, Adrian. You have no idea what trouble this may have brought down on me. I'm happy for you, I really am. But for tonight, I'm done talking. I need to sleep on this and the possible fallout. We'll get you set up with a place to stay and—"

"Hold on a minute." So help me, my own father stepped forward now, and judging from his expression, it was a wonder he hadn't been right there to argue with Jared Sage. "You're saying you're letting this . . . this . . . *marriage thing* just slide? That you're treating it as . . . real?"

Lissa, who really did look exhausted, sighed. "It seems very real to them, Lord Ivashkov, and that's good enough for me."

"I thought you were just playing along to get those Alchemists out of here! There's no way you can act as though this is a legitimate marriage. No civilized Moroi has ever stooped so low in—" My father bit off his own words as he gave Sydney and me a once-over. He swooped toward us with speed the guardians might have admired and had the audacity to grab Sydney's left hand. "I recognize those! Those are your aunt's! How dare you! You had the nerve—the sheer audacity—to put a queen's fortune in jewels on this . . . this . . . *feeder's* hand!"

I jerked Sydney away from him. "Dad," I said quietly, "I've always made it a rule in my life not to pick fights with children, cute animals, or ignorant old men. I will, however, make an exception for you if you ever touch or insult my wife again."

"Nathan," warned my mom, moving to his side. "She's your

daughter-in-law now. Show some semblance of respect."

Now my dad turned his rage on her. "I will do no such thing! This is preposterous, not to mention insulting. This is—"

"What our son wants," my mother stated. "And I stand by him."

I met her eyes and felt a swelling in my chest. I'd never made amends with her after our bad parting. I'd never even made any attempt to acknowledge her many calls and messages. It hadn't been a lack of love, so much as preoccupation with Sydney, but as I looked at my mother now, I was surprised to see something in her that hadn't been there before: defiance.

"For God's sake, Daniella," my father growled. "Don't add one more stupid mistake to the list of those you've already made. Now, if you want to come home with me tonight, be quiet and—"

"No," she said, interrupting him again. "I actually don't want to go home with you, tonight or ever again."

"You have no idea what you're saying," he hissed. "Or what the consequences will be."

"Actually, Nathan, I understand it all perfectly."

I looked up at Lissa, who appeared more than a little surprised at this new turn in drama. "Your majesty," I said. "You mentioned hooking my bride and me up with a place to stay. Any way we could get one for my mother as well?"

Lissa might worry what fallout would come of her actions with the Alchemists, but she had no such fears regarding my father. "Yes," she said. "I'm sure that can be arranged."

When we finally left for the night, a small crowd had gathered outside the palace. Gossip had spread in just the short time we'd been there, and curious onlookers had shown up, despite the late hour. The wedding clothes spoke legions, and I could see the shock and disbelief on their faces—including Nina's. I hadn't expected her to be there. Like my mother, I hadn't spoken to her since leaving Court, and it was obvious nothing could've prepared her for the sight of me with a human bride. She looked so stricken, I worried she might faint. Her hands were squeezed tightly together, and as we passed by, I thought I caught a glimpse of blood on them from where she'd scratched herself.

Not far from her stood Wesley Drozdov, and he, unlike everyone else there, didn't look shocked. He looked gleeful—maliciously so.

Uneasily, I remembered what I'd told Sydney on the plane, about how it was smooth sailing from here on out. *Life at Court's going to be a breeze*, I'd said. With a pang, I wondered if I might have inadvertently lied, and I was glad when she, my mother, and I hurried past the gawkers.

Rose and Dimitri escorted the three of us to guest housing and had enough tact not to badger us with questions—though I could tell they were eating Rose up. She maintained her self-control admirably until Sydney sat down in the guest-housing lobby as I checked us in. The toe of one of the blue shoes peeped out from under her gown, and Rose couldn't help herself.

"Those are badass shoes," she declared. "Is there a story there?"

Sydney smiled at her. "There are lots of stories."

"Tomorrow, Rose," I said. "Give us the rest of the night off, and we'll give you the whole scoop tomorrow. Plus it'll give you a chance to get us a wedding present. We're not registered anywhere, but we could seriously use some china and a blender."

"Lord Ivashkov?" asked the desk attendant, looking embarrassed at having to interrupt us. "I'm actually afraid we're short on rooms, between renovations and a tourist group from Bulgaria. We don't have two single rooms, but we do have a larger family suite that would hold your whole group."

I glanced between Sydney and my mom, both of whom seemed to be keeping their faces extremely neutral. I shrugged. "Well, we *are* family now."

Rose and Dimitri bid us farewell once everything was settled, and the three of us made our way up to the suite we'd been given. I unlocked the door and, on impulse, swept Sydney into my arms and carried her inside.

"I know it's not technically our real home yet," I said. "But with as many irregularities as we've had with this wedding day, I feel like we need to keep some traditions."

"By all means," Sydney laughed.

I carefully set her down, and my mother smiled politely. She might have stood up for me and thrown her lot in with us, but I knew her well enough to understand it would take her a while to warm to a human daughter-in-law. "Thank you, Mom," I said, sweeping her into a hug.

"I thought I'd learned my lessons in prison," she said. "But it wasn't until after you left that it all really and truly sunk in. I can't say this is my ideal situation, but I'd rather make this kind of life with you than not have you at all—or my self-respect."

I released her from the hug. "I'm proud of you. We'll make it work. You'll see. This'll be great. We'll be one big happy family."

The two women in my life seemed a little unsure of that, but both seemed certain of their love for me, and for now, that had to be good enough. My mother soon found she could hide her discomfort by finding things to criticize about our accommodations, which were every bit as luxurious as my last ones, only bigger. I left her to it and was more than relieved to finally get Sydney away for some privacy.

She sat on our bed and kicked off the blue shoes. "I don't know which part of this day seems the most unreal."

I sat beside her. "That's the thing. It's *all* real, especially the most important part: you and me, together forever, our marriage recognized in the eyes of human and Moroi alike."

"But not happily." Her smile faded. "Half my family never wants to see me again. And the half that does want to see me . . . well, I may not be able to see them again."

"You will," I said. "I'll make sure of it." I was acting more confident than I felt, and I knew she could tell. She'd just cut herself off from her family—from her race—for me, and although I couldn't entirely relate to what she was going through, I silently vowed to help her through it as much as possible.

"You were right." She pulled me closer to her. "About us getting protection. Even with all the complications, you made everything work."

"*We* made it work, and those complications won't last. For now, we can sit back and enjoy the rewards." I spoke gallantly, not giving voice to some of the fears I'd picked up. After seeing the reactions of her father, my father, and even Wesley, I had an uneasy feeling that we wouldn't be getting the peace she so longed for anytime soon. I refused to show that, though. At least not tonight. "And I have all sorts of rewards in mind. Unless you want to get some sleep."

She wrapped her arms around my neck and brushed her

lips against mine. "Depends. Did you stop at the drugstore, along with your trip to the wine store?"

"Stop there? Hell, I bought that place out, Sydney. I'm having no repeats of last time."

She laughed and let me lay her back on the bed, where I began the exciting, albeit slightly frustrating, process of trying to figure out how to get that elaborate dress off. It turned out to be worth the effort, though, and when we fell asleep in each other's arms much later, naked except for our wedding rings, I knew it had been worth *all* the effort. All the trials and ordeals we'd experienced had led to this moment, this perfect moment. We were exactly where we were meant to be.

I was awakened hours later by a knock at the door and my mother's gentle voice: "Adrian? You have visitors."

Sydney stirred in my arms, looking beautiful and content as the light of late afternoon spilled in through the blinds, illuminating her features. She was so gorgeous and sexy that I was debating pretending I hadn't heard my mom, when a second and more forceful knock sounded. "Adrian? Sydney? It's Rose. We have to talk."

That brought Sydney around and eliminated whatever romantic morning encounter I might have pulled off. We got dressed and eventually made our way out to the suite's living room. There, my mother sat with both Rose and Dimitri. I nearly chided Rose for not having been able to wait to hear the stories of all our exciting adventures . . . but then I noticed her face.

"What's wrong?" I asked.

She and Dimitri exchanged looks. "Jill's missing."

"What do you mean Jill's missing?" I demanded. "She's still

at school. I had a text from her yesterday. She set up our trip."

"And she's got all her guardians," added Sydney. "Eddie's back, right?"

Rose nodded. "All three dhampirs were there on campus. Angeline was even in her room when she was taken."

"Wait . . . did Angeline see it happen?" I asked.

"No," said Dimitri. "That's what's so strange. Angeline went to bed with Jill in the room . . . and woke up with her gone."

"She didn't hear or see anything. Jill just disappeared like magic." Rose snapped her fingers for effect. "Angeline feels terrible."

I felt a tightness in my chest, and the room reeled. Jill . . . missing? It wasn't possible. Not after everything I'd done for her. I'd brought her back to life! This couldn't be happening. There was some mistake. Eddie wouldn't have let this happen.

You see? asked Aunt Tatiana. *I told you there'd never be peace for you. One way or another, there'll always be something to torment you. Good thing you have me to help you.*

Sydney sank into a chair, hands clasped in her lap. "Angeline feels terrible? *I* feel terrible! Jill was my first responsibility, the whole reason for me going out there! If I hadn't left—"

"Don't start that," I warned, putting my arm around her. It was as much to comfort me as her. "Because you didn't leave. You were taken. This is in no way your fault." I turned back to the others, trying desperately to make sense of this. If I could think logically, I wouldn't panic. "We have to find her. Do you have any leads?"

"Not yet, but we have people scouring every inch of that place like crazy, looking for some clue." Rose sighed in dismay. "She was only a month away from coming back here."

"Well, we'll go help," I said. "Get us on a flight out there." Sydney nodded eagerly.

"Are you guys crazy?" asked Rose. "Don't answer that. Look, you aren't going anywhere. There's nothing out there you can do right now."

"Plus, that protection you fought for so hard last night doesn't extend past Court," Dimitri reminded us. "You need to stay here—for your own safety—until more precautions are in place. That, and we don't want any unnecessary attention going toward Jill." He looked over at my mom. "That means, Lady Ivashkov, that what you've just heard cannot leave this room. No one can know Jill's gone, because as long as she's missing, we can't prove she's alive or dead. And if we can't prove that—"

"Then you can't prove the queen has one living relative," Sydney finished.

I hadn't been quick enough to think that far ahead. I was still stuck on Jill—Jill, my sweet, compassionate Jill— missing without a trace. Now, I suddenly grasped the other consequences.

"The vote hasn't happened yet," I murmured. "The vote to change the law."

"Exactly," said Rose, her face grim. "And if word of Jill's disappearance gets out, Lissa could lose her throne."

ONE

I FELT HER FEAR BEFORE I heard her screams.

Her nightmare pulsed into me, shaking me out of my own dream, which had had something to do with a beach and some hot guy rubbing suntan oil on me. Images—hers, not mine—tumbled through my mind: fire and blood, the smell of smoke, the twisted metal of a car. The pictures wrapped around me, suffocating me, until some rational part of my brain reminded me that this wasn't *my* dream.

I woke up, strands of long, dark hair sticking to my forehead.

Lissa lay in her bed, thrashing and screaming. I bolted out of mine, quickly crossing the few feet that separated us.

"Liss," I said, shaking her. "Liss, wake up."

Her screams dropped off, replaced by soft whimpers. "Andre," she moaned. "Oh God."

I helped her sit up. "Liss, you aren't there anymore. Wake up."

After a few moments, her eyes fluttered open, and in the dim lighting, I could see a flicker of consciousness start to take over. Her frantic breathing slowed, and she leaned into me, resting her head against my shoulder. I put an arm around her and ran a hand over her hair.

"It's okay," I told her gently. "Everything's okay."

"I had that dream."

"Yeah. I know."

We sat like that for several minutes, not saying anything else. When I felt her emotions calm down, I leaned over to the nightstand between our beds and turned on the lamp. It glowed dimly, but neither of us really needed much to see by. Attracted by the light, our housemate's cat, Oscar, leapt up onto the sill of the open window.

He gave me a wide berth—animals don't like dhampirs, for whatever reason—but jumped onto the bed and rubbed his head against Lissa, purring softly. Animals didn't have a problem with Moroi, and they all loved Lissa in particular. Smiling, she scratched his chin, and I felt her calm further.

"When did we last do a feeding?" I asked, studying her face. Her fair skin was paler than usual. Dark circles hung under her eyes, and there was an air of frailty about her. School had been hectic this week, and I couldn't remember the last time I'd given her blood. "It's been like . . . more than two days, hasn't it? Three? Why didn't you say anything?"

She shrugged and wouldn't meet my eyes. "You were busy. I didn't want to—"

"Screw that," I said, shifting into a better position. No wonder she seemed so weak. Oscar, not wanting me any closer, leapt down and returned to the window, where he could watch at a safe distance. "Come on. Let's do this."

"Rose—"

"Come *on*. It'll make you feel better."

I tilted my head and tossed my hair back, baring my neck. I saw her hesitate, but the sight of my neck and what it offered proved too powerful. A hungry expression crossed her face, and her lips parted slightly, exposing the fangs she normally kept hidden while living among humans. Those fangs contrasted oddly with the rest of her features. With her pretty face and pale blond hair, she looked more like an angel than a vampire.

As her teeth neared my bare skin, I felt my heart race with a mix of fear and anticipation. I always hated feeling the latter, but it was nothing I could help, a weakness I couldn't shake.

Her fangs bit into me, hard, and I cried out at the brief flare of pain. Then it faded, replaced by a wonderful, golden joy that spread through my body. It was better than any of the times I'd been drunk or high. Better than sex—or so I imagined, since I'd never done it. It was a blanket of pure, refined pleasure, wrapping me up and promising everything would be right in the world. On and on it went. The chemicals in her saliva triggered an endorphin rush, and I lost track of the world, lost track of who I was.

Then, regretfully, it was over. It had taken less than a minute.

She pulled back, wiping her hand across her lips as she studied me. "You okay?"

"I . . . yeah." I lay back on the bed, dizzy from the blood loss. "I just need to sleep it off. I'm fine."

Her pale, jade-green eyes watched me with concern. She stood up. "I'm going to get you something to eat."

My protests came awkwardly to my lips, and she left before I could get out a sentence. The buzz from her bite had lessened as soon as she broke the connection, but some of it still lingered in my veins, and I felt a goofy smile cross my lips. Turning my head, I glanced up at Oscar, still sitting in the window.

"You don't know what you're missing," I told him.

His attention was on something outside. Hunkering down into a crouch, he puffed out his jet-black fur. His tail started twitching.

My smile faded, and I forced myself to sit up. The world spun, and I waited for it to right itself before trying to stand. When I managed it, the dizziness set in again and this time refused to leave. Still, I felt okay enough to stumble to the window and peer out with Oscar. He eyed me warily, scooted over a little, and then returned to whatever had held his attention.

A warm breeze—unseasonably warm for a Portland fall—played with my hair as I leaned out. The street was dark and relatively quiet. It was three in the morning, just about the only time a college campus settled down, at least somewhat. The house in which we'd rented a room for the past eight months sat on a residential street with old, mismatched houses. Across the road, a streetlight flickered, nearly ready to burn out. It still cast enough light for me to make out the shapes of cars and buildings. In our own yard, I could see the silhouettes of trees and bushes.

And a man watching me.

I jerked back in surprise. A figure stood by a tree in the yard, about thirty feet away, where he could easily see through the window. He was close enough that I probably could have thrown something and hit him. He was certainly close enough that he could have seen what Lissa and I had just done.

The shadows covered him so well that even with my heightened sight, I couldn't make out any of his features, save for his height. He was tall. Really tall. He stood there for just a moment, barely discernible, and then stepped back, disappearing into the shadows cast by the trees on the far side of the yard. I was pretty sure I saw someone else move nearby and join him before the blackness swallowed them both.

Whoever these figures were, Oscar didn't like them. Not counting me, he usually got along with most people, growing upset only when someone posed an immediate danger. The guy outside hadn't done anything threatening to Oscar, but the cat had sensed something, something that put him on edge.

Something similar to what he always sensed in me.

Icy fear raced through me, almost—but not quite—eradicating the lovely bliss of Lissa's bite. Backing up from the window, I jerked on a pair of jeans that I found on the floor, nearly falling over in the process. Once they were on, I grabbed my coat and Lissa's, along with our wallets. Shoving my feet into the first shoes I saw, I headed out the door.

Downstairs, I found her in the cramped kitchen, rummaging through the refrigerator. One of our housemates, Jeremy, sat at the table, hand on his forehead as he stared sadly at a calculus book. Lissa regarded me with surprise.

"You shouldn't be up."

"We have to go. Now."

Her eyes widened, and then a moment later, understanding clicked in. "Are you . . . really? Are you sure?"

I nodded. I couldn't explain how I knew for sure. I just did.

Jeremy watched us curiously. "What's wrong?"

An idea came to mind. "Liss, get his car keys."

He looked back and forth between us. "What are you—"

Lissa unhesitatingly walked over to him. Her fear poured into me through our psychic bond, but there was something else too: her complete faith that I would take care of everything, that we would be safe. Like always, I hoped I was worthy of that kind of trust.

She smiled broadly and gazed directly into his eyes. For a moment, Jeremy just stared, still confused, and then I saw the thrall seize him. His eyes glazed over, and he regarded her adoringly.

"We need to borrow your car," she said in a gentle voice. "Where are your keys?"

He smiled, and I shivered. I had a high resistance to compulsion, but I could still feel its effects when it was directed at another person. That, and I'd been taught my entire life that using it was wrong. Reaching into his pocket, Jeremy handed over a set of keys hanging on a large red key chain.

"Thank you," said Lissa. "And where is it parked?"

"Down the street," he said dreamily. "At the corner. By Brown." Four blocks away.

"Thank you," she repeated, backing up. "As soon as we leave, I want you to go back to studying. Forget you ever saw us tonight."

He nodded obligingly. I got the impression he would have walked off a cliff for her right then if she'd asked. All humans were susceptible to compulsion, but Jeremy appeared weaker than most. That came in handy right now.

"Come on," I told her. "We've got to move."

We stepped outside, heading toward the corner he'd named. I was still dizzy from the bite and kept stumbling, unable to move as quickly as I wanted. Lissa had to catch hold of me a few times to stop me from falling. All the time, that anxiety rushed into me from her mind. I tried my best to ignore it; I had my own fears to deal with.

"Rose . . . what are we going to do if they catch us?" she whispered.

"They won't," I said fiercely. "I won't let them."

"But if they've found us—"

"They found us before. They didn't catch us then. We'll just drive over to the train station and go to L.A. They'll lose the trail."

I made it sound simple. I always did, even though there

was nothing simple about being on the run from the people we'd grown up with. We'd been doing it for two years, hiding wherever we could and just trying to finish high school. Our senior year had just started, and living on a college campus had seemed safe. We were so close to freedom.

She said nothing more, and I felt her faith in me surge up once more. This was the way it had always been between us. I was the one who took action, who made sure things happened— sometimes recklessly so. She was the more reasonable one, the one who thought things out and researched them extensively before acting. Both styles had their uses, but at the moment, recklessness was called for. We didn't have time to hesitate.

Lissa and I had been best friends ever since kindergarten, when our teacher had paired us together for writing lessons. Forcing five-year-olds to spell *Vasilisa Dragomir* and *Rosemarie Hathaway* was beyond cruel, and we'd—or rather, I'd—responded appropriately. I'd chucked my book at our teacher and called her a fascist bastard. I hadn't known what those words meant, but I'd known how to hit a moving target.

Lissa and I had been inseparable ever since.

"Do you hear that?" she asked suddenly.

It took me a few seconds to pick up what her sharper senses already had. Footsteps, moving fast. I grimaced. We had two more blocks to go.

"We've got to run for it," I said, catching hold of her arm.

"But you can't—"

"*Run.*"

It took every ounce of my willpower not to pass out on the sidewalk. My body didn't want to run after losing blood or while still metabolizing the effects of her saliva. But I ordered my muscles to stop their bitching and clung to Lissa as our feet pounded against the concrete. Normally I could have out-run her without any extra effort—particularly since she was barefoot—but tonight, she was all that held me upright.

The pursuing footsteps grew louder, closer. Black stars danced before my eyes. Ahead of us, I could make out Jeremy's green Honda. Oh God, if we could just make it—

Ten feet from the car, a man stepped directly into our path. We came to a screeching halt, and I jerked Lissa back by her arm. It was *him*, the guy I'd seen across the street watching me. He was older than us, maybe mid-twenties, and as tall as I'd figured, probably six-six or six-seven. And under different circumstances—say, when he wasn't holding up our desperate escape—I would have thought he was hot. Shoulder-length brown hair, tied back in a short ponytail. Dark brown eyes. A long brown coat—a duster, I thought it was called.

But his hotness was irrelevant now. He was only an obstacle keeping Lissa and me away from the car and our freedom. The footsteps behind us slowed, and I knew our pursuers had caught up. Off to the sides, I detected more movement, more people closing in. God. They'd sent almost a dozen guardians to retrieve us. I couldn't believe it. The queen herself didn't travel with that many.

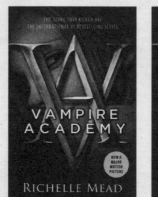